"COME, MY BELOVED," HE WHISPERED. . . .

My terror had given way to a strange, composed sense of purpose. I knew that I must find a way to lead him back down the stairs.

He grabbed me roughly and pulled me through a small door that led to the outside of the tower. I could still hear the bells chiming as he took my hand and led me past the bell tower. "Come," he said quietly. "Come to me forever."

He guided me closer and closer to the edge of the snowy, slippery parapet. I could see over the low edge. We were dangerously close to toppling and I tried to shrink back from the brink. He pulled me forcibly closer to the edge, so that we were standing there side by side, and I knew that no one could possibly save me . . .

"Come, my beloved," he whispered once more, and I felt his hand pushing at the small of my back . . .

GOTHICS A LA MOOR—FROM ZEBRA

ISLAND OF LOST RUBIES
by Patricia Werner   (2603, $3.95)
Heartbroken by her father's death and the loss of her great love, Eileen
returns to her island home to claim her inheritance. But eerie things begin
happening the minute she steps off the boat, and it isn't long before
Eileen realizes that there's no escape from *THE ISLAND OF LOST RU-
BIES.*

DARK CRIES OF GRAY OAKS
by Lee Karr   (2736, $3.95)
When orphaned Brianna Anderson was offered a job as companion to the
mentally ill seventeen-year-old girl, Cassie, she was grateful for the non-
troublesome employment. Soon she began to wonder why the girl's family
insisted that Cassie be given hydro-electrical therapy and increased doses
of laudanum. What was the shocking secret that Cassie held in her dark
tormented mind? And was she herself in danger?

CRYSTAL SHADOWS
by Michele Y. Thomas   (2819, $3.95)
When Teresa Hawthorne accepted a post as tutor to the wealthy Curtis
family, she didn't believe the scandal surrounding them would be any concern of hers. However, it soon began to seem as if someone was trying to
ruin the Curtises and Theresa was becoming the unwitting target of a
deadly conspiracy . . .

CASTLE OF CRUSHED SHAMROCKS
by Lee Karr   (2843, $3.95)
Penniless and alone, eighteen-year-old Aileen O'Conner traveled to the
coast of Ireland to be recognized as daughter and heir to Lord Edwin
Lynhurst. Upon her arrival, she was horrified to find her long lost father
had been murdered. And slowly, the extent of the danger dawned upon
her: her father's killer was still at large. And her name was next on the
list.

BRIDE OF HATFIELD CASTLE
by Beverly G. Warren   (2517, $3.95)
Left a widow on her wedding night and the sole inheritor of Hatfield's
fortune, Eden Lane was convinced that someone wanted her out of the
castle, preferably dead. Her failing health, the whispering voices of death,
and the phantoms who roamed the keep were driving her mad. And although she came to the castle as a bride, she needed to discover who was
trying to kill her, or leave as a corpse!

*Available wherever paperbacks are sold, or order direct from the
Publisher. Send cover price plus 50¢ per copy for mailing and
handling to Zebra Books, Dept. 3273, 475 Park Avenue South,
New York, N.Y. 10016. Residents of New York, New Jersey and
Pennsylvania must include sales tax. DO NOT SEND CASH.*

THE SHIMMERING STONES OF GLENDOWER HALL
CONSTANCE WALKER

ZEBRA BOOKS
KENSINGTON PUBLISHING CORP.

For my brothers and sisters—
Larry and Irene and Frank and Lois

ZEBRA BOOKS

are published by

Kensington Publishing Corp.
475 Park Avenue South
New York, NY 10016

First printing: January, 1991

Printed in the United States of America

Prologue

There is a magnificent, huge house close by the moors and closer still to the sea. It is made of limestone and slate and at one particular time of the year, on a day in late December, when there is snow on the ground and the sun is low and the shadows are in the right position, the structure takes on a peculiar color and glow — simultaneously that of shimmering darkness and glistening brilliance. At such moments it is the most beautiful sight that I have ever seen. The house stands isolated, in the middle of a vast estate, and from the topmost story of the structure one can see both the moors in front and the turbulent sea at the back. The serenity of the hazy meadows and the angry conflict of the water present a seeming contrast, but those who know the area well understand that both pose the same treachery; the seductive rhapsody of the misty fields and the rhythmic siren's call of the crashing waves lure the traveller and stranger to the forbidden, the unknown. And though I have seen the house clearly and know each and every room, though I have walked the grounds and smelled the flowers surrounding it, I know not where this wondrous estate stands, for it exists only in my deepest dreams.

Chapter One

There was a chill in the spring air. A distinct northern wind swept past me, swirling about me and sending showers of pale springtime flower petals to the ground so that in some parts of the isolated side of the hill it seemed as if the winter snows had lingered well past their time. Oh how I wished that it were still the season and that my life was still caught up with the commonplace winter chores without a hint of what was to come in the early seedtime. Would that my life had continued on its ordinary course so that I would not be standing here, hearing the recitation of the sorrowful words. "Grant eternal peace to Thy servant, oh Lord, we beseech Thee. Grant us, his friends, the strength that will replenish us so that we may remember our dearly departed." The gentle elderly voice intruded into my thoughts of times past, recalling me to the reason I was away from my daily tasks this cheerless April morning. I heard the Reverend Jenkins say the final words of the service and yet I could not bear to hear them spoken. "Ashes to ashes . . . dust to dust," he began and we small band of friends and family stood there, shivering as the wind ruffled our clothing, listening to the concluding prayers for the dead. I pulled my cape close to my body as yet another current of cold air rushed past me. "The Lord giveth and the Lord taketh away," the minister said and we all whispered, "Amen," and then he came close to me and gently touched my hand. "Come, Gwynneth, for it is time for you to say farewell." He urged me toward the open grave and I approached it, knowing that everyone was watching me, yet not wanting to face these few last moments. I could not bear to say good-bye and yet I knew I must. I hesitantly reached out to finger the golden pine coffin, wishing with all of my broken heart that I could embrace the dear man who lay shrouded inside.

I bent my head so that no one could see the tears on my face that were rapidly falling on the rough wood, staining it dark as surely as if it had been rained upon. "Good-bye, my sweet father. God's speed, dear Mathias Morys," I said softly. "Good-bye and thank you for keeping me as your daughter . . . for giving me a safe home . . . and for loving me." I looked up and into the cloudless sky as though my words would be carried to my parent by the early spring breeze. "Farewell, dear Father," I said and then wiped the teardrops from my eyes and turned away from the casket. Mr. Jenkins once again held fast to my arm so that I would not stumble on the soft, wet earth as he guided me down the hill, past the still sharp-etched headstone of Mathias's wife, Molly—my mother—who had died only four months before. "CALLED HOME" read the simple epitaph. The consequences of the harsh winter had taken its toll on my small family.

"What is to become of me now, Reverend Jenkins?" I asked as we entered the modest cottage where I had lived these past seventeen years. "I do not know if I will be able to stay here." I looked out at the farmland. "It is a difficult life for one person. And I have no other relations to whom I can turn." I sat down at the sturdy table that my father had made many years ago and traced the grain in the oak.

The kindly minister nodded his grey head. "Aye, I know there are no others—no relations—to care for you." He paused in thought. "Many the time Mathias would tell me of your . . ." He did not need to finish the sentence, for the story he referred to was familiar to me. I had been

8

told many times, since my age of reason, how I had come to live with the Morys couple. How I had been an abandoned babe when they found me at their doorstep and how they had taken me in and cared for me and loved me.

Reverend Jenkins took a slice of the cake that one of the village women had sent in remembrance, and sat opposite to me. "How do ya feel about service, Gwynneth?"

"I have no choice, sir. Do you know of a position?"

"Nay, not yet. But I shall look about for ye. And in the meantime you will stay here. Our valley people will look to you." He stood up to take his leave. "Be ye at peace, Gwynneth. Be ye at peace, girl."

I was left alone in the cottage. I pretended to myself that my parents were still alive and were merely completing chores about our small farm, but when it grew dark and I had lit the solitary candle on the table, I had to come to terms with the stark fact that, for the second time in my life, I had become an orphan.

Reverend Jenkins visited me a week after my father's funeral. "It is almost a miracle," he said. "I have been told of a position, that of companion to a noblewoman in the north of Wales." Mr. Jenkins saw my look of alarm and he held his arm out to me. "I know, Gwynneth, that it will take you away from this land, but the times are rough and it will at least be a secure position. I am told that the mistress is kind and civil. It will not be an arduous or especially hard life for you, my dear, for there are other domestics. It is an extensive estate and there is a large staff with many inside and outside attendants, as befits the manse. You will be needed upstairs to assist the lady's nurse. She is an old retainer who, I am told, has been in the employ of the household many, many years and is now not able to do all the work required by the mistress." He raised his eyes to the heavens. "It is the Lord's hand," he said simply. "The woman who wrote the letter asked me especially if there was anyone . . . a young person . . . who would be available." The minister fell silent. "It is strange. Indeed strange. It was as though they asked for ye especially. Indeed, they asked if there were any young orphan girls here. It is almost as if they knew of your circumstance, of your need."

I do not know if I was relieved or alarmed at the news. I had always thought that I would spend my entire life here among the country folk of my village. It never occurred to me to look to the outside of my shire or even beyond the valley where I lived. My father and mother were the seventh generation of Moryses to till the land, and I had never entertained thoughts of leaving these lowlands. I had expected to live my entire life here and, when my span came to an end, to be buried on the hillside next to my parents. It was not an unhappy prospect, and when I looked past the small window out toward the barn where the animals were bedded, I felt a surge of heartache for what I had loved and would now have to leave.

The Reverend Jenkins saw my crestfallen face, for I could not hide my despair. "I am sorry, Gwynneth, that you will not be allowed to stay here. The land is yours and belongs to your kin, but . . ." He bent his head and placed his folded hands on the table as though in prayer.

"Is there not anyone here who could help me with my farm?" I asked. "With the plowing and seeding? Perhaps share in the crops?"

Mr. Jenkins shook his head. "Nay, girl, I have inquired. But ye know our people. There is plenty to do on their own lands. I had hoped someone would come forward and offer to take you in and preserve your farm until you have married, but . . ." Mr. Jenkins's voice trailed off and I knew of what he spoke. Our little hollow and the surrounding countryside were austere, and the earth demanded much care and attention. It was a life of harshness and it was only because of our great love for this portion of Wales that we all endured. The rugged land claimed all of our time from sun up to sun down, but it was a price we inhabitants gladly paid for the privilege of being our own keepers. And now it was to be mine no more.

I had no choice but to accept the offer of companion to the woman in the upper north of Wales and later, after the Reverend Jenkins departed, I walked round the cottage and fingered all the precious and priceless articles that had belonged to my parents while remembering the stories that had been told to me about each and every one. I knew I would only be able to take a few personal belongings with me when I moved on and I committed to memory all those that I would leave behind. The crazed blue cups and saucers that we used every evening at the supper meal and the sturdy pots and pans forged by my mother's father as part of her dowry were all to be crated and given to our neighbors, never again to be included in a Morys household. I remembered my mother's sweet, gentle voice telling me of her excitement when her father had brought home the vessels one after another, all bespeaking his skilled craftsmanship. I touched the faded but still serviceable embroidery on the kitchen and bed linens and blinked back the tears as I remembered my mother's speech instructing me in the intricacies of the tiny stitches and knots.

I sat up late that night and watched while the light of the pale half-moon flooded through the single window in my cottage. And as the colorless beams of light fell upon each and every small treasure they were etched forever in my memory. I heard the cattle low contentedly in the barn and through the night remembered the stories that were told me by my parents. In the silent room it was as though the echoes of their voices had been summoned to recite the tales one last time before fading into eternity.

"Tell me the story again, Father, of the time you found me. Of how you discovered me," I heard my six-year-old voice inquire of the darkness. "Tell me," I would plead until my father reached out to take me upon his knee. There we would sit, the two of us, in the big wooden rocker he had crafted, and he would look over at my mother, sewing by the light of the fire, and smile.

"Again?" he would tease me before beginning the narrative anew, for though I had already heard it many times, I never tired of it. "Well, Gwynneth," he would say after drawing on his pipe, "it was an early autumn's eve—a little into the time of the harvest—and I had gone out to tend to the cows and sheep. Your mother was here inside the cottage working on her own household chores and when I had fastened the gates to the barn I had to walk slowly although, mind you, I well knew the land. For it was a rainy evening, child. So thick-rainy that it was difficult to see one hand in front of you and there was lightning and thunder all around. The cattle were uneasy and I spent an extra few moments with them patting them down and speaking easy to them, reassuring them, and when I got back to the house I thought I spied something or someone moving away from the porch but then I thought it must be my old eyes failing me in the night." He would pause then and look down at me, tightening his arm about my thin, bony shoulders. "You must remember, girl, that I was an old man even then," he would say and I would laugh and kiss his cheek and protest that he wasn't old, he was my father, and then he would look at my mother again and laugh. "That be reason enough, wife, for us not to have aged like the normal people," he would say, and my mother would nod her head in agreement.

"Well, I looked through the rain but I could not see too much, it were that heavy, only the outline of the house and the glow from where the candlelight shone through the window. I thought then that it was a play of the water and the shadows of the clouds and half-covered moon that belied my eyes, and it weren't until I had come directly in front of the door that I saw something was resting on the step. It were sheltered, this object was, by a woven basket and a bit of coarse, slick cloth, and I were puzzled for I could not see anyone about the house. I thought perhaps my Molly had set out a saucer of milk for the stray cats that roamed the farmyard and when I bent down to move it better away from the heavy rains I heard a small sound—just a wee one, mind you, and it

12

reminded me of a litter of kittens mewing—and I pushed away the material and saw a tiny babe. The most beautiful babe I had ever seen and I was so stunned that I picked up the basket and burst into the warm cottage."

My mother would put down her stitchery then and continue the story. "Your father stood there, dripping water on the floor and holding out this basket to me and it was as though he were struck dumb. And when I asked him what he had, for I thought it was a few more eggs that I had missed in the chicken coop this early morning, all he could do was shake his head and rock the basket ever so gently. 'Mathias,' I said three or four times, 'what is it you hold?' and he just remained there like the cat had gotten his tongue and finally he looked down and into the basket and he said in a whisper, 'It's a babe!' I thought he was jesting me and was about to say something snappish but just at that time you cried out in a soft voice and I rushed over to him and took the bundle from him."

She would pick up her cloth once more, knot a thread, and plunge her needle into the weave as she continued the tale. "Of course I didn't know what to believe—except for mine own eyes—and then you cried once more. We took you out of the hamper and you were none the worse for the weather, for you were well protected with layers of clothes—beautiful, fine clothes with delicate stitches and patterns. We searched and searched among the blankets and the provisions that were packed at the foot of the basket and we finally found a note, although it gave us no clue to your family identity nor who placed you there."

My father would then continue the narrative. "It were just a short writing. It said, *'Her name is Gwynneth. Please take care of her.'* That be all. *'Her name is Gwynneth. Please take care of her,'* " he would repeat and then he would shake his head and draw on his pipe. "And under all the covers, folded in a lady's handkerchief, was a gold sovereign." My father would shake his head once more in remembrance of the discovery and hug me even closer. "As though that would be the real reason we would

13

take you in and care for you." He would look down at me as I sat protected by his arms. "Make no mistake about it, Gwynnie, from that moment we first saw you, ye were ours and there be no amount of money in the whole of Wales to take ye away from us. Especially when we unwrapped you from your swaddlings and saw your hair." He would become silent for a moment. "Remember, Molly?" he would ask of my mother and she would look up at me and nod her head. "The hair was always a magnificent color. A red—like copper fire. And curly. And your eyes were the same color as they be now—the green of an emerald sea."

"Did you love me right off?" I would ask, knowing what they both would say.

"Indeed we did!" my father would reply immediately, knowing that the speed of his answer delighted me. "There weren't no two ways about that. Molly and me were always wanting a babe and when you were delivered to us we knew that you were to stay with us forever."

I always looked at my mother at that part of the story. "Even though I did not appear like you or any others about here?" Early on I had recognized that I was different from the others who lived here in the valley. While I was fair, our neighbors were dark, and while I was thin, their children were solid.

My mother would nod her head again. "Even though. You were sent as a blessing to us," she would say and even from across the room I could see the shimmer of a tear in her eye reflect the candlelight.

I would hug my father. "I love you so much," I would say. "I don't care who my real family is—even if it be that of a king or an emperor or a nobleman who lives in a fine house. I will never leave you." My father would squeeze me once more and then my mother would have me finish my milk and bread and butter before bed. I would sleep then, contented, in my room, safe from all the wild beasts and spirits we village children would conjure up in our fantasies whenever we met on market days.

14

I closed my eyes against the recollections of the past and then I picked up the small wooden doll that my father had fashioned for me and my mother had dressed. My father had painted the carved head of hair red—like mine—and had drawn the eyes of green on the face, and many nights I would fall asleep in the small bed in the second room with my hand fastened tightly on the doll's arm. I cradled it now as though the contact would call me back and bind me to the times when I had been just a little girl. I hummed the lullaby my mother had sung to me and which I in turn had sung to my doll, and I heard in my memory those five strange notes that recalled me to my earliest moments. My parents had pled ignorance on the few occasions when I had crooned the melody, and my father had sworn that I must have heard the air while roaming too near the shepherds on the hills. "Sure, it must be a tune one of them lads is always a'playing on his tin whistle," he would say, and then he would warn me once more not to stray too far on the bluffs.

I ran my finger across the painted red head of the doll, feeling the familiar grooves that were whittled to resemble my own curls. "And what will you call your babe?" my mother had asked when I had first been presented the wooden figure.

"Lucy. I shall call her Lucy," I had said, and both my parents seemed perplexed.

"Lucy? It is not a name known hereabout, child. How did you come to choose it?" they had asked but I could only shake my head and continue playing with the doll.

"Because I had to," I had answered and then added, "because it looks like her . . . like us."

My mother had glanced at my father again. "Who, Gwynneth? Who does it look like?" she had asked, but by that time I had forgotten, for there were far more important matters at hand in the dressing and undressing of my Lucy.

From somewhere in the distance I heard the song of a familiar nightbird and I was summoned back to the present and to my sorrow. The bird sang only a few dulcet notes and then it was stilled and the night was quiet. For many hours I sat and watched through the window as the hushed, dark sky turned first into shades of deep, then pale, grey and blue. Finally the heavens glowed with streaks of pink and rose and bleached yellow. From the hen house a cock crowed, and still I was not sleepy. In just a few short days, I knew, I would leave this valley and would never again hear the familiar sounds nor see the dear sights attendant to it.

The Reverend Jenkins saw to my departure, and after a final visit to the place where my father and mother lay, I was ready for the coach that had been sent for me. I glanced up just before I left the cottage and saw on the arch above the doorway the initials and date that had always fascinated me. *"I.M. 1657"*. I remembered my father holding me upon his sturdy shoulders so that I could trace the cuttings while telling me proudly that Ivor Morys, his "great, great, great, great grandfather" had carved his initials and date in the wood the day that he and his wife, Mair, had settled onto the land. "This earth was beloved to him and to all Morys kin," he said. "I had thought it lost to our clan but now you," he would tell me and then swing me around, "you will inherit Daear and pass it to your own. It is a happy prospect," he would say, laughing, and my mother would smile that sweet smile. Daear— "earth and people as one"—my father had explained the name many times. I had understood and had promised to cherish it as he and our other relations had through the years.

And now it would all be gone, lost to our tribe forever. The heaviness of the thought overwhelmed me as I reached up and gently touched the carving one last time.

"All is in readiness, Gwynneth," the minister said as I

watched as my small trunk—once upon a time included in my mother's marriage portion—was loaded on board the stage. I looked around the farm, now strangely silent, for the cattle had been sold to the neighbors and our dogs handed over to them for safekeeping. "I shall write to you and let you know who has taken over the mastery of the land here."

I clutched my reticule close. "I already feel a stranger here in the valley, Reverend Jenkins, for it is an unaccustomed feeling to be saying good-bye to Daear. To be leaving it. To no longer be a part of this land." I put my fingers to my lips. "I know not if I ever shall pass this way again," I said as I tried to conceal my tears.

"We are all strangers in all valleys, Gwynneth," Mr. Jenkins said and then handed me into the coach. He bowed his head. "Be ye forever at peace, Gwynneth Morys. Be ye forever at peace." He closed the door, the horses moved forward on command, and I waved good-bye to the religious gentleman who had guided me for all my years in the ways of the Lord. I waved until his large figure seemed small and then finally disappeared, and I knew my life would never again be the same for as long as I lived. There was to be no reprieve for me—I had to leave—and once again all I had known and loved was lost to me. Thus with a bereft heart I left the valley where I had lived all my days and prepared to take up residence as the companion to Lady Jane Glendower in Caernarfon in the north of Wales.

The journey took us three days through the heart of the country. Long, winding, silver strands of rivers gave way to sparkling clear lakes. Newly plowed fields, reminiscent of my former rural home, merged into lush, green villages dominated by their distinct, plain chapels. Lengthy ranges of mountains, their misted peaks touching the heavens, and half-ruined Norman coastal castles came and went in our purview, and the riven hills parted as if to purposely allow us our journey. And all around us, on farmland and windswept plains alike, were the rocks and stones of Wales

17

that rise from out of the earth, reminding me of the harsh life the land demands of those who choose to take the riches and the blessings from it.

In the evenings we stopped along the highway at those hostels my coachman deemed appropriate. When the stage driver made mention of our destination we were treated with much respect. Hence we were never given inferior meals or lesser accommodations; rather, our innkeepers made us particularly welcome and provided a quiet room for me far from the rowdies who sang and wagered and fought lustily and loudly, well into the nights.

By the morning of the fifth day we had come to the last part of our journey. "We will be reaching our destination in another four or five hours, if there be no trouble along the way," the driver yelled into the window on the side of the coach. I saw him glance up at the sun. "It looks to be like fine weather that will hold up another full day at least. It be more than enough time for us to complete our journey."

There indeed was nothing to delay us. The toll roads were opened almost immediately upon our appearance and the carriage rolled along lazily through the countryside. At each new turn or twist in the road another part of my beloved Wales was revealed to me, and although I had never before been in these areas, somehow they all seemed familiar. At midday my stageman stopped, and while we refreshed the horses and ate a hasty picnic meal together, he told me of the splendor I would find at the house.

"Glendower Hall be one of the finest estates you'll ever see in the whole of Wales—indeed, in the whole of the British Isles, miss," he said. Later, back inside the coach, I dreamily recalled this and, continued to watch as the landscape stretched for miles and miles. The horses' hooves on the dirt roads and the rhythmic turning of the carriage wheels soothed me into a peaceful slumber and I slept for I know not how long.

"Miss . . . miss . . . we be a'comin' up to the estate soon. Rouse yourself, miss." The coachman's mannerly voice called down to me and I realized I had fallen asleep. "We'll be a'comin' up to where you'll be able to have a first glance of it just round the bend there up ahead. You'll see . . . you'll see it in just a moment, miss. And then ye can judge for yourself as to its grandness."

We turned the curve in the road and I now understood the excitement of the driver's words, for I was instantly entranced as I gained my initial glimpse of what was to be my new home. It was a view that shall remain forever in my mind, for as we rounded the bend, and although it was still away into the distance, I could clearly see the tall, angular stone structure made of rock the cast of which could not be called by a definite color.

The house was set high on a hill with a huge expanse of lawn surrounding it, and further in the background I could see the mist rise up from what I discerned to be part of the seacoast. The towering main residence seemed to shimmer in the late afternoon sunlight, sending gleaming sparks of luster out into the air as though it were a shining beacon.

The coachman knew I was overwhelmed with the beauty of the mansion, yet he took delight in puzzling me by foretelling the future. "Aye, this be magnificent, ma'am. This indeed be beautiful, miss. But mark my words—there be no comparison to what you will regard in the cold season. Then, miss, then you'll see the most extraordinary spectacle. A view that will stun and mystify you. A most extraordinary sight you'll see, ma'am. A most extraordinary sight. Some folks say it either be the work of the Devil or of the angels, but there be no tellin', ma'am. Never has been for all of these years. But you'll see it, miss, you'll see it, and then you'll understand why the locals call it Winter's Light. Then you'll understand, miss." Having said all he wished to me, he spoke next to the horses, urging them on in anticipation of the rest due him.

A wave of disquiet washed over me as we approached the carefully laid out private lane which led to the estate.

It seemed to me I had observed the stone fences, the briar patches, even the neatly stacked woodpiles before, although I knew such a thing was impossible. I narrowed my eyes and looked out the coach window for a clue as to why I believed I had already witnessed these scenes. Perhaps they were reminiscent of a story told to me by my parents which, somehow, I still retained in my memory. I concentrated but I could not recall it to my mind, so instead focused my eyes on my immediate surroundings, hoping to push away the disturbing impressions.

Our carriage moved quickly but before we reached the carefully manicured green that led to the broad steps and expansive balconies of the entrance of the house, we had to pass within the confines of a long wood. It was a darkened spot. Patches of diffused sunlight peeked through the spaces between the leaves on the gigantic trees so that the entire forest was not unduly ominous, yet still there seemed to be an air of dolor about it. It was a melancholy more felt than witnessed, and a chilling anxiety swept over me. I shivered and knew I would be glad when we emerged into full, warm sunshine.

The house on the hill loomed even larger now, and as we advanced toward it the strange glint emanating from it seemed more subdued, as though the temperate spring breeze that just then touched it had quieted it. Despite its grandeur, the manor did not appear a forbidding home, but nevertheless I felt curiously disturbed about it. Perhaps, I considered, this was due to the emotions I had experienced these past three weeks—to my trepidation at beginning a new way of life in an alien home with no friends or family as allies—and I made a resolution not to mistake the natural for the uncanny again.

Through the trees I could see that the carriage was drawing nearer to the great lawns, and my resolve was short-lived. I put my hands to my temples—no longer able to avoid or quiet my thoughts—and I shuddered once again with the deep knowledge I did not want to admit. For there was now no way to deny the truth: I had seen this house before . . . seen it far too many times in my dreams, whether awake or sleeping. I knew it quite intimately and could have told you of the interior rooms and elegant furnishings and the color of the damask and velvet and of the crystal lamps that hung on the walls. I knew the trees that we were passing as we travelled up the secluded land, the mighty oaks set in a double row on each side almost one-half mile straight in length. I knew, too, that to the left the copse gave shelter to a large variety of small, wild animals, and knew where it shielded a patch of wildflowers.

I took another deep breath and recognized even the scent of this particular earth—its fresh, wet, damp smell seemed comfortable to my nostrils and throat. And then when we cleared the woods and approached the lane leading up the hill I felt another tremble flicker through my body. The house was even more magnificent seen at this range . . . more majestic . . . and more familiar.

"The Glendower estate, ma'am," the coachman said proudly, and this time my whole body shuddered with certainty. This was the house I had dreamed about all my life. This was the house that had haunted me, that had called to me through my days and nights, I knew not why. But in a strange and puzzling sense I was relieved, for I had finally a name for the manor.

"This be it, ma'am. This be your new home," the coachman said as he brought the carriage to a full stop in front of its main doors. "This be Goleuni Gaef. This be Winter's Light!"

Chapter Two

The staff of the estate was expecting me, and no sooner was my luggage unloaded from the stage and brought into the entry foyer than an old woman in a starched and stiffened dark dress appeared in the doorway.

"You're Gwynneth," she said after staring at me for a moment. "You're Gwynneth Morys." I curtsied while the woman peered at me. "You're Gwynneth come to help me. I'm Nanny Hoskins." She walked closer to me and I could tell that, as I stood with the full bright sunlight at my back, this elderly woman could not see me well due to both the blinding light and the feebleness of her aged eyes.

"How do you do, ma'am?" I said curtsying again, for I wanted this woman to know that I was not deficient in good manners.

The nurse's tone softened. "I am glad you have come, girl. We have been waiting a long time for ye."

"But we are on time," I said lest she think that we had dallied on the trip here.

"Aye, I know," she said and then moved toward the staircase railing, which she grasped to support herself. "My legs," she said. "My body is old and tired and is betraying me." She nodded her head. "Aye, I am glad you are here." She turned to the footman who had stood by the door waiting for his orders. "Quick, take Miss Morys's trunk to the room next to mine. She'll be wanting to change and wash before she meets the mistress." She turned again to me. "You'll take dinner first with me and then we shall make your presence known to Lady Glendower," she said. She gestured for me to follow her up the broad mahogany staircase.

The meal was neither plain nor fancy but quite sufficient, and though I thought the boiled vegetables and rice much more suited to Nanny's elderly digestion than to my young one, I ate the food with pleasure. Nanny was not given to conversation during the meal. "Encourages stomach pains," she said by way of explanation, and already I knew not to question the woman's words. But that did not deter me from thinking or from examining the woman and the servants who waited on us. Already in the space of the half hour we had taken to eat our meal I had begun to distinguish two of the maids who passed in and out of the room, each time curtsying or nodding their head in Nanny's direction. "Undermaids," Nanny said in a loud whisper. "Just learning their positions." She took a forkful of the boiled potato onto her plate. "Some of these girls know nothing when they arrive here and we have to teach them." She shook her head as a young girl approached her from the right. "No, no, girl. From the left. From the left. When will you ever learn?" She paused as the girl walked to the other side. "What do they call you?"

The young girl looked frightened and barely pronounced her name. "Meg, ma'am." She curtsied once again as though that would take away the fright.

Nanny stared straight ahead. "Well, Meg, we shall have to work on your duties." She took another small portion of the potato and then wiped her lips and spoke to me in a low voice as though the maid could not hear. "Always, Gwynneth, the breeding of the person shows. It's a proven fact." I did not answer for fear of calling attention to my own clouded birth, and instead lowered my head and finished the rest of the meal in silence.

Nanny took her time, finishing two cups of strong hot tea and pouring out a third before she indicated my duties in the house. "It's not that I'm not strong enough," she said, extending her thin, blue-veined hands to show me them. She moved her fingers up and down. "You see, my hands are not gnarled nor twisted like some. And, it's not that my mind wanders. Oh, no. You'll find, girl, that I'm sharper than most, even at my age, and none take exception to my orders." She sighed. "No, it's that the work is more demanding now that my lady has taken to her bed for almost all the day and night." She stirred the cream into the teacup. "Aye, my lady has lost her strength . . . her will." Nanny squinted her eyes at me though the light in the room was shaded. "Perhaps . . . ," she said and then she took a sip of the brew.

"I will work directly with you then?" I asked.

"Only for and with me, girl. You'll have no other duties except those that I give you. You'll take no other orders save those that I direct to you. The mistress trusts me in all decisions of the house. We have travelled life's road together and my lady knows that I'll never betray her." Nanny's voice was strong and I wondered what reason she could have for revealing these thoughts to me, so newly come to the estate. Then I put such doubts aside. Though she still had not explained my duties precisely I hoped that Nanny would quickly guide me into the niche I was to occupy in Winter's Light.

"Come away now, girl. My lady will be awake soon." She pushed back her chair and when the cook, Mrs. Padley, appeared in the doorway Nanny stopped for just a moment to compliment her on the meal and to introduce me to her before the two of us went to the second-floor master suites.

Nanny recited my duties quickly, as though she had not thought fully about what was to be my place.

"I'm sure you've been taught that you serve the elders, Gwynneth, and I'll teach you what needs to be done our way. Try not to make too much noise and see that none comes through the door. Mistress used to like to hear music and sounds but lately has closed everything from her

24

mind." She peered at me. "And don't be listening to servants' gossip about Lady Glendower not being in her own mind. That's foolish talk from foolish maids." She looked me up and down. "We'll be getting you an apron to put on over your frock. Do you have another dress? A darker chambray, perhaps?"

"Yes." I looked at my worn but still presentable gray muslin. It had served me well when I attended the local school near Daear.

"Good. Tomorrow you can wear it. It's more useful than that dress you're wearing. That will do well on Sundays for chapel." She pushed open the door and went through it. "Now we'll meet Lady Glendower."

The bedroom that we entered was dark although it was early afternoon. All the windows were heavily curtained, and these were drawn so that no rays of sunshine or light could penetrate them. Despite the pale light given off by the fire which burned in the grate I had to adjust and focus my eyesight to my somber surroundings. Already the gloom trapped within the chamber had cast a pall on my spirits, but I tried hard not to show this on my face. I was sure Nanny would not tolerate discovering her new helper already disheartened and discouraged, and I vowed that never would she suspect me of these thoughts.

The fire's flames lit up part of the room and I could see that there was a massive wooden bed at its far end. Nanny moved toward it repeating the same phrase over and over again: "Lady Glendower, Lady Glendower, are you awake? Lady Glendower, Lady Glendower, are you awake?" There was no sound from the bed. I followed Nanny, and when I too had come close I could see that there was a very slight woman arranged against the pillows. I could not see her clearly because of the dark, but Nanny soon remedied this by walking to a window and gently pulling back the heavy velvet drapery so that from one source, at least, the golden sunshine poured into the room in a warm stream of brightness. I blinked my eyes at the dancing rays and when I turned back to the bed I saw that the woman who

25

lay there was handsome, with a mass of silver white hair that had already been dressed and fashioned atop her head. The woman's eyes, though heavy-lidded, and ringed with dark circles, still seemed extraordinarily alert, and when inadvertently I caught her eye, I saw a flash of curiosity in them. I turned my head and glanced down, for I was embarrassed that I had been caught staring at my new mistress.

Nanny walked back to the bed and rearranged the coverlet on it so that it was more comfortable for the woman who had yet to speak to us. "My lady, this is Gwynneth," she said simply, and again I saw a flash of curiosity flicker across the woman's eyes. "Gwynneth," Nanny repeated. I took it for a summons, and when Lady Glendower looked at me, I curtsied low.

"How do you do, ma'am." The woman nodded her head slightly and then looked at Nanny.

"She will suit us," she said in a stronger voice than I expected to come from so frail a person. Nanny smiled at the words and motioned me back while she pushed away a stray lock of her mistress's hair that had fallen across her pallid brow.

"There," she said as though she had completed a great task and then beckoned to me to step close again so that I could help her. Together the two of us straightened the silk-wrapped pillows and sheets on the masssive oak bed, all the while mindful of Lady Glendower's delicate body. "Careful. Careful of the mistress," Nanny kept cautioning. After we had pulled the linens tight on the bedframe she sent me to the kitchen to tell Mrs. Padley that Lady Glendower was now ready to be served her noon meal.

"Why she didn't just use the bedpull, I'll never know," the cook grumbled when I appeared in the kitchen. "Aye, but that's Nanny's way. Forever sending people to fetch and carry." She put a kettle of water on to boil and pulled out and dusted a tray. "But still, no one can question her reasons when she's been right all the time." She took down a china teapot and carefully doled out the tea leaves

26

into it. "Jasmine," she said. "From the Orient." She poured in the boiling water. "Mistress has loved it since she was a little girl, I'm told." She put a silver tea cosy over the pot and set it on the lacquered tray and then turned to the large kettle of soup that was simmering on the black stove. She lifted the lid and stirred it so that little puffs of aromatic steam wafted into the air and then she ladled the golden liquid into a bowl. I wondered why she did not ask some of the kitchen help to collect the food for the luncheon tray.

"I don't allow anyone to do this for my lady," Mrs. Padley said as though she had read my thoughts. "I always fashion the luncheon tray for the mistress myself." She set a vase with a small sprig of early flowers in between the dishes. "It was one of my first duties when I came here as a young girl. I was hired then to be second cook some twenty years ago," she offered as she quickly sliced some heavy, dark oat bread and slathered it with fresh-churned butter and arranged it in a dish. "It was my honor to prepare the luncheon trays and although things be different now and I'm head cook," she said pulling her body a little straighter as though to assume the posture which befitted the title, "I still intend to prepare this meal for Lady Glendower." She placed the bread plate upon the tray and covered it with an embroidered white damask cloth before handing it carefully to me. "See that you don't drop it," she said, and then she turned back to the servant, Meg, who was busy polishing the copper bottom of the big pots on the second range. Already I was understanding that the routine at Winter's Light never deviated or changed despite promotions and positions within and among the house staff.

I knocked softly at the door to Lady Glendower's bedroom and entered without waiting for an answer. Nanny and the mistress were speaking quietly in an easy, friendly manner, and when I approached the bed Nanny stepped back and indicated that I place the tray on the small table near it. All the while Lady Glendower watched from her

27

position in the bed, never taking her eyes off me as I went about the chore. I felt clumsy under her gaze and was in fear that I would upset the soup bowl or make a clatter. When I had finished Nanny nodded to me and I, not knowing what was expected of me, started to leave the room.

"No, no, girl," Nanny spoke softly. "You remain here in case the mistress needs something from us." She poured the tea into a dainty china cup and handed it to Lady Glendower. "This will warm your bones," she said and again and I was struck with the familiarity that the nurse enjoyed. Well, I thought, the woman has been with the Glendowers for many years and should, through benefit of time and service, have established a certain degree of intimacy with the mistress.

While Nanny and I watched in silence Lady Glendower finished a part of her meal, and when she signalled that she was no longer interested in the food, Nanny dismissed me, giving me the tray to return to the kitchen.

"Mistress will be taking her nap now," she said as she tucked the blankets around the thin body. "There be nothing more for you to do for a bit. No harm will come to the house if you take a few moments to see the estate. It's always to the better if the young girls know their way about the house and grounds, but mind you, don't go near the bogs—they're treacherous—or wander too far afield. And see that you don't lose yourself in time. There'll be plenty to do later on in the day." She turned back the quilt at the foot of the bed and looked at me. "If anyone stops you or asks about you, just tell them you've come to work for Nanny and no one will bother you."

It was a respite I was pleased with for, since my arrival, I had not even been given a moment alone to form my thoughts or to see my new home. *My new home.* How sad the words made me feel, yet I could not allow myself the luxury of despondency. I checked my sadness and soon, in more adventuresome spirits, was prepared to see the estate.

It was a lovely afternoon. The sun was still high enough so that thin, elongated shadows of tall trees and parts of the house's gabled roofs were cast over the grounds. I fastened my cloak over my shoulders and head—there was still a chill in the air—and stepped out the back door with a deliberateness borne of necessity, for I had resolved that I would find in Winter's Light and its surrounding grounds much to my liking.

There was, indeed, much to be admired on the estate. The straight-bordered flower gardens, now thick and redolent with sweet spring blossoms that had just recently burst into bloom, waved in concert in the gentle breeze. These same flowers, in what I determined to be the early blooming beds, were thoughtfully and purposely massed by colors so that the full effect of their vividness could be experienced with one quick glance; the clusters of golden yellow jonquils to one side, the sections of white and red tulips in the middle, and the deep blue hyacinths on clustered stalks opposite them were all precise in their patterns. As they swayed and bowed in the wind the groups of flowers seemed much like a colorful banner of silk displayed at a country fair, one that had been caught by the wind and rippled as it hung high upon a standard. The flowers were remarkable to me, for all seemed to have been set down here in the ground at the same time, fully branched and blooming, and I remembered these same species of bulbs as they burst only one and two at a time through the hard dirt at Daear so that every new blossom seemed cause for celebration to my mother.

These were not the only flowers in bloom at the estate. Small purple crocuses still randomly peeked through the spring-green grass close to the burgeoning rhododendron and azalea shrubs next to the house. And at selected parts of the grounds, close to the house on one side and more to the manicured back, there were carved beds of newly turned and mulched earth from which vivid green shoots were already emerging, harbingers of the riot of colors that would surround the manse in the summer. The care given the outside grounds was not lost on me, for never had I seen such precision in the placement and arrangement of plants. At my own beloved Daear Father always preferred to let some of the flowers grow wild, though they were always kept neat and never allowed to go to seed. *"If the Good Lord had intended that everything be rigid and tidy, Gwynneth,"* he would say holding a buttercup or a jack-in-the-pulpit out to me, *"then there would never be wildflowers growing in the meadows in the golden sunshine or mushrooms popping up in the dark."*

I looked about me at the exactingly maintained shrubs. No, I thought, Father would not have had his own small plot of flowers this way. I stretched out my hand to a daffodil and stroked its soft petals before continuing my walk.

"And who be you, girl?" The voice was behind me and when I turned I saw that there was an odd sort of man watching me, an older stableman, I thought, for he was dressed in a long dark apron and wore heavy boots with pieces of straw stuck to the soles. "Ain't never seen you before," he continued as he moved closer to me.

"I'm Gwynneth. I've just come to help Nanny . . . to assist her with Lady Glendower."

The old man nodded his head. "Aye. They said that a new girl would be a'coming from a far place to help her." He continued to nod his head as though it would justify his words. "So you be her?" He took a corn pipe from his mouth and knocked it against his boots so that the residue of ash fell to the ground. "Nanny will need your help what with the lady taking to her bed." He continued to pick at the bowl of the pipe with a metal pick while a sharp wind swirled about us, tossing his apron strings in the air and flapping at my cape and ruffling my hood. I pushed the cloak back off my head and shook out my hair, running my fingers through the now-tangled windblown locks.

"I did not expect the wind to be so strong," I said and smiled as I smoothed the errant strands into place. I turned toward the house. "There, by the residence it was gentle, spring-like."

The man continued looking at the ground and rapping at his pipe. "Changeable, that's what it is this month. Changeable like this every year. You'll get used to it. You'll see next—" He had lifted his head to look at me and had immediately fallen silent, his words ceased in midsentence. I could see a puzzled look in his light eyes as he stared at, and through, me as though, our initial introduction for naught, he was just now meeting me.

"What is it?" I asked, but the old gentleman just stood there, his mouth open and his wiry, freckled hand shaking so much that I worried that he would drop his pipe. "What is it?" I asked again but he did not answer me. He continued to gawk and then he stepped back as though . . . as though he had been struck dumb by the sun so that he could neither speak nor hear. I could not comprehend the man's action and turned round to look behind me, to see if there was anything to frighten him, yet I saw nothing but the stables and the barns in the far distance down the hill.

"What is it?" I asked him a third time but the man just shook his head, watching me, and when I moved closer to him, he took another step backwards as if to escape from me. I stopped, confused by his actions. "Is there something wrong?" I was now beginning to feel a small stirring of fear myself, for I did not know what had prompted the poor man's fright.

The stableman stood there, squinting his eyes at me and then, in an accusing gesture I knew I would remember for the rest of my life, he raised his mud-caked hand and pointed it toward me.

"Ye have been here before," the old man said in a slow and raspy voice. I shook my head.

"No . . . never."

But the man persisted. "Ye have been here before," he repeated, his voice now cracking, and I shuddered for, in truth, somewhere in the far recesses of my mind I thought the man was correct. I, too, felt as though I had been here

31

before, had once upon a time stood in this same place and had felt the sharpness of the wind and the same warm spring sun on my face. It was only a fleeting feeling and yet it was as real and as vivid as any other memory I had.

"Ye have been here before," the elderly gentleman repeated once more, and it was now my turn to step back, mute, afraid to answer because somewhere, deep in my own heart and soul, I knew that this man had spoken the truth. But how . . . and when? It was much too much for me to ponder and I wrapped my cloak about me and ran toward the back of the house to the safety I hoped I would find in Winter's Light. Yet I knew that someday . . . some evening . . . and soon, I would have to face these strange feelings and acknowledge them. I would have to find out why certain ideas and memories coursed through my body and mind, for indeed, in just the few short hours that I had lived at Winter's Light, there were curious thoughts already forming in my reason.

Chapter Three

The care of Lady Glendower was neither difficult nor strenuous. Nanny hovered constantly near the woman, talking in bits and pieces, and all that afternoon my duties consisted mainly of being in the master bedroom with her in case she needed extra help. *"The extra pair of hands,"* as she had told me. But that seemed quite unnecessary, for Nanny seemed completely in control and capable, and at times I wondered why she indeed felt the need to have me, or anyone else, assist her.

I stayed mostly in the bedchamber, sometimes running to the kitchen with requests for hot tea or crackers or a sweet treat that Nanny anticipated might be wanted by her Mistress, but again I felt that I could probably be of more use to either Mrs. Padley in the kitchen or in another part of the house. But I was not asked for my opinion, and I was sure that ultimately Nanny planned for me to be more genuinely useful. To that end I expected that a large part of my duties in the future would be to wait upon Lady Glendower or sit quietly by while Nanny attended to other personal chores.

"I don't like for the mistress to awaken without some-one here—someone who cares, that is, expressly for her. To meet her needs." The nursemaid stared at me. "I think it best that you be here in case she needs you." She turned her back to me and checked the low fire in the grate, poking at the hissing split log on it. "And she will . . . she will," she said softly. I was puzzled at the strange statement. Lady Glendower had never met me save until this late afternoon, but already Nanny was presuming that she could and would trust me far beyond the extent accorded the servants already established in the house.

But again it was not for me to question. If Winter's Light was to be my new home then I should be thankful for, and deserving of, such trust.

I had my supper alone in the same dining room where I had eaten before, for all the other servants were still about their evening duties. When I had finished Mrs. Hoskins directed me to the small sitting room which adjoined the master bedroom and instructed me to stay until she returned, "in case my lady should awaken." She looked over at the peacefully dozing woman. "The mistress will sleep for about an hour and then she shall have company. We have guests in the house who have come to pay their respects and who will be taking dinner with me." She said the words forcefully, and I thought that she seemed almost regal and quite pleased with herself — as though the callers were coming to see her as well as her mistress.

The small woman straightened her lace cap and pinched at her cheeks to redden them a bit so that there were two small, faint circles of color in her thin, bony face of white.

"Gwynneth," she said lowering her voice lest she awaken her mistress, "if she rouses, see that you fix her coverlet so that she doesn't chill. She'll remember that today is Tuesday and that we will have company." Her voice lowered even more. "Then you'll see the bit of luster in her eyes later. Lady Glendower enjoys seeing the Price-Joneses when they visit with us every week. They are old friends — leastways, Mr. Charles is. Mr. Owen, his only nephew, is too young to be considered a long-term friend, but he is just as kind and solicitous as his uncle." She adjusted her shawl. "They'll be up to speak with her when our meal is finished." She looked over at the sleeping woman. "See that she's not disturbed, and if she awakens, fetch me."

The woman readjusted the fringe on her shawl just as the downstairs great clock tolled six. "We—Mr. Charles and Mr. Owen and I—will be up in one hour." She looked once more at the slumbering woman. "Aye, if she wakes up, she'll be glad to see you, too, I expect." She squinted her eyes at me. "Leastways, I hope she will . . ." She shook her head and gently closed the door behind her.

Though there was a fire in the sitting room it still seemed slightly chilly, and having checked to make sure that Lady Glendower was sleeping peacefully, I moved closer to the fireplace and the chair that was placed close to it. There was a book on the seat—a volume about our country—and I turned the pages carefully, looking to find my own county on the maps that were printed on the pages. When I found my shire I traced the darkened lines which marked its confines with my finger, thinking that I could almost follow in my mind each turn and curve in the reproduction.

The heat of the fire made me drowsy yet I dared not fall asleep, for I did not want Lady Glendower to awaken without my attentiveness or Nanny Hoskins to return and find me forgetful of my duty. I occupied my mind with all that I had seen this day, reflecting that perhaps life on this estate might not prove abhorrent. At least here, if fate served me well, I would find a permanent home. It was not what I would have chosen for myself, but as an orphan now, I knew I could not be too fussy about my future.

I had sat thus for almost an hour—for I heard the great clock strike seven chimes—watching the fire and dreaming secret thoughts of my own, when I heard someone knock softly at the door. I stood up thinking that Nanny had returned, but before I could cross the room, the door opened.

"I beg your pardon, ma'am. I did not mean to disturb you." The voice belonged to a young man who had moved to the middle of the room, near the bedroom, and now, in the light of the candles and the fire, I could see him clearly. He bowed once to me and I curtsied in his direction.

"Is Lady Glendower still asleep?"

"Yes."

"Then I shall not bother her yet. If you don't mind, ma'am, I will just sit here and wait until she rouses herself."

"I do not . . ." I was perplexed. Nanny had not said anything about a gentleman coming on his own to see Lady Glendower, and I looked at the open door. "Mrs. Hoskins . . ."

The young man smiled at me. "She gave me permission to come up. I have been doing so for almost two years, ever since I came to stay at Cynghanedd Hall, my uncle's estate." He nodded toward the doorway. "My Uncle Charles has been visiting with the Glendowers for more than twenty-five years. Even when Lord Glendower was alive. Those earlier times were happier, I'm told."

I understood all now. "Ah. Then you are one of the guests Nanny spoke about."

The young man bowed once again, more in jest than in courtliness. "Alas, I am found out by everyone," he said and then laughed softly. "Everyone on the estate knows us and of us," he said and then looked at me once more. "But, of course, you are new here and do not recognize me." He inclined his head toward me. "I am Owen Price-Jones, ma'am, and we—my uncle and I—live on the neighboring estate. It is our pleasure to visit with Lady Glendower almost weekly and inquire as to her health and her happiness." He gazed at me and I knew that he saw my skeptical look. "But I did not mean to disturb you, ma'am," he said again and began to back out of the room. "I shall wait until Nanny comes up with my uncle before returning." He made a formal bow now. "Ma'am. And again, my apologies."

I knew I had behaved rather foolishly and once more had to remind myself that this was not my home. "No, sir, please wait. It is not for me to question you and your pur-

36

pose, for it is I who am the stranger. It is I who apologize. And I am sure that you are most welcome in this room. As you have pointed out, you are much more familiar with the ways of this estate than I." I gestured toward a chair close to the table. "Please. Wait upon Lady Glendower. As you tell me that this is a regular visitation, I am sure she will awaken soon."

"I shall wait quietly if it does not inconvenience you, ma'am, or intrude upon your time." He indicated the book I had been reading.

"No. You only startled me, for I was lost in my own thoughts, and, indeed, you did me a service in calling me back to my work." I indicated the volume. "I was trying to educate myself in the ways of world," I said, and when the young man smiled I knew that at least I had assured him that I bore no more suspicions. I tried to distance us further from my initial misapprehension by speaking of the book's content. "The ways of the world are indeed mystifying—"

"Though perhaps more often banal," he said and I smiled.

"Indeed."

He bowed formally to me again and introduced himself. "I am Owen Price-Jones," he repeated anew, "and my Uncle Charles and I regularly attend on Lady Glendower. We live not ten miles from here, at the neighboring estate. Perhaps you have seen it." I inclined my head toward him.

"No, I am afraid not. I arrived just this afternoon and have not seen too much of this area. I am not from here." I smoothed down my dress. "I am Gwynneth Morys, come today to Winter's Light to help Nanny Hoskins care for the lady of the house."

Young Mr. Price-Jones stepped forward so that I could see his features more clearly. "Yes, I know. A pleasure, ma'am," he said before making a deep, formal introductory bow to me. "Mrs. Hoskins mentioned you to us." I bent my head and then looked directly at the gentleman so that I could better see him within the circle of light. He was a young man, perhaps twenty-four or twenty-five years of age, and was tan in complexion much as though he had been too long in the sun, with dark hair and light eyes. In the fire's illumination I could see that his features were strong and purposeful and that there were no discernible defects in his profile or carriage.

"Please, sit," I said, then moved to my own chair by the fireplace. Mr. Price-Jones remained standing, and before there was time to speak on any other subject, we heard Mrs. Hoskins coming toward the room, speaking to someone else. When she had entered the room she turned to a rather tall, robustly built, older gentleman, who took her arm and guided her toward the fire. She patted the senior man's hand and then indicated me with a glance and her words.

"This is Gwynneth," she said in the same tone that she had used when introducing me to Lady Glendower. "She has come to help us. She has come for my lady's sake."

What a curious way to express my arrival, I thought, and I looked down at the floor and then up at the gentleman before I sank into a low curtsy so that the stiff fabric of my dress wrinkled.

"Sir," I said and I saw Nanny's look of approval.

"This is Mr. Charles Price-Jones, who has been a friend of the Glendower family for many years." The formally clad gentleman bowed and I thought it strange that a gentleman would act thus to me, just another servant in the home.

"I have heard many good things about you, ma'am," he said. "Mrs. Hoskins has sung your praises already." He glanced at the door to the bedroom. "I am very pleased that the good lady will have two loyal people in her household." I moved my head slightly in recognition of his words and then was glad that it was dark so that the trio could see neither my confusion at so fine a reference nor my heated face which was, I felt, pinkening quickly at the spoken words.

"You have already met Mr. Price-Jones's nephew, I am

sure," Mrs. Hoskins said. Then she led us all into the bedroom. "My lady," Nanny turned to her mistress, who was stirring, "it's Mr. Charles and Mr. Owen come to see you." She moved quickly around to the head of the bed and smiled tenderly at the woman as both the gentlemen stepped forward to gently lift the frail woman so that she was leaning comfortably against the pillows.

"My dears," she said, and just as Mrs. Hoskins had predicted, Lady Glendower's voice was stronger and there was a glint in her eyes that had not been there before. Surely, I thought, there is a wonderful bond between these people, and I hoped that one day I, too, would be included within this tiny circle.

The uncle and nephew seemed most comfortable in this setting, and from bits of their conversation that I overheard I could tell that this was a pastime familiar to all parties. There was an ease about the four, one that effortlessly leant itself to smiles and gentle laughter. Mr. Charles Price-Jones took the lead in the conversation, first inquiring of Lady Glendower's health, then progressing to the state of the weather, and moving on to recount the latest *bon mots*. The gentleman's manner was solicitous and correct, and at times I saw that Lady Glendower would reach out and stroke his hand in an act born of long-standing friendship. I could not help but observe that Mr. Charles must once have been a very handsome gentleman, for even now, though he was in his mid-fifties and his brow was characteristically furrowed, his profile revealed a noteworthy intelligence, and his dark hair with its streaks of grey well suited him. Taken together with the fact that he was owner and master of his own vast estate, these material qualities had, I was sure, put him in the forefront whenever the list of the most eligible bachelors was recited for honored guests at cotillions and debuts.

His nephew, Owen, would, I presumed, also be included in that catalogue, for though at present he only resided at his uncle's estate, the mothers of maiden daughters would not be unmindful of the future benefits that would accrue to the young gentleman as Mr. Charles's rightful heir.

I watched both gentlemen as they continued their conversation with Nanny and Lady Glendower, and mused that neither man would lack for marriageable partners if either so desired; their striking looks, their wealth, and their impeccable manners would serve them quite well in that regard.

The four spoke quietly for nearly a half-hour and I was much taken with the kindness that was bestowed upon both women. Short anecdotes were told, a few small laughs were sounded, and by the end of the visit all four were smiling. From my place near the door I heard Lady Glendower thank her guests and ask for their assurance that they would again look in on her the following week. It was not a tiring visit for the woman—the gentlemen were much too cognizant of her condition—and I could see, from her face and manner, that it was much appreciated and cherished.

Once they had taken leave of their hostess and bowed in my direction, Nanny showed the gentlemen out of the bedroom, and together the two of us prepared the woman for the night's sleep. When all the candles save the ones we would use to guide us to our own rooms were snuffed and the grate in the fireplace had been turned down, Nanny walked me to the door of my own small bedchamber next to hers.

"Ye have done well for your first day, Gwynneth," she said to me. "Ye are what I expected you to be." She held out a candleholder to me. "Goodnight. Goodnight Gwynneth Morys. I am glad ye are here."

I went into my room and sat on the bed. This had been an overwhelming day for me, and I lay down even though I was still fully clothed. The events of the past few days were more overpowering than I had thought. Exhausted, I watched the flame of the candle in its brass stand flicker until it mesmerized me, and I became drowsy, then fell asleep.

I must have slept for several hours, for when I awakened I saw that my candle had nearly burnt completely. I hurriedly blew on the remaining wick to extinguish the small flame and preserve the rest of the wax. It would not do, I thought, for Nanny to think me wasteful, and I could almost hear my own dear sweet mother chastising me for allowing the tapers at home to burn needlessly and foolishly.

"I have always loved the light," I remembered telling my mother, who would smile indulgently at me and later quietly replace the wax candle while I was at school or on my rounds of work in the vegetable garden. *"It's only one small candle,"* I would hear her telling my father late in the evening. *"And isn't she the light of our lives?"* she would ask him, and then he would laugh and agree with her.

I touched the small stub in the holder. There would be no secret replacements any more, I thought sadly, and then stared up at the ceiling while I watched as shadows of the leaves from a nearby tree danced on the ceiling. My eyes grew heavy-lidded and before I slept once more I traced the outline of a single leaf that was emphasized on the wall opposite my bed. *"The beech tree,"* I said aloud, remembering when it was planted on that cold, rainy November day. I closed my eyes, recalling the damp afternoon so long ago, and then suddenly I sat up and stared out into the dark of my chamber. I could feel the heavy pounding in my body and I took two quick breaths to quell it but it was to no avail. I put my hand over my chest and could feel the beat of my heart as it pounded faster and faster. *The tree.* How did I know it was a beech? And how did I know when it was planted?

I heard the old man's accusing words pass through my mind once again. *"Ye have been here before."* I shuddered once more in fright. How could I possibly remember events I had had no part in? Events that had happened long before I was born and in another part of the country? My heart seemed to throb through my bodice.

"It is happening again," I said into the empty room and

I felt my hands go cold. I hunched my shoulders and drew the coverlet all around me to ward off the sudden chill, but I knew that the strange feeling that had haunted me all of my existence now loomed more pressingly. I had no choice but to accept it and wait until the reason was revealed to me.

Chapter Four

Days passed quickly. Nanny taught me my duties, light as they were, and although I keenly missed Daear, I soon fell into the ways of Winter's Light and found that my own loneliness could be diminished as I learned about my new home.

Winter's Light was a strange estate. Though the day-to-day housekeeping assignments ran smoothly, and peace and quiet were the order of the times, I could not help but feel that something else—a gloom, for want of a better word—persisted throughout the manse and its grounds. Though everyone went about their work efficiently and cheerfully there was an undercurrent of melancholy that seemed to pull at me. What made me sense this I cannot describe, but I felt that once upon a time there had been much pain in this house. It was always just a momentary feeling, brought on by a fleeting sound or a spoken word perhaps; then the mood would swiftly pass and all would seem serene once more.

I did not let this feeling of bleakness overcome me, for there was nothing tangible that I could suspect as its cause, and as for me, I could not have been better welcomed into the camaraderie of the estate workers or into the small circle of Nanny's favorites. Though I did not gossip with the maids or stand about and take up time when chores needed to be done, I did find that the companionship of the younger girls allayed much of my loneliness.

Nanny Hoskins, I soon learned, was the guiding force of the household. The inside staff took their orders only from her, although these were sometimes relayed by Mrs. Padley in respect of her own station within the house. The outside help—the gardeners, farmers, stable people and the like—deferred to the old woman, and all quoted Nanny's orders as though they were gospel truth. Few disobeyed the woman, and circulated among the staff were many stories about Nanny's temper when crossed. "Sharptongued," I once heard the stablemen say behind her back as we passed them by after Nanny had given them an order. It was no wonder, they told me, that even the stern Reverend Walker, the estate's private curate, was known to avoid the woman when he made his weekly rounds of the homes on the property.

I could not find any fault with the way Nanny treated me. I did not fear her words, for when she spoke to me they were quiet and practical, and whenever we two sat alone, after Lady Glendower had retired, I found the older woman to be a good and wise friend.

"Aye, Gwynneth," she said one evening as she rocked back and forth in her tiny room. "I know what they say about me hereabouts. But I pay them no mind. Words can never hurt me, not even the words they'll say over me when I'm gone. I know my place and I keep to it. That's the way it has been and always will be." Nanny looked over at me. "We all have our places."

I nodded. "Yes, Nanny, we all have our special places, and I'm grateful to you," I said, "for I surely know mine in this household."

Nanny squinted her eyes and I was reminded of the old hawk that used to soar above our farmhouse in the evening. "Perhaps," she said and continued to rock in silence the rest of the evening while I proceeded to stitch on a sampler for my room.

I continued to grow more accustomed to Winter's Light and to the routine of the house. My memories of Daear,

44

though beginning to blur with time, still seemed fresh and sweet in my mind, and every so often I found myself reminded of my past life there. I knew that I was fortunate to have found a position here with Lady Glendower, yet I secretly longed to return to the shire where I grew. It was but a fond hope, and I kept reminding myself to accept what had been sent my way by Providence. A short note Reverend Jenkins had sent further counseled me regarding this obligation.

"Dear Gwynneth," he wrote. *"I still think of your employ in Winter's Light as a gift that the Good Lord has provided for you. We had all hoped when Mathias and Molly took you in that rainy night that you would remain forever as one of us in our village. But now that that cannot be I am sure that the Lord has wisely guided you to your present place. Be trustworthy to all you serve and we shall remember you in our prayers. Daear remains empty and the land fallow except for those few grains that have re-seeded themselves. I often pass it on my way to the parishioners and think of you and your dear parents. Trust in the Lord, Gwynneth, and know that I remain your faithful confidant, Rev. Frank Jenkins."*

The letter, short as it was, still served to remind me of my clouded birth and of the love and generosity of my parents. I stored the note away in my trunk, knowing that on sentimental occasions I would be inclined to read it again.

Nanny and I had fallen into the habit of having high tea in the small parlor next to Lady Glendower's room. It was a pleasant interlude within the work day, and we spent much of the time conversing about the vagaries of the weather and the work necessary to keep up the estate. Nanny had not broached the subject of my family or my upbringing and as for me, I had not spoken of them because I thought her uninterested. Thus I was not expecting her question this day.

"Well, Gwynneth," she said as she set her cup of tea on the table, "I hope you do not miss your own home too much."

I bent my head and mumbled the answer. "I will always remember it, ma'am, for I had wonderful times there."

Nanny seemed pleased with the reply. "Of course you will and of course you must. But now, come and tell me what you think of our home." I had already learned that Nanny, who had not lost any of her sharpness with age, could ask blunt questions in the way of her ancestors, and woe to those who did not answer in truthful style. I had already heard her biting tongue in action when some poor household girl had brought up an afternoon tray without its full complement of sweets — Nanny's favorite — and had made up excuses about their absence. After the call-out the young girl, Meg, as it happened, had retreated hastily, and I suspect in tears, back down to the kitchen, and the missing treats were soon brought up by another, more experienced, servant.

Mrs. Hoskins's question was therefore not one I had anticipated, and I stammered before I answered. "I have not seen too much of it, Nanny. What I have seen is a wonder, and I am sure I will gradually get to see more." I hoped that perhaps this would suffice.

"Have you not inspected the rooms?"

I shook my head. "I have not had the time, and I felt it was not my place to poke about," I replied truthfully, for as I spent most of my days and some of my early evenings in the master wing of the house, I had not had a chance to very thoroughly explore my surroundings. What I had seen so far had been garnered instantaneously and superficially as I passed through rooms and halls when sent on errands by Nanny.

The old woman clucked her tongue. "That will not do," she said more to herself than to me. "That will not do at all." She put down her teacup. "Visit the house," she said looking at me. "Know it. Come to love it like . . . like we all do." She had a peculiar way of peering at me that made me uncomfortable. "You need to know about Winter's Light, for you, by the grace of the Almighty, will

46

most certainly live here for the rest of your natural life." She pushed back her dessert plate, unaware that to me her words sounded not like a prediction but rather a judgment. "Soon, girl," she said. "Learn about it as soon as possible."

The next day Nanny gave me time to explore the house fully, telling me to carefully examine all the furnishings and to take notice of all.

"The portraits and the appointments and the books, Gwynneth. Especially the books about the family. Their history. Their people." She gave me a small smile. "From the way you place the flowers in the bowl I can see that ye have an eye to detail, girl. Use it now. Look to the furnishings. Ask anyone about the history of the house. Most of us — we old ones, at least — know each and every object in it. We have polished and cleaned and cherished most for a long, long time. That is what you should do, girl. Cherish each and every piece." She looked toward the ceiling. "Pray heaven, you'll be here a long, long time."

It was an odd choice of words, but still I thought I understood Nanny. Her own service here at Winter's Light had been the most important thing in her long life, and I knew she wanted me to come to realize my complete turn of fortune in having been chosen to work and live here. In her way Nanny was kindly offering me the best of all possible situations for someone in my circumstances.

I took advantage of the opportunity and began my exploration on the first floor of the house, taking in the entire scope of the house rather than concentrating on singular items. The individual pieces, the bibelots and wall hangings and crystal, could occupy my time some other day. I surmised I would have many hours and many days and years to see everything if, as Nanny had it, Winter's Light was to be my lifelong home. But for now I wanted to see all of the mansion as an invited guest would, in all its grandness.

I pretended that I was a summoned visitor and started my tour at the front door in the grand foyer. Seen from this view the house's breadth and height made me appreciate those who originally had had the task and pleasure of completing the home. Everywhere—from the broad staircase that was set back and yet in the middle of the room to the several doors on either side of the Great Hall that opened to reveal various parlors and sitting rooms and formal halls—everything gleamed with gilt and crystal. The effect was made even more spectacular by the spring sunshine that streamed through the Palladian windows flanking the front door and caused the polished glass and gold to flash and glimmer.

I opened a door nearest me and found myself standing at the entrance to a large room, a grand and sumptuous ballroom now darkened and shuttered against the daylight. Huge, ornate chandeliers—ten of them in two rows of five—hung from the ceiling, their unlit and unburnt candles clustered within hundreds of faceted drops. I stood in the middle of the hall imagining guests arriving for supper or for a ball, and had I been sure of being unseen I might have swirled and turned in the manner of the dances I had heard about in school. We had been forbidden to practice these steps in our shire, for the Reverend Jenkins had been inflexible on the subject; country dancing—rounds—had been encouraged in the village, but I was sure that the dances performed here at Winter's Light were of the type in which a gentleman and lady danced together, swirling and turning in time to the music of violins and cello and the pianoforte. I closed my eyes and imagined that I could hear the soft harmony that must have come from the musicians' places off to the left. The sweet, clear melody seemed to swell, and for an instant I believed that I saw a handsome couple, a young girl dressed in a pale green satin gown and a gentleman in a formal suit, as they bowed to each other and began dancing in time to the music. The light from the burning candles caught the beading on the woman's dress and train so that it gleamed, brilliant as diamonds, as she moved gracefully in her partner's arms. They were alone on the dance floor, and it was as if I could hear the murmurs of the other guests as they whispered their approval of the partners. *"Beautiful." "Lovely." Wonderful match."* The two made a turn around the room and at one point danced close to me. Who the couple might be I did not know, for I could not glimpse their faces even though in my imaginings I could almost reach out and touch them as they passed by.

I opened my eyes and still the fantasy continued, as it seemed I stood and watched the man and woman until they had mingled in with the dozens of other couples who now were dancing in the warm and perfumed room. I knew it must be fancy, and yet I had the feeling that this was not just my imagination, that sometime, long ago in the history of this house, the scene had been real. Why I felt this way I cannot tell, but many times before in my life I had suspected things that proved to be true, and thus I knew to accept this feeling.

But then the vision passed. The dancers faded and all seem quiet in the dim room once again, the music silenced, the melody stopped in mid-note. I stood in the doorway and looked into the stilled, darkened ballroom where covered furniture — sidechairs and small pier tables — was arranged in mute testimony to the splendid parties that had once been given in this home. Although this had been designed to be a happy room, now the fringed, dark silk throw-cloth atop the closed piano, the heavy linen dust-wrappers on the furniture, and the mirrors turned to face the walls contradicted its purpose. No, this was no longer a gay room. Rather, had there been musicians sitting upon the stage at this moment, I knew that they would play music more in keeping with its present somber tones, perhaps a dirge. I shuddered and, suddenly chilled both inside and outside my body, I walked from the room and closed the door wishing that I had not entered here and disturbed its ghosts.

I opened other doors to other rooms; it was all as I had imagined. The furniture arrangements and even the vases of flowers brought in from the estate hothouses seemed to me to be duplicates of those from another time, another year. Before I had even looked around the rooms, *I had known where each and every piece of property was placed.* This is not a statement I make lightly, for often I had been accused by my parents of having a too lively imagination. And when I had protested to them, most vociferously, that what I saw and felt seemed more than made-up child's play, I had always been cautioned not to take too seriously all that I seemed to know. I had learned then not to fully speak my mind, and now it was this way again as I walked in these rooms. I already knew too much about them, and wandering through them had made me quite uncomfortable.

In truth, I did not like these extraordinary feelings of mine, for I had no rational explanation for them, and Reverend Jenkins had always cautioned us to accept nothing unseen save the Lord God. I had often before wished to cure myself of this easy acceptance of invisible entities, but it was one more aspect of my character that, eventually, I had been forced to acknowledge, and now it had continued to exert its power here. I did not know the reason, but once I stepped inside these rooms of Winter's Light, I had known instinctively and without hesitation where certain furnishings would be placed and arranged.

I did not want to continue with my exploration this day. The mood in the house had turned heavy for me and although all was beautiful and dazzling to the eye I could not help but feel once more, that there was a tremendous sense of dolor and gloom overshadowing everything in the manor. What it was I could not tell, but in certain parts of the house and in certain of the rooms I had investigated, it was as if a cruel, cold wind had suddenly passed through and banished the sunlight and warmth from all that it had touched. Why I felt this way when all appeared right I do not know. But I had learned to bide my time in arriving at answers to these sorts of questions, for I knew, as it had already been proven several times in my lifetime, that some day in the future I would have an explanation. With this knowledge, I tried to reassure myself.

Nanny was standing by the bed attending Lady Glendower when I returned, and when I set about my duties I saw the two women nod to each other as though they were indeed pleased that I was there to help. It was something lovely to witness, this silent communication between the two women. It was as if the two elderly ladies knew the other's thoughts and wishes and, breeding and family notwithstanding, each treated the other with utmost and kind respect for the person rather than for her position. I suspected that, had their roles been reversed, neither would have chosen another mode of companionship. No, the bond between the two old women was secure and fast in friendship and dedication, service and loyalty.

For something to do, I rearranged the flowers in the vase next to Lady Glendower's bed. She smiled at me.

"They are quite lovely for this season, are they not, Gwynneth?" I bent my head, for I was still not used to Lady Glendower speaking to me directly, and I kept looking at the blossoms.

"Yes, ma'am. I noticed the flower beds when I first saw the grounds."

"I remember when I was a child I used to want to pick them as soon as they bloomed. I wanted to have them for my very own. Even Anne would . . ." Lady Glendower's voice trailed off and she spoke no more. I saw a flicker of sadness cross her countenance. Who Anne was I did not know nor would I ask. Instead I busied myself with the pillows and looked surreptitiously at Nanny for guidance, but the old nurse pretended not to notice the exchange. I recognized her nonchalance as feigned, for Nanny was never deficient in hearing and seeing everything that goes on within this chamber. Indeed, at odd moments while working I had sometimes caught the nurse watching me as she went about her duties, and I knew not what interested her so much in me. At first I had told myself that it was natural for her to oversee me in my tasks so that no errors

51

were made, but now I found her observance rather peculiar. It was as though the old nurse waited for me to make certain moves, certain gestures, and frankly, I wondered if she were perverse. I saw her sometimes, her mouth moving in words only spoken to herself, her snowy head nodding to her own sentences and thoughts. On the few occasions when I had caught her, she had pretended to be daydreaming, and I had not questioned her. Whatever was in her mind and thoughts, I considered it best to let it be, for she continued to be kind and amiable to me.

That evening Mr. Owen Price-Jones and his uncle, Mr. Charles, paid us another visit, and again Lady Glendower appeared more than pleased with their attention. Although she was bundled up against the cold air and although her room was heated by a fire in the cavernous grate, Lady Glendower seemed to be taking a chill and Nanny, in her determined way, gently and carefully guided the two gentlemen out of the bedchamber for a few moments until the proper bedclothes had been discretely settled around her mistress.

After all had been arranged, I returned to the outer room and to the book I was reading while the guests conversed with their hostess in her chamber. Thus I did not notice that the younger Mr. Price-Jones had come in and now stood close to my own fireplace.

"I see that you are taking great delight in that book, ma'am." Mr. Jones's voice seemed genuine, and I was beginning to feel as though I had found another friend at Winter's Light.

"It is instructive and informative." I closed the volume. "I have always been a reader, Mr. Jones. Even when I was younger and in school, I enjoyed the accounts of other countries." I blushed and became quiet, for surely I was speaking much too much.

Mr. Owen seemed not to notice. "Then you must allow me to send over some texts on the subject of traveling. I myself, though not an extensive traveller, enjoy reading about other lands, too."

I looked down at the closed book. "You mustn't go to any trouble, Mr. Jones. I am sure that there must be other manuscripts in the library here."

"Even so it would please me to know that someone else enjoys my collection. Tomorrow I shall remind myself to send you some reading material." He turned to his uncle, who had just entered the room. "I have just promised Miss Morys to send her a book, Uncle Charles, and you shall hold me to my word."

"I doubt that I will have to remind you, Owen," his uncle replied, smiling kindly at me. "But now, come, it is getting late and I don't think we should overstay our welcome." He looked at Nanny, who watched us curiously. "Mrs. Hoskins might not allow us to visit again if we linger too long this evening."

Nanny shook her head. "Lady Glendower and I would never forbid you this house, sir. Not for however many times you would want to visit us. It's a pleasure, sir, just to see the two of you." The gentlemen bowed to me and followed the woman out of the room. When Nanny returned a few minutes later she said no more about the gentlemen's visit, and after damping down the fire we each went to our rooms.

My sleep was not worry-free, for strange images pierced my slumber, images of people and places that I had never seen and could not recognize. The configurations seemed to have been sketched in light shades of charcoal and then filled in with pastel colors to give form and substance to the scenes. In one, the most predominant and most vivid, I could see the bare outline of two grey horses, their breath steamy in the cold air as they stood, snorting, tethered to a post outside a small rustic inn. They were hitched to the front of a black coach and inside the carriage there was a woman who sat back away from the window, the brim of her plumed hat pulled firmly down to cover her eyes as though she hoped to escape detection. She seemed nervous and apprehensive as she sat alone, and every once in a while she would peek from the side of the window toward the inn. Soon I saw a young man emerge from the hostel with a stout older man I assumed to be the keeper. This portly gentleman bowed low and opened the coach door and extended his gloved hand. "We are at your service, miss, and at your discretion," he said, and I could see the young woman move forward and out of the carriage. Her long, deep green cloak curled round her legs as she stepped down so that momentarily it reached only halfway to her boots before falling to its proper length.

She stood beside the younger man—a rather good-looking person—and smiled nervously at him as he took up her hand and patted it by way of reassurance. The woman appeared to be young, no more than sixteen or seventeen, and seemed quite beautiful, although it was difficult to see all her features clearly, for it was as if I were viewing the incident through a heavy veil. I saw her turn to the young man with a question in her light eyes, but her companion barely shook his head and in this act gently silenced her. The young woman understood the gesture and turned her eyes away and stared straight ahead as the two men escorted her inside the square, stone building. Even in my dream I questioned who these people were and what connection they had to me. I had never seen them or the surrounding area before, nor had they ever appeared in any of my earlier dreams.

I began to awaken, but as I did so I heard the young woman softly ask her companion, *"Do they suspect? Can we trust them?"* She seemed anxious for the answer and I, too, wanted to know the reply, but I never heard it, for the vision was gone and no matter how much I tried nor how hard I closed my eyes I could not recall it. Yet I knew that in their own time these same people would return to my dreams, would return some night to haunt me once again.

Chapter Five

The next afternoon a small package arrived for me with a card from Mr. Price-Jones. True to his word, he had sent me a volume which pleased me and which I read in my spare evenings after I had completed my tasks for Lady Glendower. When first I sat with it Nanny had questioned me about it, her only comment being that the Price-Joneses were "fine, faithful men proven through the decades to be true gentleman to their word. Especially Mr. Charles, for he has been tested these many years." I agreed with her, for even in our brief encounters the two had been most courteous and I could find no fault with the gentlemen. No more was said about the book until the two neighbors rode over for their scheduled dinner with Nanny and conversation with Lady Glendower. Even though I had sent a note thanking him for his kind gesture, I had planned personally to convey my appreciation to Mr. Owen for his kindness and had asked Mrs. Hoskins to be given the opportunity.

Nanny surprised me by inviting me to sit with the three of them at the supper table. It was an invitation I had not expected, and I demurred, thinking that Nanny was just being kind to ask me. Yet the woman would not take a negative answer and I relented when because I had expressed concern that there would be no one to stay with Lady Glendower, Nanny claimed Meg for the duty.

"See that you call us right away if my lady awakens,"

she said over and over again to the poor frightened girl. "And see that you don't fall asleep and leave the mistress to attend to herself." Meg kept reiterating that she would obey all the instructions and I think she was more than relieved when the four of us went off to dinner.

I was quite bewildered that Nanny would ask me to share the dinner with her and her guests. Obviously the three were on familiar terms and I kept thinking that I would feel the outsider in their conversation. But this was not the case. Mr. Charles Price-Jones included me in many of the stories he told, pointing out the different connections and interfamilial alliances of those involved in the tales.

I was intrigued with the generational stories and instead of feeling a stranger I began to find out the ways of the Glendower family and those who had lived at Winter's Light, for Mr. Price-Jones was most adept at recounting snippets of long-ago information regarding many of the family ancestors who had inhabited the house.

"Mind you, Miss Morys," Mr. Owen said, after we had heard a particularly enchanting tale about a great-grandparent of Lady Glendower's. "Uncle Charles has many stories to tell. I have not heard half of them, I suspect, although I have lived with him for the last two years."

"Aye, and ye never will, either." Nanny had joined in the merriment. "Mr. Charles has always been known as a teller of anecdotes. He has a keen ear, Gwynneth, and the saying in these parts has always been that he never forgets a quote or a name."

"An exaggeration, to be sure, Miss Morys." He bent his head toward me and smiled.

"I am sure, sir, that your excellent reputation is well-deserved." I turned to Nanny and then back to the two men. "Mrs. Hoskins has already informed me as to your character. And as to yours, also, sir—" I added for Mr. Owen's sake. I saw Nanny beam at me as I repeated her words to the gentlemen.

"That is because Nanny in her goodness has forgiven

56

me my many imperfections."

"Ye have none, Mr. Charles," Nanny said. "Never have had a one in all the years I have known you." She took a piece of cake that was being served to her.

"How long have you known Nanny?" I asked and Mr. Price-Jones paused as if to count the years.

"Miss Morys, I have been visiting this house for many many years." He looked over at Nanny. "Just how long has it been, Nanny?"

"Now just give me a minute and I'll be able to tell you for sure." She wrinkled her forehead. "At least twenty-five years, wouldn't it be, Mr. Charles?" She blotted her lips with her napkin. "You came calling on us first in the summertime, as I remember it. A July or August, it was, I believe. When Miss Anne was near to eight or nine, it was." She looked at him and frowned. "It was a garden party, I remember, and we always teased and said Miss Anne was taken with you right off, what with the way she followed you around all day. Do ye remember, Mr. Charles?" she asked and Mr. Price-Jones nodded his head slowly. "Aye, a long time ago, that was," Nanny continued and then she paused and suddenly I felt the mood turn somber. She looked down at the table, and I could see that her face became downcast for a moment. "A long time ago, it was," she said once again and then she fell silent. "But, enough of that. What's past is past," she said and then motioned that the two men were expected in Lady Glendower's rooms. "Come. We'll go up now to see the mistress, if you're finished with dinner."

The men rose and Mr. Charles took Nanny's arm and led her out of the room. His nephew and I lingered for only a moment.

"I did not understand that remark," I said. "I hope it was not something that I inadvertently caused."

"No, Miss Morys. You must not fault yourself. You can not be expected to know the history of Winter's Light or of any of us. It was not an insensitive comment on your part. Please believe me. It is only that sometimes

57

when Lady Anne's name is mentioned the conversation is halted. It is a natural thing when one begins remembering too much." He took my arm. "Now put it aside and let us hurry to catch up with the others, for I suspect Lady Glendower will be awaiting us."

I did not have the opportunity to tell Mr. Price-Jones that I had no notion of the memories to which he referred. I knew nothing of Lady Anne or of the sadness that seemed connected with her, I had heard her alluded to only once before, in Lady Glendower's company. I held my remarks, for now was neither the time nor the place to begin such a deep conversation. Perhaps another day I would ask him to explain, or if I had the chance, I could ask Nanny about this mysterious woman.

The following afternoon my opportunity to inquire about the woman presented itself. Nanny had instructed me to go through the drawers of Lady Glendower's chiffonier in order to find a silk shawl, and when I had pulled it from its place a small framed painting that had been caught in its folds fell onto the floor. I retrieved it and started to put it back into the drawer, but when I turned it over and saw the features of the person depicted I was dumbfounded and bewildered. The portrait was of the woman I had seen in my dream, the sad young woman in the coach who had appeared anxious and afraid. Only in this painted pose she was smiling, a gentle, soft smile that might have lingered on her lips some summer day when she had just bidden someone good morning.

A sick feeling came over me and I held the portrait away from me as though, if I inspected it too closely, it would harm me. It was indeed the same woman who had entered the small inn and I instinctively knew that this was Anne, the mysterious Anne whose name brought sadness to so many in this house. I took a deep breath, for I could almost hear the soft voice ask the question once more—
"Do they suspect? Do they suspect?"

I turned to Nanny and found her staring at me again in that peculiar way that she had, and yet she made no move to take the picture from me.

"This woman? Who is she?"

Nanny flattened her lips together and waited a few seconds before answering me. "The Mistress Anne," she said quietly, and I trembled at this confirmation of my intuition.

"Anne?" I looked at the features of the woman in the painting and it was as though the light grey eyes that I had seen in my dream stared back at me from the portrait.

"Lady Glendower's daughter. Her only child," Nanny said and I shivered at the flat way she spoke the words.

"What happened to her?"

Nanny stepped forward then, took the painting from me and gently fingered the gold frame surrounding the beautiful, youthful face.

"She died a long time ago, Gwynneth, a very long time ago." She looked at me and seemed to peer right through me. "It was a tragedy—a terrible tragedy." She held tight to the frame. "She was much loved in this house by everyone, be it staff or family or friends. You couldn't help loving her. And after her death there was no more joy at Winter's Light. No more laughter." She put the painting into a pocket of her starched white apron. "Best it be kept away from the mistress for now."

"Will you tell me more about Anne?" I asked, because for some inexplicable reasons I suddenly needed to know more about the woman.

Nanny folded her hands in front of her and nodded her head. "Aye. If you want. Some other time."

"Yes. I would like that."

"So be it then." She gestured toward the bed where Lady Glendower was stirring. "You'll not be mentioning this to her at this time," she said, and I motioned in agreement and went about my chores. I knew Nanny would keep to her word when there was time.

Later, when all was quiet and we were at tea, I sat across from the old woman and I think she knew what I was going to say, for she made no attempt to speak of other things.

"Tell me about Anne," I asked, and she hesitated for only a few seconds. Then she pulled the small frame from her pocket. She swallowed hard as she stared at the picture of the young woman.

"The Lady Anne was the love of her parents and of all of us who worked here. There wasn't one of us who wouldn't have done everything for her. She was a sweet young thing, all happy and charming and full of light, and this whole house, Gwynneth, would echo with her laughter. With her songs. When any of us were in her presence we felt as though it could never be better." She took a deep breath. "For you see, the heart of this house — the heart of Winter's Light — had been captured by this little golden-haired girl from the day she was born." She sighed as she finished the words. "But that may have been the problem. We may have loved her too much. We may have guarded her too well, so that she never knew the real ways of the world."

"What an odd thing to say, Nanny. How could one be loved too much?"

Nanny poured herself another cup of tea. "Aye, ye listen sharp to me, Gwynneth, child. There are such things as too much love for one person or too much dotings and too many promises. People can be too protected, too unworldly, if ye take my meaning."

"No. I do not understand."

Nanny set her cup down on the table. "Sometimes it's best to be told of all the harsh realities of the world. To be told beforehand, so that when things — don't be asking me now to explain them — so that when certain things happen, they won't hurt you. They won't fool you."

"Nanny, you speak of matters I do not understand."

The old woman looked down at the picture and then up at me as if in explanation. "Anne was young and weak," she said simply. "She was young and romantic and allowed life to carry her along without too much worrying." Her small hand tightened around the portrait. "She was

60

kind and loving but oh," she said, "she had such a be-dazzled idea of life. Not a real worry or care in her fair head because, you see, we never allowed her to be trou-bled." Again there was a pause, and when she spoke next it was with regret. "That is what killed her, I always said. She never knew the true life."

"Lord Glendower, the master, he agreed with me after his daughter's death. We didn't tell the mistress though, for it was too hurtful by then and she already had the look of sickness that would make her frail. But Lord Glendower knew it, and when Anne died he knew he couldn't right it and it was as if he, too, died on that day." She licked her lips. "Aye, he lived for a few more years but all the substance of the man was gone. He was a big man, he was, powerful built and a keen rider, but the death of Lady Anne touched everyone and most especially her par-ents. Ye can appreciate that." She swiped at her eyes. "I wonder sometimes if we could have . . . if it could have been any other way." She looked again at the picture of the sweetly-smiling girl. "She was so gentle and so accept-ing. Not a real trouble in her head because of our guardi-anship and then when adversity came to her she didn't know how to handle it." She held the picture tighter and seemed to forget that I was in the room with her, for her words were more for herself than for me. "If we had only been able to help. If she had only . . ." She licked her lips again and looked at the portrait. "If ye had only waited, little mistress. If ye had only waited and given us the chance." She made clucking sounds as though she were talking to her juvenile charge. "The poor girl. She didn't know what to do when her young man never came back," she said, and I could barely hear her words. She pushed back a strand of her snowy hair under her cap and spoke more loudly, yet I was too confused by her words to un-derstand her at that moment. "Poor Lady Anne, if only she had had the strength and spirit of her great-aunt. That would have served her well." She looked at me as though I should understand her.

"Anne was such a lovely and innocent child and we all spoiled her. Whatever she wanted we gave her. Whatever she craved was brought to her." I was quiet, for Mrs. Hoskins was now recalling for her own sake and not for my benefit. "Not that she was a demanding child. Oh no. She was a good child, obedient, and it was so easy just to tell her stories and to let her think that all was right in the world. For in her universe it was, Gwynneth, it was. For her there would never be a worry or care however long she lived. We were all there for her and we would see to her every want and need. And not because we had to or because we were employed to, but because she was so sweet and charming and . . . and innocent." The old woman's eyes clouded over. "Aye. She was too innocent, that was her trouble. We failed her by allowing her to believe in only innocence and good." The old woman blinked back the tears that were brightening her eyes.

I refuted her statement. "I do not think that a failure, Nanny, to believe in right and goodness. I do not mock them. They are the values we all wish for and strive for. Reverend Jenkins has always preached that, and my parents always guided me in those ways."

"Aye, but gal, you had guardians—parents—who also knew the ways of the land. Who not only worked it but in addition knew how to master life. Earth and life, they be the same. Both made up of cruel rocks and soft dirt. Everyday a new twist and turn. A stone to be dug out or a patch of sod to be planted. Yet ye learned how to work with it . . . how to survive with it. Even the name of your home—Daear—represents the bond between the two."

Her knowledge puzzled me, but I did not ask how she had learned so much of my background. Perhaps she knew of my life before I came here because she herself had come from a rural home similar to mine. For all I knew the woman might still have relatives and family settled there.

She thrust out her chin to me. "Ye survived, Gwynneth," she said strongly, as though she took great pride in my life. "And you learned well. That be one of the differences between you and her. Between you and the Lady Anne."

I blushed, for of course it would be much too bold of me to ever compare myself to a lady in the same breath. But Nanny did not shrink from the comparison.

"If only she had had a bit more spunk." She squinted her eyes directly at me. "Like ye."

I looked at the small portrait that was half-covered by Nanny's hand and suddenly had a great urge to find out more about Anne. It was as though it mattered to me . . . as though it would behoove me to find out about the promise of a gentle life that seemed not to have been fulfilled . . . as though it were vital for me to know that she had been loved.

"Tell me more about her, Nanny." I was curious about Anne and the way she spent her days. "Tell me about her daily life and the life at Winter's Light while she lived."

Nanny poured herself a half-cup of tea and offered me a still-warm scone, then sat back and smiled a secret smile, and I knew that she was beginning to enjoy speaking about the young girl. She told me about Anne's childhood and the happiness she had brought to the Glendowers and how the girl had been wanted and loved though she had come late to the Glendowers. And as Nanny unfolded the story in her own way—jumping about from Anne's birth to her schooling and then back to her nursery—I listened carefully, reveling in the account as though it were a story that was being read to me. Anne's life of luxury and ease was foreign to me, and I was curious about how one could adjust to being pampered and waited upon. It was beyond my ken and Nanny saw my look of wonderment.

"Can ye comprehend it, Gwynneth? Such an existence?"

I shook my head and Nanny seemed saddened at the gesture. But I was truthful in my answer, for while my parents had loved me and nurtured and sheltered me, there had been more than enough work for three hands plus the extra planting-season help on our land. Though love had been in abundance at my home, still there had been chores to do around the farm—cattle to be cared for in both the early morning darkness and late evening sunsets, and earth to be tilled and planted, and food to be gathered and cooked for the meals. I could not imagine any life where there was more than a hour a day of idle time. No, a life of Anne's ease I could not fathom.

"Would ye have liked that life, Gwynneth?" Nanny's voice cracked a bit as she busied herself with the collecting of her plates.

"I suppose it would have been lovely," I said. "But that is not for me to reflect on. My parents were not aristocrats." I stood up and brushed the scone crumbs into my saucer. "But, Nanny," I said remembering the wonderful days of my childhood, "we three were happy. Very happy."

Chapter Six

In all my exploration of the grounds of Winter's Light I had yet to venture close to the moors. Although they were beautiful and, yes, strangely alluring with the high, smoky grey haze that hung above them, I must confess that I was frightened of them. It had always been this way. Even as an adventuresome child I had needed no discipline to keep me from the bogs. I had always heeded my parents' warnings that I was not to attempt to travel the misty fields alone lest all sorts of dire things happen to me.

I had needed no extra admonitions, for my imagination was quite acute, and I was content to stay at a distance from the moors. Not even the seductive and eerie sounds that emanated from within them were reason enough to disobey my mother and father. The mist-veiled trees with their twisted trunks and bare branches outstretched toward me seemed more frightening than my worst nightmares, and no amount of coaxing or threats from my playmates could get me close to the edge of the swamps.

Thus the lessons that I had learned in childhood kept me from showing anything more than a passing interest in the vast fields of moors that lay close by to one side of Winter's Light. Instead, I preferred the lush, green manicured lawns and clipped hedges for diversion, and the onset of the warm days did much to increase the pleasures these offered.

Summer had come to Winter's Light gradually. The trees had slowly unfolded their leaves, buds appeared and blossomed on the purple, white, red azalea and rhododendron bushes, scenting the air all about them, and the brownish patches of earth were now full and luxuriant with thick blades of grass. Pale spring green gave way to deep summer hues; the paths and walkways surrounding the gardens were paved with small white pebbles, and the annual flowers were beginning to burst forth in profusion. Butterflies and bees hovered near the plants and shrubs and lazy hot afternoons found the estate workers pacing themselves in completing their chores. It was quite a peaceful time and as Nanny had not extended my duties beyond the care of Lady Glendower, I found that I had much time to think my own thoughts and dream my own dreams in the lazy afternoons.

I settled into the routine of the house and my life became calmer. I had begun, with Nanny's approval, taking small walks about the estate since the weather had begun to turn warm and clear. I had always liked the advent of the hot weather, and now especially enjoyed surveying its effects on the gardens. As their yellowing green leaves had begun to wither, most of the spent tulip bulbs had been staked and wrapped. Their places in the cultivated beds were taken with summer flowers and shrubs and bushes just beginning to blossom. Climbing and trellised roses that had been mere twigs and spindly vines only a few short weeks ago had now turned into leafed slivers of green stalks and bulging buds redolent with a faint perfume and peeping promise of deep crimson, scarlet, and pink petals. Cutting beds massed with zinnias and marigolds and nasturtiums were already in place—the blossoms hothouse forced and then planted in the places where the spring flowers had bloomed. If summer had not yet fully come to Winter's Light, surely the mild sunshine and the pungent smell of peat humus heralded its imminent arrival.

I looked at the mounds of fresh sod stacked round the plants and I had a foolish urge to touch the earth, as though touching the warm, moist soil would renew my spirit. I moved my hand about so that it spread the dirt close to the plantings and for one brief moment it was reminiscent of my own flower garden at Daear. I closed my eyes and imagined myself back at the village.

"Are you searching for treasure, my dear Miss Morys?" The gentleman's voice was playful and as I stood up. Mr. Owen Price-Jones made a gentle bow.

"There is so much fortune here already," I said and pointed toward the house before realizing that my palm had several dark, wet spots where the moist earth had clung to it. I put my hand behind me but Mr. Price-Jones was too swift for me. He wordlessly handed me his silk handkerchief and I took it and blushed as I brushed away the errant pieces of sod.

"The earth . . . and the warm weather," I tried to explain but Mr. Price-Jones only smiled, and I could not help but feel that, for the moment, all seemed right in the world.

"You have nothing to explain to me, Miss Morys. A sudden whim? Or perhaps a sudden urge in keeping with the exhilaration of the season?" His eyes seemed bright and full of merriment and I could see that he was taking great delight in teasing me.

"Yes. Yes, that is it."

"Then," he said, "perhaps you will indulge me in my whim." He held out his arm. "Will you do me the honor and walk with me around the gardens?"

"I must decline, sir. Nanny will be expecting me."

Mr. Price-Jones shook his head and bent down to me in a conspiratorial manner. "I have a confession, Miss Morys. I knew my uncle wanted to discuss something of a very private nature with Lady Glendower, and when, from the window I saw you walking here, I was instantly taken with the sunshine—and with the thought of having a lovely woman as companion for a stroll. It thoroughly appealed to me. Half-jestingly, I expressed a wish to be outside on such a fine day, and this was taken as a reason to excuse me, although I suspect that my uncle was able to ascertain my true motives." I glanced down, for I was now thoroughly embarrassed, but Mr. Price-Jones took my hand gently and then glanced up at the windows of Lady Glendower's rooms. "And I bring you word from Nanny." He smiled at me and I could see both a mixture of merriment and true concern in his eyes. "I am to convey to you the message that my uncle and the ladies would be pleased if you were to take a turn around the estate with me. I suspect they think that you might be the diversion I need while they speak confidentially."

"I am sure there is much on this estate for you to amuse yourself on an afternoon, sir. I don't think you need me to pass the time."

Mr. Price-Jones stopped. "You take my words too seriously, Miss Morys. Actually I think the women were glad that I proposed walking with you."

I was perplexed at this suggestion and Mr. Price-Jones noticed my expression, yet he tried once more to amuse me. "Come now, Miss Morys, I do not think I should lead you astray."

"No, sir. You take my bewilderment too personally. It is only that I do not understand why they treat me so. For after all, I am only the assistant to Nanny. I am clearly one of the staff." I looked at him and felt the warm flush on my cheeks again. "Even now it seems that I should not be here with you. You . . . we . . . we are not of the same . . . ," I stammered.

Mr. Price-Jones nodded his head. "I take your meaning well, Miss Morys, but I have the feeling that both Lady Glendower and Nurse Hoskins feel that you are more than your station. Indeed, my uncle and I discussed this very same subject last week, after we all had sat at table together. I do not know, ma'am, but I have the feeling that your coming here to Winter's Light has greatly improved the spirits of the ladies." He shrugged, although it was not a dismissive gesture. "But why do we not just enjoy the day and think of it no more."

It was my desire, too, and so we continued walking while speaking of pleasantries and mundane things. It was a delightful time for me, for it gave me a chance to get a more thorough reading of Mr. Price-Jones's character, and I must own that I found the humor and the intelligence of the gentleman much to my liking. We spent more than a half-hour discussing the vagaries of the shire and its inhabitants, and in the course of the walk it was in fact Mr. Owen who proved *my* diversion, as he succeeded in making me forget my own momentary longing for Daear.

"I am glad," he said when I laughed at his teasing, "that you and I get along so well, ma'am. If I might confess to you, Miss Morys, sometimes I find the prattling of some of the young women in the area a little strained, a little forced. But you, ma'am," he said and then stopped and looked at me, "you are easily one of my favorite people already, for you see the significance of this whole scheme." He spread his hands wide. "You are truly a delight, Miss Morys, and I, for one, am glad that Nanny needed your help." I was touched by Mr. Price-Jones's choice of words, for I was beginning to realize that, even at Daear, I had never met anyone so easy and so, for want of a better word, charming.

"Perhaps you are led to feel this way because we understand the same things," I said, taking his arm. We continued to stroll leisurely and resumed speaking of everyday life at Winter's Light.

I confess to having lost myself in our conversation, and I was surprised when I looked around and saw that before us, a scant quarter of a mile away, began the moors. I had not realized we had walked so long or in this direction, and so the location startled me and a cold chill passed over me. I pulled my shawl close around my shoulders to ward off the draft, yet I still felt the coldness wash over my body.

"You'll do well to shudder and avoid the bogs, ma'am." Mr. Price-Jones raised his hand to indicate them. "They truly are beautiful and mysterious and, for some, even enticing. But they are treacherous, and their beauty belies their anger. They say that scores of people have vanished in them, that, despite all the warnings posted, the villagers still foolishly take shortcuts and chances, and that some, unfortunately, do not succeed in arriving at their destination." He shielded his eyes from the gleaming sun so that he could better see the moors. "Do not attempt to best them, Miss Morys. They say the fen claims its victims quickly and quietly."

I shuddered once more, for I knew the description to be accurate.

"Please do not worry for me, sir. I have always been afraid of the marshes. I have always been wary of them."

Mr. Owen took my arm. "Good. You'll do well to remember your own fear at this part of the estate." His eyes scanned the vast fields. "My uncle has charted these moors as an exercise, Miss Morys, and even though he is considered to be an expert in this particular area, he has always impressed upon me an appreciation and avoidance of this form of nature. I hope I convey his feelings to you." He looked once more at the distant swamps and then smiled at me, trying to allay my nervousness. "And now I believe we should return to Winter's Light," he said as he began to guide me back toward the house.

"*Anne.*" I stopped, frozen at the sound, and at that moment I would have taken an oath that I had heard the cry of a wounded man calling out from the moors. I turned back to look at the mire and scanned the broken line of dead trees standing sentinel in front of it. All remained still and unmoving, and yet I heard the faint voice call out a second time. *"Anne."* I drew my thin shawl even tighter around me but my entire body was icy with a chill that penetrated deep into my bones.

"Is there something wrong, Miss Morys? You seem frightened."

"I thought I heard someone . . ."

Mr. Price-Jones answered me immediately and decisively. "No, it is only an illusion, ma'am. It is only the bog. There is no one and nothing alive there."

I nodded and then was embarrassed at my fear. "Of course you are right, sir. Please, let us return to the house." I looked once more at the silent moors and I hoped that Mr. Price-Jones was correct, that what I had heard was indeed only a trick of my overactive imagination.

The next afternoon was an even more glorious delight, and while walking the grounds I began playing with one of the outside dogs, a mixed breed, half terrier, half hound, full of enthusiasm and endless energy. Solomon's favorite and perhaps only game, I soon found out, was chase the stick, and since it only required my throwing a piece of wood ahead of me so that he could hunt after it, it was another way of amusing myself while enjoying the warm sunshine.

The game continued for quite a long time and when at last I called a halt to it I could see that I had taken the same path as the day before and that I was now, once again, close by the moors. My first inclination was to walk quickly and carefully away from the expanse but there was something compelling me to remain, and thus I did so even though there was much trepidation in my heart.

I waited, yet nothing was revealed to me. I did not hear a voice, or indeed, any sound coming forth from the land and, again reassured that the previous afternoon's happenings had been only a trick of my imagination, I turned to return to Winter's Light.

At that moment, however, Solomon spotted a hare and gave chase to it, yelping and baying. I yelled after the dog, entreating him to stop and come away with me. Solomon, unfortunately, paid me no mind, and I walked quickly after him, holding my skirts high so that they did not trail in the pale, low waters that served as a prelude to the bogs. I continued to yell the dog's name and finally, much to my amazement, he scampered back past me, easily giving up on the chase of the rabbit who now crept along the marsh and disappeared into the woods close by.

I raised my skirts a bit higher, for the soft earth now held more dark and thickened water, and I gingerly tried to make my way back to the safe land. But it was not to be. In chasing the dog I had lost my bearings, and suddenly I realized that I had passed a little way beyond the edge of the moors and into them. Panic engulfed me as all my childhood fears assaulted me at once and I tightened my hands into fists to keep them from trembling. I knew that to escape unharmed from here I would have to employ all my wits to the problem, and my first concern was to calm myself.

The bog was eerily silent and still. The tall, pale sea grasses that edged the vast holes of oozing marshland remained stiffly upright, serving, at least for the moment, as a guide to safer and more substantive earth. Bleached-grey dead branches were strewn about near the gaping mud craters, resting there only temporarily until the ever-seeking muck fumed up and over in its quest to claim its lifeless nourishment. It was as though the scene displayed nature waiting to replenish itself, waiting to recover that which long ago had sprung from it, and I stepped carefully around anything I perceived as a danger.

The only sound in the bog—a soft, thick gurgling— came from the small, round bubbles of air that in various places boiled up from its slimy bottom and deposited their dark, oily bounty upon the top of the sludge with a hollow, explosive *plop*. At another time in another place the sound would have been almost comical, but here among the silent, shroud-like, stripped and blanched vegetation it seemed only grimly ironic.

I sat down on a small space of bare earth still protected from the marsh and looked up to the skies. Even though a blue-grey cloud hung low and close to the bare skeletons of the tall trees, I was able to detect the full sunshine that remained high above it all, and I perceived that I had at least two or three more hours of light. I gathered my thoughts and attempted to contrive a plan that might take me back to safer land. I felt a slight breeze invade this subdued territory, rippling the thin, jagged limbs attached to the top of what perhaps once were elms and yew trees, but still no sound apart from the menacing gurgle radiated from the surroundings. It was as if the haze contributed to the forbidding silence, capturing and enfolding foreign noises before they disturbed the deadly tranquility.

Within the confines of this incredible stillness my mind began playing tricks on me, for suddenly I thought I could hear the faint voices of two men discussing the treachery of the bogs. I could not hear well enough to recognize either gentleman's voice, but one seemed to be assuring the other that their journey through the moors would be safe, that this would be a shortcut to Winter's Light, and that he should trust him to lead the way.

I looked around hoping to place the voices, but the swamp had many hiding places and I could not ascertain where the words were coming from. It did not occur to me that the sounds were not real or were imagined, for even though they seemed far away, I could still hear the gist of the conversation. It was the precision of the gentleman's instructions to his companion that truly made me believe that there were two others also caught in the mire. Perhaps, I reasoned, these two unknowns were of the clan of fieldhands or villagers oblivious to warnings. In any event I was glad to hear their voices, for I hoped that they would be able to guide me out of the marshes.

I called out into the fog but there was no response. I tried again but still no one answered, only my own voice endlessly echoed back to me. The men's voices seemed to grow faint again and I strained to hear them, but there was a long lapse and I feared that they were moving further away from me. I listened hard but I could only hear occasional words now.

I started to move off cautiously, picking my way around the fulminating chasms and moving toward the direction in which I thought the two would most likely be attempting their way. But — perhaps because of my fright — I was not mindful of my own direction and soon I found myself deeper into the moors, the heavy clinging malordorous mist now swirling all about me.

I took a deep breath to stifle my fear and panic. The men's voices were no more and I knew that truly I was totally and frighteningly alone. I made one more attempt at finding my way out of the mire but it was short-lived; I knew I did not have the resources to extricate myself. What little determination I did still possess was crushed when I tripped on a small stone and it skittered toward a marshy fissure where it was immediately swallowed up by thick ooze. I involuntarily cried out in fright at what might be my own fate, and stood holding fast to a thick, dried stalk in the middle of my solid earth-island, for it seemed my entire body was now gripped in dread. The dank fog seemed oppressive and blurred my vision and I pushed at it, hoping to agitate it so that it would dissipate and I would be able to see more. But it did not clear, and it was as if I were half-blinded by the mist.

A snippet of trailing vine drifted down close to my head and I could almost believe that I felt a soft glove touch my face and caress it, but of course it was only another trick of the swamp. This would be one more fable to add to the lore of the bogs should I ever have the opportunity or desire to tell the countryfolk about this experience.

I know not how long I stayed by myself. I only know that somehow, within the space of a few moments, I felt a calm presence come over me which practically commanded me to stay clearheaded in the face of all this adversity. It was as if someone or something was there with me, trying to tell me that help would be coming and that I was not alone.

I hunched my body to ward off the descending chill and suddenly the little melody that I had sung as a child was recalled to me and I hummed it softly to myself. I did not know why the melody took hold of me now, but as I repeated the song I seemed to gain courage and somehow I knew that help was indeed on its way. I knew that I only had to remain where I was and that I would be rescued.

It was to be! Very shortly afterwards I heard the voices of the Price-Jones gentlemen calling out to me, calling for me. "Miss Morys, Miss Morys." This time it was no trick, for I surely heard my name being called over and over again. I looked about me but I could see nothing save the heavy mist. "Miss Morys, Miss Morys." I recognized Mr. Charles's deep voice shouting for me and I turned toward the area where I thought him to be.

"Here, sir, here I am," I called, but I must not have answered loud enough, for they did not hear me and, to my dismay, their voices soon grew distant. I was afraid to move toward them, for now most of the ground by where I stood was in deep shadow.

"Miss Morys. Miss Morys." Mr. Charles Price-Jones's voice was insistent and I cried out in a louder voice this time, determined to attract their attention.

"Here. Here I am, sir." My mouth was parched and dry from fright and when I called it seemed to burn my throat.

"Uncle Charles, she is here," I heard Mr. Owen yell out to his uncle. "She is in the deep section, sir." Then he called to me, "Do not move, Miss Morys. I beg you to be alert. Do not take another step no matter how safe it appears. We are here now. We have torches and we will come to you. Please, Miss Morys," he cautioned me again, "do not disobey us. We will come to you." I heard the deep concern in the gentleman's voice and I must confess I was overwhelmed with a sense of relief that it was he who had found me, for I knew that he would do all possible to rescue me from my predicament. I took a deep breath trying to dispel the feeling of faintness that was overcoming me and stood still, afraid to move even my arm to wipe away the damp on it. "I will stay," I promised and then I fell silent, praying that they would quickly find me.

"Good," Mr. Owen called back to me. "Do not be afraid, Miss Morys, for my uncle and I well know the bogs. We have been trained to judge the dangerous spots. Only, pray, continue to speak so that we can identify your whereabouts."

I did not know what to say or to call out and instead found myself loudly humming the strange tune once more, though I felt foolish that that was the only thing I could think of to guide them to me.

The gentlemen did not think it silly. Instead they continued to encourage the song.

"Good, Miss Morys, good." Mr. Charles's voice was coming closer to me. "Keep up the tune so that we may find you." I continued to hum, for no real words would come from my throat, and soon I heard, at my back, the sound of footfalls upon solid earth. My voice became louder and stronger as I realized I was about to be rescued, and involuntarily I took a step toward my rescuers. Too late I recalled the gentlemen's caution as my foot sank into a small quagmire and I felt the pull of the shifting wet earth. I watched, horrified, as the quicksand covered the heel of my shoe, sucking at my ankle and drawing my leg tighter into its grasp. I screamed and the two men, each approaching from different sides, heard my cry. Within a moment both appeared close to me.

"Miss Morys, please," Mr. Owen called out to me, "do not struggle. It only pulls you deeper. Try to take a deep breath," he said, all the while advancing carefully toward me.

I looked up, frantic at the sensation that was paralyzing my limb and yet trying to heed their words. "Mr. Charles. Mr. Owen . . ." I said and I knew they caught the urgency in my voice. "Help me. Help me, please."

Mr. Charles reached me first, skirting the dark pools of innocent-looking ground so that he came to me from the front. "It will be alright, ma'am," he said, and I saw him briefly glance at my frightened face before he looked around and saw his nephew on my other side. "Quickly, Owen," he called to the younger man. "Throw me one end of your rope. I will stand on this side while you stand there and we will make a line that Miss Morys can cling to. Carefully now," he said to his nephew, "throw me the end." He stood there with his arms outstretched. "Do not move, Miss Morys," he said softly. "You have no need to be frightened now. We are here." He smiled at me reassuringly, and yet I was not convinced, for the pull on my foot was more pronounced now. "We are here, ma'am," he said again and then he looked beyond me. "Quick, Owen, throw me the end of the rope."

Mr. Owen tossed the stout cord to his uncle but its length was too short by several inches and the end of the line fell into the bog. Mr. Charles went to his knees to try to retrieve it, but already the rope's knotted end had been sucked under into the oozing slime.

Mr. Owen's face betrayed him and I knew he was dismayed. "I thought there was enough line," he kept saying until his uncle sharply checked him. "Do not waste time in explanations," he said. "We must have another try at this." I began to breathe quite heavily and felt giddy but I knew I had to use all my energy to keep from having my body pulled under by the wet peat. I shivered, but Mr. Charles remained calm, cautioning me at the same time to hold steady. "I have another plan," he said to both of us before disappearing into even deeper, more mysterious territory. Finally he emerged with a thick piece of a decaying tree limb.

"We will have to use this," he said to his nephew, and the tone of his voice did not reassure me. "Quick—close to the left of her." He crossed over close to my right side, circumventing the bog that had captured me. "Now, Miss Morys, this is what I will do. My nephew will lean on the upright limb to steady it and at the count of three you will take hold of it, too, and pull your foot from the bog. At the same time, with your permission, I will take hold of your ankle, ma'am, and attempt to free it." He looked at me and I could see the strained lines around the set of his mouth. "Do you understand me, ma'am?"

I nodded, for it seemed as if I were struck dumb. Somehow I knew, though it was not said, that I had only this one chance to free myself, and I took a deep breath in preparation.

"Now, Miss Morys," Mr. Charles said. "At the count of three, pull." I did as I was told, exerting all my pressure to loosen my foot and somehow we were successful; my leg instantly came free from the draw of the bog.

I do not remember too much that happened immediately after I was released. I felt my body go limp at that moment and vaguely recall Mr. Owen's strong arms catching me as I fainted. "It is all right now, Gwynneth . . . Miss Morys. You are safe now," he whispered to me and I just barely nodded my head. "You are safe," he repeated and still I could not answer. "Thank God we found you," he said, and I closed my eyes against the fading half-light of the day knowing that I was now free of the bog. Only after I had been carried to safe ground and lifted upon Mr. Owen's horse did I realize that I was still quietly humming the tune that I had hummed long ago when at Daear. Again it had served me well.

I learned later that Fergus, the stableman, had seen me in the early afternoon as I played with the dog and that he had thought I was not paying enough attention to my whereabouts.

"Aye," he told me several days later when I was out walking again, "I thought that perhaps you were going a bit too close to the bogs, that perhaps you did not know that the animal was leading you too close to the marsh. That be the way of romping with Solomon. A wise name for a stupid dog," he said and then affectionately cuffed the animal that was at his side now. "He be knowing better than to go down there to the swamps. He's been shooed off from them parts." He stroked the dog's dark, flat fur. "Not that he's ever crossed into the marshes. He's funny, he is. Chases the squirrels and the rabbits in the woods for long stretches, but he has a keen sense and I suspect he knows that there be trouble that way." He nodded toward the moors so that his almost bald head captured the pink light of the sky. "Nay, never once has he gone past the trees. Dogs be funny that way. Know right off, they do, if there be any hint of trouble or the like." He threw a long stick several feet and the dog bounded happily after it, fetching it and dropping it at our feet. I picked it up and threw it again so that the game continued.

"Mr. Fergus, have you ever heard any sounds from the moors?" I felt foolish asking the question, yet I had to know if I was the only one to be deceived by the bogs.

Fergus wiped his brow with his sleeve and did not hesitate. "Now I can see from the look in your eyes, miss, that you'll be wanting the truth." He crushed his hat in his hands. "So, aye, miss. There be a few of us who have heard what some call 'the voices.' There be certain people who say they are the voices of the *Tylwth Teg*—the elves. That perhaps long ago there was a group of them little people who had their spirits stolen and were consigned to the bogs forever. Like Satan to the underworld." He wiped his brow again and nodded his head. "Never can say, miss. But, to answer your question. Aye, there be one or two of us who would have sworn we heard cries and whispers come from that there land." He took up the dog's stick once more. "Not that any of us are willing to testify before the curate but . . ." He shook his head. "Who's to say, Miss? Who's to say what be in those lands? What be in those worlds?" He fell silent for a moment and I did not move, but waited for him to complete his sentence. "Once, oh I would say about fifteen or sixteen years ago, one of the villagers got hisself lost over there and he were fortunate. Like you, ma'am. We heard him and it was daylight so we were able to watch our step as we searched. We got to him, miss, and he was none the worse for wear, but on our way to him we found some bones—human bones, they were, miss, and some pieces of cloth. They must have been given up in a powerful shift of the earth."

He touched the front of his jerkin. "We could tell the fragments were of a good cloth, Miss. Even the color, though mud-caked, we could see was of a dark blue. Heavy serviceable fabric it was, like it were a cloak or a greatcoat. Not like what a working man would wear. Not like he was a person used to rough work and wearing rough clothes. But neither were they of such quality befitting a gentleman." He ran his hand down the line of buttons on his vest. "We asked hereabouts if there was news of a missing person but there were none. The men who were not at home were all accounted for in various ways. Nay, none were missing that spring and so what we finally had to do, Miss Morys—what we finally did do— was ask Reverend Walker to say a few prayers over the remains and then buried them in an unmarked grave in the churchyard." He looked up at the cloudless sky.

"Seemed a right shame that there be no name on a stone or a piece of wood to identify him, but there was none to affix to it. We figured him to be a wandering man—mayhaps a minstrel who would never be missed. For a few weeks afterwards some flowers appeared near the site of the resting place but fairly soon that stopped, too, and it was all forgotten. Now I doubt if anyone even knows where the grave would be. Somewhere on the estate."

He threw the stick ahead of him in the direction he was beginning to walk and the dog followed, bounding in front of him. "Seems a shame, though, don't it, that there be no one to mourn for the soul, for the person that once was?" He put his cap back on his head. "But, dust to dust, the good book says." He touched the brim of the hat. "I must be getting back to the stables, miss. I'm glad you be all right."

Chapter Seven

My escape from the moors was soon forgotten as the household became occupied with other matters. Summer was now fully upon us and there was much to be done if we were to keep the mansion cool and restful. Lady Glendower continued to languish in her room and once I asked Nanny why her mistress did not sit outside on a comfortable chair in the hot, healing sun or even move to another, more pleasant room.

Nanny paused at the window and looked out. "She's not yet ready to do that, Gwynneth. But she will be . . . she will be." She stared at me and I wondered if her answer had been a rebuke, but her next words were soft and I thought no more about it. "She's getting stronger. She'll be better, you'll see. Of that I'm certain. But it will all be in her own good time." She wiped at a smudge on the glass pane. "Just as soon as she sees a sign," she said cryptically, "she'll be fully recovered." Mrs. Hoskins gave no clue as to what sign was to be expected and I did not ask, for I believed it none of my concern. Truly, at times I had found Nanny secretive and withdrawn—as though she were in charge of very private matters that pertained only to her mistress—and I had no wish to intrude upon those confidences.

She pulled the heavy drapes back even more so that the full, bright sun could be seen. "She was a very sick lady, she was, and sick in more than body. Her mind, Gwynneth. She took heart-sick and mind-sick." She looked at me and half smiled. "That be long before you came here to us. But now . . ." her voice trailed off, and though a bit mystified, I went about pouring fresh water into the glass beside Lady Glendower's bed and then set the pitcher beside it on the table.

Lady Glendower had indeed been regaining her strength and displaying much more concern for the estate. When Mr. Charles and Mr. Owen came to visit she showed more interest in current events and county matters, and I could see that Nanny was much encouraged as to her well-being. I made an effort to tend to my own light duties without disturbing Lady Glendower, but even when busy I could see that her eyes constantly followed me. On several occasions she asked me to stop working and sit with her a while, and Nanny encouraged such visits, although I personally could not imagine why my mistress should be interested in the prattling of a young girl. I was careful in my conversation and we spoke only of casual things, never discussing topics of much importance but rather making small comments about the gardens or the day's weather. And I was surprised and thankful to see that the good lady seemed to enjoy my company, to be interested in me and my thoughts. Such solicitude recalled to me the afternoon when I was rescued from the bogs. Nanny had sent me to my room — "orders from the mistress, herself," she had said — and when I had protested that I was fine, Nanny would not hear of it. "If mistress wants you to rest, so be it," she had said, folding her hands in front of her. "Go, girl. The mistress is looking after your health."

I had not protested to Nanny that it was I who was employed to watch after Lady Glendower's health, for I knew it would be of no use to argue with her. And truly after that harrowing adventure, I had found that I was tired and needed the rest.

I had intended only a short nap to refresh me and had lain down on the bed, but I could not fall asleep. The strange five-note tune had continued to play in my head, and I found myself humming the melody, unable to forget it, as though the music had taken hold of my mind and would not leave it.

Subsequently the tune haunted me, and on several afternoons I found myself repeating those same notes over and over again—as though now, more than ever, I *had* to recall the melodic phrase—but for what reason, I did not know.

I was no longer surprised at the song's strangely persistent recurrence, for this was only one of several extraordinary things that had been happening to me at Winter's Light. On several occasions I had been awakened from a peaceful sleep only to realize that my dreams were still plagued by images of unfamiliar people in unfamiliar places. In most of them I saw men and women in conversation, and sometimes I was able to recognize the profile of Lady Anne as she spoke with the young man who had been at the inn with her. Within the dreams I was able to distinguish voices totally unknown to me, and I listened for clues as to who these people were and why they should appear to me. The voices were not those I thought I had heard in the bog—they were neither alarmed nor frightened—and none of these persons seem intent on harming me, yet the dreams frightened me. They appeared so real, so vivid it was hard to believe them purely of my own imagination.

Indeed, several times I awoke with the feeling that these men and women were actually here, in Winter's Light, but though I searched the faces of the people that I daily met, I could not detect any similarities. It was foolish, I knew, but coupled with these fantasies—for I knew not what else to call them—was the frightening accusation that Fergus had cast at me so many months before, upon first meeting me. Even now, I continued to recall the stableman's haunting charge, *"Ye have been here before,"* and at times it seemed that he must be correct. I was grateful that he had seen fit not to broach the subject again, but I knew that he still watched me with a peculiar eye as I wandered the grounds of the estate.

As for the explanation of these occurrences, I had none. I tried not to let the puzzle possess my thoughts unduly, although sometimes, after an especially troublesome dream, I wished I could speak of it in the open. But I dared not tell anyone here—not Nanny or Mrs. Padley or any of the maids—for though some of my thoughts might be attributed to the excitement of all that had happened these past months, many of my fanciful dreams were quite inexplicable.

I was especially mystified by still one more thing—the strange feelings I had which led me to believe that I was never truly alone. As had happened when I was on the moors, I often had the impression that there was someone or something close by me. Perhaps I mistook quite ordinary occurrences—a sudden moment of coolness while I was in the hot sun or a soft touch on my arm when there was nothing around me but the breeze—for something sinister. I had told myself many times that it was foolish to feel such sensations, that they were really only in my imagination. I had hoped I could attribute my perceptions to my horrible experience in the bog, but in truth, these feelings were not new to me. I had felt a shadowy companion before at various times in my life. When I was a child I had spoken of this with my parents, but they were perplexed and, I think, alarmed and could not offer any explanations. I had seen the fear in their eyes, and so I had not pursued the subject, and after a few times I stopped speaking of the phenomenon to them.

It was the same here—I was afraid to share my thoughts with anyone for I did not know how Nanny or the housemaids would take to these imaginings. I wished I did not attach much importance to these strange phenomena, but it seemed that the longer I remained here at Winter's Light, the more pressing their importance became. This distressed me, and some evenings, in the quiet of my own

85

room, I could not help but wish that my life had not taken this turn, that my dear, beloved parents were still alive and I was safe with them, and that the shadowy attendant — whatever it was — would go and leave me in peace. But I knew that such days were never again to be. Deep in my heart and soul I knew that I had been bound to this manor and to this unseen presence in some strange way that I would someday be forced to remember. *I had to remember.* But I knew not what.

Chapter Eight

Despite such cares, I still found Winter's Light a beautiful estate, and I continued to feel more and more secure here, for my duties were not hard and I was treated most civilly. When I wrote to Reverend Jenkins, I strove to assure him that I understood the necessity of this move and had begun to settle into the ways of my new home.

Mr. Owen and Mr. Charles Price-Jones had left encouraging notes when they returned me to Winter's Light after rescuing me from the bogs, and each day since they had sent sincere inquiries as to my health. I found that I was growing fond of both of them, for they seemed to be genuine in their affection and care. I noticed that the younger Mr. Price-Jones especially went out of his way to comfort me, and in truth I must confess that I found random thoughts of the gentleman invading my mind in a most pleasant way. The gentleman continued to inquire about my health and mental state, and made it known that I should not dwell on the experience in the bog. "It can serve no good purpose, Miss Morys, and I only wish that the adventure had never occurred," he said to me as we walked about the estate one afternoon. "I only regret, ma'am, that we did not rescue you sooner and that you had too long a fearful time in the bogs." I assured him that I was well, quite recovered from my adventure, but he continued to be so solicitous of my health that even

Nanny remarked on it.

"I have noticed," she said to me one bright morning, "that Mr. Owen is spending much more time here." She glanced at me without a hint of a smile and I took it to be a rebuke.

I hurried to explain lest she think I had forgotten my position. "I do not encourage it, Nanny. But I confess I am glad that he considers me a friend."

Nanny sat in her chair and rocked, and her face softened. "I do not think it a bad thing that you have someone near to your age for company. Mr. Owen is a fine young man—his uncle has seen to his remarkable education—and neither of them would do you or our house harm."

"Nanny, I sometimes wonder at your choice of words." I smiled so she would not think I was finding fault with her advice. "Of course Mr. Owen and Mr. Charles would not harm me. I do not fear them. And as for their relationship to this house—why, I have never seen such faithful and devoted friends."

Nanny continued to rock and then nodded her head. "Aye, that they are. Even when things turned sour for Mr. Charles, never once did he complain or blame the Glendowers. Any other man would have sought recompense of some kind, but not him. He stood by the family—never once censuring—and bestowed his help in their time of need. Aye, he was the model of a gentleman, he was. No one will ever doubt his kindness."

I looked at Nanny hoping that she would explain her statements but again she chose not to, instead pretending to lightly nap. It was as if she wanted only to drop hints of what was dark in the family's history, as though she were testing me to see if I showed interest in her words. *"Ah, Nanny,"* I thought, *"if only you did not speak in partial truths. If only you would once explain yourself."* I sighed, for there was no way that I would loosen her tongue if she did not desire to do so. I could only wait and hope that someday all these mysteries about Winter's Light and the Glendower family would be cleared for me.

It was another lovely day—the sun bright and the air warm and pleasant—and later that afternoon I sat next to the window in the sitting room adjacent to Mrs. Glendower's chambers watching a bird as it rested on a branch of a nearby tree. It was a small songbird and its blue color against the green leaves seemed to be a statement of nature at its most glorious. I thought it a charming prospect to sketch, and although I had no paper or colored pencils at my disposal, I remembered a small slate that I had found in a cupboard in the room. When I had questioned Nanny about it she had told me that it had been needed when Lady Glendower's throat was inflamed, that at the time they had used the chalkboard to communicate with each other. But now, I thought, it would serve me well, for the black and white of the board and chalk would suffice for my sketching.

I sat at the open window, intent on my subject as it sat upon the leafy branch. It was difficult to draw, and I was soon filling in the features of the bird's body with long strokes of the chalk while thinking that perhaps I could keep the slate in my room. It would be a diversion for me and would keep my hands busy when I grew tired of embroidering pillowslips and table linens.

"What's that you be doing, Gwynneth?" Nanny's voice startled me, for I had been occupied in capturing the likeness of the scene outside the window.

I held the drawing for the woman to see and I saw her eyes narrow. "Have ye always done that? Have you always known how to hold a crayon?"

"Yes. It was just something to do when I was waiting in the house for my parents or when I wanted to amuse myself. My father even bought me some rough paper so that I could make fancy designs to hang upon our walls." I smiled in remembrance of the drawings I made of our farm and our animals and the way both my parents had encouraged me in my ability. *"Sure the flowers seem almost real,"* my mother used to say when I presented her with yet another picture. *"It's as though they're growing right on the wall,"* my father would add when he saw the sketches propped against it.

Nanny moved closer to where I sat and looked over my shoulder. The singing bird sensed her presence and flew to another branch as though it thought that it might be in danger.

"Aye, it is a good likeness," she said. "I did not know that about you. That you had talent."

"Nanny, you can't possibly know all about me. We did not meet until a few short months ago." I handed the chalkboard to her. "Would you like it?" I asked.

The old woman took the slate from me and held it away from her so that she could see it better. "Aye, I would like it very much." She patted my arm. "Very much," she repeated before she left the room.

The next morning I found several books of classical art and a small quantity of sketch paper and colored pencils on the desk in my room, and I knew that Nanny had put them there.

"They're just some old books that we had in the house," she explained when I thanked her. "The paper has been there a long time and the crayons may be old, but they are still quite serviceable. Do ye think you could use them?"

I was touched by the woman's kindness. I assured her that I would make good use of the articles and promised her my first drawing.

"Make a pretty picture for the mistress," she said and then folded her arms in front of her. "Mistress has always loved flowers and paintings."

"Of course," I said and then pressed Nanny as to where she had gotten the art supplies.

"Never you mind," she said and I knew that again she withheld something from me. "Just use them to make your pretty pictures."

"Does Lady Glendower sketch?" If Nanny would not answer my other questions perhaps she would at least tell me more about her mistress.

"No, not now. But she once did and she was fairly good at it, too. It was just one more thing that young girls in high stations learned. Surely you know that, Gwynneth," she said and I nodded my head in agreement. "Manored women all know the rudiments of colors and artwork. It's a part of their education."

I had laid the pad of paper in front of me and now touched the pencils and their blunt points remembering how I always loved the feel of the chalks in my hand. "Even I, in my village church school, learned how to use colors," I said, and Nanny sat down in her little rocking chair.

"That was a good school ye went to. The reverend was a good man. Ye learned much." She slowly rocked so that her words were in time to the action. "You're a smart one, you are, Gwynneth. Anyone could see that."

"Nanny, how could you know that about me?" I teased, thinking that she had made a good guess as to my education. I looked over at the woman but she was not smiling. Instead there was a frown upon her face and her lips moved in soundless words. There was something more of sadness then displeasure about her look, and I tried to jolly her. "Come, let me sketch you." I pulled out a piece of paper and took up my colors. "I have not done this for many months. You will be my first portrait subject here at Winter's Light."

Nanny stopped rocking and sat motionless while I spent nearly half an hour trying to capture her likeness and sketching in all the strands of white hair that escaped from her lace cap.

"See that you get me at my best," she said once suddenly and vainly, and then she continued to be silent as I drew.

When I had finished the likeness—it was not really up to my full capabilities—I handed it to her and waited for her opinion.

"You'll put your name on it," she said, and when I had written my first name, she put her hand on mine. "That be enough. Just Gwynneth. That's all that you'll need." She looked at the likeness and I could see that she was pleased with it. "I'll hang this in my room next to the chalkboard," she said gently. "It will remind me of these times forever."

The July day was warm, and that afternoon I took some time away from my duties while Lady Glendower slept. Nanny had often encouraged me to seek the sunshine. "Ye mustn't get too pale, gal. You need color in your cheeks, a young girl such as you," she would say, shooing me out of the rooms.

I knew now to avoid the path to the moors and instead walked in the direction of the stables, where I could hear the horses pawing in their stalls. Solomon and the other mongrel dogs roamed the fields nearby and every once in a while would approach me to be petted or played with in the laziness of the day.

Near a stand of old pines close by the barns I had found a special spot, one that I had purposely sought out as if I had already known of its existence. It was secluded and quiet and when the sun hit its peak in the afternoon I was able to sit, alone and with my own thoughts, in the shadows of the feathery needles that helped catch the slight breezes which all too seldom fanned the land. This was a place I somehow seemed to know well, and whenever I sat there I felt an incredible sense of peace and quiet.

My secret place afforded me a long-distance view of the manor house with the seas behind it and the moors to the front. It was an intriguing prospect and I had vowed to capture the scene on art paper and give it to Lady Glendower as a present. Thus this afternoon I carried my drawing book with me. I would try sketching the house in charcoal as it looked this clear day.

It was not an easy task. Although I had no trouble with the sharp angles of the house, or the inset of the leaded glass windows, or the placement of the bushes and shrubs, I was stumped as to how best to convey the manor's color. The house was such an unusual hue of stone that no amount of blended colors could possibly do credit to it. I made several starts in my sketch book, each from a different angle but it was no use. I could capture neither the glint nor the tone of Winter's Light.

The continual gleaming of the manor's exterior dazzled me so that at times I had to screen my eyes from the brilliance. I had early on recognized that there were both tiny specks and long veins of glittering mica embedded throughout the stones of the house. The bright sunshine of the day was somehow able to extract a faint blue sheen from the limestone. At the same time, as the blazing summer sun struck the mica in the stone, it caused it to shimmer and sparkle with dazzling silvered hues. It was as though an unknown artist long ago had taken a huge life-sized canvas and painted it dark, then washed over it with a blue dye, and then dusted it with silvery light before sketching in doors and the windows and balconies.

I tried blending several chalks but the color still eluded me. There were too many dark and light shadings throughout the exterior of the house and no sooner had I colored one part than the slow-moving sun would highlight another section, throwing my perception off and rendering my drawing incorrect.

I held my sketchbook in front of me, lazily giving up my quest to capture the house's likeness. My attempts seemed to have been of no merit and I became drowsy as I sat in the warm sunshine contemplating my problem. Perhaps I would draw Winter's Light some other day when the sun was not so bright and the glistenings weren't so shining and the summer warmth did not cover me so that I wanted to close my eyes for a few moments and doze.

"It's a difficult subject, miss." Fergus came quietly from around the bushes near the barns and startled me from my reverie. He pointed to the house. "Many another has tried, but not many were able to draw Winter's Light in the true." He indicated the grounds surrounding the house. "Even master painters would try, those with fine reputations for salon portraits of noble men and women and the like. They would come here with their confidence all puffed up and saying that they could paint anything and anyone, but after three or four months they would give up on the undertaking, telling Lord Glendower that it were too hard to capture on canvas. They all fell into the same trap, they did. They were bedazzled by the color of the stones. Aye, we folks watched a long line of them start out arrogant-like with their pads and chalks but us that worked here could have told them that it was near to impossible to do."

He picked at the slender needles of a yew tree and laughed. "Anyone who has been on this land and worked it and seen it year-long could have told them that Winter's Light never looked the same any two days in a row." He scattered the needles on the ground. "Not even any two hours in a row." He looked down at my half-drawn picture and wrinkled his nose in what I took to be a negative critique of it. "Ye aren't the first one to be defeated by it, miss." He was quiet for a moment and

94

then he stroked his chin.

"It is the color, Mr. Fergus, that has me stumped," I said agreeing with him. "You are right. It doesn't seem to be of any one true shade."

Fergus nodded. "Aye, that's it, miss. You see it already. The color is what gives the house its name. Why it's called Winter's Light." He peered at me. "You do know the story, don't you, ma'am? The reason?"

"No. No one has told me."

Fergus planted his feet apart and I could see that he relished the opportunity to tell the story. "Well, ma'am, 'tis very simple. Though it be beautiful and somewhat elusive-like now in the summer, it be a better sight yet in the cold weather. A far better sight. When you see it happen you'll know why, miss. This here manor got its name from the light of the frosty winter sun setting on it, setting on the stones. It's a special coloration then, it is, with the winter's light on it. The stone that's been used—it's peculiar to this area." He dug at the dirt underneath the tree with the toe of his boot until finally I saw bits of brilliance flash in it. "All of the slate and limestone that was used in this estate was found on this land. It's always been here, and the first Lord Glendower wanted to build his house from it." He bent down and scooped up a handful of the dirt and let it sift between his fingers so that every so often I saw the mica twinkle.

" 'Tis said he liked the fact that it wasn't foreign soil. That when he first saw the flashings on the ground he remarked that it was as though all around him the land had been lit up by fire or struck by lightning. And then when they built the house the glint remained in the rocks and stones—never to be leeched from them—and it just added to the color of the manor. Gives it that smoky cast." He looked toward the main house. "It's not only in the daytime, Miss Morys, that the house takes a different look. Did ye ever look out at it in the night time?

When all was dark?"

I shook my head.

"Well, take the time to do it this evening, miss, and you'll see a fanciful sight." Fergus spread his hands wide. "It's like, miss, like the house captures the moonbeams and starlight and it glints a bit mysteriously. But it's not a frightening sight, ma'am, and sometimes it's downright comforting if you've been out all night and need to find your way home. It's as though the house had purposely been placed to take full advantage of all the times of the day and the night and the winter and the summer. You'll see what I mean, miss, ye will, if ye stay here year-round."

I was struck by the eloquence of the man's speech and realized that he too, like Nanny, loved the house and saw the depth of the beauty of the land. It was clearly a source of great pride for him to work on the estate. I told him my thoughts and he put his head down briefly—embarrassed, I thought, at my words of praise—and then raised it to me.

"Aye," he said proudly, "my family and I have been fortunate to spend our days here in the kind of occupation that pleases us. My grandfather, my father, me, my son, and now my grandson. Five generations of Fergus's have all been part of this land. Been here through the happiness and the sadness."

I looked at my incomplete drawing of the house. "Well, who am I to paint this picture, since you tell me that others, all of them more talented than I, have failed?" Fergus laughed and touched his fingers to his cap. He started to move off but then stopped and walked back to me.

"There be one sketch of the house, though, now that I'm reminded. Perhaps you've seen it hanging in the Great Hall. A little one?" He positioned his hands to indicate the small size. "Framed in silvery gilt?" he asked.

I bit my lip trying to remember.

"No. I don't recall it."

He shook his head. "Used to be there. Near the door to the ballroom." He clicked his lips together. "Ah, well, maybe they've taken it away. Hidden it like." He shook his head. "Aye, that's what they probably have done. Probably they wouldn't want it up there as a reminder after all that has happened."

I listened quietly, for I did not want to interrupt his words. "Miss Anne's gentleman—her tutor he was at the time—sketched it. Professional-like it was, too. Like some of those other pretty scenes of cottages and the like that hang in the house." He pulled a piece of clinging hay from his sleeve. "There be other scenes he did, miss. Real pretty they were and there were some that he did of us who worked here in the fields and gardens. Lifelike they were of us. Someday, miss, when you have the time, search them out. You'll appreciate them. I even have one that he pictured of me. I'll show it to you sometimes, if you'd like."

I thanked the man and told him that I hoped he would indeed show me the drawings. Then I hurried back to the house and to Lady Glendower's chambers. Nanny saw my sketchbook and I turned it over so that she could see the unfinished sketch.

"It's more difficult than I thought, Nanny. I wanted to do a picture of Winter's Light but I could not. I wanted to give it to Lady Glendower as a gift so that she could look at it when she is in bed."

Nanny nodded at me and then looked out of the corner of her eyes at her mistress, who reclined against the pillows. "That would be nice, Gwynneth. Very nice," she said, as much to Lady Glendower as to me. She then turned her face away but not before I had seen its momentary look of alarm. The thought of her expression perplexed me for several hours.

97

That evening as I prepared for bed I remembered Fergus's advice and, looking out the window, saw the two wings of the manor as they stretched back toward the seas. The blue-grey stone of the house appeared subdued and wrapped in dark smoke, yet because of the flickerings of the mica it still seemed to be of an uncommon color. For a moment it looked as though a hundred—no, a thousand—fireflies had descended upon the home at the same time, but the light was not sustained and the radiance subsided into random flashes that glowed only briefly.

The warm humid night had settled onto the cliffs and in the moonlight I could see the mist that had risen up from the cold sea beyond them. The pale moon played with the rapidly moving clouds, peeking in and out of them so that it first appeared full, and then half, and then disappeared entirely before reappearing in another, not-too-distant place in the sky.

I could smell the hint of a summer storm coming from the north and I could hear the whisper of the trees as the occasional soft wind touched their tops and made them sway ever so gently. There was a quiet in the air, a natural harbinger of the imminent rain, and as I watched the clouds descended even lower, until they entirely enveloped the edges of the jagged cliffs.

Soon the black clouds hovered over the entire manor. Everything was quiet—the house was hushed, its rooms now darkened. Even the glint of the mica embedded in its stone facade seemed to have been stilled so that only an occasional twinkling radiated from it.

I thought of all the strange things that I have witnessed since my arrival here. Of my strange dreams. Of Nanny's half-finished sentences. Of Fergus's words and of the tragic story of a young woman named Anne.

"Oh, Winter's Light," I said as I glanced out the window once more. "Though you are but of hard rock and limestone, you have secrets embedded deeply within you, like the mica in your stones." I closed my draperies against the first heavy drops of rain. "Someday I will learn them," I said to myself, for I was certain that someday I would have to unlock the secrets of this house.

Chapter Nine

The bit that Fergus had revealed to me about Anne's tutor—"Miss Anne's gentleman," as he had called him—intrigued me and I regret that my nature is such that I must always find the answers to all that perplexes me. I knew Nanny could tell me what I wanted to know, but I would have to wait for the right time and moment to ask the questions. The life of Lady Anne fascinated me, for never had I heard of a household more affected by the pain of one person's death. In my village the dying were treated with respect, yet the process was taken as a matter of course, and after the proper spell of grief, life was to be got on with. We all knew that the end had to come for everyone.

When I returned from my walk today the old nurse was standing next to Lady Glendower's bed, my sketch of her in her hands. Lady Glendower had continued to make rapid recovery from her illness, and I thought that Nanny was trying to aid her convalescence by diverting her thoughts to things other than her sickness.

I did not go directly into Lady Glendower's room but stayed in the sitting room for a few moments and watched the women as they talked. There was nothing I had to do immediately in the chamber, and there was something in the way the two women looked at each other—as though they were sharing a secret—that made me hesitate to interrupt their conversation.

Nanny's voice was such that I could hear her. "See here, my lady, the way she has done my hair and my eyes," she said, and I moved closer to the door so that I could see her as she held up the portrait that I had sketched of her. "There be real talent there. There's no denying her on this count." She held the drawing so that her mistress could see it better. Even though she did not know I was near, I smiled knowing that Nanny was pleased with my work.

Lady Glendower took the little sketch from the nurse and turned it in several ways, and then finally nodded.

"Yes. You are correct, Nanny. I can see that." She looked up at the other woman. "Did she say when she learned this subject and how, or who taught her?" I was astonished that they were talking about me and I stayed quiet while the nurse looked at her portrait.

"Just that it was something that was taught her in school and that she likes doing this work." She pushed back a lock of hair from in front of her eyes. "It just came natural to her, she said." She scratched at a finger. "My lady, it's like a sign. It's what we were looking for."

Lady Glendower was silent and then she touched Nanny's hand. "We'll wait, Nanny. Just to make sure. Yes, we'll keep this to ourselves for just a little while longer." She looked once more at the sketch and handed it back to the old woman. "The likeness is well done." She turned her face to the flower-papered wall. "Oh, Nanny, it is both bitter and sweet to think of what this might mean."

Nanny pulled the covers around her mistress. "Aye, I know. But it's time, my lady. It's time to forgive Mistress Anne."

They say that people who eavesdrop never hear anything to put them at rest, and I now was sure that this homily was correct. I heard Lady Glendower sigh at Nanny's words, and I began to feel a sickness in my stomach. What was the sign they were waiting for? And why was it to come from me? Why should they think me that interesting or important? And though I had never known Lady

101

Anne, I wondered what she could have done that she remained unforgiven after these many years. Why had Nanny and Lady Glendower withheld their mercy up to now? What terrible thing could a young girl of such high birth have done? These were more questions that I would someday have to discuss with Nanny if I were to be comfortable at Winter's Light.

By the time I entered the bedchamber the conversation has been concluded, and I pretended that I had heard nothing of it. I remarked on my sketch being in the room and Nanny replied that she had not had time to put it away and that she would take it back to her bedroom later. I did not question her further and we both went about our work, speaking only a few words to each other.

That evening the Price-Joneses came to the house. My joining them for the evening meal was now taken as a matter of course, and I confess that I looked forward to the evenings, for I was beginning to think fondly of the younger gentleman. Pleasantries were exchanged, and while the four of us ate and laughed and teased, I debated whether I should reveal my questions to Mr. Owen. I wondered if he knew of the tragedy that at one time had occurred here in Winter's Light, and I wondered further if he would discuss it with me.

After we had been served the sweet course and Mrs. Hoskins and I had had our tea and the gentlemen their wine, Mr. Charles stood up and held out his arm to Nanny.

"My dear Miss Morys," he said, "I pray that you will again occupy my nephew's attention for a few moments. I have something of importance to discuss privately with Lady Glendower." He bowed to me. "If you will see that my nephew has company . . . We will try to be brief." He smiled and made a formal bow to me. "With your permission, ma'am," he said, and he and Nanny left the room.

"Well, Miss Morys," Mr. Owen said when I had poured myself another cup of tea and he sipped his small glass of port, "what interesting things have happened to you since your escape from the bog?" He laughed and looked at me. "Surely you have not done anything else to warrant rescuing?" He sat back in his chair and I saw his eyes sparkle. "Not that I would not enjoy rescuing you again, ma'am."

"Would you rescue a lady from a puzzle?" I had asked the question, unable to resist, and Mr. Price-Jones seemed astounded at my request. He tilted his head to one side.

"A game, Miss Morys?"

I had to explain then. "No, sir. A puzzle of the mind." Mr. Price-Jones raised an eyebrow and waved his hand airily.

"You pique my curiosity, ma'am. What puzzle? Tell me," he said and settled back against the chair.

It was easy to speak to him and I told him of some of the things that I was interested in—some of the tales that I had heard in snippets about Winter's Light—and about the Lady Anne and her tutor. I asked him if he knew why the house seemed hushed now. Why was it not an open estate, with visitors, friends and family coming in and out?

Mr. Price-Jones listened respectfully and waited until I had finished. "As to why there is so much sadness here, Miss Morys, Gwynneth, I can only tell you that it was like this when I came and that I, too, have been struck by the gloom of the estate." He sat up straight. "Please do not mistake my words, ma'am. This is not to censure Lady Glendower. Never would I want my words interpreted as such. This is a lovely estate and no one can ever speak against its upkeep. Nothing has been spared in that matter."

"You speak, then, of the closed rooms? Of the darkened rooms?" I suggested, and the gentleman nodded his agreement. "But it is not the seen aspects of Winter's Light that I question, Mr. Price-Jones, but the unseen. I have a feeling—" and here I hesitated, for I did not want to reveal too much at this time. I regarded Mr. Price-Jones as a special friend who kept his word and could be trusted with my conversation, but I knew that what I was revealing was so seemingly absurd that until I had found out his own way of thinking along these lines, I did not want to tell him about the mysterious things that had happened to me since being here.

"As to that other aspect, Miss Morys—the sadness I presume that you refer to, the invisible current that exists here—I cannot truthfully tell you. I suspect Mrs. Hoskins would know more about that than I, for in the scheme of things I am really just a newcomer, too."

"Has your uncle never spoken of these matters?" I asked and then blushed. "I am sorry, sir. I do not mean . . . Please forgive me, sir, I did not mean to ask personal questions." I could feel the heat in my face. "I truly am sorry, sir. It was unwise and impertinent of me to press for answers to those questions." I sipped my tea. I was mortified at my own audacity and I wished that I could find some way to escape from the room.

"No, please, Miss Morys. I do not take any offense from your inquiries. Were I in the same position I can well imagine myself asking the same questions." He held up his glass of wine to the light. "I agree with you, ma'am, that this house should be the focal point of the entire shire, yet it is not. I once, when I thought about it, attributed it to the fact that Lady Glendower had retired now that her husband was no longer alive, but at other times I dismissed the theory. She is too lively and genteel a woman to relinquish the kind of life I have heard once existed on this estate."

I stirred my tea in its cup. "I do not know anything of those times, sir. I do know that there is a magnificent ballroom and furnishings but the room is always kept closed."

Mr. Price-Jones frowned. "I am sure, Miss Morys, that at one time in our conversations my uncle has let slip that there were balls and fetes that had taken place here." He squinted his eyes. "I do not know whether it was Uncle

Charles or someone else—a friend from the area, perhaps—who once mentioned an extraordinary one." He shook his head. "I seem to recall that my uncle was involved in it somehow." He shook his head once more. "No, I don't suppose I paid too much attention to it. I cannot recall too much of the conversation about it. Perhaps it was just said in passing or to make a point."

"I am curious, sir. When did your uncle meet the Glendowers?"

Mr. Owen poured himself another half-glass of the deep red wine. "This answer I know well, for Lady Glendower and my uncle often referred to it. My Uncle Charles and the Glendowers became acquainted when he moved into Cynghanedd. It was when he assumed the inheritance upon the death of his own parents many years ago. He was, I understand, not much older than I am today. That he became the master of the house at an early age was in itself extraordinary, but that he was a gentleman used to learning and studying and that the estate did not suffer in his apprenticeship seems to have been held even more remarkable. Indeed, I have been told many times by the general manager of the estate who advises us even now that he took my uncle and taught him everything within a few months." He smiled at me and I could hear the satisfaction in his voice. "I know that to be true, ma'am, because it is a source of pride for my uncle that he learned so quickly and so successfully."

He drummed his fingers on the table. "I," he said, "was fortunate in having been invited to come and live with him two years ago when my father passed away." He sipped his wine. "My mother still lives in the country but she has no ideas as to how to raise a son. So when Uncle Charles asked me to come here, my mother was relieved that I would have an older male relative to respect. It was a generous gesture on his part, don't you agree, Miss Morys?" He looked at me and smiled a full smile that I was sure had won over many a person. "It is much like your own situation."

I shook my head and looked away so that the gentleman could not see my expression. "I think not, Mr. Price-Jones. The Glendowers are not related to me. True, they sent for me—not expressly for me, you understand, but for a person in my situation. Still, I am only a hired help here. I have no legitimate connection to Winter's Light. Were it not for Lady Glendower's kind generosity, I would still be living in my own village hoping that I could sustain my small farm."

It was Mr. Price-Jones's turn now to apologize, and he seemed plainly disconcerted. "I did not mean, ma'am . . ." He briefly touched my hand. "I did not mean to hurt you, my dear Miss Morys. Please forgive me." Mr. Price-Jones seemed genuinely concerned that he had pained me and I felt affected that someone—so soon a treasured, dear friend indeed, but still relatively a stranger to me, for I had only known him a few months—would be disturbed that he had wounded my sensibilities.

"Please do not worry, sir, for it is the plain truth that I speak. One cannot change circumstance. And I thank you for your considerations, for I know they are confided honestly." I stood by the table. "But I think it is time that we went up. I am sure your uncle and Lady Glendower have sorted out their business by now."

Mr. Price-Jones took my arm. "Please, Miss Morys," he said, "please consider me a friend . . . and perhaps even more . . . ," he said and I blushed at his words. "Please know that all I say or do for you I say and do with honor and in total, consummate friendship."

I could do nothing but thank him for his words, for they were indeed comforting, but I felt it best to ignore his veiled implication. The thought of this gentleman considering me even as one of his circle gladdened me and through the rest of the evening, in Lady Glendower's chambers, I found myself looking at the young man and recalling his words. Perhaps, after all, there was someone here that I could not only trust but admire.

After the Price-Jones' had taken their leave and Lady Glendower had fallen asleep I sat in the parlor of the chamber looking through the art books that had been given me. Nanny came and sat across from me in her rocking chair and the two of us sat by candlelight, she with a knitting needle and a ball of yarn in her hands, and I enjoying the paintings in the volume.

"I am glad to see you with the pictures. 'Tis a shame that things go to waste. It's time for someone to use them." She rocked and with each movement the nurse's head lowered more and more to the side until it was almost touching her shoulder. "Yes, it's time for someone else to have them," she said drowsily and I did not know if she was truly sleeping or again pretending.

I decided to speak in the eventuality that she was only playacting. "Nanny, these books belonged to Lady Anne, didn't they?" I asked. Nanny did not reply and continued to rock slowly as though she did not hear me. I took a deep breath and asked what I thought was a forbidden question. "Or were they the property of her tutor?"

I was correct; the query was one that should not have been asked casually. Nanny's head jerked up and she peered at me, her manner was sharp and attentive, and I knew that she had not been dozing at all.

"What do you know of the tutor? About Mistress Anne and her tutor?"

Stunned at the tone of her voice, I closed the book and prepared to defend myself. "Nothing. I know nothing about him. Only that there was one and that he loved painting Winter's Light and its workers. Only that he once did a remarkable painting of the house.

Nanny's face softened and she bit her lower lip. "Aye, he did that."

"I have not seen it hanging on the walls. Where is it? I would like to see it."

"It's away. Put away. It's not to be seen just yet. It

107

wasn't right anymore and the mistress . . . it has nothing to do with you right now." She stirred the sugar into her cold cup of tea. "Who has been talking about it?" she asked, and I could see that she was like a terrier who had gotten hold of a bone and would not let it go. "Who told you about it?"

It was not in my nature to invent falsehoods, for I had been taught well by my parents and Reverend Jenkins. "Fergus. He saw me struggling with the portrait, trying to capture its color."

"Ye shouldn't be wasting time gossiping with all the folk on the estate." I did not know why Nanny was angry with me and thought it best to retreat to my own room so that we could not continue this conversation.

I put my book on the table and rose. "I am sorry, Nanny, I did not mean to gossip. That has never been my intent. If you will excuse me, ma'am, I'll see to my household chores."

Nanny licked her lower lip and took a deep breath and then spoke in a more rational and gentle manner. "Nay, stay a while, child. Don't go. I did not mean to be so hard on you. It's only that whenever Lady Anne's name comes up there be foolish people talking against her. Telling malicious stories about her. There were those who were not kind, those who do not hold their tongues when someone is in pain and trouble. Those who did not know her well condemned her mightily." Nanny's eyes began to glisten. "I understood her, Gwynneth. I knew her and her gentlehearted ways. She was like my own child to me. I was here when she was born and . . . ," her voice caught for a moment, "and here when she died. And for all those in-between years of her young life. She was so young. And then to be denounced for something that she could not help. Something that we all fall victim to at one time or the other. It was terrible. Just terrible. And then all those blaming her and making sport of her good name and gentle ways." The tears spilled over her wizened face and I poured her a fresh cup of hot tea hoping that she would compose herself. It gave me no satisfaction to see the poor woman cry and I was already beginning to regret my query.

I tried to offer a consoling word. "Fergus did not say anything of Lady Anne's plight, Nanny. We only spoke of the painting and of the tutor's talent."

"Aye," she said and wiped her nose with her handkerchief. "I suspected such. He wouldn't speak ill of her. Fergus is a kind man. He understood." She sipped from her cup. "Oh, if you had only known her, Gwynneth."

I had finally summoned the courage to ask the question. "Please tell me all about her, Nanny," I said, for somehow it seemed that this was the time to know her story.

Nanny, now mellowed and, I could see, much calmer, looked down at her hands in her lap. "There is nothing more to tell you. I've told you all about her already." She began to rock her chair. It was something she did whenever she had a mind to think about questions and problems. I had noticed right away that one could tell by the quickness of the rocking and the periods of silence between her words that there was something on the woman's mind. It would do no good, I knew, to hurry her or to implore her for answers, for Nanny was stubborn and set in her own ways. No one, perhaps not even Lady Glendower, would be able to pry into her thoughts and be given the answers to questions that needed answering until she was ready to supply them.

I suspected the mistress knew this quirk about her nurse and therefore she never pushed her, never attempted to hasten her into speaking or giving an opinion. I followed Lady Glendower's lead now, biding my time and waiting for Nanny to think about what she wanted to reveal to me.

"All right, Nanny. If that is what you wish." The old woman looked at me and I saw a certain hesitation in her eyes and then it seemed to disappear.

"Sit, Gwynneth," she said, "for I will tell you a little about her." I took up my embroidery hoop while she spoke. "I have told you about Anne's ways, how she was not used to life's harsh times."

"Yes."

"The little mistress was a bright young girl, quick to learn and good at her studies. And when she was approaching her fifteenth year she began to show extraordinary interest in art and music and her parents were truly proud of her accomplishments. But her governess did not have the resources to educate her further in these subjects and recommended that another, more able person be brought in to guide her.

"The master and mistress interviewed several skilled people, both men and women, but in the end it was a young man, a Mr. Jeremy Donne, no more than twenty-five he was, who seemed the best suited for the position.

"All went well and Lady Anne thrived on the instruction even to the point where she gave small recitals on the pianoforte for her parents' most intimate friends. You should have seen her, Gwynneth, as she sat at the pianoforte, her golden hair dressed so and her parents proud and happy for her. She played as if she had been born to the music, and all the time her tutor, Mr. Donne, would sit by her side on the piano bench and turn the music pages for her. It all seemed so innocent then. All so simple.

"In the morning she would study her music and then in the afternoon it would be her drawing lessons. Mr. Donne would spend hours with Anne instructing her in the arts. Showing her which colors were best suited to her drawings. Talking about things like forms and figures — things I don't know about and only remember because I heard the words so much. And then giving her these books of his so that she could study them. She did, Gwynneth. Make no pretense about that. She was interested and talented and she wanted to do it all correctly. The two of them, the tutor and his pupil, would spend long days in the conservatory and she would paint the flowers and the vases over and over again until they were just right, until they were nearly perfect. But it wasn't until Mr. Donne would approve them in their entire that she would feel satisfied and give them to her parents for viewing."

I looked around the room as though I would see some hanging.

"They are not here any longer. They have been taken down, put away with the rest of her things."

"With the painting of Winter's Light?" I asked and Nanny nodded her head.

"Aye. That too." Nanny looked into the empty fireplace as though she could recall the ghosts of past years from the ashes. "They were wonderful times for all of us, Gwynneth. Especially for the young mistress. We had never seen her so happy as she was when she was with her music and painting. Aye, now we realize it was because she was with him, too, that there was such a glow in her eyes." She looked at me then. "Do ye understand, Gwynneth? She fell in love with Mr. Donne just as surely as day follows night.

"None of us saw it or suspected it for a long while but one time I remember remarking to Lady Glendower that there was something about Lady Anne that made her seem so gay, so giddy. Not even her mother supposed it was due to a love of the tutor because, you see, it was still so innocent. I think if any of us even noticed we might have just attributed it to the young girl having a crush on her teacher. That's all. Just a schoolgirl's fancy." She bit her upper lip.

"As for Mr. Donne, he well knew his place. He knew he wasn't of the same station as Mistress Anne and so no one can fault his conduct and behavior at first. He was very principled, he was, for his way of life, and never a word, not even a small one, nor a look or glance would pass between him and the young mistress that could ever have been mistaken or taken wrongly. He kept to himself, going out and about and painting when Mistress Anne was at her other studies. Just like Fergus said, he would draw the workers. But I think he probably knew his pupil's feelings for him and was trying to avoid them.

"One day, I remember, when some friends came to call on the family, Mr. Donne excused himself and I saw him as he stood in the Great Hall looking at the closed door to the drawing room where Miss Anne and the family was entertaining. He had a strange look on his face and I think, if I had paid attention to it, that it probably would have been my first key to his feelings. He went into the music room then and set about his composing and you could hear the notes despite the closed doors.

"That same afternoon when I went in to the parlor to see about something, there was Mistress Anne being quiet and companionable but I could see she was listening to the music that Mr. Donne was playing. She was so quiet, Gwynneth, that her mother had to remind her of her manners at one point, as she had not replied to a question put to her by one of her elders.

"Then one day I saw them as they both came in from riding. They had taken the horses—she had her beloved Empress, the grey mare—and they had their sketchbooks with them and they said they had been out and about the estate looking for scenes to draw. She was smiling and oh, the radiance in her eyes." Nanny looked once more to the flames. "Brighter than that fire, it was. Brighter than the fire and it was then that I saw it for the first time. Saw their love.

"And when I asked to see the sketches she had done, they made up some excuse about how they were so terrible that she dared not show them to anyone, and I saw that she lowered her eyes when she said it as though she wasn't telling me the full truth, and that was unusual for the young girl. But I truly didn't know what to do, Gwyn-

112

neth. I thought maybe I should tell the mistress of my suspicions but I delayed it because, I think, it was because I wanted the young mistress to have all her happiness. And perhaps I hoped that this fancy would run its course and then go away when she became sensible again.

"But, Gwynneth, I think in my heart of hearts I knew that Miss Anne's love for Mr. Donne would always remain. She was that taken with him. And I was afraid for her — afraid for both of them because I knew that it could never be." Nanny rocked even more slowly now, and I knew she would not — could not — tell me anymore, for the emotions of those times were still with her.

I had worked at my embroidery the entire time Mrs. Hoskins spoke, and when she had finished I looked down at my stitching. For some reason the white and gold daisy that I had created on the green velvet cloth reminded me of the Lady Anne. I touched it gently and somehow I knew that the story I was hearing would someday become important to me.

Nanny stood now and picked up her candlestick and I could see that she was tired. I did not press her for more details of the young couple's love. I was certain that when she was ready she would tell me the rest of the tale, for I knew that the old woman had much more to recite, that the full story of Anne had still to be told.

"Please, I have only one question at this moment."

"Aye?"

"What color was her dress, Nanny? At the recitals?" I asked and I could see the surprise in her eyes at such a strange query. She was silent for a moment, but even before she answered I had the word on my lips.

"Green," she said. "A pale, pale green. It were her favourite color and all her clothes had some tint in it."

Green — the color of the woman's dress in the dream of the spectacular ball. Grey-green — the color of the woman's cape in the coach scene. It was as if I had always known that the young woman was Anne. Anne had been captured within my dreams — had wanted to be captured within my dream for a reason I did not yet know. Soon. Soon I would know. Of that I was certain.

Chapter Ten

I did not press Nanny for any more of the story and Nanny did not volunteer details. We went about our work at Winter's Light and although I still felt the loss of Daear, I often marvelled at my good fortune in being taken into this household.

I continued to join Nanny with the Price-Joneses when they came to visit, and the four of us continued to enjoy pleasant dinners together. Several times Nanny and Mr. Charles had gone up to speak privately with Lady Glendower, leaving Mr. Owen and I to continue the conversation alone for the next half-hour or so.

When this occurred one evening, Mr. Owen brought up the subject about which I had queried him weeks before.

"Have you learned anymore, Miss Morys? About the puzzle?"

I did not want to break my trust to Nanny. "No, I am afraid not, sir."

"Perhaps, ma'am, this is a sign that you are not to know."

I took his words as an admonishment for my curiosity and could not help blushing. Quickly I held my hand to my face to hide the reddening. Mr. Owen saw my gesture and seemed horrified that I had been stung by his speech. He immediately set down his glass and started an apology.

"Miss Morys, I am truly sorry. I did not mean it as it sounded. I only meant to suggest that perhaps it's best to let the past lie. For surely neither you nor I can do anything to change the course of what has happened here. Not even Nanny or my uncle, who are both devoted to Lady Glendower, can undo the pain. I have often wondered since we last spoke what devices could remedy it, but I have no answers." He stood up and came close to where I was sitting. "Sometimes, Miss Morys, it is best to let things be, for we never know what suffering we may recall." He held out his hand to me. "Please, take my hand as a sign that you forgive me and my truly innocent words. I did not mean to hurt you, ma'am. I only mean to protect you," he said and I looked at him at his suggestion. "To protect all of us who are fond of Winter's Light," he amended and smiled his wonderful smile again.

How could I do other than forgive him? Never in the few months that I had known him had Mr. Owen displayed any animosity or meanness toward me or anyone else in the house.

I took his outstretched hand as a sign of peace. But I did not accept his suggestion that we should let the past lie. The past was what continued to hurt Lady Glendower, and there seemed but one way for her to be rid of her grief: she would have to open the hurt to the light in order to be rid of the darkness that enfolded her. But how could I help? Why did I feel that I could be the instrument to end her sadness and the gloom that seemed to surround all of Winter's Light? I did not yet know the answers.

Mr. Owen and I clasped hands in a show of friendship and trust but, even still, I was not able to forget all the uncanny things that had happened to me in this house.

The next afternoon I again took up my sketchbook thinking that I could capture the beauty of the day. It was a calm afternoon. Sweet-smelling newly mown grass perfumed the air, and the sun was warm enough to keep the animals lying near the barn indolent. I passed close to the stables and could hear the pawing of the horses as they beat against their stalls out of boredom. They, too, seemed affected by the languid day.

Outside the building Solomon and several fat and scruffy dogs chewed contentedly on either twigs or old bones until they, too, succumbed to the heat and fell asleep. It was a peaceful scene and one that did much to bring back the memories of my native village. I half expected at any moment to look up and see my parents coming toward me from out of the fields, but alas, it was only a trick of my imagination, brought on by the hot sun. I sometimes daydreamed about those days past, but I knew they could never be repeated.

I walked aimlessly about the grounds enjoying my moments of leisure. Although I did not find my inside work difficult, I still appreciated the time to be on my own that was given me. If only Lady Glendower could be out here in the warm sunshine, seeing the bright green of the grass and trees and hearing the sounds of the day! I resolved to speak again with Nanny about the restorative powers of the summer season. Perhaps the two of us could take it upon ourselves to move the lady outdoors for an afternoon.

I had been rapidly growing fond of the manor's mistress, and although we did not say too much, I felt a kinship, a warmth between us. When we did speak, she had a kind voice and yet there was something that shone from her eyes—worry, perhaps. I still did not know what sign she and Nanny were expecting to see from me. I knew of nothing secret or healing that I

117

could offer them. But I willed myself not to think too seriously on this subject, for I did not want to mystify things this day. It was too lovely, too peaceful, and my only inclination was to spend an hour or so restoring myself.

I stopped to investigate a small flower in the middle of the field—a weed, I was sure, that had escaped the gardener's attention. I hesitated to pick it. Surely all things, animal and vegetable, have a right to live in their own environment, I thought, and taking one more glance at its blue, velvet petals, I continued on my stroll.

These few hours away from my duties allowed me to think my own thoughts and form my own conclusions, and while I enjoyed the companionship of Meg and the rest of the staff, and the attentions of Mr. Owen, I cherished this time alone. It was as if I needed these periods of restful solitude, for although I could not recall most of them, I was still plagued by the strange dreams that invaded my sleep. Every night I awakened and tried to recollect what I had seen in my dreams. But most of the time my attempts had been in vain; I could not summon what seemed only to appear to me when I was supposed to be at rest. Sometimes I tried to attribute my dreams to my overly active imagination coupled with the hint of the tragedy that had befallen Lady Anne, but in truth, I knew better. I dimly perceived that I was destined to know more about this house in due course, and that someday I would understand all.

Moving now toward the manor, for I did not want to leave Nanny and Lady Glendower alone too long, I ambled through the fields. I half searched for a section to draw, but in reality, I was lost in reverie, musing on both the wonders of the day and my fortune in having my work defined so that I was not kept indoors all the time like the rest of the staff.

"Miss, miss, stand out of the way! Stand out of the way!" I heard someone hoarsely call out to me and I turned while at the same time I heard the sound of hoofbeats coming quickly towards me. I looked out at the golden fields down below where I was standing and saw Fergus shouting out to me and waving his arms to get my attention. "Miss, miss," he yelled again. I saw him gesture me away from the path I was taking and obediently stopped.

"Stand where you be," the old man warned again. "It's Empress. She's out of control. Something has set her off." I watched as a beautiful grey mare ran, seemingly bent on charging at anything in her way. I stood still, as Fergus had commanded, and hoped that the horse would not think me threatening and come at me.

"Do not move, Miss Morys. Stay where you be." Fergus ran toward me just as the animal galloped close and then abruptly stopped a few feet away from me. "Stay where you are, Miss Morys. She'll not harm you. She'll not approach you. And don't you go near her either, ma'am. There's something wrong with her. She's in a panic." He cupped his hand over his eyes so that he could see to the animal in the sunlight. "Empress," he called, but the animal just picked up her head briefly and continued to dance in one place, her hoofs stomping at the ground in a tattoo. She turned her head from side to side and the large muscles in the sleek upper part of her legs seemed taut, as though she were about to run off once more.

Fergus moved cautiously toward the frothing animal. "Empress," he said softly, so as not to further upset her, but the animal did not respond. The stablemaster scratched his head. "This is not the same horse that I've known. Something has been about her. She acts as though she's been frightened." He walked slowly toward

119

the animal. "Look at her eyes, miss, and the way she's holding her tail. As though she's ready to run again." I understood exactly what Fergus was telling me. Although I had not seen this animal before, I recognized that the look in her eye was not calm like that of most horses I had encountered. Her eyes were large, dulcet brown—the hint of her gentleness still visible—yet there was a wild gleam in them that I knew should not be there. "She's never like this, ma'am. She's the sweetest, most gentle mare that we have. We used to trust her with the little mistress all the time. I don't understand it. Something at the stables must have set her off."

We both glanced around toward the barns yet we saw nothing unusual. It was quite calm and still and now that it had quieted again we could hear the vague neighings of the other horses in their stalls.

Fergus held out a hand to Empress. When she ignored it, the stablemaster scratched his head.

"It's devilishly strange," he said. "Usually she'll come to me no matter what. Skittish, she is, but not around me." He wiped his head with a bandana. "She's usually very docile. Sweet and calm. She's a lovely animal. Gentle and willing to please. Although no one rides her now."

He continued wiping his perspiring brow. " 'Tis a shame, too, what with her used to always going out on the fields and even near the seas. The sound of the surf never bothered her like it did some others. Although she hasn't been near it for a long, long time. We only saddle her up and lead her around the grounds now." He shook his head. "No one has the heart to ride her these days. And then Lady Glendower never wanted to see anyone mount her after Mistress Anne. Maybe she just wanted to run again."

Once more Fergus put his hand out to the animal. "Here, girl," he said, trying to coax her toward us, but

Empress stayed her ground, pawing at it, still obviously agitated. She snorted a few times, her wide nostrils flaring out, and try as Fergus would, Empress kept moving away when the man approached her.

Suddenly she reared up and Fergus stepped aside quickly. " 'Tis a puzzle, it is," he said watching while the horse settled back down again. "The only other time I've seen her act like this was when . . ." He did not finish the sentence, and now was not the time to question him about it.

"Here, Empress," he said reaching into his pocket and extracting a sugar cube. He held out his hand and placed the sweet into his palm so that the horse could see it.

"She'll not take it," he said as the animal backed away. "It's her favorite, too." He looked back toward the stable. " 'Tis a funny thing. She isn't usually like this, miss. She's one of our finer animals. We always used to show her off, she's that gentle. She'd no more do this than run off with someone on her back. Nay, there's something that bothered her." He sighed and I could see the man was trying to devise another attempt to pacify the animal.

"May I try?"

Fergus shook his head. "That wouldn't be the best idea, miss. She's never seen you and, like I say, she's usually coy around strangers. That's always been her way. But now, I just don't know. I don't want to force her to do anything right now. I'd like her to just calm down again until we can lead her back to the stables." He looked at the cube in his hand and then closed his fist over it.

"I promise I will do nothing to startle her again. I once had a horse. Before I came here. I would ride every day in the early morning. I used to get up early before school and chores. Even when I was young—a

121

little girl—about seven or eight years." I looked at the stablemaster. "I am an accomplished horsewoman, sir. I will do nothing to hurt her. I promise."

Fergus squinted in the sun. "Aye. Go ahead and try, then. I'll be here, just in case." He gave me the lump of sugar. "Here. She loves these."

I walked slowly to the small, grey mare as it stood there pawing the ground, nervously trying to slip its reins. "Steady girl, steady," I said and held out my hand to offer her the sweet cube. "Steady Empress, steady."

The horse stopped digging at the earth and reared its head, staring at me with her big, brown eyes, watching as I moved slowly toward her. She was still hesitant about me and stood in place watching me as I held fast to my ground. "Sweet Empress," I said to her in soothing tones. "Sweet girl, sweet Empress," I repeated and suddenly the song that I had heard in my mind throughout my years came back to me again. The same notes that I had hummed to myself and to my parents. The same five notes that I had sung to guide the Price-Joneses to me when trapped in the moors seemed to be needed on this occasion, too. I voiced them faintly and then the same few strains repeated themselves in my memory until I realized I was saying words that seemed to fit the melody: "Pretty Empress mine, Pretty Empress mine." The syllables fit into the notes and without pause I sang the words louder. I saw that the horse was watching me, her breath no longer labored. "Pretty Empress mine, Pretty Empress mine," I sang as the now docile mare came slowly toward me, her head held high, her gait purposeful and proud. I stayed my ground now and waited for the animal's next move.

I saw Fergus watching me from the side, his fringe of white hair blowing gently in the wind, nodding slowly at me, his own eyes keen.

"Sweet Empress," I said again as the gentle animal came to my hand and gingerly took the sugar treat from my palm and chomped on it. She sidled even closer then and nudged my extended hand, neighing once, as it seemed, happily. "Pretty Empress mine," I sang again and the animal, now quiet and compliant, licked the few remaining granules of the sugar from my palm with her rough tongue and then came closer to me so that I could stroke her slick flanks.

"Good girl, good girl," I said picking up her straps and holding them in my hand while leading her in the direction of the stable. She seemed contrite and tame, as Fergus had said was her true nature, and I knew that there would be no more trouble with her.

"She has calmed," I said to the stablemaster while I stroked the mare's head. "She's quiet now." I whispered into the animal's ear. "Sweet Empress, sweet Empress."

"She's never done that before, miss," Fergus said as I walked the animal to her stall in the stable. "It's as though she . . ." He took off his faded kerchief once again and wiped at his eyes, then shook his head. "She's taken to you, Miss Morys. She trusts you." He looked round to the house. "If you would like, miss, I'll see if you can take her out. I'll speak to my lady, if you'd like, miss. She should be your horse, ma'am. Aye. Yours, now that she no longer has a mistress," he said, peering curiously at me. I turned my head back to the care of the now complacent mare but it was not fast enough, for I saw in Fergus's wizened eyes the accusation he had made upon meeting me: *Ye have been here before.*

The news of Empress's bolt and my ability to restrain the horse quickly circulated throughout the house, both upstairs and downstairs, and when I returned to Lady Glendower's bedchamber after dinner I overhead Nanny and her mistress speaking about it.

"Imagine," I heard the nurse quietly say to Lady Glendower when she thought I was some distance away from the bed. "Fergus said she was able to stop Empress, that he could do nothing with her but that Gwynneth sang to her and calmed her. The mare had no fear of her and went directly to her." I could not hear Lady Glendower's words, but I sensed that she was excited. Nanny continued, "Well, we shall see. We shall see. Of course, in my heart I know what is truth but we shall bide our time, my lady, and we'll surely know."

This time I heard Lady Glendower's reply. "Do you think that there can be any doubt?"

Nanny looked straight at her mistress and her tone was definite. "Nay. None whatsoever, my lady. There are too many signs. Too many ways. There is no mistake. I did not make a mistake. Mark my words, we shall have our proof soon."

Lady Glendower smiled at her trusted attendant and friend. "I pray that it will be so."

Nanny, not knowing that I had overheard her and Lady Glendower, praised me later in the day for my handling of the horse.

" 'Tis a good job you did, Gwynneth. The mare was frightened or else she would have stayed in her stall. But it was a good deed you did for all of us, and the mistress thanks ye. She told me to tell you so." I thanked Nanny and set about finishing up my chores in the room.

Fergus easily secured permission for me to ride Empress. "Aye, they — Lady Glendower and Nanny — were all for it, they were," he said the next day as he saddled up the mare for me. The two of us rode off to see the full glory of the grounds. It was an exercise that pleased both the animal and me, and in the course of our exhilarating ride on that warm summer day, Empress and I came to act and react as one. It quickly became a habit that, in the late afternoon while Lady Glendower slept, I would slip away, with Nanny's approval, and ride the small mare across the fields, always letting her lead me at her own speed.

On one such sojourn I was joined by Mr. Owen, who, having seen me riding one of the trails near the main road of the estate, rode over and asked permission to accompany me. It was a reasonable request but I still was not used to having a gentleman such as he pay attention to me, and when I tried to retreat from his company, I felt that he suspected my dilemma.

"My dear Miss Morys, Gwynneth," he once said to me. "I do not annoy you, do I?" I could tell by the way he spoke, using my Christian name, that his sense of humor had overtaken his sense of propriety, and I answered much too quickly.

"You can never annoy me, sir. But just now, Mr. Price-Jones, it appears that you were trying to."

Mr. Price-Jones looked away and then at me and I could see a small smile form about his mouth. "In truth, Miss Morys, I probably was, and I do beg your pardon. But you are so serious, so reticent, when speaking with me. Do you not enjoy our conversations?"

"But of course I do," I blurted out before I realized what I was saying. I put my hand to my face and spoke in a calmer voice. "Recall all our evening dinners together. Mr. Price-Jones, I think that you mistake me. Please let me explain." I pulled gently at Empress's reins. "I am sometimes quite confused, sir. There are things that I find inexplicable."

"The puzzle again, Miss Morys?"

"Indeed."

"Does it help when you ride?"

"Yes, for then I have time to sort things out."

"Do I dare ask what?"

I had begun to trust the gentleman and I decided to speak a little more about my dreams. I also told him about the presence I sensed and how I sometimes knew more than I should, and explained that even Empress seemed to respond to me.

Mr. Price-Jones listened intently as we rode side by side.

"Miss Morys, I confess that at first I thought that you were imagining things, that seeing Winter's Light in its glory together with all that has happened to you might have affected your judgment. But now I acknowledge, ma'am," he said, pulling his horse up short, "I admit that what you say . . . that what you tell me . . . makes confusing sense." He smiled at me and I signalled Empress to stand.

"Thank you, Mr. Price-Jones. Perhaps I shall tell you more some other time. But for now I must return."

Mr. Price-Jones took off his hat and bent toward me. "I will look forward to that day, Miss Morys, for I enjoy our conversations."

I turned Empress toward the house and the two of us rode in happy silence back to Winter's Light.

Lady Glendower was awake when I returned; I heard her sigh just as I entered the room. She opened her eyes slightly, then closed them again, and I thought that perhaps she had not seen me, but I was wrong. Her eyes again opened, I smiled at her, and she moved her arm toward me, motioning me close to her bed.

"Gwynneth," she said and I stood up at her words. "Please. Come here and tell me about your ride. About the day."

I did not know what prompted the woman's request. I looked around at Nanny, who nodded her head, urging me to comply with Lady Glendower's wishes, then went and sat by the bed and began to tell her about all that I had seen this day. If Lady Glendower noticed my initial nervousness she did not communicate it to me. I spoke about the beautiful weather, holding up my sketchbook and showing her my drawings to illustrate my words.

Lady Glendower seemed truly interested in what I was saying and I saw Nanny smile at the two of us. Suddenly I felt very comfortable and very wanted, as though I were finally beginning to enjoy being with Lady Glendower and Nanny. It seemed the most natural thing in the world for the three of us to be together at Winter's Light on this hot August day.

Lady Glendower fell asleep shortly after I began speaking to her, and when I gently pulled the coverlet up close around her neck, I had an urge to reach out and touch the woman's cheek. But of course I did not do this—such a gesture would have been too familiar. Still, as I looked at her the sleeping old woman seemed to be more than just my employer.

"She has taken to you," Nanny said from behind my back. "She thinks well of you, Gwynneth, and I know she likes your being here."

"I do not know why, Nanny. She has many friends, and I am sure she has family who would do much for her."

Nanny shook her head. "Her family is all gone now except for two distant cousins." She tightened her lips so that they pouted. "And we don't talk about those people," she said. "They are not worth the time of the new day." The nurse poured from the tea tray that had just been placed on the table by Meg. "You are the one who is making our mistress happy. Who has given her the will . . ." She looked over to the dresser where the small portrait of Anne was placed.

"Nanny, do you think she confuses me with Lady Anne?"

"No." Nanny set the teacup down with a loud clatter.

"No, she knows you are not Anne. Just look at your coloring. She was blonde and grey-eyed. My lady has not lost her senses. Despite all that some people would like her to do. Nay. She knows you are not Anne." She picked up her cup and sipped from it. "You are not Anne," she said in a strong voice and then fell silent. We both finished our tea and continued with our work.

Chapter Eleven

The long summer days all seemed remarkably the same—all cool, flower-perfumed mornings, lazy sun-drenched afternoons, and nights so warm that slumber was impossible. I could not sleep this night. Perhaps all that I had been hearing about young Lady Anne excited my mind, for I was restless and a score of questions flooded my head. Nanny's reluctance to discuss Anne and then her sudden turnabout teased my mind, and I questioned, as I lay in bed, what she and Lady Glendower could have meant when they spoke of waiting for a sign.

This evening Nanny had surprised me with a question I was not prepared to answer.

"Tell me, Gwynneth," she said as we stitched by candlelight. "When you first heard about Winter's Light, how did you feel about the offer that the good Reverend Jenkins made to you?"

I held my thread high for a moment and wondered what had prompted the nurse to ask me such a question. I thought for a moment and did not know how to answer. I hesitated, unsure whether I should speak of the strange coincidence of the offer with my need of employment, and then thought better of it.

"I did not think about it, Nanny," I lied and Nanny continued rocking, taking my word for the truth.

"Ye felt nothing about coming here?" the nurse spoke

in an even voice and yet I had the feeling that she was baiting me, that she wanted me to say certain words and to express certain feelings.

"I was apprehensive, of course, but I had no other recourse. My parents were dead. No one offered to help me on my farm. I had no marriage prospects and this was the only opportunity I had tendered me."

"Aye." The old woman continued to rock. "You are truthful to a fault, girl." She seemed lost in thought. "Truthful to a fault," she repeated. She closed her eyes and I saw that she was about to fall asleep. "Ye are much like . . ." Her words trailed off and the chair rocked only a few more seconds, then stopped while the nurse slept on.

Nanny's questions had stirred up many thoughts, and it now seemed imperative that I write to Reverend Jenkins and ask about the way my employment here at Winter's Light had come about. I had a score of questions for him—queries I had not asked at the time—and it seemed essential that I receive his explanation.

Rising from my bed, I went to my little desk and lit a stub of a candle in the holder. I wanted to write Mr. Jenkins immediately to see if there was anything to this mystery that he could clear up for me. I wanted to know if anything had been said to him that could possibly shed light on the circumstances of how I had been chosen to work at Winter's Light.

A fortnight later a letter arrived from the good man, but it did not reveal much to me. Although Mr. Jenkins had complete recall of the occasion, it had not entered his mind to question the way in which what he called a miracle had come to be. The coincidence had merely signified to him the faith of his lifetime.

"When the letter came asking about needing help at the estate," he wrote, *"about a position open at Winter's Light, I did not question. My first thought was that the Dear Lord had answered your prayers and was showing*

130

us the way. I just assumed that one of the staff people employed at the mansion came from this land, although I do not know that to be truth. I preferred to think that this person was found satisfactory and that the mistress of Winter's Light thought that all of the people in our area were hard-working and trustworthy, and thus wanted another individual of the same qualities. (Of that, I know I was not mistaken, for what you tell me, Gwynneth, leads me to believe that you are doing well and serving your mistress with loyalty in your new position.)

"The letter, as I recall, did have specific requirements. All, I may say, happened to fit with you and your position. The woman who wrote—I believe it was actually composed by Mrs. Hoskins and sent at the direction of Lady Glendower—specified that they needed a young girl, a strong girl who would be diligent in her duties. They then listed some of the tasks that the girl would assist in at the manor. These included helping in Lady Glendower's bedchamber, assisting the nurse, and small, miscellaneous duties that might crop up from time to time and did not need recounting. I don't think there was anything more, except that the young girl should be about sixteen years of age and in need of a home and employment.

"There was a bit in the letter that an orphan girl would do quite nicely and a promise that the staff and mistress of the estate would give the young woman a good home for the rest of her life. In fact, now that I recall, I did get the impression that it was an orphan child they expressly desired, for I supposed they wanted no encumbrance of the helper.

"The only skills that were required for the position were obedience, a sunny disposition, and willingness to work, and now that I think back on it—perhaps they requested a person with knowledge of reading and writing. These skills you had, and I did not hesitate to recom-

131

mend you immediately. Now I am convinced that it would have been much more prudent of me to examine all the particulars, but at the time, you will remember, Gwynneth, there did not seem to be a way out of your misery and circumstances. Fortunately, all turned out well for everyone and there is no need for regret on anyone's part.

"I hope you are well and happy and I remain with all kind wishes for your life, Reverend Frank Jenkins."

I read and reread the letter hoping for more than what Mr. Jenkins had written—perhaps I had missed something—but I discovered nothing. The minister's letter was straightforward and did not deviate from the recital of fact. I was disappointed that he could not supply me with more information about the inquiries, but at least I had some clue as to what Nanny and Lady Glendower had been searching for when they employed me. Although the skills listed seemed rather general, they were, as Reverend Jenkins had pointed out to me, entirely within my ken.

I settled further into a routine at Winter's Light, helping with Lady Glendower's care, riding Empress, and having dinners with Nanny and the Price-Joneses and summer seemed to continue endlessly.

Nanny did not press me more for information as to my feelings about Winter's Light, although I did let it be known that I had no objections to spending the rest of my days here. Many times, when we were working or having tea together, I would speak about the glories of the manor, and the nurse, smiling, would rock in her chair, seemingly relieved to know that I was taking great pleasure in the estate. I did not tell her my sense of the house's gloom still persisted or that at odd moments I felt a mysterious sadness. There was no way for me to explain these emotions to her, and I did not want to risk being viewed as eccentric or unstable.

In the early twilight, before I retired, when there was

still a pale grey cast to the sky, I would sometimes sit at my window and muse about the way things had been ordained for me. Some days I would recall a fragment of an incomplete dream or the profile of a person, but more often the five-note tune would come into my thoughts and I would try to remember where and when I first had heard it.

Other evenings I would think that I saw the same dancing scene that I had seemed to witness in the ballroom downstairs. The illusion, lifelike, had become familiar to me, and no longer frightened or alarmed me. Thus the hidden anguish of Winter's Light influenced my thoughts, but it was something that I had come to accept.

There was another thing that preyed on my mind. All the talk about families—the Glendowers and the Price-Joneses—weighed upon me, for it had always been a source of unhappiness to me that I did not know the identity of my true parents. I wrote another letter to the minister hoping that he, now that I no longer was his parishioner, would be able to supply me with more information about my birth. Perhaps he had been entrusted with secrets that he could reveal to me now that I no longer lived at Daear. Although I knew the story that my father and mother had told me, I hoped that the good man had found out or had been told the exact circumstances of my birth. I did not ask outright for the name of the man and the woman involved, but I hoped that there had been some news—some gossip, perhaps—from around the parish that would have reached the ears of the cleric at the time.

But again, when I received Mr. Jenkins's reply, it provided no help in ascertaining who my real father and mother were or from where they came. The minister knew only what my parents told him and, because they had been such honest people, he did not question their words.

"I do not remember Mathias or Molly telling me any more particulars about your birth. I suspect they did not know more, or if they did, that they were of the opinion that it was not for the village people to know. Not that anyone, dear Gwynneth, would have questioned, for the Morys's were always two of our most respected parishioners and you were just naturally accepted as their daughter, no matter whether you were their natural child or not. But I have always felt—nay, I have always prayed, that someday you would learn about your real parents, or, failing that, would know that your adopted family and all those who wished you joy and peace were here at Daear and within our village. We were all of one mind when you appeared to your parents as a babe and we all loved you and rejoiced when Molly and Mathias presented you to our congregation.

"There was never anyone who came forth to claim you, nor was there any hint or rumor regarding your birth. Even now, after all these years, no one has ever reported a lost child, and so we must assume that you may never know, on this earth, those who gave you life. I know Mathias and Molly at first feared that someone would petition for you but that fright abated after two or three years. Soon after that the circumstances of your coming to Daear were never questioned or included in casual conversations. You became another villager, much like all others living here.

"I know nothing more than that, girl, and am sorry that I can not help you more. I pray you are happy and that you know that you have my best wishes and prayers. Yours sincerely, Rev. Frank Jenkins."

There was a postscript written in the minister's spidery handwriting along the edges of both sides of the piece of paper.

"Perhaps, Gwynneth, this bit of information can help you, although I do not know how it can be so. Maybe sometime you will be able to use it if there are other *things revealed to you. For the last fifteen or sixteen years there has always been someone coming about in the winter time—always in the winter time—to just poke about the records and the graveyard and the church ledgers. I remember that there was always this same one man who rode into the village and stayed a few days at the inn near the rectory. He was not a land surveyor, for I recall that I once had asked him if that was his profession, but I recollect that he replied that he was merely a working man come to search out odd jobs and the like while on his way to his family home, although he never did identify his village. I thought it rather suspicious that the same man showed for all the time but I put it down to the fact that the man might have been in an occupation such that it was seasonal and that the winter months offered no promise of a job. He was not of a garrulous nature and therefore kept to himself and his own mind, and I doubt that even the innkeeper or the patrons had much to say to him for all the times he has visited at the hostel. This same gentleman, I know, has even been here this past year, for I remember seeing him in the church for evening vespers.*

"I have not questioned what he searched for, for all our records are open. I even thought once that perhaps he was just a country person come to look up his ancestors—perhaps there was something black in his family history and he did not want to own up to it—although why he comes every year, I cannot guess. I remember once asking if I could assist him and offering to tell him the history of the church and cemetery, but he seemed not to be interested in either at the time. I have no clue as to what he was looking for or if he was checking the records for something precise, for it was not my place to ask that of him once he declined my attempt to help.

"I had also once thought him an emissary and that he was interested in buying extra property for some landed gentry from another shire, but no one has ever tendered

an offer for any parcel of land. Who this man is I cannot tell you except that he has repeated the same search every year. He rides about the countryside seeming to call at no specific cottage, and yet he appears to know the territory well. He never speaks to anyone and asks no questions of any who are working the fields or gardens, and I do not know how long this inspection will continue. And that is the only peculiar thing that happens in our village and I am still not aware if he is an agent come to find land or birth records. Again, I do not know if this bit of information will help you in later life. Yours in God's faith, FJ."

I shivered at the footnote, for what the minister wrote seemed to fit in with what I had learned in one of my last conversations with my father. Reverend Jenkins had unknowingly supplied me with information that seemed in keeping with my father's words, and I read the letter again hoping to sort out the connection. But I could not, and even though I perused the letter several times, I gleaned no further knowledge from it. I read it once more and then put the letter with the small mementos I had carried away with me from Daear.

The next evening, in the waning moments of light, I again sought out the letters Reverend Jenkins had sent me and reread them, looking for I know not what. Once more I examined every word that the good man had written, but there were no clues hidden within the missiles.

I sighed and thought back to the last winter that I had spent with my parents. They had become very tired and enfeebled by that time and I suspect that both knew they did not have much time left on this earth. One day my mother had asked to see my father in private. I had left the cottage to tend the animals in the barn, then returned, entering the room just in time to hear my mother speak to my father.

"Tell her, Mathias, tell her," she had urged, taking hold of his hand. "Ye cannot deny me this wish—my deathbed wish. The child has a right to know."

I remember my father nodded, but when my mother died, grief overcame him and my father forgot for a while his last promise to his wife. Although I did pose the question once or twice, I had not wanted to press the matter at that time. But when, after three months had passed and he had taken ill, I had had to speak once more and ask the questions that only he could answer.

One night, when it was late and all the surrounding hillside was dark, I had sat by my father's bed as he called out, in delirium, to his dead wife. I wiped his forehead and he opened his eyes and smiled at me. "That question," he said to me, and I had known to what he referred. "Ye still want the answer, don't you, girl?" I nodded and my father sighed. He hesitated and then spoke. "I cannot say too much, Gwynneth. Only that the story that I have always told you is a true one." He put his wrinkled hand out to me and I took it and pressed it to my cheek. "I cannot reveal too much, my dear, for I am still bound by an oath I took many years before." I implored him to tell me whatever he knew of my ancestry, but it was of no use—it was said in the village that whenever Mathias Morys gave his word, it was enough for any man. Nothing, not even my tears and his approaching death could change his mind.

But that night I suspect he saw that there would not be many more times for us to speak. Thus he had given me some information about my birth without revealing anything that would break his sacred pledge. He could not disclose the names of the people, he whispered, for he truly did not know them, but he said he had once been visited by a man after he and my mother had taken me in. He had been told by this person, under strictest secrecy, that I had been an unwanted child and that my presence at my real home would only have been an embarrassment and a reminder of matters better left alone. This version seemed in keeping with my own childhood fantasy, for I had always assumed that I was the child of some prominent gentleman and had had to be sent away lest I dishonor a noble name. I considered myself fortunate that such kind and loving people as Mathias and Molly had adopted me and raised and cherished me as their own.

My father also told me that money had always come to them—that every year, in the middle of winter, the same man would ride up to the house and deposit a small bag of gold coins at the door. "He never spoke to me, Gwynneth, except that once and then one other time. He directed that the money be used for your care," my father said, "and we abided by those terms. Your mother was very strict about that, and no matter what the situation was on the farm or in our household, the money was never touched for any other purpose than to keep you." He started to cough so that his whole body trembled. "That's all the man ever said to me about the money. Just that it was to be used for you.

"And then one time more, again in winter, I met that same man near the chapel, and he seemed to know all about you and your mother and me and about Daear and the way the plantings and harvest had gone the previous year. He seemed to know your accomplishments through the entire year and I remember he spoke about you as 'the little redhead.' I thought it queer but to be truthful, Gwynneth, we did not press the gentleman as to his source, for your mother and I were afraid that if we probed too deeply he would somehow take you away from us." Father started to cough again and I waited until he had caught his breath. "We knew nothing more. Only that every year a bag of coins would be propped up against our door—in the spot almost identical to the place where I found you—and with no note."

So he was the man that Reverend Jenkins had seen in the church. I felt it only right that the minister be told what I knew of the stranger, and I wrote him another

138

letter describing in detail my last conversation with my father.

Reverend Jenkins's reply came by the next stage.

"I am glad you have cleared up the mystery for me, my dear Gwynneth, and now, I suppose, the gentleman will no longer visit us, since you are gone from the village. We shall see if the man returns and questions me as to your whereabouts come next winter.

"As to your father not revealing any more to you, I suspect it is because of the oath and the fact that all is in the past. I do not think, my dear girl, that at this time of your life there is any longer a need to know of your natural family, for you had the good fortune of having kind and loving parents. It is best, Gwynneth, to let the past lie, for surely no good can come from it now."

I folded the paper into thirds and put it with my other letters. Perhaps Reverend Jenkins was right. Perhaps it was best to let the secrets of the dark die and be buried. I had always trusted the just man's words before; I had always believed him. Yes, I thought, Reverend Jenkins must be right. Had I been destined to know the circumstances of my concealed birth then surely I would have been made privy to them long before now.

I blew out the candle flame and stared into the dark. I was disappointed that I had found no answers to the questions that had always plagued me, but apparently there was to be no help for me. I had always thought that in some manner my true origin would be revealed to me, but now this hope seemed just another of my fancies.

I lay awake for a long time thinking of my clouded birth—contrasting it to the Lady Anne's—and I felt an overwhelming sense of sadness. I closed my eyes, hoping to still my thoughts, and I remember hearing the clock in the Great Hall strike ten chimes before I fell asleep.

It was not a restful sleep. Faces and sounds appeared to pass before me until it seemed as if my head would burst. I remember tossing and turning on my bed, yet I was powerless to awaken. A montage of unknown people continued to parade in front of me, and at times it was as if all the noises blended into a cacophony of sounds and all the people's features became one. And then suddenly everything faded and there was only one person in the scene, a young girl. I could not see her features, for she was not facing me. She appeared to be walking away from me toward the estate chapel near the main house. An unbearable melancholy seemed to envelop her, there was such sadness visible in her step and the manner in which she held her body. Her long grey-green cloak trailed behind her over the newly cut blades of grass and the hood of her cape was bent forward as though her head were bowed to her unhappiness. She was surrounded by beauty, the speckless blue skies and golden sun and deep green of the grass combined in cruel contrast to her somber and inconsolable mood.

She walked slowly, as though even this was too much effort. Finally, when she had come to the chapel, she paused and looked around, checking to see if there was anyone near. I could see that the area was clear of people and she, too, must have noted it, for in one quick movement quite unlike the other steps she had taken, she opened the door of the stone building and vanished.

But the dream did not end, for in a few short seconds I saw the same female figure emerge from a door at the top of the chantry onto a balcony that encircled the whole of the structure. The summer breeze had picked up and I could see the trellised red rose bushes near the chapel sway gently. The wind seemed to play about the girl's head, ruffling her hood about her face so that I still could not identify her. I saw her brush at her face with her gloved hand, but it was just an idle gesture and was not done out of annoyance.

I think it was that careless gesture that alerted me. A coldness came over me even in my dream, and I knew

140

what was in that young girl's mind; I sensed her intent, and I wanted to stop her. I felt a powerful pull of fright in my stomach. I was powerless. All I could do was watch, for I knew there was no way I could breach the distance between us. I felt desperate and yet I knew that I had to let the scene play out to its inevitable tragic end. I had to watch as the girl ended her life. There was no stopping her, no matter how much I wanted to . . . how much I tried.

Still I cried out to the figure under the bell tower.

"Please stop. Please don't do this. Please don't do this," but the woman, of course, neither heard me nor faltered in her mission. I saw her pull her cloak close around her and tug at her hood and for just a brief moment she turned and I saw her face. She had blonde hair — errant curls twined up and over her cheeks — and I shall always recall that her light grey eyes were wide and sad.

When she turned I finally recognized the woman's face. It was as I expected! It was the same face as that in the small painting kept in Lady Glendower's cabinet, one of the several hidden artists' renditions of a young woman with innocent eyes and a dainty, shy, smiling mouth. Only, as she turned in my dream in these last few seconds, there was no more sunlight in her eyes or on her face. Now there was only darkness and despair.

I realized that somehow I was witnessing the last few moments of young Anne Glendower's life. It was evident that the girl was in torment and despair; the small, labored steps she took as she walked were those of a saddened and disillusioned sweetheart. The figure was Anne — I had no doubts about that — but why I had been chosen to witness her death, I did not know. Not even the last tragic look she gave me revealed the reason.

Anne moved purposely to the edge and I became frantic. I was powerless to stop her and I watched in horror as she approached the low parapet of the upper level of the chapel and without hesitation stepped gracefully up and out into the air as calmly as if she were stepping onto the step of a staircase. There was no urgency or fear about the fatal move, nor was there anyone other than I to witness it.

At that moment the vision vanished and I was left with the fading view of the thin young figure in dark grey-green cotton hurtling from the glimmering stone balcony.

I awoke to the sound of my own voice moaning and calling out, "No. Please stop. Please don't do this," and I clasped my hand over my mouth to quell the words. I touched my face and found that there were tears on my cheeks and that my fingers were trembling with the horror that I had just experienced in my sleep. The vision of the figure falling from the balcony would not leave my mind.

Eventually I became more calm, but once, as I sat there in bed in the dark night, I thought that I had almost pronounced a word or a name while in my own agitated state. But when I tried again to form the word, no articulation came forth. The name or notion that had flitted through my memory was now gone.

Whatever had happened to that young girl, I felt inextricably bound to her fate, and yet I knew not why Lady Anne's life—and now, her death—should affect me so.

I positioned the light sheet around me and closed my eyes, but there was to be no more sleep for me this evening. I heard the downstairs clock chime every hour until it was time for the household to rise and begin another day.

Chapter Twelve

The next morning at breakfast Nanny noticed my fatigue and questioned me for the reason. I knew I had to offer some excuse to hold off her probings.

"It was nothing, Nanny. I was disturbed last night by a dream—a silly dream, I'm sure," I lied, for I did not want to speak of the nightmare just yet. To reveal it would be to open up to her all of my inexplicable dreams and feelings, and now was not the time for this. Perhaps some evening when we were more at leisure and Nanny more receptive, I would explain.

The old nurse looked at me suspiciously and I knew that she would not let up on her questioning. "About what, Gwynneth?" She stirred her bowl of porridge. "What could have disturbed ye so?" I could see the lines around her eyes deepen so that it seemed the dark pupils searched out the answers from me.

I pushed away my morning meal, for the recollection of last night's dream had taken away my appetite. Nanny saw my gesture and frowned.

"What disturbed you, Gwynneth?" Her voice was gentle yet demanding. I knew I had to tell her something, but how could I account for my bizarre dreams and my feelings of gloom here at the estate that she loved so well? "Say straightout what it was, girl," she urged.

I tried to make light of it. "It was just a strange dream, Nanny. I am sure it occurred because I imagine too many things when my mind is not occupied."

Nanny would not be put off. "A dream, you say? What kind of a dream would disturb you, girl?"

It was no use attempting to keep it to myself. I could see Nanny would have none of my excuses or stories.

"I dreamed about a dreadful death that may have occurred here at Winter's Light. It was not real, and yet it unsettled and frightened me. It was a violent death. I cannot tell you any more than that, except that I am sure it took place here on the estate." I did not have the heart to tell the poor woman that I had dreamt of Lady Anne. I did not want to open more wounds for her—it was bad enough that the young girl died. Perhaps the truth would come out at another time, when I felt more courageous.

"Did it happen on the bogs?" Nanny's eyes were wide with curiosity. I blinked at her question. Shadowy impressions of the nightmare seemed to appear in my mind and I again saw the young girl about to take her fatal step from the chapel balcony. I wished I could shake the memory from my head but it persisted as though it would be with me forever. As though there was something I was to glean from it.

"Did some of the hands tell you about a death on the bogs?" Nanny's piercing voice recalled me to her question and I thought it easier to let her think that this was the cause of my fright.

"Yes, I have been told that there are supposed to be people who have not returned from the moors. And that one body was found there several years ago."

"Sixteen. Sixteen going on seventeen years ago," she said softly and I was amazed that she remembered the number.

"Yes, I know about that person. A man, they say, although no one was able to identify him. Fergus told me."

Nanny stirred her hot tea. "But that is not what upset you, is it, girl?" She looked at me through slitted eyes. "This death that you dreamt about—it did not take place

144

on the moors, did it?"

I had no choice but to confess the truth. "No."

Nanny sat back and seemed satisfied for the moment. "Ye know now, after your own fright, not to wander too near them, don't ye, Gwynneth?" I assured her I did, but Nanny was not about to let the other matter recede. "The nightmare. The one that frightened you. What was it about?"

I was of a mind not to speak any more about it, but very gently and quite skillfully the old nurse pulled an account of it from me. I spared nothing but the fact that I had recognized the woman to be Lady Anne. As I spoke I watched Nanny's face and once I thought I detected a look in her eyes which seemed to indicate that what I recounted was, if not the entire truth, at least the half of it.

The woman listened attentively and said nothing until I had concluded the recitation. I don't know if I expected her to confirm my story or to tell me that my imagination was quite lively but she did neither. Instead she stood up and nodded her head to me.

"Best we get to work now, Gwynneth," she said easily, then excused herself from the table without uttering a word about what I had just revealed to her.

I was disappointed in her reaction. I had hoped that she would confirm my story and maybe tell me, herself, that the woman was Anne Glendower.

"Come, Gwynneth. The pitcher needs fresh water in it." She handed me the vessel. "Ye can fill it at the same time you fetch Lady Glendower's breakfast," she said and indicated the door. But I was not fooled. I knew Nanny wanted me out of the way so that she could discuss my tale with her mistress as soon as possible. Perhaps someday I would find out why my doings were so important to Lady Glendower.

That evening Nanny released me from my duties early, saying that she remembered that I had not had a restful sleep the previous night. I must confess I welcomed the break, and no sooner had I put my head upon my pillow than I fell asleep.

But this night soon proved exactly like the last; the same nightmare played in the darkness of my mind. Over and over again I saw Anne tumble from the chapel balcony. The frightful scene was eerily silent — even the summer wind I saw rustling the leaves of the trees made no noise. The dream was even more frightening this second time, for I anticipated everything that was about to happen and still I was unable to break the spell. I could not save Anne from her fate, but again was helpless in the face of her death. I awoke, stricken.

I wished I could rid myself of these visions, but I knew I had no control over what was brought to the forefront of my mind while I slept. I was powerless against the images. What disturbed me even more was the thought that this particular nightmare would recur. I felt somehow no matter what I did or thought, this awful spectacle would haunt me for many more days and nights.

I was thoroughly confounded by the many things that had happened to me since coming to live on this estate. Daily I looked about me at the other staff members wondering if they, too, felt the strangeness and the gloom. Although I had not spoken of it to them, I could not believe that others here were unaware of the mysterious currents, that I was the only one. I wished I could discuss this with someone, but how could I tell another all I believed? How could I voice my feeling that a spirit hovered here, in the light of day and the shadows of night alike? How could I confide in anyone my suspicion that evil surrounded this house and this estate?

Evil. It was a word I had never uttered lightly, and I hesitated to use it even now. But I did sense evil here at Winter's Light; I was forced to admit it, though I knew not from whence it had come or for what reason. Its implications were much too complicated to sort out quickly, and I resolved to keep my fears to myself for the moment.

The next day I made a concerted effort not to think of Lady Anne's death, and whenever Nanny or someone from the staff made light of a situation or spoke in jest, I confess I may have laughed a bit too loud or smiled a bit too much. It was my way of warding off the darksome thoughts in my mind.

In the late afternoon I took my sketchbook and rode Empress to my secret place on the estate hoping that I could make a more creditable drawing of Winter's Light. It was only an exercise for me and I did not expect to depict the manor perfectly, but I was stubborn enough to want a try at capturing its color on this sunny day.

Again, though, I was defeated, and somehow I knew that my drawing skills alone were not to blame. Rather, it was as though all the pain and sorrow of Winter's Light had blighted my endeavor. The gloom was beginning to permeate my very mind, and I was afraid that no matter what I did, I would never be able to escape it.

That evening as Mrs. Hoskins and I sat by the firelight and I stitched on my cloth, I was preoccupied with my morbid thoughts and Nanny, ever perceptive, again questioned me carefully.

"Ye seem not to be the same self that you were this morning, Gwynneth. Is there something else troubling ye? Has the nightmare come again?" The words were said kindly, but I knew the woman would persist if I did not offer some excuse. I was weary and did not want her to delve too deeply into my inner thoughts, so I claimed that my inability to get a good likeness of Winter's Light was the reason for my silence. I was careful to lay the blame for my artistic failure on myself, telling Nanny that it might have been my outlook.

"Aye. Sometimes the way you view the happenings of life colors your imagination. But ye are a fine artist,

Gwynneth. Perhaps you are too hard on yourself. Maybe you expect too much on your first try." She picked at the threads of her shawl. "Maybe we all do," she said quietly. She pulled at the fringe so that it ravelled.

"I shall show you my sketches of the house sometime," I said trying to put the conversation on a lighter plane. "And then you will see for yourself that I am not the artist you credit me with being."

Nanny nodded her lace-capped head. "Sometimes we see more than we want to . . . more than we ought to," she murmured, more to herself than to me.

I did not want my gloomy attitude to settle on the old woman, and so I started to speak of other, more cheerful things — of the way the gardens were growing and of the birds that had flocked to the fields and woods near the house.

Nanny continued to rock in her chair as I spoke and I saw a look of consternation cross her face. I could tell that there was something that the woman wanted to ask me, and I waited, knowing that, in her own time, she would find the correct words.

"Have ye seen the dream again, Gwynneth?"

I did not answer for a moment, but I knew I had to tell the truth. "Yes. Last night."

She continued to rock slowly, and though she asked nothing more, I spoke about the dream, striving to explain that, though quite unaccountable to others, it was quite real to me.

"I often have strange dreams, Nanny. Of things I cannot explain." The woman seemed not to hear me and I continued. "It has always been so. I don't know why it happens, but I pay them no attention," I lied. "Perhaps when I grow older I will no longer be haunted by them."

"Haunted, ye say?" Her white head jerked up at the word and she looked at me with narrowed eyes before glancing down at the dainty gold ring on her middle finger.

"Perhaps that is the wrong word," I said, and even I was rather shocked at my choice of expression, for I knew not what had made me allude to the supernatural.

"And be there anything else?" Nanny's hands now were in her lap, calmly lying there as though I had said nothing unusual.

"No," I said and then smiled at her in hopes of dispelling her interrogation. I did not want to reveal to her that I had also dreamed of Winter's Light long before viewing the estate. Even though the subject had been broached, I most certainly did not wish to tell her that this estate had haunted me throughout my life. For how could I? Such a thing could be neither easily explained nor readily accepted, and I had learned long ago that to justify its occurrence was much too difficult. Even my parents, who trusted and believed in me, had not been able to comprehend my meaning the few times I attempted to speak of the phenomenon. No, I had decided long ago that my inner visions were best kept to myself.

Nanny continued to rock in a rhythmic fashion and I worried that I had made a mistake in confiding even a small amount to her. I had always lived in dread that someday someone would think my truthfulness odd, and my mother had often cautioned me not to speak of my uncanny experiences with those outside the family circle. I did not want to seem eccentric to the woman who had given me a trusted position, and when she said nothing I feared I might have already jeopardized my position in this household.

"Witch." I closed my eyes and even now, so many years later, I could hear the shrill voices of the village children. *"Witch!"* The accusing, hurtful word had been cast my way many times before I had learned to control my tongue, before I had learned that there were secret things of which only I must know. The appellation had brought my innocence to a bitter end, but thanks to the goodness of the adults in my village, the cruel taunts had ceased

149

within a few months and I was encouraged to forget all the times when I had been frightened and angered by the accusation. Reverend Jenkins had explained that the children had just been teasing me because I looked different, but mercifully, he had not questioned me regarding the things I had confided to them. I do not know how he would have received my confession.

I put my stitchery aside and allowed my mind to wander back to the past. The memory of the schoolchildren's jeers still lingered within me. I could see, in my mind's eye, the boys and girls of yesteryear as they stood some distance away from me, pointing. *"Beware of her. Beware of her,"* they had screamed. Then they had run around each other pretending to hide their eyes. *"Don't look at her. Don't look at her hair. She'll rob you of sight!"* They had laughed and giggled until they finally tired of the wretched game and moved away to other, more interesting sport.

I touched my head as I remembered all the times I had been taunted and teased about the color of my hair, the bright copper that was so singly mine amongst the dark Welsh heads of my country. While growing up I had constantly been tormented by my peers about the brightness of my locks. And even though I knew it had been only an amusement for the children, the remembrance of it still hurt.

"Witch. Witch," they had called after me as I made my way to and from school, for in my part of the country it was widely thought that only witches and harlots were born with red hair. *"Witch,"* they would call me when they were finished with their chores and needed a diversion. They would find me on a path going towards my farm and then they would surround me and sing the harsh chant that someone, I cannot remember who, had made up. I could still recite it now, although no one had spoken the words since my childhood. *"Hair of gold, Heaven's fold. Hair of red, Devil's head! Witch. Witch."*

150

It was heartless, and many an afternoon I had run home to my father and climbed onto his lap to tell him of my hurts and fears. He would stroke my hair—" 'Tis a beautiful shade," he had said to comfort me—and I would fall asleep as he held me, gently rocking back and forth in front of the peat fire.

"Ah, child," I remember hearing him say one evening when, no more than four or five years old, I had come running home, tears streaming down my face. "Ah child, 'tisn't fair. You belong at—" He had held me tightly and I did not hear the rest of his words, for I had buried my head deep into his jacket, and in truth, I had wanted nothing more than to be at Daear, with my parents and my doll, Lucy. Wherever it was that my father thought that I belonged, I did not care. To sit there with him in the warm room, drowsy with the firelight flickering, to feel his gentle arms about me and to smell his pipe tobacco, was all that I wanted or needed.

I was awakened from my reverie by the sound of Nanny's rocker as it scraped against the wooden floor, and I looked at her as she continued to sit, straight and tall, her aged eyes trained on the dimly lit wall across from her.

She spoke and her words astonished me.

"Do ye have the gift," she asked in a voice that seemed to penetrate the dusky stillness. I inhaled quickly and did not answer, for truly I did not know of what she spoke. "The gift, child. The gift," she repeated, and this time I could hear in her voice the agitation that came from frustration. She turned toward me and I could see her mouth working to form the precise words she wanted to use. "The gift, Gwynneth. Do ye have it?"

"I do not know of what you speak," I said truthfully. I saw the old woman's face tighten and I could tell that she was pondering her sentences.

"The gift, child," she said so quietly that I had to strain to hear her. "The gift of understanding . . . of

151

knowing."

I shuddered and dared not move. I was puzzled and frightened, for it seemed that Nanny had pierced my innermost secrets and thoughts. I felt a cold chill pass through my body and I shivered and pulled the sleeves of my dress down to cover my wrists.

Nanny, watching me now with hawk-like eyes that seemed to glisten by the candlelight's glow, continued in a voice that was composed though strained. She thrust her head forward towards me and reached out a hand as if to touch my arm.

"Tell me, girl, did ye ever before *know* of things that were about to happen? Or of things that happened many years ago? Much like your last night's dream?" she asked. Instantly I stiffened with apprehension. Nanny saw my motion and I could see a small smile play about her mouth. "There, I was right. Ye have it. Ye do have it," she said triumphantly. "I could tell. I knew. I knew," she repeated. "Ye do have the gift, don't you, Gwynneth?" she said, rather than asked, and then she put her arms in front of her, her hands placed together as though in prayer. "I knew it. I knew ye would," she said. Then she fell silent once more, and the predominant sound in the room was the summer breeze rustling the sheer lace curtains at the window.

I put aside my needle and stared down at the cloth that I was working. It was no use now inventing stories to deny the old woman's words. I had opened the entire Pandora's box myself by speaking of the dreams I had had. Now I knew what I had had all my life—*the gift,* Nanny had called it. Of course it was a gift, but still I did not want to speak of it. To verbalize it would be to accept it, and for the moment, I was much too frightened to do so.

Nanny continued rocking and I could hear only the sound of her chair moving to and fro on the bare floor.

"Ye do have it, don't you, Gwynneth?" Nanny's voice

was calm, so calm that I wondered at its import.

I did not know how to answer her vague yet pointed question, for the challenge had never been put to me before and I did not know Nanny's opinion of such intangibles. I hesitated, afraid that if I admitted to the terrible secret I had carried with me since I was small, I would be condemned . . . or worse. And in that moment's delay I recalled two of the biggest mysteries of my life: I heard once again the mysterious tune that I had hummed when a child and I remembered the way I had named my doll Lucy as though it had to be so.

In this atmosphere of recall I did not know how to answer the old woman. What would she say if I admitted to my "gift"? Would Nanny, who had surely seen many things in her time, consider me a fraud or, worse still, a heretic? No, I thought, it is best not to speak yet of these things. I would let a longer time pass before trusting anyone with my deepest secret. Otherwise, how could I—how would I—explain Winter's Light and my dreams?

Nanny peered at me, the question still posed in her bright eyes.

"No. None. I have nothing. No gift . . . nothing," I lied. I took up my cloth again and counted out threads, aware that Nanny sat staring at me as if she could read my mind. As if she did not believe me.

"Say you so," she said. She remained silent until it was time for us to go to sleep.

In the days that followed I tried to avoid speaking of anything except the mundane to Mrs. Hoskins. She accepted my decision and so we spoke not of me but of the household and the help—of Meg, who was becoming a valuable asset to Mrs. Padley, and of the other girls who were beginning to find their places among the staff of Winter's Light.

"They're good girls," Nanny said, "although they can never rise above their level. Breeding will always out." Again I was uncomfortable with the tendentious phrase, just as I had been upon hearing Mrs. Hoskins utter it the first day of our first meeting.

"We are all not in the same class as the Glendowers, Nanny, but that does not mean we are of any less worth as people."

"Maybe. Maybe not." She opened a window and looked out. "But breeding always tells." Alas! The old woman would not give up her prejudices.

Chapter Thirteen

One afternoon Mr. Owen Price-Jones joined me as I was exercising Empress, and the two of us took a long ride to the cliffs that looked out upon the sea. I was impressed with the view; the spectacular beauty of the deep blue water as it crashed against the rocky coast, then sent its ruffled whitecaps to search in and among the rocks was something entirely new to me. I was in awe of the water's roaring, and I liked feeling the faint sting of the salt spray upon my face. These sights and sounds and feelings brought to mind all the ragings of heaven and hell, and I wonder if Reverend Jenkins had ever imagined that his sermons would cause me to see this particular spot as the gateway to eternal salvation or damnation.

Today, though, the ocean was calm, as was the day itself, and the gentle, splashing, almost playful waves against the rocks seemed neither frightening nor intimidating. Seabirds rested on the edge of the cliff and on some of the higher rocks in the middle of the sea, giving it a tranquil look, and I regretted that I did not have my sketchbook with me to capture the sight.

We set our horses to grazing and then walked close to the brink of the cliffs and looked down, watching as the water gently cascaded over the jagged promontories, then receded, leaving little, white bubbles to bob on the surface until they exploded and were consumed by the rest of the sea.

"I wonder how many others have watched these same rocks." Mr. Price-Jones moved close to me and pointed below. "When I was a child and came to visit Uncle Charles, we would often sit at the water's edge and spend entire afternoons watching the sea. It was a pleasant time for me, and I remember . . ." He stopped and looked around. "It is funny, Miss Morys. I just remembered something that I've not thought of in many years." He stared off at the coves along the coastline. "We once climbed all the way down there, my uncle and I, and I remember now that when I told someone what we had done, he said it had been a sign that my uncle was sad, that when my uncle sat at the sea edge he was trying to recapture something that had passed."

"Sad? That is not a word I would ever choose in connection with Mr. Price-Jones. I think of him as one of the most contented of men. For what reason would he have been dejected, sir? I imagine that your uncle is and always has been in one of the most enviable positions in the area."

The younger Mr. Price-Jones nodded his head. "I know he has everything one could ask for, but I do seem to remember hearing from my mother or another relative that Uncle Charles was to be left alone until he had emerged from his gloomy state. In fact, I seem to recall someone saying that he was to be left alone with his sorrow until it had straightened itself out." He cocked his head. "I wonder what they were talking about." He smiled at me and his smile was reminiscent of his uncle's. "As I said, ma'am, I was but a child, and yet I do recall watching him for signs of unhappiness, expecting to see I know not what on his face. But he never spoke of his feelings, and neither his face nor his manner betrayed a heavy heart."

"Perhaps someone romanticized him, sir, for he is indeed a handsome and distinguished man. Perhaps the myth of his melancholia was invented to excuse his unwedded state. Perhaps it was an invention of some of the mothers of eligible young women. It could have been, particularly if their daughters had not been able to capture your uncle's eye."

Mr. Price-Jones chuckled. "Miss Morys, what a delightful suggestion. I had never thought about that."

"I think women are sometimes more inventive than men, sir." I laughed and Mr. Owen touched my hand in agreement.

"I do believe that, in some ways, they are, ma'am." I was embarrassed at the slight sign of affection, but Mr. Price-Jones withdrew his hand immediately and I gave it no more thought.

We watched as a gull flew close to us, then headed off toward the water to land on a small stretch of sand near a curve in the shore.

"But there is no denying that your uncle is an attractive and intelligent man, Mr. Price-Jones. I myself have wondered why he never wed. He is well born, amusing, and witty, and he has a hundred other qualities that would serve him well in marriage. I am sure there are many mothers here in this neighborhood who would seek him out for their daughters."

"I am sure that that has been done through the years, Miss Morys, but I cannot answer your question. I do not know why he never wed. I think I did hear once that there had been a woman who captured his heart. The banns might have even been read, but obviously something must have gone wrong, for there is no Mistress of Cynghanedd. I do believe that the gossips intimated that the woman had broken off the engagement."

I could not believe the suggestion and I shook my head. "I find that difficult to comprehend, sir. Mr. Price-Jones is quite a catch, and I cannot fathom why any woman would fail to reel in her line. Come, come, Mr.

Price-Jones," I chided, "do you not know more? There seems to be a story here, sir. A love story, Mr. Price-Jones." I began to laugh but then I bent my head, distressed that I had made light of the subject. "I do beg your pardon, sir. I did not mean to trivialize your uncle's past, I do beg you to believe me. I only meant that, given his attractiveness, his inheritance, and his estate, it seems quite remarkable that his betrothed should have failed him."

Mr. Price-Jones waved aside my apology. "I did not take it wrongly, Miss Morys. I wish I knew the answers to your questions."

We walked once more along the edge of the cliff. "Do you truly not know why the marriage did not take place? I am fascinated that a gentleman such as Mr. Price-Jones could have had trouble persuading woman to walk to the altar with him."

Mr. Price-Jones kicked at a pebble and watched while it rolled dangerously close to the bluff's edge.

"I cannot enlighten you, Miss Morys. I only know that in my home we never questioned my uncle's unmarried state, never even spoke of his bachelorhood."

"Do you wonder at it?"

Mr. Price-Jones kicked at another pebble, which also stopped short of the brink. "Well, yes, I remember that as a young boy my curiosity was aroused by it, and even now when we are at a dance or fair and a young woman is introduced to him, I find myself questioning whether my Uncle Charles will fancy her. But at such times he always manages to turn the conversation away from his private affairs and then includes me in the discussion. Especially if the lady in question is young and nearer to my age." He looked at me and smiled again and I could see his eyes brighten with self-mockery. "I suppose he thinks that I should be the one to entertain the notion of marrying. In fact, I have heard him joke—in gentlemen's company only, of course—that his fate is to live in the single state and that he believes marital bliss should be accorded, instead, to me."

"I see. And," I asked teasingly, "is there a special girl who has taken your heart or your fancy?"

Mr. Price-Jones looked sidewise at the ocean. "None yet, I fear, Miss Morys. And of course, no matter what my uncle encourages, I am in no position to even think such thoughts, for I have no inheritance and no real means of support for whomever I take to wife. Were it not for the goodness and the kindness of Uncle Charles, my place would not be in such magnificent surroundings."

He paused and turned and looked out at Winter's Light in the distance. "If it were not for my uncle's generosity and the fact that he and his solicitor have drawn up a will that passes Cynghanedd to me on his death — pray that it not be for many, many years — I would have only modest prospects."

I, too, looked at Winter's Light as it glimmered in the afternoon sun. "In my village, sir, we only concern ourselves with whether a man is kind and generous and whether he has sense enough to earn a living for his family. We only ask that a husband provide for his wife and family in a suitable way."

Mr. Price-Jones bowed to me. "I understand that, ma'am, but that is in your homeland. Here — and please understand me, ma'am, for I cast no aspersions on your country or its ways — here we are a bit more proud." I turned and looked straight at him, for I was rather insulted. He bowed again very slightly. "We simply do not choose a wife until we are in a position to support her in a — if you will excuse my words, Miss Morys, support her in a grand manner." He held up his hands to me. "It is what we have been taught, ma'am."

"So be it, Mr. Price-Jones. We all have our differences in style."

"Exactly, ma'am." He pulled at a blade of grass and

159

dropped it over the edge of the cliff and we both watched as it fluttered downwards and into the waters until finally it was pulled under by the current. Somehow this reminded me of my nightmare and of the young Anne as she fell from the chapel balcony. I clasped my hands together, shuddering, and Mr. Price-Jones misinterpreted my gesture.

"You are chilly, ma'am? It must be the spray of the sea."

"No. It was only that I recollected something that has been disturbing me these past nights, but I am all right now." I watched as the waters gathered force and I knew that as the day wore on, the waves on the rocks would become more powerful and demanding.

And then I heard the sound of a woman's laugh come from the sea—a powerful, deep-throated laugh that seemed to mock both the heavens and the waters. The laugh continued for a few more seconds and I turned, half-expecting to see someone standing next to us on the cliffs. But there was no one there except Mr. Price-Jones and he saw me stiffen.

"What is it, Miss Morys? You seem to have—"

"To have heard a ghost, Mr. Price-Jones?" I said the words before I had had time to think, and now I shuddered again.

"Had I been allowed to complete my words, yes, 'ghost' might have been one of them." He peered at me and I did not avert my eyes.

"And if I were to tell you that I had heard a ghost, Mr. Price-Jones, how would you take it?"

Mr. Price-Jones put his hands behind his back and looked down at the rocks and the slowly assembling waves.

"I do not know, Miss Morys." He waited while a small crest gathered energy and then feebly spilled over the rocks, a mere portent of the force that was to come within a few hours. "Have you heard a ghost, Miss

Morys?" he asked. I could not determine whether he expected an affirmative or negative answer. I did not want to tell him the complete truth, for I still could not trust him, or anyone, with my secrets. "You have spoken of hearing things before, Miss Morys," he continued, I thought, censoriously. "In the bog, ma'am. Do you remember?"

"Yes. You told me then that there was nothing alive and hidden within them."

Mr. Price-Jones nodded his head. "Exactly, ma'am. And there is no ghost here." He spread his arms out to the sea. "There is only the ocean, Miss Morys, and surely there is no one who speaks to you from it." I could not tell if the gentleman was truly angry with me, or simply annoyed by my fright. He motioned toward the horses. "And now I think it time we returned to the house."

As I picked up Empress's reins I again heard the laughter, as though it sought to lure me back. I turned to look at the edge of the cliffs. I saw nothing else. And yet that enticing, tempting laughter remained in the air, though impalpable, real as the seacoast.

That evening it was a balmy night—the kind best for remembrances—and as Nanny and I sat together, I could not help but think about Lady Anne. I did not reveal to Nanny that I had heard laughter on the cliffs this afternoon. I did not know whose it had been. Indeed, the sound might have been, as Mr. Price-Jones insisted, a figment of my imagination. Or perhaps my hearing it had been a manifestation of what Nanny called "the gift." I did not know and I could not decide just yet.

The sultry air wafted in through the open window and both the nurse and I were complacent, she with her ball of yarn that had not dwindled this past month and I with my velvet cloth and embroidery needle.

I was growing more and more at ease with Nanny, although I still did not want to answer her questions about my life. The nurse had respected my feelings since our last conversation, and as we sat, each with her own thoughts, she did not turn the conversation to further probings. Instead it was I who asked questions, for since she had begun to tell me something of Lady Anne's life, I had come to want more.

"Nanny, you have never told me what happened to Lady Anne."

Nanny kept rocking in her chair and I wondered if she had heard my question.

"About Lady Anne," I repeated, and, putting her feet firmly on the floor in front of her, the old woman stopped her rocking for a moment.

"Aye, I heard ye. I was just collecting my mind to tell you some things about her, for ye should know about her." She resumed rocking and I found the silence before she spoke her next words interminable. "I told ye, didn't I, Gwynneth, that no one suspected Lady Anne had fallen in love with Mr. Donne?"

"Yes."

"Aye, well it progressed to the point where it was difficult for the lovers to keep their secret, although they still did or said nothing to betray their private thoughts." She licked her lips. "No, they did not betray each other. Nor did they do anything that could have brought reproach to the Glendower name." She paused and then said ominously. "At least not at that time." She shook her head. "One time the young mistress came to me and I thought she was about to tell me of her love, but then we were interrupted and she never again approached me. I was a favorite of hers, you see, and she used to tell me little secrets. Just little things about what she thought about people, and I would listen and let her talk. She knew she could trust me, Gwynneth. She knew I would never say anything against her. But," she smacked her lips together, "she never spoke to me of Mr. Donne. Never told me a thing.

162

"I was worried about them, for I knew that what they were doing was dangerous. That it would all come to nothing and then both would be hurt. But I was powerless to stop them." She looked at me. "How can ye stop someone from falling in love, Gwynneth? Even though all the forces are against it and ye know that it isn't to be, how can you stop it?" Mrs. Hoskins stared off through the window. "I prayed and I prayed that it would all end, but it did not. And each day I could see her now falling more and more in love with the young man. And he the same. Just to look at him when she was in the room—if you had paid attention, you would have guessed.

"And Anne! You should have seen her, Gwynneth. As happy as she ever was. Her eyes sparkling and her step sprightly. You must remember that a lot of us were here when she was born. We were devoted to that small girl, and if any of us had suspected anything, none of us would have spoken about it. None of us would have revealed it.

"And Mr. Donne. He was a fine-looking man, make no mistake about that. Clean-cut he was, sandy hair and medium height. He made a good figure." The nurse looked down at her hands. "And talented. In both music and art, and there were so many evenings when it was just Lord and Lady Glendower and Anne and Mr. Donne in the music room and all through the manor you could hear him playing his songs. And sometimes Lady Anne would join him at the piano and they would play duets that had all of us humming and singing.

"Aye, Gwynneth, they were happy times. No one can ever take them away from us. They were happy times. If only it could have stayed that way." She sighed. "But then everything just seemed to come apart." She looked to her ball of yarn. "Came unravelled as surely as a sweater that a kitten was playing with. It all came undone." She rocked so slowly that the chair barely moved.

"I don't know what it was—maybe a glance or a word—but somehow Lord Glendower sensed something and I heard him and the mistress speaking about it in their private rooms. Lady Glendower could hardly believe it—she was still thinking that her daughter was too young for love-thoughts.

"She asked me the next day what I thought and if I had seen anything pass between the two young people and I was caught, then. Caught right in the middle, for I didn't want to lie to my mistress nor did I want Lady Anne to have troubles. But Lady Glendower noticed my hesitation in answering and then she started to pay close attention to whenever Mr. Donne and her daughter were together. Always insisting that someone be in the same room with them and having Fergus ride with them when the two wanted to take to the horses.

"It was amazing and so innocent that the two lovers never suspected they were being watched and so they weren't as careful as they should have been. And one day when they had returned from riding and were showing their sketches to Anne's mother, Lord Glendower came into the room and asked to see Mr. Donne in private.

"I think Anne and her young man knew then that they had been caught, and I don't think I'll ever forget the look of alarm that came over her face. She turned all pale and shaky and whenever she was frightened, we used to tease, her light eyes seemed to vanish from her face. And that's how it was this evening—her eyes just went blank and seemed to fade into the rest of her coloring.

"Well, after the master and Mr. Donne spoke behind closed doors, the young tutor came out of the room and there was this stern look on his face and he didn't even glance at Lady Anne or her mother. He bowed formally to all of us and then he went straight up to his room. Whatever was said to him by the master were strong words, and when Lord Glendower joined his wife and daughter he just announced that Mr. Donne would be leaving Winter's Light at the end of the month." Nanny put her hand to her heart. "Poor Mistress Anne. She seemed about to faint and shook her head and cried out. 'No, no,' she said, but her father was not the type to be moved by a young woman's tears, and presently she went off to bed still crying. Her father would not relent." She sat still for a moment. "He never did," she said softly, and I detected a note of regret in her voice.

"I went up to her later, with a glass of warm milk, but there was no consoling her. She just sat on the edge of the bed and stared at the picture that she had brought in that afternoon. It was a picture of the chapel. Done beautiful, it was. I hurt for her, Gwynneth. I hurt so much for her because I could see she was in pain and I worried that she would not ever get over it.

"As for Mr. Donne. He never said a word about his dismissal and I felt sorry for him, for he had no one to talk to nor turn to and I could see he was hurting, too." Nanny bent her head. "Ah, Gwynneth, they were so young and so in love and if Mr. Donne had only been born into a more secure background, there would never have been any question as to their betrothal. They were that much in love that in that final month we all could see how they were in misery.

"Even when Lady Glendower would try to coax her daughter into a happier state Mistress Anne would have none of it. She spent the last days with her tutor all proper-like, in full view of the staff and her parents, and they kept their respectful distances—with him calling her Lady Anne and she addressing him as Mr. Donne. Not once—not once, Gwynneth, did they give a hint that everything wasn't proper. And Lord Glendower kept saying to his wife that he had put a stop to it and that it was only a puppy-love sort of thing. He wasn't a mean man, Gwynneth, just a man caught up in his family's best interests. Make no mistake about it, he loved his daughter. But not enough to give her what she wanted—Mr. Donne." Nanny put her hand into her pocket and pulled out a tiny gold frame. She gazed into it.

"Ah, Lady Anne, you should have had your wish. You should have had your love."

"And then what happened, Nanny?"

The old woman seemed startled. She stared as though she had forgotten me for a moment.

"What happened, Gwynneth, was that the master gave Mr. Donne a fine letter of recommendation. Even got him another position in another shire." She squinted her eyes.

"And he just left? They never saw each other again?"

Nanny seemed disconcerted. "What?"

I repeated my question and Nanny continued to stare off into space as though she were muddled. "No. No, there was something else," she said very quietly. And then I know I could ask her nothing more. Recounting the story had reopened her pain.

Chapter Fourteen

Mrs. Hoskins did not bring up the story of Anne for the next few days, although I was sure that she had still more to tell. When we were together in Lady Glendower's bedchamber and the woman slept, Nanny would fuss about the room as though she wanted to avoid talking to me, as though she was loath to reveal anything more about Winter's Light.

Often the two older women spoke together in hushed tones, excluding me from their conversations although I was in the room. They did not mean to ignore me, I was sure, nor were they distant. But I did feel sure that they observed me as I went about my duties. I had often caught Lady Glendower staring at me, and yet there was no meanness in her looks. Rather, I sensed expectancy in her, as though she waited for me to say or do something—what, I could not fathom.

There were times when Lady Glendower asked me to sit with her and tell her about my sketches. Then, though embarrassed, I would tell her of how I had etched the face of an estate worker or drawn a particularly odd-shaped tree. Several times I had seen Lady Glendower look at Nanny as I spoke, and I presumed that she feared I would speak of the paintings that had at one time hung at Winter's Light. I once turned to Nanny to find her staring at me, and I took her look as a silent warning for me to mind my words. It was an admonition I did not need, for I was careful not to mention that I knew of the study of the manor that the tutor, Mr. Donne, had completed many years ago. I did not want to speak of anything that would bring unhappiness to the woman.

More and more I saw a change in Lady Glendower's health. She appeared stronger, and I suspected that soon she would be able to leave her rooms. Dr. Lawrence—who weekly attended her—himself held out the promise of her recovery.

"Aye, she'll be better now," Nanny would say after the physician had gone. "Her body and her mind have been mending." She would look at her mistress and then at me. "She'll be better now. You'll see." She would smile at the prospect. "You'll see, Gwynneth. Lady Glendower will be up before the year is out."

The warm summer days had begun to turn cool and brisk, one of many signs that autumn was fast approaching. The last several days the crispness had begun to chill me, and I had taken to wearing a cloak over my dress to help ward off the cold when I left the house. The days were growing shorter and soon, I knew, intemperate weather would deprive me of my time outdoors. Thus I took advantage of the waning summer days to sit outside and draw. My sketchbook rapidly filled with drawings of trees and flowers in deeper hues—scarlets and oranges and browns—and then with studies of bare branches and of leaves which now lay on the ground.

The advent of another season had done nothing to change the atmosphere that I believed penetrated the house; the air of bleakness still loomed over Winter's Light. I had felt this several more times as I passed the darkened ballroom or rode to my secret place in the woods, and now had come to expect it in odd moments. Whatever it was that brought forth this dolor, did not relent, but continued to hover over the estate.

I had not gone back to the cliffs since being there with Mr. Price-Jones. On the contrary, I avoided them as I had continued to avoid the bog. Just as surely as I knew myself to be Gwynneth Morys, I knew I had heard voices and laughter call out to me, and no amount of Mr. Owen's teasing could dissuade me. The unknowns were there at both places and it seemed they waited for me to sort them out. But the task remained a puzzle, for I did not know why I had been chosen for this assignment.

A day came when I could no longer deny my calling, and I rode Empress to the edge of the cliffs. Although I was afraid of what I would discover, it was as if I were compelled to return to the place where Mr. Price-Jones and I had stopped.

The sea was no longer calm, the autumn winds fomenting the waters into dark, angry waves that rushed forcefully toward the rocks and then just as quickly ebbed back into the ocean. Even high above I could feel the cold bite of salt sting at my face so that it seemed there were hundreds of tiny, sharp particles that pricked at my skin.

I went close to the edge of the cliff hoping that I would hear the laughing voice call once again, but the only sound was the steady crash of the surf as it fell upon the huge slabs of rock that protruded from the waters. I remained on the bluff several minutes, the strong wind lifting my cape and rippling the dress underneath it, but no voice spoke, no name was called, and there was no laughter. Finally, disappointed, I returned to the house. Perhaps some other day I would investigate again.

Later, when the two of us sat at the tea table, Nanny clucked her tongue at me. "Ye seem to be distant, Gwynneth. Is something more troubling you?" She took a piece of the apple cake Mrs. Padley had sent up to us.

I debated whether now was the time to tell her about the strange voices and sounds I had heard on the moors and by the sea, for still I wondered if I could trust her with my secrets. Would she, I wondered, attribute all that I revealed to what she had called *"the gift,"* or would she think me deluded? Despite my fears, I decided to test her reaction.

"I will tell you something, Nanny, and I hope that you

will keep my secret." The woman put down her fork, folded her hands in front of her, and gave me her full attention.

"Aye. That I will, if such is what you want." She stared hard into my eyes and her gaze made me think that she could see into my thoughts. "If ye want me to hold my tongue, I shall." She picked up her cup of tea and took a few sips from it, all the time watching me as though she expected some enormous revelation. "There are many secrets that I know that have never been repeated to anyone. Not to anyone, God help me!" she said emphatically. Again I wondered at Nanny's words, but I thought it best not to comment on them for the moment. Indeed, I already had enough on my mind.

I looked out the window and saw a leaf spin past it, twirling as it moved from branch to ground, and I reflected that sometimes I felt much like that leaf as it spun round and round. Too many strange things had happened to me here at Winter's Light. It was dizzying. Why did I hear things? Why did I know of places I should not know? Why was I so curious about young Anne?

Perhaps Nanny had some answers for me. Perhaps my "gift" was the source of my confusion. I would tell her only some of the simpler things lest she think I was lying, or worse, unsound in mind.

"What would you say, Nanny, if I told you that there are times when I believe I see things or hear sounds that seem not to exist?" I asked. I watched the old nurse as she put aside her cup and stared down at her napkin. The woman's face remained unconcerned and she did not seem excited or disturbed at my question.

"What things do you see, Gwynneth?"

"Scenes. Scenes of people I do not know, like the death watch I dreamt about a few weeks ago."

Nanny nodded her head. "Aye. And the sounds? What are they?"

"Strange things that have no meaning for me. Voices that I cannot place. Laughter when there is no source. And a tune that has been with me since I was a child. It comes into my mind when I need comfort or help."

"A tune?"

I nodded my head. "The melody came to me on the moors when I was lost, for example. I hear it only at times of significance. Even now as I try to tell you of it, I cannot recall it — it is that elusive." I told the nurse about the times I had hummed the strange notes when young, and that, since my parents had no recollection of it, they had credited it to the shepherds on the hills.

"Can you hum it, lass?" She poured herself another cup of tea yet did not stir it. When I did not answer, she asked the question more loudly. "Can you hum it for me, lass?" I wondered what she thought of my revelations, and if they fit her own description of "the gift."

"Do you believe me, Nanny?"

She looked up to the ceiling. "Aye, I do, for sometimes there are things that take no explaining." She poured milk into her cup. "This tune, Gwynneth. Can you sing it to me?"

I thought for a moment and even formed my lips so that I could hum it, but no sound came from my throat. I tried again to remember it for her, and could only shake my head.

"I'm sorry, but I cannot, for it only comes to me at odd moments and never on command. But I would swear on the Holy Book I have never heard it played at village fairs or in chapel." I became quiet, hoping the song would echo through my mind once more; again I could not conjure it. "No. I am sorry, but I cannot remember it just now."

Nanny Hoskins nodded her head and seemed not at all excited or disquieted by my disclosures. She only smiled, and soon she seemed lost in thought. I got up from the table and fastened the windows tight, as the cool, autumn breezes had begun to invade the room.

I wondered if Nanny truly believed me, for I saw her turn and look at me several times and then shake her head. But

171

still I did not interrupt her meditation. Whatever her verdict, there was nothing I could do now to take back my words.

She sat for a few moments longer, looking down at her hands in her lap. "Ah, well, girl," she said quietly, "when you hear the tune again, do try to remember it and sing it to me. I have always had a good ear for music and could perhaps identify it for you," she said calmly. Then she resumed drinking her tea, and changed the subject to matters of the house. The two of us talked for a few more minutes before she excused herself.

"I must be checking on my lady now, Gwynneth. See to the curtains and draperies so that the room remains warm." I did not know whether Nanny had believed me, but I was grateful that at least she had not dismissed my words out of hand.

That evening the Price-Joneses came to dinner, and as we sat at the table Nanny seemed almost merry. One of Mrs. Hoskins's great delights was to hear the senior Mr. Price-Jones reminisce of the bygone days of Winter's Light, and Mr. Charles, ever mindful of Nanny's wishes, continually told us about the grand dinners and the music recitals that had once taken place here on a regular basis. I did not respond to Mr. Price-Jones's stories except to comment that music seemed to have played a great part in the lives of the personages who had lived at the estate.

"Always, Miss Morys, always there was music, for we Welsh have a fondness for songs, as you well know. Every Welshman can hum or sing or whistle a tune from almost the time that he is born." I glanced quickly at Nanny, fearing that she had betrayed my secret, but the woman returned my look quite innocently, and then I knew she had not given away our private conversation.

Mr. Price-Jones continued to tell of parties that had been held at Winter's Light, and I wondered if he had known about the love between Lady Anne and Mr. Donne, if perhaps he had been one of those who suspected the

172

attachment.

"Many an evening the music room was filled to overflowing, Miss Morys, and the candles would burn out before all of us had left." He raised his wineglass to Mrs. Hoskins. "And, Nanny, you will bear me out, ma'am, there was not a month that a visiting artist, be it a musician or a poet or a painter, did not entertain the guests." He sipped from his glass of wine. "Is that not so, Nanny?"

"Aye, Mr. Charles. You tell the story correctly. There were many celebrations here."

"The holidays, Nanny. Do you remember? I do believe I even danced a turn with you on Christmas Day."

Nanny laughed and I could see the sparkle in her eyes. "Yes, ye did, Mr. Charles. You came up to me in the hall and you made a fine, gentlemanly bow and you said 'your servant, ma'am,' and you asked me to dance. I remember it well." The elderly woman began to laugh. "Aye, you said, 'your servant, ma'am,' just as if I were a grand lady."

"Your servant, ma'am." The words seemed to come not from Nanny's mouth but from another's — a gentleman's — and I moved my eyes around the table, then beyond it, searching for the source. But neither of the men had said it, and no one else seemed to have heard it. *"Your servant, ma'am."* Again the polite phrase sounded, and I tightened my hand about my water goblet for I knew that the voice was only speaking in my mind.

Mr. Price-Jones continued to tell of the galas that had taken place at Winter's Light, unaware that I had been stunned.

"Many a young man and woman met here and owe their marriages to these gatherings. Lord and Lady Glendower were always asking the young people to attend, always wanting them to show in their finery." He fell silent while he poured his nephew and himself another finger of port. "If we were to count, Nanny, how many marriages would you believe to have been first thought about here at Winter's Light?"

"There would not be enough fingers and toes, Mr. Price-Jones," Nanny said, laughing and I could tell that this was the merriest of times for her.

"But *you* were never caught, Mr. Price-Jones," I interjected without thinking. "How come that is so?" I smiled at him and Mr. Price-Jones looked at me as I continued. "You never married. Did no one ever catch your fancy?" I inquired, and then when I realized that everyone had become quiet, I lowered my head, mortified at the impertinence of my question. I saw Owen Price-Jones frown at me and Nanny seemed startled at my tactlessness. I was humiliated, and immediately began to apologize profusely.

"I am truly sorry, sir, for asking such a personal question. I do beg your pardon. I had not meant to be rude." I wished I could run away from the table, but to have done so would only have added insult to injury.

Mr. Price-Jones waved aside my apology. "Do not trouble yourself with embarrassment, Miss Morys. Every mother in this shire has at one time or another asked me those same questions." He smiled at me graciously, but at the same time I saw a slight grimace on his face, as though I had wounded him. The latter expression jolted me, for it seemed that I had seen that look upon his face before. And yet I could not recall another occasion upon which it had appeared.

Mr. Price-Jones continued to speak, assuring me that I had not offended him. "It seems, Miss Morys, that I have been consigned to a single life," he said, then indicated his nephew, "As for wedded bliss, I will leave that to the younger generation."

I vowed not to say any more, for I was still truly distressed that I had been so foolish and so rude as to ask my silly questions. Again my own mouth had betrayed me before I had had a chance to think.

Mr. Charles noticed my silence and attempted to cajole me. "Come, come, Miss Morys. It was not an unreasonable question, and indeed I have heard it many, many times in my life. I assure you, I am not insulted." Again he smiled at me, though there remained a rueful expression around his dark eyes. He appeared somehow defeated, and I was angry at myself for causing him pain.

He twisted a heavy, gold signet ring on his finger as though he gained strength from it, and again I seemed to recall this gesture of his from before, and yet it could not be possible. I half closed my eyes, willing the recollection to appear to me, to tell me where and when I had beheld the gentleman's expression, but it was for naught. The fleeting picture had vanished.

"Please, Miss Morys, do not disturb yourself. No damage has been done," Mr. Price-Jones said. "I assure you, you have not offended me." He stretched his hand toward me in reconciliation and I blushed at his kindness.

"I thank you for your pardon."

His brow wrinkled only slightly. "I tell you, Miss Morys, you have not affronted me, and to prove it I ask you—with Nanny's permission, of course," he said bowing to the woman, "I ask that you allow me to show you the gardens on my estate. I am sure you will enjoy them, for the fall flowers have already blossomed and are spectacular this year."

Nanny beamed at me. "Ah, Gwynneth, go and enjoy the gardens. The days are beginning to turn rapidly and there won't be many more days to enjoy them."

I accepted Mr. Price-Jones's kind offer.

"Tomorrow afternoon then. I will have Owen call for you, if you please."

"Yes, thank you." Mr. Price-Jones was being exceedingly gracious, but there were still vestiges of that strangely familiar expression on his face, and I kept trying to place it. Even the way he spoke seemed suggestive of another time and another place. I wondered that I had not noticed it before.

"You seem to be thinking of many other things," Mr. Price-Jones teased and then laughed. "Is it something that

I said?"

I shook my head, not wanting to compound my stupidity in front of the uncle and nephew. "No, it was only that I thought I remembered something for just a moment."

"And what was that, ma'am?" Mr. Charles had been given Nanny's silent permission to move away from the table, and now he came and stood by my chair. "What is it that you remembered that would cause you to be, shall I say, many miles away?"

I shook my head. "It was just something foolish — just something foolhardy, sir."

Mr. Price-Jones bowed and turned to his nephew. "She is as you have told me, Owen. Charming and fresh and straightforward in her ways. Miss Morys, your candor is a virtue in these days of guarded talk. We shall make sure that you enjoy the gardens tomorrow." He walked to Nanny's chair and extended his arm to her. "And now, Mrs. Hoskins, shall we go up to Lady Glendower? I understand her health is improving so rapidly that it seems we may have the pleasure of her company at this dinner table soon." He turned to me and bent low over my hand. "Your servant, ma'am. Until tomorrow afternoon. Until we meet again."

There . . . there they were again . . . the same words as before. Why should they disturb me? *"Your servant, ma'am . . . until we meet again."*

Later, after I had seen to Lady Glendower's toilette and Nanny and I had gone into our separate apartments, I sat by the small fire that had been set in my room to ward off the chill. I listened to the logs pop and as I felt their heat upon my face I heard Mr. Price-Jones's voice once more. *"Your servant, ma'am . . . until we meet again."* It was as though I knew the words from before, as though I had to remember, had to keep alive the memory of the times past.

When would I know why I had these glimpses of the past? When would I know why Winter's Light haunted me so?

"Your servant, ma'am . . . until we meet again." The sentence played over and over again in my mind until finally I fell asleep.

Chapter Fifteen

"You will see why the gardens are well known in this area, Miss Morys." Mr. Owen Price-Jones and I had set off on this cool autumn afternoon for the promised tour of Cynghanedd. "You will understand why they are spoken of in exclamatory terms and why my uncle takes great pride in them. When he first became its owner Cynghanedd had lovely gardens, but nothing to match what they have become these past seasons. Uncle has spent several years laying out the plans for all of the bushes and plants, and you will see, ma'am, that it was time well spent. Many of our neighbors have brought their visitors here, for I believe Uncle Charles has planted varieties and species that are not known in this part of the country. Even Lady Glendower has come and admired the blossoms, though Winter's Light, as you well know, is certainly famed for its own."

We directed our horses toward the path connecting the two estates. "I am truly glad you have come to Cynghanedd, Miss Morys, for I have wanted to show you our home and grounds since the summer." Mr. Price-Jones looked at me. "I think you should see them, ma'am, for . . ." Mr. Price-Jones did not finish his sentence and looked away for a brief second before continuing. "I am glad you will see the gardens in their full autumnal splendor. The plants still retain many of their finest qualities. In fact, Miss Morys, the fall flowers are just reaching their peak, I am truly pleased that you will do us the honor of enjoying them."

As Mr. Price-Jones and I rode across the fields to Cynghanedd I could not help but be puzzled by my great good fortune. I was but an assistant to Nanny in her domestic chores to Lady Glendower, and by all accounts I should be confined to the house and treated the same as the other staff members. And yet here I was, astride a beautiful animal that had once belonged to the young mistress of the estate, and visiting with a gentleman at his uncle's palatial home. I did not know why I should be allowed to carry on this way. It was as if this were all a dream from which I would awaken to find myself still at Daear and still in meagre circumstances, with no one to help me.

"You seem preoccupied, Miss Morys. I assure you that whatever is troubling you will disappear once you view the estate." Mr. Price-Jones guided our horses through one of the wrought-iron gates that opened to his uncle's property.

"No, you misread my countenance, sir. I was just thinking that it is a beautiful day and that there is nothing I would hope to do more than to be here with you and your uncle."

Mr. Price-Jones laughed. "Well done, Miss Morys. I think that you must have practiced that speech, for it seems too perfect."

"It is better, is it not, Mr. Price-Jones, than my asking foolish questions of your relation as I did yesterday?"

Mr. Price-Jones pulled up his horse next to mine. "Miss Morys, Gwynneth, we will have no more apologies. My uncle made no mention of your remarks on the ride home last night, and I think you, too, should forget them." He pointed to a group of oak trees. "They are Uncle Charles's pride, Miss Morys, although I grant you

179

they are not exactly stately. They are very old, and their twisted forms might even be called grotesque, but my uncle has resisted all suggestions from the gardeners that he cut them down, for he says their shapes remind him of the moors and the mysteries of the land. They have been on this estate for one hundred and fifty years or more, and I suspect that once upon a time they were part of a much bigger stand than they are now."

We rode near the stunted trees and I remarked that their contorted shapes were still beautiful in their imperfectness.

"They are much like us, Mr. Price-Jones, in that our bodies too become misshapen when we grow old." I touched one of the overhanging wind-smoothed branches as we passed under them. "And hidden within our deformed bodies is our past, no matter what it may be. Viewing something like this allows us a sobering glimpse into the dark side of life."

"And death." He glanced back at the oaks. "You speak as a philosopher, Miss Morys. I am afraid that all I see is a group of decaying trees that do nothing to cheer the estate. But my uncle will be glad to hear that you also appreciate the woods." He patted his horse's head. "However I will agree with you that the oaks may indeed hold the secrets of yesteryears. When I was younger and just a visitor here, there was many a day when, restless and in search of adventure, I would ride out to the oaks only to hurry back to the house as quickly as possible. I always seemed to fear that patch of the estate. I think the bent trunks were menacing—especially to a young boy—and perhaps they reminded me of irrational things, like ghosts and spirits, that existed in stories told to me by my parents. And yet I was always compelled to return to those trees again and again. Possibly I wanted to conquer my dread, Miss Morys."

"Perhaps that is so, sir." I did not want to make a

comment that Mr. Price-Jones would think silly, and thus I made no mention of apparitions or things unseen and unexplainable. It was enough that I had trusted Nanny with my secret.

"Did you never fear anything, ma'am?"

"Yes. The moors at Winter's Light have that same fatal attraction for me, sir."

"You have reason to be alarmed by the bog, ma'am. You have been caught there. But those," he said, casting a backward glance at the oaks, "those hold another form of terror. One that is not so real." He laughed. "No, theirs is only a childish horror, ma'am, one certainly of no issue to me now." He eased his horse into a gentle run. "I think my uncle will be waiting for us."

Mr. Charles Price-Jones greeted us at the steps of his home and I could see that he was eager to be an attentive host.

"Welcome. Welcome to Cynghanedd, Miss Morys. May I offer you some refreshment before we start?" I declined the suggestion, for I was anxious to view all the flora, and Mr. Price-Jones saw my impatience. "Then, ma'am, will you not take a turn with me around the gardens? I promise you a treat." He turned to his nephew. "Owen, there is some small matter that needs your attention. A dispatch from your mother that needs immediate answering. It should only take a few moments and then you can join us. If it suits you, ma'am, the two of us will walk together until my nephew returns." Mr. Price-Jones extended his arm to me and his nephew laughed.

"Best you watch out for my uncle, Miss Morys. I have heard that his commentary on the gardens is considered poetic and romantic, and that many a female companion has lingered too long in the mazes in order to hear him speak. I do not vouch for that, ma'am, but I will be interested in how you rate him. You must tell me if

181

you think his recitation is worthy of Lord Byron or Mr. Shelley."

"Come, come, Miss Morys," the elder Mr. Price-Jones said to me. "Pay no attention to my nephew. He believes that I should be married. He is on the same side as you," he said and I felt my face warming as I was reminded of last night's *faux pas*. The reference was made in jest and Mr. Price-Jones, unaware of my embarrassment, continued in a light vein. "Owen thinks that every pretty young girl in the shire has set her cap for me. As usual, he has judged incorrectly." Mr. Price-Jones smiled graciously at me and I bent my head slightly. It was all too easy to fall into their gay, teasing mood, and I was grateful that Mr. Charles had not taken offense at my outlandish speech of yesterday.

"I do see, sir, what your nephew means, though. For just yesterday I saw the younger female servants at Winter's Light smile at you in a way I had not seen previously. I fully believe your nephew, sir, and I will watch my manners and my step so as not to succumb to your discourse. Flowers and trees and bushes have always proved my weakness."

Mr. Price-Jones laughed and then nodded his head at me. "Now it is my turn to be impressed, Miss Morys, for I did not expect your humor. Your intelligence and beauty, ma'am, are obvious. But your wit is subtle." He led me toward the trellised gardens where climbing bushes were secured to lattice-work of different sizes and shapes. Much pruning was evident in this part of the garden, as sculpted topiaries were placed at various points along the alley so that different patterns, both familiar and unfamiliar, emerged in shadow along the paths. Already some of the shoots had turned deep bronze, and the dark-colored evergreens seemed ready and waiting for the advent of the colder times. Hundreds of red holly berries glowed brightly amongst their sharp, pointed leaves, and here and there, strategically placed, were ruby and gold and purple chrysanthemums.

"I am sorry that you did not visit us in the summer," Mr. Price-Jones apologized. "The flowers and shrubs were quite significant and did the estate justice."

I assured the gentleman that even now, in this season, the gardens were spectacular.

Mr. Price-Jones nodded in agreement. "Come this way, Miss Morys, for there are truly lovely Michaelmas daisies in bud and blossom, and I do want you to see the last of the roses. There are only a few remaining, and again I regret that you did not have the opportunity to view them when they were in full bloom. Perhaps you will honor us next year." We stopped at several bushes and I admired the colors of the last of the climbers. We lingered only a few minutes in this section, for most of the roses were spent and without the blossoms, the trellises and stakes seemed wanting. I could, however, see that fat, golden-orange rosehips had begun to form and mature on the stalks, assuring the next year's supply of tea for the household.

We proceeded at a leisurely pace, Mr. Price-Jones continuing to provide commentary about the origins of the plantings, and I could discern that much care and consideration had been taken in planning this particular plot of ground. Everywhere, as at Winter's Light, there was order and strict arrangement; indeed, the layout's precision spoke more of geometric design than of ease of form and grace. Although there was method to the plan, it was a bit too orderly for my taste, and yet I had to appreciate what Mr. Price-Jones had achieved in these parcels of earth.

We walked further into the gardens and my host continued speaking of the way certain plantings had been arranged in order to take full advantage of the winds and the sun.

"Naturally, ma'am, like all things that are alive, they must be given the ideal growing conditions or they do not flourish." He touched a bright red leaf that had the full sun on it so that it seemed to flame. "Without the light you and I well know that this particular flower would never have bloomed. And without order . . ." he began, and I feared that he was able to read my mind and would censure my thoughts on artificial arrangement, but instead he stopped speaking for several seconds. His face became pained and I wondered what could have caused him to lose his train of thought and forget his guest. I did not intrude upon his meditation, and finally I saw the gentleman's countenance clear. He bowed to me and offered me a flower he had picked, saying, "Civilization itself is order, Miss Morys."

I thought it best not to speak of his momentary lapse and instead commented on his pronouncement. "Of course. It is as I have been taught by Reverend Jenkins. I am as impressed with your argument, sir, as I am with the order of your gardens. Is that why this estate is named Cynghanedd—'harmony'?"

Mr. Price-Jones took my arm and continued to guide me toward other shrubs. "I am glad you appreciate the work that has gone into the exterior of the estate, ma'am. You understand the precision with which we have arranged things." He smiled at me and I could tell that he took genuine delight in showing his work. "Now about the name," he bent his mouth close to my ear. "I will tell you a family secret about why it is called so. One that very few people know."

"Is it such a secret that I should know, sir? Should you be revealing it to me?"

"I have never been challenged as to my discretion before, ma'am," he said, and I put my head down, chagrined. It seemed I was always saying inconsiderate things to the gentleman.

"I am sorry, sir."

"No, no, please do not be embarrassed again, Miss Morys. I truly find your questioning delightful. I admire your guilelessness, your innocence." He looked away. "Sometimes you remind me of . . . of someone I knew long ago." He shook his head and sighed. "But we shall have no more apologies. And about the secret—it is not really a secret, but just part of the folklore of the house. It adds to the charm of the estate and in truth should not be hidden." He laughed and then proceeded with the tale.

"I understand that there once were writings that attested to this story, but these were lost many years ago, so that there is no guarantee of its veracity. However true or false, it is an amusing tale about the naming of this house, and I think you will enjoy it." He smiled at me and I could see the teasing look in his eye. "I have grown up with the knowledge, Miss Morys, that the first Price-Jones, who came here nearly three hundred years ago, gave the estate its name. This gentleman was the eldest of many siblings, and rumor had it that, having had enough of his constantly quarrelling sisters and brothers-in-law, he set out to build his own estate so that he could become the master of a serene manor. He travelled all over the country looking for a suitable site, and when he saw this land he decided to stay and build his residence here, far from his carping relatives. It was in this part of Wales that he found his wife—the first mistress of the mansion—and she was supposed to have been of a quiet and reticent nature. She was also very amenable to her husband's wishes, and so when the manor house was finished, the gentleman named it *Cynghanedd—harmony.*" Mr. Price-Jones looked around at the shadows that showed on the walk. "I think he was a person of much insight, don't you, ma'am?"

I laughed at the audacity of the story. "It is a delightful tale, Mr. Price-Jones, and one can only hope that your noble ancestor obtained his wish."

"I think it so, Miss Morys, for I never heard otherwise. And now come, ma'am, for there is still very much to see here." He touched my arm and again I wondered why the gentleman had never married. His strong good looks and his wit most certainly would be the envy of many men in the area, be they young or old.

We walked along the side of the gardens until we came to an area enclosed by a low, ivy-covered, stone wall. Mr. Price-Jones pushed at a small wooden door and led the way onto a paved path that wound through dwarf fruit trees and ornamental bushes and finally opened up to a sun-exposed fish pond filled with silver and gold minnows that darted around the large rocks that were placed in the water.

Carpets of deep green moss grew on the shady flat stones that formed the pathway through this section, which was, I saw, the loveliest of the gardens. The vines and the dark green plants here were allowed to grow unrestrained and unfettered, and somehow this seemed in keeping with the harmony and the peace in the area.

"I knew you would bring me here," I said as we walked past a showy scarlet bush. "It has always been your favorite spot in the gardens, hasn't it?" I bent down to touch a large fern and let my hand drift lazily over the delicate feathery fronds.

Mr. Price-Jones stopped and stared at me and I could see puzzlement in his eyes.

"My dear Miss Morys, however did you know? I have not told many people of that." He seemed perplexed as he watched me and I tensed, trying to remember the occasion when he had revealed it to me. Had I spoken too quickly? Had I unwittingly betrayed myself?

"I beg your pardon, sir, but I had thought you had spoken of it before we started out," I lied, hoping that

186

the good Lord would forgive me.

Mr. Charles shook his head in denial and I saw his eyes cloud, but then, in deference to my visitor status, he relented. "Perhaps," he said, as though to placate me, although he still seemed bewildered. He peered at me so that I was disconcerted and I wanted to turn away in shame at my untruthful reply. "Perhaps I spoke without my remembering," he said, but I knew that he was not convinced though he did not speak of it anymore. He took my hand again and guided me toward the inner rings of the gardens, close to the other side of the water, and he tried to make light of the moment. "Perhaps you will allow me to show you some other favorites of mine," he said. I nodded and stepped gently onto the brick footpath.

But I was unsettled, for Mr. Price-Jones was correct. He had never spoken to me of this part of the garden, and yet I had known it to be his favorite. But how? I took a deep breath. Did that strange knowledge, that uncanny insight of mine haunt me even here?

I tried not to let the thought upset me for too long. It would do no good to try to explain it to Mr. Jones. If he were of the same belief and temperament of his nephew the admission of my "gift," as Nanny had called it, would fall upon deaf ears. Better that I should just allow Mr. Price-Jones to think that he told me of the pool or that I had made a fortunate guess.

We walked slowly on through the miniature mazes and lanes, and as the mingled scents of spices lingered in the air, I knew we were approaching the herb garden. We came upon a white marble bench situated so that the viewer, while resting among shade trees, could smell the pleasant tang of the plants, and Mr. Price-Jones proposed that we sit and rest. I took a deep breath and inhaled the fragrance of the autumn flowers and the herbs in the vicinity, letting the various scents wash over me.

"I smell roses and asters and heather and . . . and lemon leaves and mint," I said and Mr. Jones smiled.

"They are all of the late blooming varieties."

"I especially prefer the lemon and mint. At home, in Daear, we always crushed the leaves and used them in large bowls to scent the rooms of the house." I closed my eyes in remembrance of the fragrances of my home and became silent with the memory.

"You miss your home . . . your family? I am sorry."

"It is not a rebuke of Winter's Light, sir," I said lest he think me ungrateful for my lodgings and position. "It is only that my home is no longer mine. It has been abandoned. And as for family, I have none. We were only three, and two of us have passed on this year."

Mr. Price-Jones gently pressed my hand in an un-spoken message of sympathy that went straight to my heart. It seemed an indication of the man's true strength and charity. "I am once more truly sorry for your pain," he said, and I understood then that once upon a time this gentleman must have experienced much anguish. He looked at me and momentarily I could see a bleakness in his eyes. I wished I could say some words of comfort to him, although I knew not why he was distressed, but then he stood up, seemingly recovered. He walked to-ward a small, rectangular, reflecting pool which lay off to the side. I could see the stagnant, yet not unlovely, water in the enclosure and the fading, cream-colored lil-ies that floated upon it.

"It is so cool here. So refreshing." I watched as a last lazy summer bee alighted close to a rock, disturbing the water before it landed on a lily pad so that slight ripples radiated through the moss-covered pool. "It is . . . it is so prayerful," I said, then looked away, for it seemed that the sun and shadows and vines were playing a trick on my vision. For one short instance I had thought that I saw another young woman standing near the pool, looking into it at her own reflection.

I inclined my head in the direction of the illusion but it had disappeared. Had it been another vision, or just my imagination? I hesitated only a second before answering my own question, for I realized that the cloak the woman had worn was of a green material. *It had been Anne. The Lady Anne.* I put my hand to my eyes and brushed at them, but it was as before—the figure had vanished and I was left to wonder once more why she should appear to me.

Fortunately Mr. Price-Jones did not see my expression but seemed still to be reflecting on my words. "Prayerful?" he asked me, and then he looked around and I wondered if he would have been able to see the ephemeral figure had it lingered. He gently blew on a leaf floating toward the ground so that it swirled upward before landing in the pool. "Someone other than you once said the same thing, Miss Morys. It is curious. This is the second time I have been reminded of her this afternoon after so many years."

Mr. Price-Jones offered no more and even I marvelled at my choice of words. "Prayerful" was not an epithet I would normally use to describe the scene. I smiled slightly. "It indeed is a strange description, is it not?" I tossed my head slightly trying to dispel the memory of Lady Anne. "I suppose it is because all is so serene here—all is in harmony as you call your estate—that I was caught up with the moment."

Mr. Price-Jones continued to stare past me and it seemed that a chill suddenly swept through the area. It touched my shoulders and I hunched them as though to fend it off. I then quickly moved toward the herb gardens, for it was as though the breeze had brought an unwelcome and unfriendly current to this section of the gardens. It overcame me, making me feel as though I had long ago visited in this place and now had no rea-

189

son to be here. I wanted to leave as quickly as possible, but I tempered my words so as not to arouse suspicion in my host's mind.

"Even though this part of the garden is lovely, Mr. Jones, on a bright day like today I think I prefer the full sun. It is not so hot that we must continue to seek the shade, is it?"

Mr. Price-Jones's eyes seem to cloud over as though he, too, felt the sudden turn of cold and was perplexed by it. "You are right. Indeed it has suddenly become brisk. Come, let me show you the lemon sage so that you can smell the leaves once again." He took hold of my elbow to lead me away and I could not help but notice that the gentleman's countenance had gone pale. I wondered if he had taken a chill.

We had already spent the better part of two hours in the gardens and yet the younger Mr. Price-Jones had not appeared. Mr. Charles now felt it necessary to apologize for his nephew's absence.

"I apologize, Miss Morys, but it seems that Owen has been delayed longer than anticipated. We shall not stay here too much longer, but if you are up to it, Miss Morys, there is just one other place that I would like to show you—an ornamental fountain close by that some say is the most enchanting part of these layouts." He led me past several bends in the path and then parted a bower of creeping ivy so that I could see the object in question. It was undeniably beautiful, its motif—cascading waves of water in graduated sizes piled atop each other—evoking the memory of the limestone cliffs near both the estates. Trickles of clear water fell several feet onto each curved and rounded tier so that a pool formed which intensified and reflected the glistening stone and shimmered, bright and shinning, pouring over into the next sculpted ridge. And throughout this sequence there was constantly the reassuring sound of the sparkling water gently hitting the wet rocks as it moved steadily downward in its spiral pattern until finally it collected in the circular limestone pool below the fountain.

"It is lovely, is it not?" he asked. I could only nod my head, for the sight seemed all too familiar to me, evoking shadowy memories of other days and other times. I found myself wishing that we could move out from the gardens and onto the huge lawns that surrounded the main house. My mind was playing too many tricks on me and I longed to be away from these paths, for whatever was happening to my imagination seemed to have been awakened here.

Mr. Price-Jones now appeared in no hurry to return to the house but rather seemed preoccupied with thoughts not associated with the garden. He had discontinued speaking, apparently intent on other considerations, and I was ill at ease with this turn of events. Neither of us spoke for a few minutes and then he abruptly began speaking once again.

"Miss Morys, you asked me recently why I had never married." I held my breath for I did not expect this drift of conversation and, in truth, felt uncomfortable with it.

"I have apologized for my clumsiness, sir."

Mr. Price-Jones seemed not to hear me and continued. "There is a quite simple reason for this." We moved closer to the fountain.

"Please, sir, it was not my right to ask. Let us not speak of it, for the shame of my impertinence still burns."

Mr. Price-Jones gently held up the palm of his hand to silence me. "Please, hear me out, ma'am," he said, and I had no choice but to let the gentleman speak. "I will answer your question now." He looked at the fountain and I could see he was transfixed by the waterfall.

"I was in love once, Miss Morys. Only once in my life." He put his head to one side. "Oh, I know there are those who say that love is something which can be acquired or commanded, but I am of the opinion, ma'am, that it is not so." He guided me toward a marble bench by the fountain. "I am aware, Miss Morys, that love does not always figure into the state of matrimony, but in my case, once having seen the lady and having loved her, I knew that there would never be—could never be—any other for me."

I sat quietly and watched as the fountain sent its tumbling water onto the sparkling stone waves and then cascaded into the pool below. Even though I was uncomfortable, I thought it best not to comment on Mr. Price-Jones's speech so that he could continue.

"I wonder if you have guessed by now that the woman who captured my heart was Lady Anne." I trembled at the revelation and at the fact that it came as no surprise, that somehow I already knew this information.

Mr. Price-Jones carried through with his explanation. "From the first moment I saw her grown, a young woman, I knew that there would be no other for me." He touched a leaf that hung near the bench. "I called upon the Glendowers when I first inherited Cynghanedd, having procured letters of introduction from some mutual friends, and when I arrived for an afternoon tea Lord and Lady Glendower were talking to their small child—the very young Lady Anne. She was charming, Miss Morys, ingenuous and guileless, and I confess, as I did to her after many years had passed, that I considered her a beautiful young girl.

"She seemed, even then, ma'am, to be older than her years, perhaps because she had been in adult company all her life. But yet, she had this quality—this innocence, if you will—that seemed to shine through. I was enchanted with her as one would be with a favorite niece or godchild, and on occasion when I came to visit I would bring her sweets and tiny presents."

Mr. Price-Jones stopped and silently pointed out with his walking stick a small bird that had landed in the shallow end of the pool and was bathing itself noisily in the water.

"Well, the years went by, Miss Morys. I had been introduced to more than my share of young women whose parents had hoped that I would make a match but I could not seem to bring myself to care. I knew well that it was my duty to marry and have sons to carry on the family name. But, as I said, I was not impressed with any of the eligible women I had met." He seemed to be remembering the times and when he smiled at me it seemed that the gesture was really meant for someone else. "Perhaps I was too fussy or too critical, or perhaps I was just too lazy to think of one woman in a special way.

"I went on the continent then—I saw Paris and Rome and Florence and stayed away from Wales for more than a year, and when on my return I was invited back to Winter's Light, I was stunned. For you see, Miss Morys, I had been so busy with being abroad and going my own way that I had hardly noticed that this little child was growing up. And when I went to call that next week, I found, instead of the small, innocent child with the extraordinary light eyes that I had remembered, a beautiful young woman. I could not believe my own eyes for you see, Miss Morys, she had blossomed into a beauty when I was not looking.

"I continued to visit her and her family, and several months later she was formally presented to me and to society at her cotillion. She said the most enchanting thing to me; it totally captivated . . . and captured me. She smiled that wonderful smile that she had," he said, and then something must have recalled to him that I

193

had never known the woman and he apologized. "But of course you did not know her, did you, ma'am?" He paused only briefly, and it was as though he were eager to continue and have me share in the experience. "She smiled at me, Miss Morys, and then she said, 'And have you brought me yet another treat, Mr. Price-Jones?' for you see she remembered me from all those times when I had brought the tiny sweets to her." Mr. Price-Jones's mouth continued to form silent words of remembrance, and I knew that neither I nor anyone else was meant to hear them. Finally he seemed past his reverie and he continued. "I laughed and just then I heard the music start up again and I . . ." Mr. Price-Jones's actual voice seemed to fade, for somewhere deep in my memory I heard him ask the young woman to dance and suddenly the couple that I had seen in my dreams now took on faces and became known to me.

"She wore a lovely green gown with sparkles," I said. Mr. Price-Jones looked at me and nodded, then viewed me with suspicion.

"How did you know?" he asked and I stammered out an explanation I thought would suffice.

"I have been told."

Mr. Price-Jones accepted my answer and smiled again. "Nanny. She was there. She must have remembered the occasion. And of course, Anne always wore green." He ran his finger along the bark of a tree. "Anne was young, Miss Morys, and I knew I would have to wait until she was older before I asked for her hand, but it was an honor to wait for her. She was the loveliest young woman I had ever seen. I do not mean to embarrass you, Miss Morys, but somehow you remind me of the Lady Anne," he said, and I clenched my hands tightly together for fear that they would begin to shake. "We often came here and walked these same paths," he said. As he spoke I could almost see the young Mr.

Price-Jones and the Lady Anne walking in the gardens and at one point I could have sworn I heard her shy laugh. I scanned the area half expecting to see a ghostly vision as I had only moments before, but there was none. I closed my eyes hoping to bring back the memory of her, but I could not—it had faded into eternity once more.

Mr. Price-Jones took my slightly trembling hand and led me toward the exit of the gardens. "So you see, Miss Morys," he said simply, "since I have never found another like the Lady Anne, I remain in the single state."

I could do nothing but thank the gentleman for his candor and yet I wondered why he had chosen to tell me his story. Perhaps it was as he said—that in some way I reminded him of his lost love. But this was not a completely sufficient answer for me, and I knew that at some point soon I would have to ask Nanny about Mr. Charles Price-Jones. I had to know why he had never married Anne and what had happened to her. These were things Mr. Price-Jones had avoided telling me, and I knew he had deliberately ended his tale much too soon.

Chapter Sixteen

I was determined to find out the rest of the story of Lady Anne, for Mr. Price-Jones's admission of his devotion for her had thoroughly confused me. I needed to know the answers to two questions: what part had he played in the love affair of the young couple? Had he even known of Anne's affection for someone else? I had no reason to expect answers or even to question what had happened in the past here at Winter's Light, but somewhere deep in my heart there was an overriding urge to know the true story of the lovers. There were too many scenes that played over and over again in my mind—most especially I saw the last moments of that young girl—and for my own sake I had to know what had happened. Only Mrs. Hoskins could fill in the details for me, and I resolved to find them out.

I did not rush my questions, instead biding my time until I felt that Nanny was in the mood to finally tell me all. I waited for longer than a week, the query always at my lips, but there never seemed the right time to speak. Increasingly Nanny spent more time at Lady Glendower's bedside, becoming not only her nurse but her day-long companion. More and more the woman had delegated authority in the chambers to me, and I found myself not only ordering up the meals but taking charge over Meg and the other young housemaids who came to clean and straighten. When I protested such arrangements, saying that I was in no more a position than the inexperienced girls, Nanny gently but firmly gave her reasons.

"I have taught you well these few months, Gwynneth, and now it is your place." I could not comprehend the woman's reasoning for, as she said, I had only been here a short time, but I could not argue since it seemed even Lady Glendower had concurred with the plan. Thus I uncomfortably slipped into the mode of one in authority, although I took special pains not to tread within Mrs. Padley's domain. The housekeeper had her routine set, as she had told me the first few days of my arrival, and I did not want to do anything to depose her in her own kitchen. For her part, Mrs. Padley gave me no grief and continued to treat me well, even to the point of sending up favorite treats for my meals.

This evening the weather turned appropriately sharp and cold, as we were well into the full season of autumn. Fires were now set in every fireplace and the small logs burned cozily and invitingly. This was one of my favorite times of the day. The draperies and shutters of the sitting room were pulled tight against the blustery night winds and even the occasional swirling leaf or branch that bumped against the windows served to make me feel safe and comfortable. It was strange but this small room was the only area in the house where I did not feel the evil that seemed to be suspended upon the estate. It was as though that which I could not describe, yet knew existed here, was barred from the room.

Nanny and I sat at the table drinking our tea, each of us busy with her own thoughts. In the past month Nanny had abandoned her pretense of knitting another muffler for one of the working men. Although the ball of yarn, the knitting needles piercing it, stayed on the table, she made no motion toward picking it up, and the

197

half-finished scarf remained the same length.

Nanny closed her eyes briefly, then opened them and began to watch me once again, her gaze penetrating. Her chair remained stationary and I saw her fidget and pull her shawl about her.

"Well, girl. You have something to ask me, don't you?" The accuracy of the old woman's question amazed me and I could only nod. "You want to know the rest of the story of Lady Anne, is it?"

"Yes. Mr. Price-Jones has only added to my curiosity. He told me that he had been in love with her. But, like you, he did not finish his story. He left inexplicit the fact that he had lost her." I stared back at the nurse. "Will you tell me now what happened to her?"

Nanny inhaled deeply and I could see her shoulders slump forward. "Ah, no one could have been more faithful than Mr. Price-Jones," she said gently and clucked her tongue. "It took him a long time to get over his love. A long time." She bit her lip. "Aye, I'll finish the tale for you."

I put down my embroidery cloth for I did not want anything to interfere with my attention.

"The part about Mr. Price-Jones and Lady Anne. He told you of how he had become enchanted with her? Had fallen in love with her and waited until the appropriate time to declare it?" Nanny asked.

"Yes."

"Well then. This was all happening at the same time, Gwynneth, as the infatuation between Mr. Donne and Anne, and there was Mr. Price-Jones waiting to acknowledge his love for the young girl, only no one knew anything about all the different parts of the tale. This was when the two lovers kept their secret.

"Mr. Price-Jones was truly smitten with Anne. It was written in his eyes and everyone here—from the master and mistress to Mrs. Padley and her staff—could see it plain as day. Everyone, that is, except Anne and Mr. Donne, for those two were caught up in their own attachment. Mr. Charles would come to Winter's Light on any excuse, riding over from Cynghanedd for an afternoon to bring a bouquet of exotic flowers or taking an informal dinner with the family, and it was only a matter of timing then that the inevitable would come about.

"One evening he and the master excused themselves from Lady Glendower's presence and went into the master's library for what we thought would be the usual habit of cigars and wine. But we later found out—I later found out," she said, emphasizing the singular pronoun, "for my lady confided in me, that Mr. Price-Jones had asked for and received permission to marry Miss Anne."

"But Mr. Donne?"

"None of us knew about that liaison, Gwynneth. And even if we did—and I told you I suspected—it would have been of no consequence, for Mr. Donne was only a tutor and wouldn't—couldn't—figure into marriage plans for the little mistress. It was unthinkable. And Mr. Price-Jones was the perfect candidate. It would be a union not only of two great families but of immense fortunes. There would be a joining, so to speak, of two mighty Welsh estates that would ensure that these lands would never fall to strangers." She nodded her head. "In everyone's summation it was the most excellent of betrothals.

"The adults decided not to tell Anne yet, for they wanted her to finish her education and it would only be a few more months and then she would be presented at the cotillion. And so, Gwynneth, that was one of the first mistakes everyone made—not telling that young girl of the plans for her own future. I often wonder if any of us deep down felt that that was wrong. I often

199

wondered whether, if one of the personal maids had said something to Miss Anne, there would have been time enough to stop what was about to happen." She looked down at her thin hands. "Ah well, 'tis something we will never know.

"Everyone could see the love that Mr. Price-Jones had for his Anne. He would attend on her, advise her to continue to her singing lessons and her paintings and, you see, it was one more cruel joke on the girl, for everything she was urged to do was only sending her more and more into Mr. Donne's company.

"Then came the ball and there was Miss Anne, so beautiful and all filled with promise coming down the staircase with the beads sparkling like diamonds from her bodice. She made a beautiful curtsy to her parents and everyone here was just enchanted with her and her manners. And when the music started up her father asked her to dance and when, in the middle of it, he stepped aside and handed her over to Mr. Price-Jones, everyone applauded. It was symbolic, Gwynneth, that gesture, and I think everyone in the room then realized that the gentleman was in love with that girl and had been promised to her. Everyone, that is, except Mr. Donne and Anne."

Nanny's voice seemed to diminish as I could see in my mind the now much more vivid scene of the dance and the two people—he dressed in formal black and she in the pale green satin dress—who danced alone on the ballroom floor. I heard the violins and the cellos and the violas play their lilting music and now I could see, quite clearly, the two faces of the dancers. A young and handsome Mr. Price-Jones was smiling the smile of a promised lover as he held his beloved in his arms, but Anne, although there was a modest and pleasant look on her face, searched the sidelines of the guests and I knew she was looking for Mr. Donne. I watched and now the dream expanded into a version longer than before and I saw that she spied her tutor, for there was a brilliant smile and a relaxation of her face. Around and around the two dancers turned and finally at the end of the music, Mr. Price-Jones bowed and led the girl back to her parents and I could hear the applause of the guests.

I blinked my eyes, for it seemed I was watching a series of moving pictures, and then I heard Nanny's voice, much louder now, intrude upon my trance. "You have seen them, haven't you, Gwynneth? You have either seen them or you know about them." That was all she said. She did not ask me any more or wait for my answer but instead continued with the story.

"Someone must have suspected something by then, for a little time after that was when Mr. Donne was abruptly discharged. It might have been when Mr. Donne and Anne danced a turn at the cotillion as he was urged to do so out of politeness to his hostess. I think all of us saw something then that we did not want to see shining in Anne's eyes.

"A few days after the tutor's dismissal, Lord and Lady Glendower told Anne about her coming engagement to Mr. Price-Jones. The poor thing. She was shocked and scared and frightened and I heard her imploring her parents to rescind the pledge but it was already a *fait accompli* by then and nothing could have changed her father's mind. His word had been given. I heard Anne crying out that she didn't love him and then in a slip she spoke her true mind and named Mr. Donne as the man she loved.

"Mr. Donne for his part still behaved correctly, but his departure was hurried. The evening before he was to leave he came to me to ask me to always care for Anne and to tell me he would love her forever. That was his word — *'forever.'* It was a nice speech, honest and sincere and truthful. A fine declaration of his heart, and I wished I could help him but there wasn't anything I could do. It had all been decided by then. I told him I would always stay with Miss Anne and he seemed to accept it and the next morning—early, before anyone else was awake—he rode off." Nanny licked her lips. "It was all so sad, Gwynneth. Knowing that that poor girl's heart was breaking and feeling so helpless.

"But when Anne didn't come down for breakfast the next morning at the summoning by her father, I went up to get her and I found her room empty. And we all knew straight on what had happened, for we discovered that Empress was missing from her stall. Miss Anne had either gone with Mr. Donne or she had set off on her own to find him.

"We found out they had eloped to Gretna Green—I'll tell you how we knew at some other time, for it's beginning to get late and there's more to the story." Again visions invaded my mind. I could see the scene of the young girl at the inn, and now it seemed to piece together, for it was Anne that I saw and I finally knew that the young man who was at her side reassuring her was Jeremy Donne. I was viewing their anxiety and fear—I was viewing their elopement, and I heard Anne ask the question over and over again. *"Do they suspect? Do they suspect?"*

"What is it, Gwynneth? You look startled." Nanny stopped speaking and peered at me.

"Nothing," I lied. "It was only that I was thinking . . ."

Nanny nodded. "Aye, I understand," she said, and I wondered if she did. Then she continued. "Lord Glendower sent Fergus and me to find them and we did, and our orders were to bring Miss Anne back to Winter's Light. Mr. Price-Jones wanted to ride with us but it was decided that it was best that he remained behind, for, after all, he was part and parcel of this triangle.

"It wasn't difficult for Fergus and me to trace the couple, for there were innkeepers and other carriage drivers who had spied them along the roads and who told us about them, and we caught up with them at Gretna Green. When Miss Anne saw us she was frightened. She knew why we were there and she protested, of course, and it wasn't until Mr. Donne insisted that he be allowed to accompany her on the return journey that she finally agreed to come back with us. They were going to tell her parents that they were married—that they were a proper couple."

Nanny adjusted the cap on her head. "But things didn't work out right, Gwynneth, for they couldn't. Lord and Lady Glendower were sickened at the news—Anne's mother took to her bed and really was of no help to her at the time, and her father threatened all sorts of things against Mr. Donne if they did not separate.

"It was a terrible time, it was, Lord Glendower raising his voice and Anne crying and Lady Glendower not knowing what to do. Mr. Donne stood there proud-like, trying to speak, but the master was in no mood to hear him out. Mr. Price-Jones, of course, was not privy to this scene, for he wasn't yet part of the family, and I would say that all the while it took only about one hour before it was all resolved. And finally the girl relented, for she wanted to protect her young husband from everything her father had threatened.

"They sent Mr. Donne away then for good. They wouldn't even leave them alone for a last private meeting and so he said in front of everyone, *'I love you, Anne. I always will. I'll come back for you, beloved. I promise. I promise you on my life, on my honor.'* And then he turned to her father and he said, *'No one . . . no one, sir, will ever stand in our way. We belong together,'* and the way he said it, Gwynneth, it was like a thunderbolt only it was a quiet one and it seemed to just echo and echo in the room. Even Lord Glendower seemed taken aback with the force of the gentleman's words. And then Mr. Donne left Winter's Light. And the poor little girl was crying and then she fainted and was carried to her room.

"Lord Glendower confined her to just the grounds of Winter's Light, and when she finally was able to go out and about she would take Empress and ride off to the chapel. Always going to the chapel where we all knew she was praying for Mr. Donne to return."

"Was there no one who could have helped her? Who could have spoken for Mr. Donne to her father?"

"Nay, Gwynneth. Lord Glendower was put into a position of having a blemished daughter, although Mr. Price-Jones, bless him, would not withdraw his proposal. He said he would stand by Anne and then when it was an appropriate time, he would marry her despite all. It was a most generous offer and one that not many young women would get in the circumstances.

"In three months' time Lord Glendower had his solicitor quietly annul Anne's marriage, and I suppose we all hoped that everything would settle down, but it weren't to be, Gwynneth. God help us—it weren't ever to be again. For Mistress Anne began showing and we soon realized that she was pregnant with Mr. Donne's child."

I gasped and Nanny acknowledged me but she was now too far gone into the story to stop. Her eyes were set on a place not of this time.

"It was so different from when she was born. Her parents—Lord and Lady Glendower—they waited for so many years for a babe, Gwynneth. So many years and then when the lady was delivered of Anne, there was such rejoicing." Nanny's eyes glistened. "Ye never saw anything like it, Gwynneth. Nothing ever to match it in the whole of the country. The food—oh the food. And sweets and wine and ale. And beautiful gifts. Gifts of fine silks and precious laces and the women of the estate set to making and tatting lace for the delicate things the babe would wear. Such rejoicing. It was a wonderful day and the master declared it a holiday for one and all. Allowed everyone, after their daily chores were done, to leave off in the evening and to come and join us at Winter's Light for dancing and fun and sport." Here her voice went soft and I left her to think her own thoughts for a few moments while I went back to my needlework.

" 'Tweren't the same when the young mistress herself was expecting," she said sadly, then lapsed into silence. I searched Nanny's eyes, but knew she had her own way of telling the story and that I must wait until she was completely finished if I were to ask questions. She continued to rock her chair as though I were not in the room. At last she proceeded.

"No, it wasn't the same. It couldn't be. With Anne it was all sickness and pain and tears. Hers and her parents. Holy God," she said and she looked up to the ceiling of the room as though she could see beyond into the heavens. "The babe was born in sadness . . . into dark sadness, but only for a little while. Only a little while," she said and her mouth closed tight.

I begged Nanny to tell me what had happened to the child but she only shook her head and mumbled. Finally she said, and I could hear the bitterness in her voice, "Nothing good came of it. The babe was born into darkness and sorrow. There wasn't anything we could do about it," she said. When I pressed, she merely looked through me.

"Please, Nanny, whatever happened to Anne's baby?" I asked again, for it seemed imperative that I know.

Nanny folded her arms in front of her as though she was guarding still another secret. Then she answered me in a deadened voice.

"The babe died. That's all. The little babe died and the strain of it was what killed her mother not three months later. Killed that precious young girl. Make no mistake about that—that wee one was all that Anne had then, and when it died it was too much for her. It was too much of a pain for such a young girl. She couldn't bear to lose two. Not two that she loved so much. She was too young to take all that sadness."

I wanted her to go on and tell me what had happened to Anne—how she had died—and I wondered if people actually could die of a broken heart.

"Could no one save her?"

Nanny looked at me and her eyes were dull. I doubt that she even saw me.

"No one. It was not to be."

I was horrified at the story and along with shock I felt an incredible surge of sadness throughout my mind and body. It was as if I, too, had known Anne, as if her pain was now my pain, and I turned away from Nanny for I did not want her to see my tears.

Nanny was too quick for me. "Gwynneth," she said and there was a fright in her voice. "Gwynneth, why do ye cry for her? What reason for your tears?"

I shook my head. "I do not know, Nanny. I only know that it is a sad story and somehow it hurts me, too. Lady Anne . . ." I put my hand out to the air. "It's as though I almost knew—" I said and then for some strange reason amended it quickly, "It's as though I know her, Nanny. God forgive me, but it's as if I know her well."

Nanny sat in her chair, her eyes wide. She shuddered and bowed her head and I wondered if she, like my schoolfriends, believed in the Devil. I did not have time to ask her.

"Gwynneth," she said when she had regained her composure, but then she closed her mouth and remained watching me until I quieted my tears. I did not want to hear any more of the Lady Anne. It was all too much for me to comprehend, but Nanny wanted to continue speaking now, as though the rest of the story should be revealed.

"He never came back for her, Gwynneth. Mr. Donne never showed his face around the estate again, and I think everyone wished it were different, for the young girl just kept walking and walking from here to the chapel and back again like some poor caged animal.

"She even took to leaving a lighted candle in her window and I knew it was to be a secret signal to her lover. I think even her parents knew about it, but they were so sure that nothing would come of it that they didn't say anything to her. I think they thought that anything that would get the poor thing through this time—her time—should be tolerated, for now there was the babe to be considered.

"Anne never gave up hope that Mr. Donne would come back for her. I remember she stopped me in the hall one day when she was about six months gone. 'Nanny,' she said to me and her eyes were all dark ringed and lifeless, 'Nanny, tell me he'll come for me. Tell me he loves me.' I remember I replied—despite Lord Glendower's notice to us not to encourage foolish ideas—that she was right, that the young tutor would be back for her, would claim her for his own when he had enough money to make her proud. Her faith in him made us all almost believe that it were so, though how and when this would happen we could not imagine. But when I listened to Anne I thought he really meant to return and claim her. She was like that, Gwynneth. She had such pure and simple faith that we all believed for her. And then when the days kept getting longer and the wait going on and on and she was getting bigger and bigger

207

with the child, even then she didn't lose her faith. Even then she would make us all feel that she was right. That the young man would come back for her and claim her and his child.

"Lord and Lady Glendower were worried about their daughter and they were in a quandary, too, for how to tell about the babe and how to explain to all the neighbors and family about the secret marriage. They were caught, too, Gwynneth, in their own way. I could see that Lord Glendower was heartsick, for Anne was his one and only child and he loved her only he didn't know how to resolve it for her, for he could not relent. After all, she had disobeyed him, and no matter that he was hurting, he couldn't go back on his own words." Nanny began rocking in her chair. "It was a dilemma that had no solving, for in the end someone was bound to be hurting.

"Miss Anne took to keeping to herself, eating only when we would remind her of the baby and the consequences, and even then it was hardly enough to keep her alive. Mrs. Padley made all kinds of favorites of hers but they were always left sitting on the sideboard or on the table with not even a small bite from them. And all the time, Gwynneth, the gloom was settling over the house and the family. Where there was laughter once upon a time, now there was none. Where there was happiness and music and painting, there was none. Winter's Light had become a dark unhappy estate, bleaklike, much like those abandoned farmhouses that stand at the moor's edge. Everyone felt it. Everyone knew the reason and everyone was powerless to change the direction toward which we were all heading. Mistress Anne's broken heart had affected us all—had hurt us all." Nanny wrung her hands together as though to get them warm.

"She kept stopping me, as she grew bigger and the

days longer, telling me that Mr. Donne would be coming soon, would come to take her away from the house and then she wouldn't be alone anymore. It seemed like she was going crazed with the hurt in her heart. None of us had the words to tell her that it was now too long a time that passed without him and that not one of us now believed it to be so anymore. Oh, we lied a bit and told half-truths, but I think we all knew that we were only saying it would be so because of the baby. We thought maybe then she would cheer and at least be contented with the babe, although none of us knew what was to be done with the child and what was to be said to friends and family.

"Miss Anne, though, still lived in that dreamworld of hers and she would invent hopeful stories about how, when Mr. Donne came for her, the three of them would go off and set up a household. Or how, when Mr. Donne came back to claim her, they would all live at Winter's Light with Lord and Lady Glendower. It was all playacting, of course, Gwynneth, but she wanted it so. She wanted it to be that way.

"But then, when her time came and she went into her labor and was sick with the pain and the worry and then delivered the child, I knew absolutely that she would be alone and without a fitting husband and father for the babe. That Mr. Donne would not come. And I couldn't believe it myself, for he seemed so happy with the young Anne and so unhappy when he was sent away. *I'll come back for you,*' he told her and he was sincere and we all thought he spoke the truth when he spoke it in front of us. *I'll come for you, beloved.*' That's what he said." Nanny rocked slower, as though the rhythm had to be slowed for her next words. "But then she presented the baby and . . . and . . . it died," she half-whispered and again I gasped. She recognized my shock and nodded to me and I could see the tears in her eyes. "Aye," she said, "it died. Poor Miss Anne. Poor Miss Anne. Wanting it so, for it was Mr. Donne's child, and then it was gone. I think at that moment I knew, there in the room when she was told the fate of the babe, that the life went out of her, too. We—her mother and I, for her father was truly grief-stricken at the turn of events and was banished from the nursery for the delivery—told her gentle-like but it didn't matter. It seemed as though everything she had loved and had wanted was gone. She said those exact words to me, Gwynneth. Told me that once a few days before . . . before . . ."

Nanny had all but stopped moving her chair and body and was still. The room seemed to be getting colder even as we heard the popping and hissing of the logs as they blazed in the grate, and although the candles still burned in their holders, I would have sworn the room had darkened. I rubbed my arms and saw Nanny adjust her shawl around her stooped shoulders and I knew that it was not a physical cold that had overtaken us but an emotional cold, one that could not be cured by the layering on of clothes or the addition of hardwood logs to the fireplace.

"What happened to Anne, Nanny? After the baby's death?"

Nanny stared at the floor and by the light of the fire I saw that she frowned, her face contorted in pain for a moment.

"She died, Gwynneth. She died, too. They say there was an accident at the chapel." Hearing her voice tremble I knew that even now Nanny was not sure of the explanation. "An accident, they said." She put her fingers to her mouth and moved them delicately across her lips. "An accident, they told us. Aye, an accident."

I swallowed hard and the cold in the room now turned frigid as the vision once more appeared to me. I watched as Anne approached the balcony of the chapel, saw her step out into the air and then saw the frail frame tumble . . . tumble down to the rose bushes below, the grey-green cape flaring out behind her. I had confirmation now that the scene I witnessed had been Anne's last on this earth.

Nanny was still speaking, explaining for her own benefit as well as mine. "We — all of us about the estate — tried to believe that she had not meant to take her life and that she fell by some sort of accident. Even now we're not sure what happened. It could have been," she said hopefully. I did not contradict her, but the vision of Anne tumbling into space became more and more vivid and I knew the truth.

She said no more at the time and looked away — out the window in the direction of the estate chapel — and I could see her small body heave slightly. "We tried to lie to ourselves but we all knew, you see, Gwynnie, we all knew that she didn't want to live anymore. The lovely Lady Anne just couldn't live without her young man. It was much too much for her. Her world was nothing without him. It was too hard for her. The dear, sweet innocent. We had loved her so much and so we all had done too much for her. And we had given her no strength, no backbone, so that when there seemed to be nothing for her, when her world seemed broken and sorrowful, she didn't know how to contend. Didn't know what to do. And when that happened . . . no one . . . no one on this earth . . . or in heaven or hell," and here she raised her eyes briefly as though she was asking for confirmation from the skies and beyond. "No one in heaven or hell could have saved her. Could have given her reason to live. It were too sad. Too sad for her." The rocking chair began to move slowly and Nanny's body inclined ever so slightly toward me.

"You see, when she found out that the babe had died

211

she was like a crazy woman who had nothing more to say or do in this world. She would walk the estate—round and round she would walk—first to the moors and then to the seacoast and then to the chapel. Nothing would stop her. Not even if it be bad weather. Still she would walk the grounds and I knew . . . I knew that she was waiting and watching. Looking for her young husband—for that was what he was, make no mistake about that. Good and legal husband he was, and there she was waiting for him to return to her. But that wasn't to be. Leastways not then. Not then.

"She just went out one day and I suppose she just got tired of thinking and praying and hoping. It was a beautiful day otherwise, Gwynneth. A fair summer's noon day. Warm and the smell of heather from the gardens and the salt of the sea all mingling together. Fergus said that the young mistress stopped and talked to him for a moment—only a few words and mostly done by Fergus himself. He warned her about the sunshine not being good for her for it was so strong, it was, but she just smiled at him—she had a lovely smile, Gwynneth, so simple and faultless and heartbreaking—and told Fergus not to worry. That she would be all right. She said it twice, Fergus said. She would be all right."

Nanny took out a starched white handkerchief from within the long sleeve of her dress and wiped at her eyes.

"And of course, I guess in her own mind and in her own way, she is now. But why she had to do it, I'll never know," Nanny said, betraying her real thoughts about Anne's death. There must never have been any doubt in the old woman's mind though she protested otherwise. I did not let on I had caught the slip and she kept on with her story.

"There would have been others for her, in spite of her

212

past. There was Mr. Price-Jones who loved her and who would have married her despite all, for he was a good man, a decent and devoted man, and he was standing by her. He was like her own family and all of us — we all could forgive her her sins no matter what." Nanny squinted toward me. "Not that they were sins, mind you, even though some 'round here would like to think they were. Married they were. Mr. Donne and Miss Anne were married proper. I can testify to that.

"But that beautiful summer day she just went walking by herself like she always did, and no one could suspect — though still I sometimes blame myself for not catching her drift, not understanding where her mind lay. I sometimes think about that, Gwynneth, even though it's been many years now. I can't help but suppose that maybe if I had questioned her a bit more or listened to her a bit more or if the baby had not . . ." Nanny once again wrung her hands and even I could see them tremble.

"She was a near perfect young woman and the only time she faltered was when she fell in love with a man whose only fault was that he was poor. I often think of the unfairness of the situation." Nanny wiped the tears away from her eyes. "You would have loved her, Gwynneth. You would have loved her." She stood up and I knew she would reveal no more to me. She walked to the door, carrying her candle high, and turned back to look at me. "I know you would have loved her."

Chapter Seventeen

There was an unusual amount of activity on the second floor this afternoon. Servants bustled in and out of the guest wings with freshly laundered towels and linens and the rooms were being given a thorough cleaning and airing. Even Mrs. Padley seemed to be a bit sharper than usual and kept admonishing her undermaids to "look lively." Though it did not concern me, I wondered just who could create such fuss and turmoil among the servants. Who could be visiting us that would rally the entire staff to extra duties?

" 'Tis only the Davies, my lady's distant relatives. They'll be here tomorrow," Nanny said when I remarked on the action. Her nose twitched to express her disfavor. "Come to pay their annual duty call for the season, they have. Every year about this time they come to visit Lady Glendower, and they'll stay until well after the holidays so that they can collect their gifts." She glanced out the hall as Meg hurriedly passed by on her way to the guest chambers, two large quilts filling her arms. "They'll set everything and everyone topsy-turvy what with all their demands for attention until they leave. Tell everyone that they've come to cheer their cousin but they don't fool me. They've come to get whatever they can get. You'll meet them soon enough, Gwynneth." She shook out her shawl. "Like birds of prey, they are," she said, and then stopped and stared at me and smiled. "Aye, well, we'll see what happens when . . ." She smiled again but her eyes seemed cold with fury. "Aye, we'll see."

Mr. and Mrs. Davies arrived early the next morning and within the hour, much to Nanny's annoyance, were insisting on visiting Lady Glendower in her chambers. Mrs. Hoskins had them wait and sent me down to the kitchen to request that extra pots of tea be sent up to accommodate the guests.

"Stay and visit with Mrs. Padley a few minutes, Gwynneth, for I'd rather you didn't meet the pair until later. The Davies are snoops, my dear, and will want to inspect everything and everyone, and they'll find ways to interrogate you until they find out all the last details here at Winter's Light. And I'll not allow them to do that to you until such time that suits me."

I repeated Nanny's words about the gossiping to Mrs. Padley and the woman laughed. "Looks like there be fireworks again." She proffered a plate of seedcake slices toward me. "It's the same everytime the Davies come to call. Nanny has never taken kindly to those people, nor in truth, should she. They only come to make trouble. Always walking about, lording it over everyone here in the house as though they had already taken charge. Almost like they were taking inventory of everything here. Many a time I've suspected that it not be in the lady's best interests when they are here, for they do nothing to make her happy."

"Will they inherit Winter's Light?"

Mrs. Padley wiped her brow from the heat of the kitchen.

"Aye, they're the only ones left now from the family. It will be a sad day, Gwynneth. A sad day when they take over. They're not at all like the mistress." She tied her apron about her stout body. "Ah well, those affairs

215

have nothing to do with me."

I did not tell Mrs. Padley of Nanny's evaluation of the relatives and, after waiting a decent interval, I went back to the bedchamber and stayed in the sitting room until I heard the guests leave. If Nanny wanted me out of the way for a bit it was not for me to question. If the Davies were to stay here for the next two months there would be ample opportunity for me to meet and, if necessary, to serve them.

Lady Glendower and the nurse were once again talking in low whispers and I was struck with the fact that the mistress was smiling in a way I had never seen before.

"I have lived for this day, my lady. Serves them right," Nanny said. I wondered at the reason for her vehemence. I had only glimpsed Mr. and Mrs. Davies as they walked past the sitting room, but they appeared to be decent, respectable people.

I told Nanny this later, as we were finishing up our lunch.

"Decent? Respectable? Mr. and Mrs. Davies? Ah, Gwynneth, you have a lot to learn about the ways of the aristocrats in this family. There are some in every family more like the blackguards than saints. Decent? Respectable?" she repeated to herself. "More likely they've come to clear out the silver," she sniffed, setting her teacup down with a clatter. "Mark my words, girl, they've come too soon this year because they are in poor finances. They only come early when they want something—when their stakes have run short again or when they're being dunned by the fashion merchants. That's when you'll see them. That's when they turn up. When all their money is on their back in the latest fashions. No sense of responsibility or pride in the family.

"Mr. Davies, the late lord's cousin, was given an adequate inheritance for a younger son such as he was, but he and his silly wife have squandered away their money on foolish things. The stories I could tell about them and their ways. Their own lovely home—Y Pyn—with its beautiful pine trees that it was named for and that surrounded the home for centuries, is in a sorry state, I hear. Old Fergus and Mr. Benjamin, our own head groundskeeper, was sent there once for a fortnight out of the graciousness and goodness of the mistress to help make order and sense of it. But even after ten full days they complained that they weren't able to do too much to fix the old place up. Said the estate was in such disrepair and neglect that only another fortune could save it—that that's what would be needed to restore it. Mr. Davies," Nanny scoffed, "hasn't that kind of money. But they think they know how to get it." She looked around and up. "And this estate, too, in the bargain.

"They've been coming 'round here since the lady took sick. Never came before except on Boxing Day and an occasional weekend in the spring and then only to collect their presents that the lady had made ready for them." Nanny shook her head and I had never seen her like this, for it was more than anger that had gotten into her. "Come to look after their fortune, they have, because they know there be no other to inherit Winter's Light. There they sit—all smug, they are—thinking that all this—all these lovely old furnishings and the whole of the estate will be theirs someday." Nanny touched a cut-crystal vase that sat upon a carved oak table. "These pretty things in their possession? They'd sell the entire lot, if they could. You mark my words. That's what they're after." The old woman pinched her lips together. "Well, we'll see about that. Just let them wait a bit." She stoked the last embers of the early fire and smiled menacingly such as I had never seen her do before.

"Well, we'll just see to that." She gave the coals a vigorous shake that surely must have taken all her strength and then looked over at me. "Just let them wait and see. Just let them wait and see."

I was not introduced to Mr. and Mrs. Davies until we were all assembled for tea in the sitting room. Nanny had urged me to pay close attention to the relatives for, she said, she wanted my opinion of them.

"They're only taking tea with us, Gwynneth, because they want to observe me. To see if I'm to be retired soon. To see if my old bones are too worn to carry on." She stood straight against her own words and brushed her stiff, starched apron. "Well, they'll see me in my prime," she said and then laughed again. "And they'll see you. They'll get to meet you." Meg had come into the room and Nanny had her set the tray on the table and then leave.

"Let it be, gal, I'll pour for us." She turned the pot handle toward her and laughed that strange laugh again. "They don't know about you yet, Gwynneth. But they will. Oh yes, they will."

Nanny's words disturbed me, for I had no idea to what she was referring. Surely the addition of an aide in the chambers could do nothing to provoke interest in these two relatives. Perhaps Nanny was going to use me to offset any negative opinion the Davies might take regarding her fitness for the chores.

I added another log to the fire; the days were increasingly getting colder and the room could do with more heat. Outside, dusk was already upon us, and the curtains had been pulled against the greyness of the day. The bleakness of the early twilight had seemed inauspicious, given that I was meeting those who might be my future employers.

Nanny busied herself with the tea, making sure that

the cosy kept the pot hot and that the sandwiches on the plates were fresh and crisp.

"Never on time," she said. "Manners wanting." She straightened a teaspoon on the tea tray. They'll not be too late, though, for they always relish Mrs. Padley's teas," she said, and I wondered if the old woman was taking pleasure in speaking ill of the couple.

We did not have to wait long before the cousins came into the room with great show, apologizing to Nanny for their tardiness. I could see that they were annoyed that Nanny had chosen the head chair at the table for herself, but the Davies did not say anything. They took their places at the side and when I took a chair opposite them, they seemed puzzled.

"This is Gwynneth Morys," Nanny said by way of introduction. She gave no further explanation of who I was or why I was there with them. I saw her watch them as she said the words and it was as if she were waiting for them to acknowledge me. She seemed to have gotten her wish, for Mr. and Mrs. Davies stared at me and a slight flicker of—what shall I call it?—interest . . . curiosity . . . crossed their eyes.

"How long have you been here, Miss Morys?" Mr. Davies' voice was low and yet loud, genteel yet coarse.

"Just a few months, sir." I was already uncomfortable under his gaze.

"Gwynneth's come to help us tend my lady." Nanny smiled charitably at me. "She does a good job, too, what with her knowing how to keep the bedclothes neat and clean enough to please the mistress. A great joy she is to her, too. The mistress has taken to her." Nanny seemed to take immense delight in extolling my virtues and I could not understand her seeming to play a cat and mouse game with the cousins. It was a side of her I did not recognize.

"We didn't know you needed help, Nanny. You should have told us and we would have gotten someone to help you. To take the heavy chores from you." Mrs. Davies seemed solicitous and yet I saw Nanny bristle.

Mr. Davies took his cup of tea from the nurse and put it on the table, then sat back and folded his hands.

"Perhaps it would be best if you started thinking about retiring, Nanny," he said, and I saw the old woman's lips move as though she were speaking to herself. "You are of a certain age and . . . ," he let the rest of the sentence remain unfinished and had the grace enough to seem uncomfortable with his own suggestion.

Mrs. Davies hurried to echo her husband's words, only she made an attempt to soften the impact. "What my husband is saying, Nanny, is that perhaps you are in no fair condition yourself to help with Lady Glendower's care. It is not as though you are a young woman any longer."

I saw Nanny's face tighten at the words, though they were spoken gently. She turned toward the other woman.

"I served my lady when she was a bride and continue to serve her well now that she's a widow." She stirred her tea so that the sound of the spoon scraping the bottom of the cup was the only sound we heard in the room. Finally she looked up and glared at her adversaries. "If you're thinking that there should be a change in my service here, then I think it best that we should take it up with another." She sipped her tea and looked toward the adjoining room. "I take my orders direct from the lady, the true mistress of Winter's Light," she said, and then signaled to me to follow her as she stood up and walked toward the door. "Them's that don't like it or who cannot tolerate it needs reminding as to who they are and who they are not," were her last words as she started into Lady Glendower's chambers. I was amazed at Nanny's boldness, for even though she was a confidante of Lady Glendower, to commit such a breach of etiquette was unthinkable.

I rose, embarrassed to be a witness to such a scene, and quickly curtsied to the Davies, who paid me no mind. Evidently, in their scheme of things I was too unimportant to notice.

"Someday," the gentleman said to his wife as he took another slice of bread and butter onto his plate, "Nanny shall be dismissed." His wife coughed discreetly and signalled to him that I was still in the room, yet he hardly looked at me, for I was sure the feelings of a helper did not count with him.

"Excuse me," I said and did not wait for their reply. I had already grown to dislike the company of the Davies, and vowed to keep my distance from them. Nanny had been right—they were not nice people, and even I could tell that they were at Winter's Light only to bring trouble.

That evening when Nanny and I took our dinner together there was no mention of the relatives. We sat by ourselves in the small dining room we often used when just the two of us ate and Mrs. Padley, in a gesture I took to be meant as support for the nurse, sent in a fresh pound cake that she had just taken from the oven.

We did not linger at the table, as Nanny did not want to leave Lady Glendower alone too long.

"If they don't see me there," she said, and I realized that she had set herself up as the only defense against Lady Glendower's kin, "they will barge in on the mistress with all their fine ideas." She wiped her lips on the napkin. "Come, Gwynneth, finish up your meal and we'll ask Mrs. Padley to send up the sweet to our rooms."

221

Nanny was right. Just as we arrived at the door to the master chamber, Mr. and Mrs. Davies were set to enter.

"Mistress might be asleep," Nanny said, blocking the way to the room. "I'll see to her first." She frowned at the two. "If that be all right with you, that is," she said sarcastically. The couple could hardly protest, thus instead sat, without an invitation, in the sitting room.

Nanny was gone only a moment.

"The mistress asks that you excuse her and attend her tomorrow. She'll be rested then and will be able to speak with you at length." She took her place in the rocking chair, daring the man to oppose her.

Mr. Davies said nothing, yet made no move to leave, instead getting up to stoke the fires so that they burned brighter. He walked past the table upon which the small portrait of Anne was kept and picked the frame up, turning it toward the light of the flames. There was a scowl upon his face and I could see that this expression did not do anything to enhance his features. Although he was not an aristocratic man there was still a smoothness to his face that could at first sight be considered attractive. But Mr. Davies's eyes betrayed him. They were set far too close and were hooded, as though he would be about hiding something from friends and family alike. This evening, in addition, I could see that he had been far too long at the port, for the slits of his eyes revealed them to be glassy.

His wife, who was standing by the door, was a comely woman though, as Nanny had pointed out, she was rather too ostentatiously got up. Already I found her demeanor false and would not have trusted a secret or even a remark with her. They were not an unattractive couple but there was a coldness about them—a hint of cruelty that would, I suspected, show itself should they be crossed or deprived of a goal.

Mr. Davies set the picture frame back on the table and turned his back to it and faced his wife.

"Our cousin surely disappointed her parents and our family. She was really nothing but a bit of fluff." Mr. Davies's voice dismissed the memory of the young girl.

"She weren't nothing of the sort." Nanny's crackling voice cut through the silence and the tone of it shocked Mr. Davies, who turned and stared at the old woman. "She were a kindhearted, lovely young girl who was taken advantage of by some." The woman crossed her hands in front of her and glared at the man, daring him to challenge her words and her statement. "You're trying to disgrace the young mistress for your own purpose and I'll—we'll not have it."

Mr. Davies poured himself a small glass of wine from the decanter on the sideboard. "I do no such thing, Nanny. I am merely telling the truth. Had young Anne not run away with a man of ill intent and then returned in disgrace, her mother would not have been hurt. And probably her father, my beloved cousin, would still be alive this day, for I am not the only one who says that after his daughter died there was no will for him to live. And," he said sipping from his glass, "the family name—the proud Glendower name that has endured through centuries—would not now be whispered about the countryside in snide snickers and remarks whenever a field hand or a gossipy servant has nothing better to do with his or her tongue. Many a time, Nanny, and you cannot deny it, we all have heard the carelessly spoken words that are said when people do not realize we are within earshot." He drank his wine. "Had Anne not returned in her condition and . . ." He poured himself still another drink of wine and replaced the stopper in the crystal decanter and looked down at it. ". . . And borne—"

223

Nanny picked up the ball of yarn that was on the table and angrily squeezed it so that a knitting needle popped onto the floor.

"Hold your tongue, and say no more, Mr. Davies," she said in a strong voice as she half rose from her chair. "Say no more about Mistress Anne. There are still some of us here who will speak for her."

Mr. Davies waved his hand as though to dismiss the woman's words. "You are still protecting her, Nanny."

"Aye. And I always will. Had you given her and the family the love that you profess for them now, perhaps things would have been different. Instead you joined in her condemnation—you and some of those others who professed to be friends—and added to her and her parents' misery." She sat down again. "Aye, many a day and night I have had to think and reflect upon it, and many an explanation I have come up with," she said and then began to rock back and forth. "And many a persons could be called into account for what passed for friendship at Winter's Light that year."

Mr. Davies, I had already ascertained, was not one to be easily bested, and I could feel the tension building in the room. Even his wife seemed on edge.

"Whom do you indict, Nanny?" Mr. Davies spoke in a deadly, quiet voice. "Whom do you indict for the goings on?" He took another drink from his glass and it seemed that the wine had gone to his head, for even in the firelight I could see that his sallow complexion had taken on a flush. "Go on, old woman," he hissed, "tell us your theory as to why Anne went sour. Why she was ruined."

Nanny continued to rock purposefully and the room filled with the sound of the creaking of the wood runners against the wooden floor. Back and forth . . . back and forth she rocked, never taking her eyes off Mr.

Davies' face, and each rock served to escalate the now open hostility between the two.

"Well, old woman," he shouted, "give us your version. Tell us," he said and waved his arms toward his wife and me, "tell me and the good ladies assembled here what you think and whom you think meant harm to the Glendower name." He once again drained his goblet and recklessly poured himself more sherry, spilling it over onto the polished floor so that the wet drops glistened as the candlelight reflected from them.

This last outburst and the spilt wine was too much even for his wife, who stepped in between the two enemies.

"Mr. Davies," she said, taking hold of his arm and leading him to the door. "For heaven's sake, it is of no consequence. She is but a servant in this house. She only serves at our—at your cousin's pleasure," she said, correcting herself, and pulled her husband through the door.

Nanny continued to rock as though there had been no flare-up of emotions, but I saw a slight, almost distracted smile on her wizened face and I knew that this would not be the end of the animosity.

Chapter Eighteen

During the next several days it seemed outwardly that all was forgotten between the two protagonists, though I could see the fight and fire still in Nanny's eyes whenever she spoke to Mr. Davies. It was a civil but uneasy truce, and one that did little to allay the feelings of dread that now seemed to swirl more rapidly about the house. My own sleep these past nights had been filled with images of Anne and Mr. Donne, the vision of the two eloping seeming particularly recurrent. Each time it played in my mind I awoke to a feeling of impending terror and yet I could not explain it. It was as though someone at Winter's Light had to be on guard, but against what or whom I did not know. I did not speak to Nanny of these impressions, for I could see that the woman had had more than enough to handle since the arrival of the relatives. Instead I tried to put the premonition out of my thoughts.

One evening I went to the library in search of a book to my liking and on the way back to my room I met up with Mr. Davies. He stopped me immediately in a most polite way, although it seemed that he had been lying in wait for a chance to question me when I was alone.

"Gwynneth, Miss Morys, a moment, please," he said. His manner was calm and agreeable, yet I did not feel that I could or should trust him.

"Yes, sir?"

Mr. Davies moved close to me and I could feel a flush

on my face, for he seemed to look closely at me, as though he were examining me.

"I am curious. Do you come from around here? From this area?"

"No, sir." Nanny had warned me not to offer too much in the way of answers to him.

"Then how is it that you were taken in to Winter's Light?"

"My minister received an inquiry and I was found suitable." Mr. Davies continued to look at me and it seemed he was not satisfied with my answer.

"How came that your minister knew of the position? Did someone know of you? Or of your family?"

"I do not know, sir." I shifted my book in my hands. "If you'll excuse me, sir, I must get back to the master chamber. Nanny will be wondering where I am."

Mr. Davies stepped aside and as I walked away I glimpsed his reflection in the hall mirror. He continued to stare after me and I did not particularly like the look upon his countenance. I did not credit the man, and now I could not tell if he had been inquiring about me merely as preface to an idle gossip or if there had been another motive for his queries. I decided I would not tell Nanny about my encounter but would keep my own counsel and wait to see how it all progressed.

The next morning Mr. Davies and his wife tried to come into Lady Glendower's bedchamber while she was still asleep only to be blocked, once more, by Nanny. He seemed not to be put out with the woman's obstruction and instead began to question her about his cousin's health, and I wondered if that had been his intent all along. I suspected that the gentleman was not interested in hearing good news, for when Nanny replied that her mistress was regaining her strength rather quickly, Mr. Davies sniffed as though he disbelieved the nurse's opinions.

"You will always say that, no matter what the circumstances, Nanny." He looked at me and then signalled the woman to come closer so that they could speak in confidence. I was sure he thought I could not hear, but the room was made in such a way that when one whispered in the corner the sound carried throughout the apartment. Nanny did not tell him about the acoustics, and when I saw her soft, sly smile, I knew she delighted in this secret and fully intended for me to hear the whole conversation.

Mr. Davies wasted no words. "I fear my cousin is getting weaker," he said. Nanny made no motion to either affirm or deny his words. "Perhaps we should begin thinking of—"

The old woman's eyes flashed. " 'Tis no such thing you'll be thinking, Mr. Davies. Ye best get that notion out of your head, for if you're anticipating that Dr. Lawrence will sign to her being unable to handle her own affairs, I think you will be greatly mistaken," she said, again standing up to the gentleman. A flicker of shadow passed in front of Mr. Davies' eyes and I knew that Nanny had guessed not only his ideas but his intention.

"She is not capable—"

"She is more than capable, Mr. Davies. She converses with me when she has a mind to. These past days she has spoken to you and your wife about family matters. She speaks to Mr. Charles and Mr. Owen when they attend her, and I've seen her smile and heard her converse with young Gwynneth when the gal is working about the room." She looked at him so that her eyes held his and he could not appropriately turn away from her. "Mistress is fond of the young girl, too," she said, and I knew that there was a reason for her last state-

228

ment. Nanny was skilled at provocation when challenged.

Mr. Davies seemed to whisper even lower and I bowed my head briefly so that it was not too obvious I could hear him.

"How did you find the girl? Is she trustworthy?"

"Aye, very." She looked at me and knew that I heard her. "More than some people I know," she said, and I was sorry that I could not smile at the time. Mr. Davies pursed his lips and I knew he had taken offense at Nanny's words. In truth, their implication was obvious.

"She's just a farm girl—an orphan, I understand."

"Whatever you hear, you hear. But mark my words, sir, appearances deceive." Mr. Davies turned to stare at me, then said, "We'll keep an eye on her."

Nanny nodded in agreement. "Aye, we will." She walked toward me, giving no indication that she knew I overheard the remarks. "Besides, the mistress likes the girl about. She's gay and witty and talented and I suppose," she said sighing, "it's as though she remembers other times when there were so many here. She always enjoyed the lads and lassies and their parties and balls. I remember when she used to watch over them. When she would watch the dancing. I think it reminds her of her—"

"We'll not talk of her again, Nanny," Mr. Davies' voice was sharp, for I suspect that he understood where Nanny was leading the dialogue. "We'll have no more talk of that one. She has been dead and gone for a long time now and it's best that she is forgotten by everyone."

Nanny's black eyes flashed. "Never by me or her mother," she said and her eyes closed in anger. "Never by me or her own mother." She opened her eyes and seemed to look through Mr. Davies. "And nothing you say or do can ever take away the sweet memories of the young miss. The sweet memories of the Lady Anne." She said the name fondly and Mr. Davies, unaccustomed to hearing it spoken so, stepped back. In defiance, Nanny said the name again. "Anne. The sweet Lady Anne. Nothing you or anyone else in the world say or do will ever make us all forget her." She tugged her shawl around her and held out her hand to me. "Come, Gwynneth, take the tray and call for the mistress's luncheon now." She moved close to the fireplace so that she stood between the flames and Mr. Davies and I could see the flash and fire that must have been in the old woman's character when she was a young girl. "If you'll excuse us," she said to the man. Fascinated by this second display of bravado from Nanny, I watched as Mr. Davies turned tentatively toward his cousin's room, then thought better of barging in on her and hurriedly walked away from the chamber. He stopped, paused, then turned again to face Nanny, and it seemed as though he purposely chose his words so that they should threaten her.

"This is not the end of the matter," he said and I gasped at the hatred in his voice.

"Aye, you are correct about that," Nanny said fiercely. She watched until the door was fully closed before turning toward me. I remained quiet as she dignifiedly told me that no questions were to be asked about her latest encounter with Mr. Davies. But I knew that, given time, there would come some answers.

That evening Mr. Charles and Mr. Owen Price-Jones paid their regular call on Lady Glendower, and Nanny had no choice but to invite the Davies to dine with us in the small dining room. To her surprise Mr. and Mrs. Davies accepted and I thought an armistice had been declared for the evening. The senior Mr. Price-Jones served as mediator between the two opponents, though I did not know whether he suspected that he had been cast into that unenviable role. The dinner conversation was a bit forced, but if this was noticed by the uncle and nephew, nothing—not a word or a glance—was said or exhibited to indicate it.

Mr. Davies stared at me throughout the dinner and at one time I did catch a puzzled expression on Mr. Owen's face, as though he too had noticed that I was being given an inordinate amount of quiet attention.

At the end of the meal Mr. Davies put aside his napkin.

"Charles, when you have a moment, I would like to speak to you."

"Perhaps over cigars and wine?" Mr. Price-Jones seemed agreeable to the suggestion. "If Owen will excuse us and perhaps entertain the women for a few moments," he said, looking at his nephew, who nodded his head in assent. "We haven't had a talk in a very long time."

Mr. Davies seemed pleased with himself. "Yes, that will do nicely." He caught his wife's eye and they both turned and glared at me. I felt my cheeks pinking and directed my attention to the last bit of potato on my plate. I did not want to look up for fear that I would see Mr. Owen looking at me speculatively again, and I was relieved when the two older men finally excused themselves and went into the library.

Mrs. Davies and Nanny returned to Lady Glendower's room. It seemed that when she was not with her husband, the woman could be almost cordial. Still, I did not trust her, for as Nanny had said, appearances are sometimes deceiving.

"Miss Morys, you appear to be thinking deeply. Is there something that disturbs you?" Mr. Price-Jones had lingered at the dinner table with me. "I could not help but notice—"

"I, too," I replied, for I knew he referred to the way the Davies kept looking at me. "I do not know why they are trying to find fault with me. I have only just met them."

"I am not sure that that is their motive. They appeared much as if they suspected something in your appearance or your manner."

"I beg your pardon. I do not know what you mean." I was stunned. Up until now I had thought that Mr. Owen was my friend.

Mr. Price-Jones jumped up from his chair and came and stood beside mine. "My dear lady," he said, taking my hand in his, "I did not mean that there was something wrong. No, only that I thought that the two were suspicious of something. But I perceive that their cynicism applies to all who thwart them." He held my hand tighter. "I did not mean to imply that there is anything amiss with you or your character. Would that Mr. and Mrs. Davies had dispositions like yours. There are few like you, ma'am, that I have encountered." He stepped back and I smiled at his gracious recommendation.

"I thank you for your evaluation of me, sir. And as to the cousins, well, it is not my place to criticize."

Mr. Price-Jones nodded. "Again, Miss Morys, you respond with the most correct of replies." He held out his arm to me. "Come, let us go and visit our hostess now."

Within the hour both Mr. Davies and Mr. Charles joined us but the relatives did not stay long, excusing themselves after Mr. Davies had spent a few moments with his cousin. I suspected they were miffed that the lady favored the uncle and nephew Price-Jones in the conversation. Nanny did not speak often while all were gathered and instead watched as the Davies tried but

232

failed to put Lady Glendower's mental competence to the test. I perceived that they knew they could not consider Mr. Price-Jones a confederate in their attempts.

When another half hour had passed the Price-Joneses made their farewells to Lady Glendower, who appeared tired, and Nanny invited them to spend another few minutes with us in the sitting room. She rang for tea and soon Meg had brought up the tray and the four of us sat at the small table.

"We've spent many an afternoon and evening here, haven't we, Nanny?" Mr. Charles accepted the cup of tea from Mrs. Hoskins. "This has always been a pleasant room." He looked at the low fire that burned, pale gold and deep blue, in the fireplace. "Nothing seems to have changed here in all the years." He looked 'round and his eyes rested on a drawing which I had presented to the nurse the previous week, and which now hung on the wall. It was one I was especially proud of, for it showed in good detail the barns and stables and the workers who had been baling the hay for the animals, and I thought it captured the day and time of the year in true form.

He stood up and walked to it. "Except this is new, isn't it? This sketch, Nanny, where did it come from?"

Nanny seemed pleased to explain. "Look at the name in the corner, Mr. Charles," she said and the gentleman moved so he could better see the drawing.

"Gwynneth?" He turned to me, his surprise discernible. "You did this, Miss Morys?"

"Aye," Nanny said proudly. "The girl has talent. It's a pretty picture, is it not?"

Mr. Price-Jones continued to look at me. "Yes. There is indeed talent here. I should have asked you to sketch my gardens, also." He looked away for a moment and I thought him confused about something, but then he

233

spoke to his nephew in a jovial tone. "Owen, you did not speak of Miss Morys gift," he said. I somewhat trembled at his choice of words, for it reminded me of Nanny's question to me in another context. *"Do ye have the gift?"*

The two gentlemen were most effusive in their praise for my drawing, and then they rose, stating that it was late and they should take their leave. Owen stayed by the sketch, viewing it and commenting on the technique, and Mr. Charles and Nanny spoke quietly as they moved toward the door. I saw the nurse move her head back and forth as if she were denying something that the gentlemen had said and then, since they now stood in the space from which sound carried, I could hear everything that was said, although I think Nanny must have forgotten the trick this time.

"And what do you think, Mr. Charles? Are ye of the same mind?"

"It had not even occurred to me, ma'am, until Mr. Davies mentioned it. Even then I did not give the notion credit, for I suspect he is suspicious of everyone and anyone right now."

"Aye, that is my belief, too, for I hear from their own staff that there is trouble at Y Pyn. That the creditors are coming by to collect their due and that Mr. and Mrs. are forever putting off the repairs." She folded her hands in front of her so that her shawl lay clumsily across her bony shoulders. "I suspect they worry that they may not be the only ones in line should something happen to the mistress, may the Lord forbid. Looking for trouble where there is none, I think."

Mr. Price-Jones took up his cane. "You may be right, Nanny, for I did notice a kind of hunger when Mr. Davies spoke about this house. I think that because he is looking to eliminate anything that might impede his

234

becoming master of Winter's Light, he plays imaginative games, suspecting everybody of all kinds of ill intentions." His voice was low yet I could still hear him speak. "And about the girl. Of course he is wrong. There is no resemblance whatsoever to . . . How could there be?"

"Aye, none whatsoever, for we both remember that the sweet girl was blonde."

Mr. Price-Jones continued to watch me as he spoke. "Although wasn't there another Glendower who is supposed to have had her coloring? I remember hearing some talk about such a personage."

Nanny shrugged so that the shawl fell crookedly. "I never believed that, Mr. Charles. It was servants' babble. Foolish talk, I think. I never trouble myself with that kind of gossip, sir, for you and I know that there be enough of the regular kind to heap on our plates." I saw Mr. Price-Jones look at me once again and I pretended to be caught up in the book that his nephew was now showing me. "Probably you're right, Nanny. I should know better than to believe Mr. Davies or his chatter. The gentleman is probably too far in debt to think clearly."

"Aye, that's what I think, too." Nanny pulled the shawl so that it righted itself. "And now, Mr. Price-Jones, tell me of how you view Lady Glendower. Haven't you found her changed for the better?" She grinned. "Ye might say that her cousins' visit has had a restorative effect on her, could you not?"

Later, after our guests had departed, the Davies returned to the room where Nanny and I sat in silence, each thinking her own thoughts.

"That gentleman—Mr. Price-Jones," Mr. Davies said to no one in particular, "is the man who should have been brought into this family. A true gentleman. A man

235

who knows his way about. If you want to speak about the girl, then let us both agree that it is a pity she did not marry him. He's done well with his inheritance, too. His nephew, Owen, will receive more than enough to keep him in prosperity's way when he assumes the duties of Cynghanedd."

Mr. Davies eyes grew cold. He glared at Nanny as though to provoke her and I think we all knew that he was now far into his cups.

"The Glendower girl—and our family—would have fared better if she had had the good sense to accept him instead of that tutor."

Nanny paid the man no attention and soon he fell to talking to himself and his wife. Within a half hour they both left our company.

Later, when we were alone and the house had been closed against the cold night air, Nanny was contemplative.

"Stay a while, Gwynneth. Having those two here has made me cantankerous, and you'll soothe me." She picked up the unfinished scarf and seemed about to continue with it, but then thought better of it and replaced it on the table.

"I was with her when she returned, Gwynneth," she said to me, and though I was surprised that she should begin the conversation this way, I did not say anything. "When she returned in disgrace and in love and knowing that that love would be denied her. For although she kept a brave face, I am sure she knew that her marriage could not be. No matter that she played those little games thinking that it would be set right; I think she knew that it was doomed. Her once happy face, the one that we all loved so, was no longer bright and shining, and on the way home from Gretna Green I could see the light leaving her eyes. Mile by mile she turned inward.

236

She returned to Winter's Light with her faith in people in shreds and her love of life gone. She had been such a happy child, Gwynneth. All the world was hers, and her only crime was that she happened to fall in love with Mr. Donne."

Nanny shook her head as she addressed all the guilt in her mind. "I wonder now, in hindsight, if I couldn't see it coming from the first day he came into Winter's Light. He had the kind of face that I knew would appeal to the girl. All open and kind. Nay, I'll never believe that the young man betrayed her or that he was bought off. That's what some said. That Lord Glendower sent his solicitor to pay him a huge sum to leave the girl forever. Nay," she said louder, more to the empty room than to me, "I'll not believe that that gentleman intended to harm her. I know people, Gwynneth, and I have seldom been wrong or deceived. They were two young people in love and their only offense was that Mr. Donne was a poor tutor who had no other means of earning a large income. He wasn't the sort either who would listen to others or who needed to compete. He was a proud man. A very proud man. You could see it in his bearing.

"They did what they had to, Gwynneth, because in their eyes there was nothing else for them to do. No other way to accomplish their own will." She put her gaunt hand up to her mouth as though to cover her lips. As though the gesture would stop her from speaking. But it did not.

"They say she ran away with him and that they never were married but I know different. Fergus knows different, too. We were there. Aye," she said as she took away her hand from her face, "I did not tell you all of the story. I did not tell you that Fergus and I caught up with them right after they were wed. I went and spoke to the minister and he told me that, yes, the ceremony was all legal and proper and done according to the Bible. It were a chapel so the marriage was valid, although I don't know what kind of a God-like man would have married them without her parents' permission or without the banns being said. But either way, Fergus and I swore on our own life's mortal soul that neither of us would ever reveal the fact to the master. We thought that it would just fade away . . . that if we took Lady Anne home and Mr. Donne did not come with us that it would be all right. We were foolish, I know, to think that, but we thought that no one would ever be the wiser and that Lady Anne would always have the knowledge that she had been married. It might have been a sin, but I thought that then the girl could live with that little bit of memory for the rest of her life. We didn't know if she would reveal the fact to her father once we got her home, but then Mr. Donne wanted to come back with us and we knew there was nothing we could do about it. And when Lady Anne heard Mr. Donne's declaration, she went pale and we knew—both of us—that we couldn't do anything then. We would have to tell the master that they were wed and we thought he could just annul the marriage.

"Lord Glendower would never have consented to the union. Would never have given them permission to marry. He was a kind father, Gwynneth, a loving man and family patriarch, but he knew his place and his family's destiny and he would never give it up to someone of low birth. Nay, she was promised to Mr. Charles. She was meant to keep her father's promise, but Mr. Donne brought her love." Nanny smiled in remembrance.

"When the young man had his back to her, I would catch her expression, watching him, and I could see the

238

light in her eyes and the shining on her face and I knew
. . . yes, I knew, though I never said a word to anyone,
for I thought that Anne needed her bit of love if only
for a few days or weeks. 'Tweren't fair for her not to
have a chance at it, even though I knew in the end it
would have to be taken away. But oh, that love that was
there," she said and her voice rose to a feverish pitch,
"that love, Gwynneth, was real and genuine and spirited,
and you remember that, my girl. You remember that
and you can be proud that you knew that." Nanny
stilled and I thought she had fallen asleep in her chair
but she opened her eyes once more. "That love were true
love, Gwynneth, and my heart ached for the two young
lovers. My heart ached for them all the time. It still
does." She stood up. "Ah well, that were long ago. Long
ago."

The room seemed to have grown chilly, and although
I shivered when I moved away from the fireplace, I
realized it was not just the cold air in the room that
made me uncomfortable. I could feel the nearness of
malevolence, which had now made its way into the
sitting room. Yes, the malice that I had continued to
sense had finally crept into all the rooms of the estate. I
did not know whether the presence of the Davies had
exacerbated the situation, but I knew with certainty that
there was truly something sinister at work at Winter's
Light. Something evil was dominant, and now had overtaken the only room where I had previously felt truly
safe. I could not guess at whom this hatred was directed, but the fear abided in me that somehow I was
now caught up in the horror.

Chapter Nineteen

I was awakened one morning long before sunrise to the sound of bells. I heard the strong, distinct, rhythmical, tones pealing continuously as the clappers hit the heavy iron and I thought it a call for help. The sound seemed to radiate out from the chapel as though the entire country-side should hear the alarm, but when I put on my woolen wrapper and ran to the window to determine the occasion for the ringing I saw that everything remained dark and still. There were no lamps lit in the far cottages on the grounds nor was there any unusual activity in the house. Winter's Light remained at rest, the courtyard empty of everyone, although I had expected to look down on the bustling of the half-aroused estate staff congregating in the courtyard, milling about trying to find out why the bells had been tolled.

The carillons pealed once more—in a rush, it seemed as though there had been a dozen frantic tugs of the ropes—and I waited, hoping to see the lamps being lit in silent rooms, but all remained dark, the inhabitants of the small cottages on the estate still blissfully sleeping the chilly night away.

The bells continued to clang for a few more moments and then they abruptly stopped and all was still and when I turned back into my room only a dim echo of the tolling remained in my mind. Although it seemed that there had been no reason for the alert, I could not fathom why no one else had been roused by it.

I could not sleep anymore. The ringing that had awakened me now totally occupied my mind, and I lay in bed for the next hour trying to puzzle out the mystery, but there seemed to be no explanation for the gongs. I was now fully awake and preoccupied with the riddle, and by the time the first pale streaks of light of the new morning appeared in the dark sky, I had been up and dressed for fully an hour.

I was not able to speak to Nanny about the early dawn bell ringing, for there was a small controversy involving the Davies that morning, Mr. Davies demanding that they be allowed to consult with Lady Glendower's physician and Nanny stoutly defending her mistress. It was all done in hushed tones, and Lady Glendower herself was unaware of the altercation. Mrs. Hoskins, as usual, won out, but Mr. Davies returned to his own quarters still vowing to have his way. By the end of the disturbance I had already forgotten about the bells, and I did not remember them until I was on a short walk about the grounds and looked up and saw the chapel directly ahead of me.

"It be a right cold day, miss." Fergus was leading a beautiful, large, black horse toward me. "Days are getting shorter now. We'll be into the full winter season in a week or so."

"Mr. Fergus, a moment please, if you will."

"Aye, miss." The old stableman stopped beside me and rubbed his gloved hands. "You need something, ma'am?"

"An explanation, if you please, for I can not understand it. About the bells. About the reason why they were rung this morning."

"The chapel bells, miss?" He gave me a puzzled look. "The bells did not ring last night, Miss Morys," he said. "They were silent as usual. They haven't rung in sixteen years."

"But I heard them," I persisted and Fergus slowly shook his head, denying what I knew I had heard. "Surely you

241

heard them, too. Surely last night . . ." But Fergus continued to shake his thinning, white hair.

"Begging your pardon, ma'am, but you must have dreamed it. The bells have not rung since the young Lady Anne died, miss. Since the day of her funeral when they tolled for all to attend chapel and bid the little lady her peace in eternity. They tolled throughout the service and that was the last sound any of us ever heard from them, miss. They were ordered silent after that by Lady Glendower. The good woman could not stand to be reminded of her loss." He put his hand to his forehead and shielded his eyes as he looked up at the parapet at the top of the chapel. "I'm positive you know about her by now, ma'am. About Lady Anne?" I nodded, for I was sure Nanny had already discussed some part of our conversation with him.

Fergus continued and I could see the steamy breath of the horse as it snorted in the cold air. "The bells needn't have been rung for her that day, for all of us just naturally drifted into chapel that morning—summoning or not, we all were there. It were really all our loss, miss, for we all loved her. We watched her as she grew . . . remembered the night she was birthed." He smiled and I recalled what Nanny had told me of the rejoicing that evening.

"She was a quiet one, Miss Anne was. Liked playing with her dolls and her toys. Didn't have many friends, though. Hereabouts there weren't too many young ones and so she more or less became the countryside favorite. Nanny used to take her for long walks near the moors and the seas." He laughed and then bit the stem of his pipe. "Nanny were much spryer then, and the child would run ahead and laugh and tease. But when Nanny called to her to stop—for she knows the dangers of the bogs and the cliffs as well as we all do—the young mistress would halt just like a soldier on command and wait for Nanny." He shook his head once more. "Aye, real obedient girl she was. Only time she ever disobeyed . . ." he began, then cut himself off and mused silently, forgetting that I stood there.

"Ah well, it were a long time ago, ma'am, and there be no sense to bring it up now." He tapped his pipe against his mud-caked boot. "No sense to go over it again and again, miss. It don't do nothing to bring it 'round to another end." He bent down and picked up a small clod of dirt from that surrounding a young evergreen sapling. "Yes, ma'am, you nourish it, give it attention, give it care, and still with all the nurturing and concern you never know how it will all grow to maturity." He tapped the ball of earth around the base of the tree so that it fell scattered upon the ground. "And despite everything there are all the other parts of nature that sometimes work against you." He patted the sapling's thin trunk and shook his head and I knew that he was talking about more than the growing and tending of the forests.

"Ah well," he said, taking hold of the horse's reins once more. Now I'd best be going." He tipped his cap in my direction. "Nature," he said once more. He moved off, leaving me to still wonder why I seemed to be the only one who had heard the bells.

Late that afternoon Nanny and I stood at the window watching as the gardeners tidied up the grounds, clipping back bushes and applying heavy mulch to the beds so that the plants would pass the winter without harm.

" 'Tis almost the time when no one will go about, Gwynneth. It's a time that makes me sad. But," she glanced at Lady Glendower, who was sleeping, "the mistress keeps making strides, and Dr. Lawrence tells me that by the beginning of the year she'll be up and around. With no thanks to the Davies, either," she said, and I heard the vehemence in her voice.

"Then it will be a good holiday this year, Nanny."

"Aye." She closed the curtains and turned to me. "I see by your darkened eyes that something is bothering you. Will you tell me about it?"

"Yes," I said, for I wanted her opinion about the ringing of the bells. I told her what I had heard this morning. After

243

I had finished, Nanny bit her lip and gazed at me.

"Ye do have it, don't you, my dear?" she said, addressing the issue of the bells and all the other things that had haunted me throughout my lifetime. "The gift. Ye have it, don't you, Gwynneth?" she asked, and this time I recognized that there was sympathy and understanding in her voice and I finally nodded, still afraid to speak of that which I had come to accept as my peculiarity. And yet, looking at Nanny and her kind countenance as she asked me pertinent questions, I knew I was finally relieved of the burden. For no one—not even my parents—had tried to probe me further after the incident of the doll I had named Lucy. No one in my entire life had ever asked me to tell them of my most secret thoughts.

"Ye can tell me, Gwynneth. Ye can truly trust me," Nanny said, and somehow I knew that I could and that I would not be laughed at or scorned or told that I was foolish. Somehow I knew that Nanny had always suspected this secret about me. No, it was more than suspicion—I felt she had always known it to be there, but I did not know how she knew or why.

"Yes, I believe you, Nanny," I said, and I began to tell her of just a few incidents here at Winter's Light that had unsettled me.

Nanny listened as I related to her some of the things I had heard or envisioned that I thought could not possibly have been real. I told her of the music I had heard coming from the ballroom the first time I explored the premises and she said nothing; I told her of the scene that kept playing in my mind of that same room, where I saw Anne dancing with Mr. Price-Jones and she did not seem alarmed at my story.

"Aye," she said quietly when I described the girl's gown and the lilting music. "That was correct. That was the dress she wore," she said and I, now fully encouraged and relieved, then told her of the fragments of what I believed had been the young girl's elopement. Nanny still did not seem surprised and instead only nodded her head again. "Aye, that was her cape and her young man." She listened carefully to all I said, waiting until I had finished telling of just the few visions. I did not tell her that I had been witnessing Anne's death in my dreams, for to tell her that part of the story would have been too cruel. Instead I spoke of the voices I thought I had heard when stranded on the moors, and the sound of laughter when I had been with Mr. Owen at the edge of the sea.

"Did you recognize anyone?"

"No. It was too muddled."

"Perhaps another time. Listen—just in case," she said, and I knew that something else was in her mind. I would have liked to speak longer but she glanced up at the wooden clock that sat on the table in the room. "It's time to prepare the mistress's supper, Gwynneth, and then we'll be dining with Mr. Charles and Mr. Owen . . . and the Davies," she added in an unkind voice. "Afterwards, after our guests have all gone, we'll speak some more of this, if you are of a mind to. Until then," she said kindly, "I think it best that it still be your own mystery. I'd not be speaking about any of this to anyone else if I were you. Ye be careful, girl," she cautioned me. "There are folks here who are up to no good. Here to cause trouble." She spoke to me not only in warning but as though she possessed a full understanding of all that I said, and I wondered if she had ever known anyone like me, or indeed, if she too, had a bent for seeing into another realm. I wanted to question her about this, but she had closed the conversation for now.

"Yes, we will talk more later." At last I would be able to share what had bothered me for so long.

The six of us dined, not uncordially, and when the meal was concluded everyone but I visited with Lady Glendower. I stayed behind, for it was not my place to be included amongst those who were family and close friends. I excused myself on the plea that I needed to do some mending, and Mr. Charles and Mr. Owen accepted the reason, although they did protest, in keeping with their polite behavior, for a few seconds. Mr. and Mrs. Davies, on the other hand, were relieved at my suggestion that I be excluded from the group.

"At least," I heard Mr. Davies say to the elder Mr. Price-Jones, "the girl has the good sense to absent herself when we are with my cousin." He bent his head toward Mrs. Hoskins. "There are some who do not belong," he said, and if Nanny understood that she was also included in this summation, she paid little attention to his remarks.

I busied myself in the sitting room, mending the buttons on a tunic of mine and happy that Nanny and I were to talk further about what she called my "gift." It was pleasant in the warm room and I was pleased to think that now I had found an ally at Winter's Light. I was starting to feel less cautious of my surroundings and the people here, and suddenly I realized I had begun to hum the tune that had plagued me much of my childhood. Softly to myself I kept repeating the notes so that I could remember them and repeat them to Nanny. I was so engrossed with this project that the time passed quickly, and it seemed only a short while before the others returned to the parlor saying that their combined audience with Lady Glendower had seemed to tire her rather quickly.

I saw Mr. Davies signal Mr. Price-Jones to meet with him in the back of the room, and they stood together in the corner where the architectural flaw made the sound travel so that all of us — Mrs. Davies, Mr. Owen, Nanny and I — were able to overhear their conversation.

"Does my cousin seem too frail to you, sir? Too incapacitated to take care of her own affairs?" I blushed at the man's first comments and I realized it was much too late for any of us to avoid hearing the rest of the words. I did not detect concern in Mr. Davies voice, but rather, anticipation. Mr. Davies was apparently intent on soliciting an affirmative reply from Mr. Price-Jones.

Mr. Charles answered immediately. "I do not think so,

Mr. Davies. In truth, I think she is becoming quite well. We do not find her incapacitated at all." Mr. Price-Jones's voice was even, yet I felt sure that every one of us could discern his tension and annoyance at the design of the query as he rejected the cousin's suggestion. "I am told, by both Mrs. Hoskins and Dr. Lawrence that, thankfully, your cousin will be well enough to join in some of the holiday festivities. In fact, Dr. Lawrence has led us to believe that, by some miracle or design, she has regained the will to live and shows remarkable progress." He clasped the other gentleman around the shoulders. "I am sure you will be relieved to learn of this, sir," he said and then made a slight bow to his companion. "And now that your mind has been placed at ease, let us join the others."

I kept my head down during the entire exchange, for I was embarrassed at having the secret of the room discovered. When the conversation was concluded between the two men, I raised my head and I could see that Mrs. Davies, to her credit, had also looked away from the rest of us. Mr. Owen stood gazing first at the two men, and then at Nanny and me, and I saw an incredulous look upon his face although I did not know whether it was because of the talk between the two men or because he had now detected the room's defect. Nanny, for her part, had a mischievous look upon her face as though it had all been a bit of fun for which she had been personally responsible. I knew that nothing would be said to the two men for now, but that later that evening both of the gentleman would be told what had transpired.

When Nanny had offered refreshment — port for the gentlemen and tea for the ladies — we all carried on in the same light vein that we had pretended existed in the dining room. Mr. Charles seemed perplexed at one point and finally, it appeared that he had recalled something. He put down his crystal goblet and turned to me.

"That tune, ma'am — the one that you were humming when we entered this room — what is it? I seem to recall

247

some other melody much like it." Mr. Price-Jones looked at me peculiarly and the others stopped to listen so that I felt as though I had been placed at the center of attention.

The notes now seemed to echo loudly throughout my mind and I shook my head, distressed to have been caught singing the tune.

"It is of no consequence, sir. And I cannot tell you what it is, Mr. Price-Jones, for I truly do not know. I have been told that it is something I have hummed ever since I was a babe. My parents used to tease that I had been born knowing the notes." I felt my face burn, and I hoped that he would take it that I was too near to the fireplace. "It does not mean anything significant." I looked at him. "Why do you ask, sir? Is it something you recognize or have heard someone else sing?"

Mr. Price-Jones stared at me and I saw a flicker of alertness streak across his brow as though he were trying to recall something, and then it seemed that there was another look on his face—this one filled with trouble—but it, too, lasted for just an instant.

"No. I thought I did, Miss Morys, but I am sure now it was not the same melody. It could not be." He swirled the liquid in his goblet so that the wine made red bands on the inside of the glass. "Sometimes memory plays tricks on us, as I am sure you know, ma'am, and what we seem to hear or see is not what we really hear or see." He smiled and sipped at his port and again I marvelled at his distinguished facial features. "It is as though life were made up of little tricks such as those, is it not so?" He put down his glass and concentrated on it as though to bring to mind the melody. "And yet I remember an old tune, somewhat similiar, that someone long ago once sung." He looked at me and shook his head. "But I am sure the music cannot be the same."

"It is strange, is it not," Mr. Davies said as he finished the last of his wine and reached for the decanter on the silver tray, "that I also thought I had heard the tune?" He glanced first at me and then at Mr. Price-Jones. "I wonder, sir, if we are both thinking of the same song. An obscure melody by a minor composer, perhaps? One that Miss Morys might have heard in a chapel service?"

"No, I beg your pardon, but I think both you gentleman are mistaken. As I said, it is just something that my parents told me I had invented when I was a child. In all likelihood it is an old shepherd's tune." The five notes seemed to be playing louder and shriller in my head and it was as though everyone in the room should hear their progression. "It is one of those things that haunts you," I said and tried to laugh. "It has no significance, sirs. None at all." I did not know whether I had convinced the two of my words, and the tune was now playing so strongly within my mind that I was sure all of them could have heard it had they moved closer to me and listened.

"I remember now." Mr. Price-Jones jumped up and smiled at me and I could see that he was no longer puzzled. "That tune. It was the same one that you sang the day that we rescued you from the moors." He turned toward his nephew. "Do you not remember it, Owen?"

"I only remember that it was a frightening experience for Miss Morys, Uncle Charles, and that we were both intent on leading her out."

I turned to the Davies, happy to speak of something other than the melody that might take up their attention.

"I am afraid I was foolish one afternoon and carelessly ventured too far into the moors."

Mrs. Davies took a deep breath. "I have always been afraid of them," she said, to no one in particular.

"Miss Morys was very brave that day. She did not cry out in fear nor did she panic," Mr. Owen Price-Jones said, and again I blushed at his effusiveness. I wondered if Mr. Davies knew the area. I asked, and it was one of the few times that the gentleman had a civil answer for me. I suspect this was only because he was now able to demonstrate his knowledge of the estate.

"Know the moors? My dear Miss Morys, the bogs are like part of my own land," he said, and I heard Nanny sniff at the words. "I know them better than I know my own woods at Y Pyn. Lord Glendower, my late cousin, used to take me near them to point out the new land that had been claimed by the quicksand." His wife shivered again and he turned to her. "My dear, why is it that you don't even like speaking about the moors?"

"They frighten me, Mr. Davies, as you well know. They are so dark and terrifying. Anyone can get caught there. Anyone can die there. Why you yourself told me that a skeleton of a man was found there several years ago. I think it foolhardy for anyone to explore beyond the boundaries."

Mr. Davies took another sip of his wine. "Nonsense. The moors offer no harm if you know the territory and the lie of the land." He turned to the senior Mr. Price-Jones. "Isn't that so, Charles? Aren't the moors easily managed once you get to know them?"

Mr. Price-Jones nodded his head. "But we must recognize, sir, that what Mrs. Davies says is correct. It is best for those who do not know the marshland to avoid it."

"Or to get a good guide." Mr. Davies laughed and again I felt chilled.

Mr. Price-Jones pushed away his goblet and beckoned to his nephew.

"Again, Owen, I think we impose too much on the good graces of these people. It is getting late and we must leave."

Mr. Owen Price-Jones came close and spoke only to me. "May we perhaps go riding once more before the weather turns too bitter?" he asked. I smiled at him and he took it as an agreement. "Good. I will be in touch with you, ma'am." Both nephew and uncle bowed to all of us.

"By the way, Miss Morys," Mr. Charles said to me in parting, "please tell me if you ever recall where you first heard that tune." Even though he tried to disguise his interest, I knew that he was curious. He turned back to look at Nanny. "I wonder if you, by chance, have ever hummed that air in Lady Glendower's presence. Or Nanny's?" he asked, gazing at Mrs. Hoskins, and I thought his eyes secretly queried her. The old nurse said nothing, but instead looked at me with wide, straightforward eyes, and I remembered her admonition that I was not to tell anyone of the strange phenomena that occurred to me.

"Yes. It would be interesting." Mr. Davies leaned forward on his chair as though waiting for the answers to Mr. Price-Jones's inquiries, but I said nothing, as I now thought I truly understood the reason for Nanny's caution. It would be all too easy for Mr. and Mrs. Davies to suspect me of some plot against the Glendower family. I shuddered. I knew that the Davies would not hesitate to have me sent back in disgrace to Daear.

I waited while the Price-Joneses and then the Davies made their farewells, all the time wondering why the five mysterious notes seemed to push at the interior of my head so that their rhythm made it physically throb. I shuddered again and I wished I were closer to the fire, for it had grown very cold in the apartment. But I knew that no matter how roaring the heat, it could not fend off the evil feelings that were now quite abundant in this room. I was dismayed, and again I knew that this sitting room was no longer my safe haven.

Nanny had stayed behind in the parlor and was busying herself with the candles on the tables.

"That tune, Gwynneth," she said immediately after the guests had departed, "ye say you have always sung it?"

"Yes, Nanny, but it is only a piece of foolishness. Something that I made up to ward off the . . ." I wondered if it would sound silly were I to tell her about how I had used the music whenever afraid and anxious.

"To ward off what, Gwynneth?" The nurse had now moved closer to me and I was sure she heard the tune, too.

I stared into the fire, watching as the flames glowed blue and orange. "To ward off the fright," I said.

"And did it?" The old woman's eyes turned into narrow

lines. "And did it, Gwynneth?"

"Yes."

Nanny bobbed her head up and down as though she were pleased with the answer. "Tell me what happens when you hum the tune." She moved her hands around and about as though they were little birds in flight. "Tell me all."

We spoke for more than an hour, neither of us paying much attention to the chimes from the clock in the Great Hall. I was relieved that I could confide to someone what I heard and Nanny, fascinated and believing, encouraged me to tell her everything.

I returned to the mystery of the voices on the moors, for all the questioning by Mr. Davies and Mr. Price-Jones had brought it to the surface of my mind.

"When I was trapped in the bogs, Nanny, I know I heard the voices of two men. I told you I did not recognize them, but I could tell that there was confusion. One of them seemed unfamiliar with the land. His partner kept urging him forward and I thought he was leading him through the swamps."

"You say you thought he was? What else might he have been doing?"

I hesitated. The scene was not quite set in my mind. "I don't know." I looked down at my hands and saw them tremble, for this was the first time I had delved into the unknown with any witnesses present, then suddenly another picture came into my mind. "I keep seeing one man stranded, Nanny. A young man that I do not know but he appears to be frightened." I closed my eyes and yet I saw the man touching the bare limbs of some of the dead trees that surrounded him. He was looking around and I heard him call out, *Wait for me. Wait for me.* I repeated the words to Nanny, who sat still, the rocker now stopped so that there was no sound in the room except the shifting of the burning logs in the fireplace.

"Go on, girl," the nurse kept encouraging. "Try to bring it all to your mind. Try to find out who the gentlemen were

252

out there in the mire."

"I see . . . No," I shook my head, "it is a bit blurry. Sometimes it frightens me to have these ideas," I said. Nanny continued to urge me and so I concentrated once more on the landscape in my mind, and yet I could not distinguish the features of the two men. "I'm sorry, but I cannot quite make out the faces or the voices." I folded my hands and placed them on the table and then was panicked at something that occurred to me. "Nanny, could one of them have been Mr. Davies? Is he so enamored of this house and estate that he is capable of such trickery?"

"Aye, he is." She frowned. "But what made ye think of him?"

"I don't know. I keep hearing the voices and I know that one gentleman has deceived another." The view seemed to fade so that only very faintly could I detect one man as he walked further astray into the deepest part of the moors.

I swallowed hard and asked the question although I was certain of the answer. "Nanny, could the bones that were found so many years ago be those of Mr. Donne? Could someone — Mr. Davies, perhaps, or someone else — have led him purposely into the bogs?" My whole body began to tremble with the suggestion that I was submitting to the woman. "Could someone have purposely set out to harm him? To murder him?"

I watched in horror as Nanny slowly began to nod her head. "One of the answers I know, and the other is what I have thought for a long time, Gwynneth," she said softly. She pushed my cold cup of tea toward me. "Drink something, girl, while I tell you what I know about the skeleton."

She touched the wood of the arms of her rocker. "I have always known that the bones were those of Mr. Donne," she said, and I marvelled at her low, modulated voice as she revealed this information to me. "At first when they told me they had found the skeleton of an unknown, unidentified person who had died in the bogs, I did not suppose that it was Mr. Donne. For all the unhappiness was now past us. Anne was dead a year, her babe gone, too, and Lord and Lady Glendower had never spoken afterwards of the girl or the tragedy. To all outsiders the matter was closed, but of course, I knew that it wasn't—that the master and mistress were still heartsick.

"So when a year later we found a body—or the remains of a body, for there wasn't anything there but some old bones and part of the clothes of a man—we all were sorry that it had happened but we truly thought that it was a stranger who had wandered unknowingly onto the marshland. It was a sadness, of course, but nothing that really touched us at Winter's Light.

"Then a few days later the Reverend Walker came to see us, for he had been charged by Lord Glendower to prepare the body for a right proper funeral. Reverend Walker came in that day and I could see that he was hesitant, as though he wasn't quite sure about what he had to say. The master and mistress were sitting in the parlor with him, having high tea, and I was there just to be attentive to him, and then he reached into his pocket and pulled out some torn shreds of faded paper and handed them to the master. 'I think you best see these,' he said, and Lord Glendower took the bits and scraps and looked hard at them and then I saw his face turn pale and he looked away. I could almost swear that there were tears in his eyes.

"Well, Lady Glendower saw that her husband was troubled. 'What is it?' she asked him several times and finally he held the papers out to her, but he didn't give them to her. 'It's part of a note addressed to Anne,' he said, and Lady Glendower screamed at the mention of her dead child's name." Nanny ran her pink tongue over her lips. "Reverend Walker then said that it was clear from the scraps of the note that the bones were those of Mr. Donne. It seemed, the minister said, that the tutor was coming back for his lady but got lost in the bogs and couldn't find his way to her. He evidently had written the note on draw-

254

ing paper as a last tribute to his wife. He didn't even know that she was going to have his child. There was some sort of a mention of someone who had led him into the moors, but where the tutor had written the name, the paper had frayed and muddied so that there was no making it out." Nanny wiped at a tear and the rocking resumed at a quick pace.

"Lord Glendower directed the reverend not to say what he knew, but he asked him to say the prayers for him in a chapel service and then we buried the tutor in our small cemetery. Only the master and mistress and the reverend and I knew the identity of the corpse, and we were all pledged to secrecy." She pushed at the floor with her feet so that the chair moved faster.

"Ah, Gwynneth, it was such a shame. All that pain and hurt and then the poor girl so out of her mind what with thinking that her man wasn't going to come for her. And there he was all the time lying dead in the moors. If we had only known. If we had only known, then we could have comforted the poor lass and she wouldn't have had to die. She would have had the strength and the will to continue what with knowing she wasn't abandoned." Her voice now cracked. "All that pain for everyone." She put her foot on the floor to stop the rocking chair from moving. "Ah well. Ah well, them days are over now."

I could not sleep this evening, for too many thoughts were now crowding my mind. Too many pieces were quickly falling into a puzzle that I had not recognized earlier on. So Anne's young husband had come back for her after all, had kept his promise to his bride. But why was he found in the bogs? And now that I was sure that there were two men on the misty moors, who was the second man who had led the tutor on his death walk? Surely someone had betrayed him. But why?

I sat up in bed, my blanket wrapped around me, for it was very cold in the room. The fire had burnt itself out in the grate so that the bed of ashes held only an occasional flickering ember, and I debated whether I should try to rekindle a small flame in order to warm myself. I knew that this was to be a long night—that no restful sleep would come to me for a while. There were too many things on my mind now. Too many parts of the enigma were still missing. Most of all, I had to know what message was in this for me. Why should the events that happened long ago at Winter's Light concern me so?

I moved quickly to the fireplace and put a few more faggots on the iron grate, then stirred up the still warm, grey, powdery ashes so that the twigs flared once more into a fire. I could not help but remark to myself that that was exactly what I was doing with my mind. Perhaps if I stirred up enough ashes of the past I would be able to discover the secrets of Winter's Light.

Chapter Twenty

All day long the clouds had hung dark and heavy in the sky, and the candles had had to be lit early in order to provide some light in the house. With an air of anticipation of the winter's first significant snowfall, the servants chatted companionably and cheerfully amongst themselves while they moved briskly about their chores. Throughout the morning workmen had labored both inside and outside the house to secure the estate against what everyone knew would be a heavy storm. Logs had been set in all the fireplaces, and in those rooms which were occupied, huge blazes of blue and orange flames crackled. The sound was reassuring to those few who were dismayed at the inclement weather.

Nanny busied herself in Lady Glendower's chambers, taking out heavier blankets from drawers and closets and seeing to it that the windows in the rooms were safeguarded against the cold winds which whistled through the small openings at the corners of the panes. "Mr. Charles and Mr. Owen sent word that they'll be coming over this afternoon instead of the evening," she said to Lady Glendower. "They don't want to be caught in the bad weather." The nurse nodded to me. "This will be your first winter season with us, Gwynneth. You'll soon know what bitterness it can be here." She shuddered in dread of the weather. "It seems the longer I live, the longer the cold

257

season stays with us," she said, to no one in particular, and then folded her hands in a simple beseeching gesture. "Aye, you'll be waiting and praying for spring to come round soon, you will."

I was disappointed that the weather had turned so quickly this morning. "I had hoped to take Empress for one last ride," I said, for already I was beginning to feel depressed about what was to come. If Nanny were correct this would probably be my last chance to ride until the stormy weather had passed.

Nanny heard my frustration and peered out the window at the grey skies. "There be a few more hours before it turns completely dark. If you hurry, girl, you'll be able to take that ride and be back before both the snows and the gentlemen come." She held up her hands. "But mind you, don't ride too far, for you don't want to be trapped anywhere where we can't get to ye."

Fergus again warned me as he was saddling up Empress in the stable. "Now, miss, only a short canter about the grounds. And stick to the known areas. I've seen times when the ground was clear one minute and covered with snow the next so that even experienced people lost their way." He helped me onto the horse's broad back.

"I shall not be longer than a half hour all told, Fergus." I looked at the darkening sky. "You'll not have to come after me," I said as I rode off for a short gallop around the gardens. Surely I could not lose my way such a slight distance from the house.

Although it was blustery and the wind was cold, the ride was exhilarating and I rode further than I had anticipated so that by the time I realized it, I had ridden close to the estate chapel. I could see the balcony around its top—the exact spot where I kept seeing Anne plunge—and to ease my mind about it, I decided to explore the structure despite the threatening weather. I tethered Empress to a tree close by, promising her that I would be only gone a few minutes, and went to the huge, weathered, wooden front door of the stone building. I pulled at it and it gave way easily. It was dark and chilled inside the main room and, although it was silent and abandoned, a feeling crept over me which warned that inside the nave I would come upon a scene of great sadness. I moved down the deserted aisle and as I did so it seemed I had stepped into another age. The room was no longer deserted, for now I could see shadowy people dressed in somber clothes sitting in the straight, wooden pews, attending to the service and listening to the Reverend Walker as he preached his sermon.

I walked further into the dim room, hearing the echo of my boots as they trod on the stone floors, and still I did not flinch at the darkness. I seemed to have no control over my own motions, it was as if I were being compelled by someone or something to walk through that room where the ghostly figures sat hunched over their hymnals. I heard a choir from the loft and a sobering hymn and then just as sharply I heard once again the slow, deliberate tolling of the bells.

I edged my way further into the chapel and it was as if I now oversaw the entire setting. I could see Lady Glendower and a gentleman whom I knew instantly was her husband sitting in the first pew. They both wore plain, black clothing—mourning dress, I knew. Seated right behind them, in a place of honor, I saw another woman, and I knew that this was a younger Nanny although I could not see her features, which were entirely concealed by a heavy black veil.

I heard the sounds of sobbing while all the while the pealing of the bells became louder and clearer and as I walked down the aisle, past the grieving people, I wondered that they did not pay attention to the carillon. No one seemed to notice me, and I realized that for them I did not exist, that I was an unseen spectator at this unhappy event. Somehow I had intruded upon another era, and now I was witnessing the mournful service of the dead, which had been performed for the Lady Anne some sixteen years before.

I was able to pick out the faces of some of the older household staff — Fergus, Mrs. Padley and a few of the gardeners and stablemen — sitting in their accustomed places in the church. On the other side of the aisle there was a solitary man — Mr. Charles Price-Jones — who sat stoic and alone in his dark suit, a black satin armband fastened around the upper sleeve of his coat.

In front of the altar several small bouquets of golden roses covered what I was sure was Anne's plain, wooden coffin, and for a moment I thought I could smell the sweet scent of the soft yellow flowers.

I marvelled at my own calmness. I was neither frightened nor bewildered for although I could not explain it, it seemed my destiny to view the scene.

I felt a dryness in my throat and I moved away from the musty main room toward the spiral staircase that led up past the choir loft to the bell tower. It was as if I had to prove to myself that the large, iron bells were unquestionably silent, to affirm that I was only hearing the echoes of yesteryear.

I moved cautiously, for it was now very dark on the stairs. I had no candle to guide my way but as I passed the loft I could see, up above me, a small window that allowed some of the dingy, dusky light into the chapel. I progressed slowly. The steps were of well-worn stone and I did not want to risk a fall here where no one would find me.

I finally reached the window at the top of the steps and stood looking out of it, adjusting my eyesight to the partial light before continuing further up to the bell tower. I could still hear the methodical chimings and I suddenly felt very cold — colder than was necessary because of the winter weather. It was as though a spectral chill had run through me and I shivered and for the first time this afternoon wondered if I should abandon my goal to climb to the bell tower. I could always wait for a warmer day, I reasoned, but still something seemed to drive me forward up the winding steps.

I moved away from the window, for there was a force emanating through it . . . as though something unseen had been flung or hurled from it. A dizzying compulsion guided me toward the tower . . . toward the last few steps that led to it. I wanted to cry out in fear that I knew not what was compelling me, taking over my body, and now suddenly thwarting my original intent. The force pushed me toward an alcove carved into the wall near the steps, setting me back into it much as one would set a stone statue or vase into the niche. I flailed and yet I was power-less to struggle against the strength of its constraints. Sud-denly I heard another sound—human footsteps from below—and although my first impulse was to cry out for help, somehow the invisible force whirled about me, si-lencing my mouth and holding me flat against the stone walls so that I was completely concealed from view.

I heard the footsteps start up the curving steps toward me, then, inexplicably, they stopped, and somehow I knew I had to be quiet and shield myself lest I be discovered. I knew I should not scream or identify myself, for some-thing either in my mind or beyond—was at me, telling me that I should stay silent and close-mouthed. I took a deep breath and in the silence of the next minutes I waited, hoping that whoever was here would soon abandon the chapel. I know not why I did not reveal myself or why I was afraid of someone who was surely mortal, and yet when I finally heard the footsteps retreat, I felt as though I had passed a great crisis. I heard the door open and close against the stone floor and I waited still a few more moments until I was sure that all was clear. Then, slowly and carefully, I made my way down the stairs, past the choir loft where the ghostly men and women sang a mute hymn, and then finally out through the door that led onto the frozen lawns surrounding the chapel, where I knew I would be safe.

It was all as I had left it moments before; Empress was still tethered to the tree, but in the distance I could hear the sound of hoofbeats—as though someone were riding away from the area.

"Miss, miss," Fergus's voice came from around the building.

"Here, sir." I breathed a sigh of relief when I saw the stableman bundled into his worn, dark, heavy coat.

"I think, miss," he said gently when he saw me, "that it's time you were coming back." He looked up at the skies just as the first few flakes began to fall from the clouds. "It's coming soon, miss. It'll be a good one."

I did not know how long the stablemaster had been in the vicinity, but I knew that whoever had been on the chapel steps a few moments ago must have been scared off by the old worker. But it was a mystery to me why I should have feared anyone here at Winter's Light and why I should have felt that I had been protected from that mysterious hunter. Again I knew not the answers or the reasons, nor could I guess at them.

I looked toward the house. "Was anyone else with you, Fergus?"

"No, miss. Everyone else has gone inside. I just came to get you before it grows too dark." He took up Empress's lead and both of us rode back to the house together.

I did not tell Nanny of the footsteps I had heard at the chapel or about the unearthly feelings I had experienced there, and all through dinner with the Price-Joneses and the Davies I tried to keep up my end of the conversation, although sometimes I could not help but look at Mr. Davies too long. I wondered if it were he who had stalked me and, if so, for what purpose.

"Miss Morys?" I heard Mr. Owen Price-Jones call out my name and I realized that because I had been daydreaming, I had missed a cue in the conversation.

"I do beg your pardon, sir. My mind was in another place."

262

"No matter," he said, smiling at me. "Mr. and Mrs. Davies have just asked to be excused, for it seems they are tired this afternoon." He turned to his uncle. "It is we who should be tired, uncle. It was a cold journey here today."

I looked at Mr. Davies. "Have you ventured out today, sir?"

The cousin closed his eyes briefly. "Only for a quick breath of air. Sometimes I find the rooms here in the house too warm—too many fires blazing." He stood up and signalled to his wife. "Come, Mrs. Davies, we have matters to attend to this afternoon." He took his wife's arm and led her out of the room.

"I think the cousins are not happy with the situation," Mr. Charles Price-Jones said. "I fear the cold weather is not to their liking." He glanced out the window and we could all see that the snow had begun to fall in earnest, for huge, fat flakes were tumbling past the panes.

"I think I should go up and pay my respects to Lady Glendower immediately," he said. "Owen, I know you were up to see our hostess while I was down warming myself, so Nanny and I will leave you two young people for a few moments." He bowed to me. *"Your servant, ma'am,"* he said and I nodded as he left the table. Again the words resounded somewhere in my mind.

Mr. Owen waited a moment until the other two had gone.

"You seemed not be intent on the talk this afternoon, Miss Morys. Is there something disturbing you?"

I took a deep breath, for I did not know whether the gentleman would think me foolish if I were to reveal my afternoon's adventure.

"If I were to tell you that I had been stalked this afternoon, sir, would you believe me?"

Mr. Owen jumped up from his chair and came close to me, then took my hands in his own. "Good heavens, Miss Morys, what is it that you say? Stalked? By whom?"

"I don't know, sir," I said. I proceeded to tell him most

263

of the story, although I did not mention having seen the ghostly recreation of Anne's funeral service or speak of the unreal feeling that had seemed to protect me.

He listened until my recitation was complete. "Surely I believe you, ma'am, but it is all too confusing. Why should someone terrorize you? And with what intent?"

"That is something I do not know and which frightens me. But Mr. Price-Jones, now that this has happened I feel that I must investigate the tower further. Please," I said and held up my hand before he had another chance to speak, "please do not ask me why I must, for in truth I cannot give you a logical explanation. I only know that I must go there—must prove something to myself."

Mr. Price-Jones tightened his hands about mine. "My dear Miss Morys, I cannot let you go alone now that you have told me of this occurrence. Tell me, please, when you intend to go, and I will make myself available to you as an escort. I know that I cannot dissuade you, ma'am, for your eyes reveal your resolve." He looked closely at me and I knew my face had reddened.

"The day after the snow stops. That's when I'll go to the chapel," I said. "I do thank you for your offer and I will most gladly accept it, sir, for I do need the company."

"Will you wait for me then? You promise you will not go without me?"

"Yes," I said.

"Good." He glanced into the hall and saw Nanny and his uncle returning to the dining room.

"Well, Owen, the day is already very dark outside. We must hurry if we are to make it back to Cynghanedd before the full brunt of the storm hits us." The two gentlemen made their good-byes to Nanny and me and we watched through the side windows, safe behind the closed door, as, within moments, the two disappeared into the rapidly swirling flakes that were already whitening the grounds.

Mr. Price-Jones was not the only person who had noticed my inattentiveness. Nanny touched my arm and stopped me as we were about to retire to our rooms late that night.

"Something has frightened you, Gwynneth," she said straight off and I had no reason to lie to the old woman.

"Yes, Nanny."

"Tell me about it."

I recited the entire scene for her, including the ghostly apparitions in the chapel and the feeling that someone or something was protecting me.

Nanny listened to it all and then spoke very slowly and very seriously to me. "See that you don't venture out alone for the next few days." Her gaze was piercing. "Mind my words, Gwynneth. Do not go out alone until I tell you it is safe."

I shuddered at her grave warnings. "You frighten me, Nanny. Whom am I to fear? And why?"

She touched my arm, patting it in pacification. "Never mind for this night. Soon you'll know." She watched as I walked to the door of my room. "See that you heed me, girl. Do not be alone just now."

The ominous words had a strange effect on me, for I now knew that someone other than myself believed all that I had been seeing and hearing throughout my life. I wondered if what I saw in my visions could be the key that would unlock the clouded past and present of Winter's Light. Somehow, in spite of my terror, I was able to sleep easily this night knowing that soon everything would be made clear.

Chapter Twenty-one

The snow had fallen the whole of the night and into the early hours of the day and when we awoke the next morning everything outside appeared white and shrouded. The flakes had begun to taper off by mid-afternoon and it seemed as though the entire staff had declared a holiday, for in contrast to yesterday's frenzied activity, all was slow and tedious today.

Nanny spent almost the entire morning sitting by Lady Glendower's side, speaking to her in low whispers. I remained away from them in the sitting room, taking care that the chores were done properly by Meg and the other servants while the two elderly women spoke together. Their conversation seemed long and, at times, complicated: every once in a while I heard Lady Glendower's voice raised so that I could tell her strength was just about nearing to normal, and Nanny vigorously shook her head at other parts of the discussion. Even I had to smile to hear her contradict her mistress a few times.

"It's the best thing for all, my lady," she said. "Best we get it over with now so that we all can begin again." Finally they both fell silent and soon Nanny joined me in the sitting room. She waited until the servant girls finished with their chores and then she motioned me to come sit by the fire.

"Sit down, girl." The nurse's voice was soft, as though

she were talking to a small child. "Sit with me a while. I have something to tell you." It seemed strange that we were to interrupt our daily chores for conversation, but Nanny was insistent. "Come sit with me, Gwynneth," she said once more, this time motioning me to her side. I took a seat near the fire and watched as she settled into her favorite chair. This time she did not even make a pretense of knitting, and the ball of yarn and needles remained on the table next to the far side of the wall.

"We—the mistress and I—have been watching you," she began and then shook her head. "No, that is the wrong way to begin," she mumbled to herself. She cleared her throat and started the conversation again. "No, I must begin at the beginning." Sighing, she hunched her shoulders so that she could be closer to me. "You remember, Gwynneth, when I told you the story of Lady Anne and her babe?"

"Yes."

"There is more, much more. I did not tell you all." She settled her shawl around her shoulders and I knew that it was really an attempt for her to organize her thoughts.

She put her hands to her head and then started. "Gwynneth, when Lady Glendower was taken sick this last time she and I talked about the fate of Winter's Light and the fact that it would most probably fall to the Davies. She was saddened by that. It seemed unfair that all the hard work maintained by the Glendowers for so many years would go to an undeserving couple. We talked a long time about that, and then one day last year she called me to her side and the two of us had a long chat about the old days—the time of Anne and the tutor and then the baby." Nanny bowed her head and I could see her mouth working, trying to form the next words. "Well, Gwynneth, the long and the short of it is that she told me that it was time to bring the child back to Winter's Light. To its lawful place."

I inhaled a deep, audible breath for the words overwhelmed me. "I do not understand. You said the baby had died."

Nanny held up her hand to silence me. "That was the story that we gave out. The story that we told Anne—and the neighbors—but, God forgive me, it wasn't true. It wasn't true." She saw me blanch at her plea and then stared straight at me. "There will be plenty of times for questions later, girl, but for now let me speak so that I may tell you all." She slowly began to rock her chair.

"When Miss Anne's time came to be delivered, I was in attendance on her, and I was the only one who knew the true story. I was the one who pronounced the babe dead, but you see, Gwynneth, Lady Glendower was clever. She suspected right off that the infant did not die—that I had really sent it away. She was right, of course, for I dispatched the babe to a family that I had once been told would care and love the child as if it were their own. I sent the little infant away the very day it was born—with a person I trusted—so as not to cause any more pain to the family. That person could be relied on to hold his tongue—he has to this day—so that I thought there would only be two of us who knew the fate of the child."

"It was Fergus?" I asked and she frowned and rubbed at her eye.

"Aye, he's the one. But Lady Glendower was skillful at knowing things and one day, a few months after the Lady Anne had died, the mistress called me into her room and put the question straight away to me. 'Is the babe all right?' she asked me and I did not lie. I told her yes, for there was no use denying the story to her—I knew that she must have found out my plan. Not that anyone spoke up, for I knew Fergus could be trusted, but I figured that she must have puzzled it out for herself." Her lace cap bobbed along with her words and I could see tears form in the corner of her eyes.

"I did not lie to her, Gwynneth, for I can't abide people who cannot tell the truth. And when she asked me if I knew where the child was, I told her that I did. She wanted to know if it was well cared for and I told her yes, and that's when she gave me a bag of gold coins to dispatch to the family for the babe's safekeeping."

I began to shiver, for the story was beginning to sound much like my own. I knew that children born clandestinely of people of high birth were often hidden, but this bit of news only confirmed what I had always thought about my own position—that I, too, was the issue of such a union. Nanny did not notice my shaking and continued the story.

"I sent Fergus to check on the family and the babe and to deliver the money, and then to report back to me about the child's welfare. The mistress, after that first time she asked about the health of the child, did not question me further, either then or in subsequent years. But always, every December, there would be a day that a bag of coins would appear on my table—this very one that we sip our tea at, Gwynneth," she said, and I rubbed my hand against the grain of the wood. I had a strong desire to cry for that innocent baby and its mother.

"Fergus always took the coins to the family and always came back and told me that the child was well cared for and was doing nicely in school and that the couple that I had selected to care for the babe were good, kind parents to it. He told me that the child was happy and healthy and had settled in nicely." She stopped and then looked at me and it seemed her eyes bore through me, while at the same time I heard the hypnotic rocking of the chair. Finally the chair stopped rolling and all was eerily silent. She continued to stare at me and then suddenly, without warning, she asked, "Do you not know who ye are, girl?" I could feel my heart pound against the cloth of my dress.

"No." The blaze in the fireplace seemed oppressive now and I was afraid that I would be smothered in the heat of the room.

"Do you not suspect?" The old woman peered at me

and it was almost as if she willed me to answer.

I shook my head and it seemed as though I was watching myself from another part of the room. Watching a bewildered young woman first sit up straight, then swallow hard, and then shake her head back and forth as though the expression would erase the question. I took huge gulps of air to calm me, for I was reluctant to even consider the question while lifelong years of vivid memories and undefined images blended together in my mind, swirling and mingling until nothing seemed sane or normal anymore.

"Gwynneth, child. Look at me." Nanny's voice seemed to thunder and echo throughout the room. "Ye are a Glendower. Ye are Anne's child."

"No."

She nodded her head and repeated the words quickly and yet so truthfully that I could not deny them any longer, no matter how I tried.

"Ye are Gwynneth Glendower—the Lady Anne's babe."

"No. No, it is not possible. I am Gwynneth Morys."

Nanny stood up and faced me. "Before that time, girl. Before that time. Ye were born here, in this house." She pointed to a room near to where we were sitting. "In that very room."

"The baby?"

Nanny nodded her head. "Aye. Ye are that babe."

"But it died," I said remembering the first time I was told the story.

"No." Nanny sat back in her chair and I could see that she was as exhausted as I—she from revealing the information and I from being forced to understand and accept it. "No, the infant did not die. I sent it away." She swallowed hard. "Sit there, Gwynneth, and drink some tea. There is still a part of the story of Anne that I did not tell you. I could not tell you before, for it is still painful to me. For it reminds me of my deception."

I could not ask any questions—my mind was trying to sort out everything I had just been told and it was much

270

easier to wait until the old nurse had told me all.

"Mathias Morys and his kindhearted wife, Molly, were known by their distant cousin who worked here, below stairs, but who is long since dead and buried. She had at one time told me about her gentle, aged kin and how they had longed for a child. I remembered that conversation when you were born and when I hatched my scheme." She wiped at her eyes. "Ah, child, I did not have the heart to abandon ye to someone I did not know, and Morys and his wife were well spoke of by their kin as people who were salt of the earth and true to their principles."

I felt my own eyes mist now. "Yes, they were. Very fine. My parents were very fine people." I smiled as I remembered the dearness of the honorable and loving husband and wife I had called Mother and Father.

Nanny took time to compose herself. "Several months ago when I realized I was getting too old to do all the work for Lady Glendower, I knew that I would be needing some sort of help. I had heard that you were now without kinfolk and it just seemed natural to call you back here, for it gave us a chance to get to know you and to see how you turned out after all these years.

"It was not a mean trick, Gwynneth. We were just protecting everyone, since there was no way to undo the original decision that I had made years ago to send you away. We did not know if you wanted to come back to us. We did not know whether to tell you about your heritage right off—for it was a big and fearful decision. We—Lady Glendower and I—did not know what would be your reaction. You might have hated all of us. You might have been a mean-spirited person out for revenge." She looked at me and a faint smile touched her lips. "But I did not think so, Gwynneth. Not ye, girl, for ye have the lifeblood of your sweet mother coursing through you. Nay, not ye." She twisted the plain, gold signet ring on her finger.

"But how were we to know of your behavior? So we decided to take you back under false pretenses, so to speak.

We would watch you. Find out if you really were Anne's daughter and make sure that you had not been substituted. All these things we had to take into account, Gwynneth, for you realize what a big task it is to be a Glendower." Here she looked about the rooms and through the open door into the hallway and I knew what she meant.

"You wanted to see if I was of the same spirit as the family to appreciate all of this. To follow the line, so to speak?"

Nanny nodded her head. "Aye. When we found out that Molly and Mathias had died, we put out the word that I would be needing help, that my old bones did not serve me well any longer. I wrote a letter to your reverend and he wrote back that there was indeed such a girl as I had requested living in the village—a young thing, he said, but strong, who had recently been left an orphan. I already knew that, of course, but it did no one any harm the way we went about bringing you home."

Home. Just the way she said that word sent panic through my body and there were a hundred questions I wanted to ask and have answered. All those times I dreamt about Winter's Light now seemed to make sense.

"Then the dreams I had about this house . . . ?"

Nanny nodded her head again. "I do not know, but somewhere deep in your heart and soul and mind there must have been the will to remember."

"But . . . ?"

"I don't pretend to know how or why you were able to recall this estate but, Gwynneth, I know you are a Glendower and Glendowers have always been able to return to their soil no matter what the circumstance."

I remembered Fergus's startled look when he first saw me and his tremulous and frightening pronouncement, *"Ye have been here before."*

"But if Fergus knew about me, how come he was so frightened at my appearance when he first saw me? How come he accused me of being here before? How come he did not recognize me?"

The old woman sighed. "Because," she said, "because he did not expect you. Lady Glendower and I both took care to let no one know our plan."

Nanny's mention of her mistress made me wince. "Lady Glendower . . . ?"

"Delighted that you are here. Ready to love you and accept you as her true granddaughter. She will speak to you tomorrow when we are alone and then acknowledge you to all. Until then, let me speak, and then you can think and form your questions and we will answer them."

I clasped my chilled hands in front of me, for I did not know what else to do to control their trembling. This revelation was far too much for me to absorb, and I wanted to go straight to my room so that I could be by myself and consider Nanny's confession.

"Ye still are confused, I know, but can you abide even more? Do you want to know all?"

"Yes. The incident yesterday. In the bell tower. Is that the reason why you are telling me all this now?"

Nanny's face contorted briefly and I thought I saw a flickering of alarm pass over her features. "Ye be a smart girl. Aye. That's the reason why we had to tell you now. So that ye can be on your . . ." She did not finish her sentence but instead took up a candle and lit it from the fire in the grate. "Come with me, Gwynneth. I have something to show you." She beckoned to me and I, astonished and wary at everything that had just transpired, obediently did as I was told. I followed the woman out of the sitting room and into the hall. She moved quickly past the guest wing, where the Davies had their rooms, and then through a small, concealed door at the far end of a picture gallery. I had never been in the area before and, in fact, had not known that it existed.

"We'll go to the attic," she said and I heard the urgency in her voice. "There's something that you must see as soon

273

as possible. The lady and I agree," she said and I thought I heard fear in her voice. "It's time for you to know so that you can . . ." Her voice lowered and again she did not finish her sentence, and I could understand what the intent was in neither her statement nor in our hurried flight up the small dark, winding stairs to the upstairs rooms.

"This be the attic," she said as she lit an unused candle in a brass wall sconce. "I know you have never been here before, but don't be afraid." She waved me closer to the back of the room, where several white-sheeted large rectangles stood against the wall.

"Ye once asked me what had happened to all of the drawings that Lady Anne's tutor had completed." She pulled the cloth from a large square. "This be one of them," she said and I recognized the likeness of Fergus and several other estate workers as they went about their daily chores. It was a bright scene, for it had a hot, blazing summer sun in one corner, and it showed the lifelike figures as they were about to pluck the wheat and take the horses down to the pastures.

"This is beautiful," I said. Nanny nodded her head in agreement.

"And this," she said, pulling another piece of white cloth away from a smaller frame, "this be the one you inquired about. The picture of Winter's Light." She moved the painting so that I could see it better and I was in awe of it. Fergus was right. No artist, having seen this picture, would ever have wanted to paint Winter's Light again. Jeremy Donne had captured the light and the glint and the color perfectly. It was as if the cast and hue had been taken away from the original stones and put forever on this canvas.

"That be what you expected?" Nanny was smiling at me. "That be a good picture?"

"Yes," I said and Nanny nodded her head, again agreeing with me.

"When it was first done, Lord and Lady Glendower marvelled at it. They were so taken by it that it was immediately framed and hung."

"In the Great Hall?"

"Aye. Fergus told you?"

"Yes." I backed away from the painting in order to see it more fully. "It is magnificent."

"The master said it was the finest that he had ever seen. He even negotiated an extra payment to the tutor—he thought it that good. Lady Glendower told me that it was only proper to offer a sum for it, for Mr. Donne's talent should not go unrewarded." She leaned the drawing against the wall.

"Ye have inherited two things from the tutor, girl," she announced, and I wondered what she would say. "That tune that ye sing—ye should know that it is one that Mr. Donne composed for Lady Anne." I took a deep breath, for everything seemed too much for me, but Nanny did not stop speaking. "Dedicated that air to her one evening in front of all of us, and for a long time she went about the house humming those same five notes as ye have sung to me. I recognized it right off, but I could not tell you about it at the time. I had to wait to talk to Lady Glendower." I blinked my eyes at the revelation but she paid no notice to my bewilderment and instead looked around at the paintings, choosing to continue with her explanations. "And the second thing in common with the tutor is your ability to draw likenesses." She patted the frame of the painting of Winter's Light. "Ye see it, don't you, Gwynneth, that ye have the talent, too? That same ability as your father."

I caught my breath once again at the word Nanny used in connection with Mr. Donne and me.

"Aye, girl, ye must consider it, for the tutor was indeed your father." *Father*. I did not know if I would ever get used to that name for Mr. Donne. Nanny finally saw my look. "Think on it a few months, Gwynneth, for everything will fall into its own place in all good time." She moved toward another stack of covered squares, and I wanted to speak more of them so that I would not have to make quick decisions about my past and future. These were things that I had to examine and question in my own way.

"And all these other paintings, Nanny? Were they all done by Mr. Donne?" I asked, for I could not use the new term just yet.

"No," she said, stammering for a moment. "Some are just poorly done pictures," she added. I knew she was finding excuses not to uncover some of the art, although I could not fathom what more there was that could be concealed or revealed to me.

"Are any of them the portraits of Lady Anne?"

"Aye. There be one or two." I saw her eyes scan the covered frames.

"Then isn't it about time that Lady Glendower hung them once again on the walls of Winter's Light? Has she too not suffered enough, Nanny?"

Nanny looked at me and a wistful smile formed on her lips. "I knew ye would say something like that, girl. I knew that you would have the same sentiments for someone else that Mistress Anne was noted for. Aye, then we are doing right," she said to herself, then led me to another corner of the room so that I was beginning to feel dizzy at the pace of all the discoveries.

"This one," the woman said when she walked close to an immense picture that was carefully shrouded in a cream-color cloth. "This be the one. This be the real reason I brought you up here." She motioned me forward. "Come, come, Gwynneth. I want you to see this in its full glory all at once." I moved closer to Mrs. Hoskins and just the way she said her sentence made me apprehensive. I could not imagine what it was that she wanted to show me now. What could be tucked away here in the attic that would be more mysterious or more revealing than all the

276

rest of the information I had been told this day? Nanny looked at me and then I saw a small, daring bit of a smile edge her lips.

"You're not to be afraid," she said and I shuddered at the dramatics of her words. She stepped forward and took hold of an edge of the heavy material, jerking it away so that in one fell swoop the entire portrait was revealed to me. I gasped and fell back a few steps. She was right to forewarn me for this was indeed the most astonishing event of a day filled with confusion.

The portrait was of a woman and, whoever the subject, she was fair, with brilliant green eyes and a heart-shaped face. She had bright red hair fashioned in a haphazard way—as though the pins had fallen from the shining tresses and it had curled around her face and spilled over and beyond the open lace collar of her bright scarlet satin dress. There was a faint, mocking smile on her full lips, as if to show that she had mastered life, and yet there was a directness in her countenance. She stood, proud and regal, and there was a mysterious glint in her eyes which seemed to indicate that she cared nothing for all the trappings and wealth surrounding her.

"Ye do see it, don't you, Gwynneth?" Nanny asked. I nodded and once again Fergus's words came back at me: *"Ye have been here before."* Now I understood the terror in his voice, now I understood his meaning—for the face depicted in the portrait could have been a likeness of me! It was as though an unknown painter had spied upon me and captured my features, then substituted the gaudy fashions of another era for my plain, grey clothes. I licked at my dry lips and stared at the canvas. "I knew you would see the resemblance," Mrs. Hoskins said.

I stepped closer to the portrait and wanted to reach out and touch it. I had never before seen another who had my coloring, yet this woman looked as if we two could be relatives. I looked for the title of the canvas but there was none.

"Who is she, Nanny?" I could barely ask the words.

"Can ye not guess?" the nurse said, and I knew that she and I had come to an unspoken understanding, for the name instantly came to my lips.

"Lucy."

Nanny nodded her head in full comprehension. "Aye, she is Lady Lucy Glendower—the late master's great-aunt."

Lucy! I did not panic at the information. Rather I remained extraordinarily calm as I recalled my long-ago answer to my mother. *"I shall name my doll Lucy because I have to."*

"You know all now." She set the huge portrait upon an old table. "There are many mysterious stories about her, and although the master never acknowledged them to be true, he had us keep this portrait up here, out of sight. She was supposed to have been more beautiful than anyone in the entire country and even when I first came here as a young woman, the old retainers who were still at Winter's Light spoke of her with awe. They said from birth to death she always had fiery red hair. They likened the sheen to the glow of a burnished copper pot on the stove—to the color when it was heated. To the way it glinted gold and red and orange when the flames leaped and danced about from under it during the cooking." She watched me as I examined the portrait. "Much the same color, I imagine, as your own."

I continued to gaze at the portrait, unable to speak.

"She died young and in a mysterious way, and they said that she loved life so much that on her deathbed she vowed to come back again. A witch, some called her. And there were many a times, I was told, when she deserved that name. It's told that once she put her hand close to a burning candle and the flame drew away from her palm as though it had taken on a life and a fear of its own. They say that three times she advanced her hand toward the burning candle and three times the flame flickered and then finally died out, though it were a new candle and there was much wick and wax still left.

"Lucy, they say, laughed when it happened—a powerful laugh that was said to have shaken all the delicate crystal on the table. *'Not even fire can hurt me,'* she was known to boast and then she would laugh again and again." Nanny lowered her voice as though speaking of the woman would awaken her spirit. "Some even said she was such a witch that in many countries, if she were allowed to say her thoughts, she would have been suspect by the clergy." Nanny shivered. "Aye, do you believe in witches, Gwynneth? And in spirits and sounds of the night?"

Nanny's question stirred my mind. *"Witch. Witch,"* I heard the voices of children from my town calling out to me. *"Witch. Witch."* I flinched as the long-forgotten memory came to the front of my mind.

"What is it, child?"

"I remember once when I was close to the village well some children had pushed and tugged at me and made a pretense to throw me down it, and I was frightened for they seemed so hurtful. I tried to run away but I could not, for they blocked my way. And then something peculiar happened. Suddenly the children stopped taunting me and stood quiet—as though they had been struck dumb by lightning. They seemed to be frozen in their tracks, and I remember I felt a current of warm air and then a gentle tug at my sleeve and it seemed, I know this sounds silly, Nanny, but it seemed as though someone was guiding me past the children, and when I stepped close to them while making my escape, they didn't even mind. I even approached one young boy who had been especially mean in his name-calling and he never said a word to me—he just let me pass him. I wanted to stop and speak to him but I felt another, more insistent pull at my sleeve, and it seemed that I was forced—although that is such a strange word, for no one was near to me making me walk the path—but it was as if I was forced to be on my way home.

I remember walking calmly down the road and when I got to Daear and told my parents, they could only tell me that I must have been dreaming, and they warned me not to speak of it again to anyone. I remembered they looked at each other—I remember that vividly, for my mother's face seemed alarmed, and I recall my father shaking his head and silencing all of her unspoken questions. Then Father put me on his knee and held me and I remember him saying, *'Child . . . child . . . ,'* and my mother came and gave me a warm scone that she had been baking for the midday meal."

I looked at the portrait of Lucy. "Could that presence have been . . . ?"

Nanny nodded her head and I could see the tension relax in her face. "Aye, that would be Lucy—come to help you. I am glad to hear of that episode. She was said to take care of her own. To protect them. Do not ask me questions of this, girl, for I am not of a privilege to tell you of those unknown things. Just be patient and wait while things are revealed to you. Accept, that is all I can tell you. Accept what is given to you."

"Do I need Lucy's help now?" It seemed a logical question and Nanny hesitated only a second.

"Aye. I think so, for there's the inheritance—the Glendower estate." I was stunned at the prospect and Nanny looked at me in a silencing way. "I was right—ye did not think of the fortune or all that would be left to you someday." She touched my arm. "Do not be afraid though, Gwynneth, for we will be watching, too. Only be sure to look about ye for the next few days. Be alert and don't be telling anyone of our conversation just yet." She held up her hand to me in warning. "Be vigilant, girl, until we know more."

"Someone then is stalking me?"

"Aye, but I do not know who. I suspect, though that is not enough, that there are others here who have seen the resemblance. Stay wakeful, girl, until we know more." She

280

replaced the covers over the painting and snuffed out the attic candle. "Now, girl, back to Lady Glendower, for I don't want anyone to know that we've been poking about up here."

I do not know how I finished my chores that evening or how I was even able to concentrate on anything other than all that Nanny had told me of my connection to Winter's Light. When, after dinner, I excused myself early, the old nurse was not surprised, and the candles and fires were dampened prematurely in the main chambers so that the two of us could return to our rooms.

I had no thought of sleep, for the import of Nanny's words weighed far too heavily in my mind. I could not discern everything although I had been told most of it in a straightforward fashion. How was I to accept that I was Gwynneth Glendower? How could I accept that I was the daughter of Lady Anne and Mr. Donne and that I was now rightfully part of the family of Winter's Light? How was I to accept that all the dreams and visions that I thought I had only imagined throughout my life had now come true?

I stood in front of the small mirror that sat upon my dresser and kept looking at myself from all angles. I reached up and took out the pins which held up my hair and let it fall round my shoulders and face much in the loose fashion of Lady Lucy Glendower—and I was fascinated with the image. It was a vain gesture, one which would not have made Molly, my mother, proud, but I was in a strange mood. The shock of seeing someone whom I resembled and the coincidence of being taken for her though she had lived and died many years ago, were too much for me to comprehend.

"This will not do," I said. I brushed back my hair and then looked once more into the mirror. I touched my cheek and my eyebrow and then stared into my eyes as though seeing them for the first time.

"Ye do favor her," I could hear Nanny say, and then it

281

was as if I heard a laugh—a long throaty laugh that seemed to fill the room, and I turned, expecting to see someone standing in a far corner. But of course there was no one there. Once more I heard the laugh and again I turned. Perhaps someone was playing a joke with me and hiding within the folds of the heavy velvet draperies. Perhaps Meg had come to turn down my bed and was teasing me. I grasped at anything that I could perceive as logical.

"Come out, Meg," I said, "for I do not like games." There was no answer. I walked to the windows and flung back the curtains so that the dark night and the small sliver of moonlight shone through the panes, and with that tiny stream of light came long-ago but not forgotten words.

"Tell me you doll's name," I heard my mother ask, and then the small voice of my childhood replied, *"Lucy. I shall call her Lucy."*

"Lucy." I spoke the name aloud into my empty room and once more I heard the laugh—this time longer than before and more full, more deep—although I knew that there was no mortal soul here with me. I sat on my bed, bewildered at the turn of events and unable to trust myself and my thoughts. I waited for another sign, but none was forthcoming. Now all seemed quiet and still so that I heard only the hissing of the small logs as they burst open and filled my room with an uneven warmth.

Was there someone here with me? Did I dare trust my own thoughts and did I dare to believe that somehow the ghost of Lucy Glendower was here?

"Lucy," I said into the void, but there was nothing—no stirring . . . no eerie breezes . . . no tangible evidence that there was anyone here with me.

My breath came rapidly and I felt faint, for I did not like the feelings that had slowly washed over me or the thoughts that invaded my mind. How could another being be in my room with me? Why would there be an unseen presence? My fancy had gone too far this time. I pulled the draperies into position once again, for I did not want the slice of silver moonlight to keep me awake . . . to remind me of whom I had now become.

The fire was dying down, its embers glowing only half-heartedly, and I bent to bank the fires. I held the slender iron poker in my hand and looked at it earnestly before replacing it in its stand. Surely I was letting my imagination get the best of me. Surely no one would wish to do me harm.

I started to pull the bedcovers around me, then saw that the small mirror was still shining, still sending back reflections of the room. I climbed out of bed and turned it toward the wall, but not before I caught a fleeting glance of myself in the glass. And in that swift second, I panicked, for there, reflected in the fragile, dying firelight, was my image, but I could have sworn that my hair was tumbling all about and curling softly around my face and onto my shoulders.

"No," I said. I closed my eyes and I thought I again heard the boisterous, teasing sound of laughter as it echoed throughout the room. I turned chillingly cold—colder than I could ever remember being—and reached out to extinguish my candle. At that moment I remembered the story that Nanny had told about Lucy. I took a deep breath, ready to blow out the wick, then thought better of it, deciding that, although it was wasteful, I would leave the fat candle to burn all night.

But it was a sleepless few hours I spent as I puzzled all that had happened to me so far. Was I really the long-lost granddaughter now summoned back to Winter's Light and was I really to live here for the rest of my life? Why did I feel that someone or something was stalking me and why was I frightened just now of my own reflection? Why? Why? Why? So many questions and so few answers. And most of all why had I always known, deep in my heart, that I would find Winter's Light?

I was afraid to close my eyes, for visions of Anne and

Lucy and Lady Glendower and Mr. Donne and Nanny and the Davies seemed to stray past me in the dark, keeping me awake and on guard until at last I fell asleep to the chirping of the morning birds.

Chapter Twenty-two

This morning there was an eerie calm about Winter's Light, as though everyone were waiting for something special to happen, as though time itself stood still on the threshold of something momentous. Voices were hushed — even the kitchen was quiet — and I could not comprehend why everything seemed to be in a suspended state. I wondered if it were simply that I had projected my mood onto life here at the house, but I thought not, for it was a bleak day — the sky had not lightened but instead, with the passing of each hour, had grown darker. The pale grey clouds that had been present earlier this morning deepened to a dark hue, a portent of another mighty snowfall yet to come. Fires were set in the fireplaces of the main rooms, and the aromas of baking bread and charred wood mingled in all the areas of the house. Normally the pleasant scents would have given comfort on such a dreary day, but today they did not and everything seemed oppressive. The tone in the house was heavy — like the clouds — and I had a sense that something formidable was about to take place. This feeling of dread penetrated even into my sitting room, and I found myself wishing that the sky would brighten so that I might take a short walk outside of the house in order to clear my mind. The events of the past day seemed to weigh on me, and I found I did not know how to adjust to them.

"You have had a shock, Gwynneth," Nanny said when she noticed my quiet. "When Lady Glendower awakens, she'll talk more to you and then everything will fall into place."

"It is not just that, Nanny. It seems as though I am being smothered. I need to get out into the open air so that I can form my own thoughts in my head." She looked at my hands and I blushed as I realized that I had been running my fingers over and over the wooden table in an act of impatience. "It is as though I must be outside on my own."

Nanny stopped fussing with her glasses and peered out the window closest to her. "I do not think that wise, Gwynneth. I am still wary for you." She indicated the hot pot of tea under its cosy. "Take a nice cup and calm yourself here instead. Maybe a turn around the rooms will help you."

I roamed the hallways of the upper floor of the house hoping that I could focus my thoughts, but it was no use. There seemed no escape from the apprehension that was gripping me. Nanny's admonition was securely lodged in my memory and I began to fear almost anything or anyone. I passed the Davies' chambers wondering if they suspected who I was and might now wish me harm, and I hurried quickly into another corridor when I heard activity from within the room. One of the cousins might emerge, and I did not want either of them to see me just yet.

I returned to the master wing and Nanny greeted me with good news. "It seems that Mr. Owen will be coming this day," she said. "His gentleman just rode over to say that he will keep his promise to you—whatever that may be—and to be ready at two o'clock." She smiled at me. "That should be pleasant for you, Gwynneth, for now you'll have safe company."

Mr. Price-Jones's message did much to cheer me, for I knew that he alluded to our proposed visit to the chapel, but by the time the hours of the appointment had come and gone, I was again in a uneasy mood. Mr. Owen was nowhere in sight, but with the thought that he would soon be about, I deemed it safe for me to take a walk outside where I would possibly meet up with him. I did not tell Nanny of my plans for fear she would try to deter me and instead slipped out the back door when I thought no one would see me. I spied Fergus in the distance, coming up the side walk, but I was careful and I was sure that the old stableman had not seen me.

The cold air was clear and refreshing and smelled of the snows yet to fall. Within its calmness, I began to lose my fright. It was as though my woolen cape protected me not only from the frigid air but also from whatever or whomever wanted to injure me. Surely, I thought, out here in plain sight of everyone no being, mortal or otherwise, could possibly stalk me or terrorize me. So brightened in spirit was I that I was sure that if I walked slowly toward the chapel, Mr. Price-Jones would arrive at any moment, see my tracks, and follow me there.

I walked carefully, my thick boots leaving footprints in the untrampled snow as a marker for him, and when I looked back at them I realized that the path I was taking must be the same as that which the Lady Anne had strolled that terrible, sunny, summer noon. It was not a long walk and by the time I reached the chapel I still did not see Mr. Jones, but rather than wait outside in the cold air, I thought that I would linger in the nave of the building.

Again the door opened and closed easily enough and I entered the dark interior, pausing for only a few seconds to let my eyes become accustomed to the drab room before letting my gloved hand guide me toward one of the inner wooden pews. I sat for several moments but I grew impatient, for it seemed as though I were meant to explore the upstairs immediately, and gathering all my courage, I moved past the empty rows . . . past the draped altar . . .

and toward the curving steps that led up to the silent choir loft. I had no candle and the only light I had to see by was that which naturally flowed through the tiny window near the top of the stairs.

I moved slowly and cautiously, taking small steps to be sure of my footing, all the time wondering if I would encounter the force that had shielded me from I knew not whom — or what — that last time. My hand moved gingerly along the stone wall and soon I had passed that tiny, recessed niche where I had hidden the last time I was here, and I shuddered at the memory of my terror.

I reached the small tower window and looked out, hoping to see Mr. Jones, and I was overjoyed at the view. Below me, on the deep snow approaching the bell tower from the back, close by the sea, was a fresh set of horse's hoofprints that led straight to the chapel. I was much relieved, for surely, I thought, it was Mr. Price-Jones, come to accompany me.

I pressed my head closer to the window but still could not see him, and I was puzzled why he did not make himself known to me. I looked closer and saw no one and a faint feeling of panic began to creep into my mind. If it were Mr. Price-Jones, why had he tethered his horse to the far side of the chapel so that it was out of sight of the main house?

I looked both ways from my vantage point at the tiny window but could see nothing, and I felt the fear rising up in me, for the church rooms below were eerily silent. I held my breath hoping to hear a call of greeting from Mr. Price-Jones and instead I detected a slight, flowing sound, and I knew instantly that what I had heard was the sound of the heavy, wooden door giving way. I speculated that perhaps the wind had pushed it open, but when I looked outside I knew it could not be so. The air was still and the snow was not blowing.

I waited for other noises and wondered why no one called to me to let me know of his presence. I felt a mixture of foolishness and fright, for perhaps, I thought, I was merely imagining macabre things. Perhaps it was only a small animal that had wandered in from the snows, or some decayed leaves that had been swept along the stone floors in a current of air. Perhaps it was nothing at all, and to satisfy myself I opened my mouth to call out but I could not speak, for something silenced my voice.

I heard another sound—this time that of muted footsteps upon the stairs—and suddenly I knew that I was not foolish, that I was in danger and that whoever had stalked me this past week was pursuing me again. I could not move—my legs seemed paralyzed, and I knew that this time there was no place for me to hide. I stood motionless, waiting for an unknown, and I heard whoever it was carefully climb the winding stairs . . . coming closer and closer toward me . . . moving up the dark, curving staircase until finally a shadowy figure came into view just below me.

I could not speak or cry out—my mouth was dry with fear, and I knew that there was no one near to hear me anyway. I clenched my fists, for my hands were trembling and the panic-born cold had now penetrated deep inside me. I was unable to move and still the figure came up the steps toward me, its arms outstretched to me so that its long, black cloak floated away from its body.

"Anne."

My scream died inside my throat.

"My Lady Anne. You have come back." The deep voice appeared intoxicated with the discovery. *"You have returned to me."*

"No," I said, trying to evade the shape that was closing in on me. "No," I cried, but the tower bells mysteriously began to toll, masking my denials. I put my hands to my ears to block out the chimes and still I heard their pealing and the heavy, searching voice which called the name of my mother.

"Anne. Anne. Beloved."

I held my hands up in front of me and backed against the wall but this did nothing to stop the shrouded outline from continuing to come toward me.

"Anne. You have returned," the voice said. The clothing of the person scraped against a ridge in the wall and caught and the hood of the cape fell back and away from the face. I could not even cry out as Mr. Charles Price-Jones moved into full view so that I saw him in the deep grey light. So besotted with his imagined discovery was he that he did not make a move to conceal his face. He smiled at me and yet I could see that there was no happiness for him. His eyes were wild and distant.

"I have waited for you," he said simply and held out his hand to me so that I could take it.

"Please, Mr. Price-Jones, I am not Anne. I am Gwynneth Morys," I said, but the gentleman was too far gone to hear my truthful words. He reached out to me and I knew that he was truly unable to discern correctly between the real and the unreal. He looked at me and I could see the hysterical pleading in his frantic eyes.

"Do not be afraid of me, Anne, do not be afraid of me," he appealed, as though all times had now been jumbled and he believed me completely to be Anne Glendower, my mother.

"Please, Mr. Price-Jones. Do not follow me. Allow me to pass. Allow me to make my way down the steps." Mr. Price-Jones paused as though some semblance of sense had passed into his mind, but just as quickly his eyes seemed to dim and I saw that at the moment all hope of reasoning with him was lost. Still I tried once more.

"Please, Mr. Price-Jones, leave me." This time he did not even attempt to listen but moved one step closer. One more space closed off to me and I felt along the wall, felt the cold, rough-chiseled stones that were assembled to construct the sides of the staircase leading to the top of the chapel. I felt the jagged edges penetrate my palms, scraping them with their roughness, and yet I did not want

290

to let go. The stones were my only means of support.

Mr. Price-Jones stopped only a step below me and stared at me. I took a deep breath and looked into his eyes and shuddered. It was as though I saw into the very soul of the man, saw his torment and pain and melancholy and, yes, his guilt, but, while I felt torn in the face of these emotions, now was not the time to offer my sorrow.

I stood still, trying to keep my wits about me, while Mr. Price-Jones watched as though I were about to disappear.

"Come, Anne," he said, taking hold of my arm so that I could not escape. "We will climb together." He tugged at me so that I was forced to climb the stairs even higher. I moved slowly up the staircase, hoping to delay our ascent, but my resistance was to no avail. Mr. Price-Jones was much too strong for me, and whenever I hesitated or lingered too long on a step, his hand tightened against my wrist.

"Come, Anne. You know I will not hurt you," he said. Even his voice seemed different, and I knew that no amount of reasoning could penetrate him, for in his mind I had now become Anne Glendower.

"The song that you sang—I remembered it. He wrote it for you." He touched the hood of my cape so that it fell away, and even the sight of my red hair did nothing to dissuade him. "I wish it were summer so that I too could give you a gift. So that I could bring you the flowers," he said.

"I do not want . . . Please, Mr. Price-Jones, look at me. Recognize me as Gwynneth." I pulled at his hand. "Please, Mr. Charles," I begged once more. "Please consider what you are doing. I am not Anne. I am Gwynneth."

Mr. Price-Jones stopped and looked at me and I saw the bewilderment in his eyes as he searched the narrow staircase.

"You are right," he said more rationally, touching my hair. "You are not Anne. You are Gwynneth, come to help Nanny." He looked around and shook his head. "I loved her, Miss Morys, I loved her more than life itself. I even tried to stop her from running away with Mr. Donne, but she only would smile, ma'am. Only smile in her gentle way and say that that tutor—that poor, unsophisticated man—was the only man she would ever love. And, ma'am, he was not good enough for her. I knew that he would only bring her to ruin . . . would only disgrace her. She had been promised to me, Miss Morys. We were to be betrothed. I know that she loved me, although I was older than she, but I know she loved me." He glanced down at his hands.

"And afterwards—when all was finished with the tutor—still, I loved her so much that I would even have accepted her child." Here he looked at me and I could see confusion in his eyes, for somewhere deep within I am sure he knew that I was Anne's daughter, but his bewildered mind would not permit him to reconcile the past and the present. "I loved her almost from the day I saw her and I know she loved me. At least, until Mr. Donne came to Winter's Light." He moved closer to me and I saw his eyes become furtive and I knew that in the half-light of his mind he retained a certain shrewdness. Even so, his face was contorted in anguish, and again, had it been another occasion I would have felt a tremendous sense of pity for him.

"I saw her that last day, Miss Morys, when she was walking toward the chapel. I had gone to visit her and her parents and I met her on the steps of Winter's Light. She told me she was going to the chapel and I said that I understood her sorrow."

The vision of the last meeting between Mr. Price-Jones and Lady Anne seemed to take shape in my mind. I saw the young girl, the hood of her light cotton cape almost concealing her face as she paused on the steps of Winter's Light. She was speaking to a much younger Mr. Price-Jones, and, like him, I saw the wan smile of a very sad woman. The chance meeting was all very proper and civilized and when it became evident to him that Lady Anne did not want to be delayed, Mr. Price-Jones bowed from the waist and touched the girl's thin hand. *"Your servant, ma'am, . . . until we meet again,"* he said, and the young girl smiled at him and continued on her way. I saw Mr. Price-Jones pause and gaze after her.

"Your servant, ma'am . . . until we meet again." These were the words that had seemed to echo when Mr. Price-Jones and Nanny were teasing, that first night we had dined together. When they had spoken of the time that Nanny had once danced with Mr. Price-Jones. *"Your servant, ma'am . . . until we meet again."* Now it seemed to make more sense why I had remembered the phrase: the words had once been addressed to Anne.

The phantom scene lengthened, and I was surprised that it was not finished in my mind; I was still the observer. I watched Mr. Price-Jones begin to knock at the door to the mansion and then, instead, glance once more at the fading figure of Anne. He seemed to contemplate his next action, then suddenly he turned from the house and began to walk in the same direction as Anne, closely following her steps. The young girl was now out of his sight and Mr. Price-Jones seemed to hurry, as though he suspected something was amiss.

I wished I could ask Mr. Price-Jones about this, but it would have been of no use—I doubted that he was able at this time to respond coherently. Still, having witnessed the entire scene in my mind, I was sure that part of the pain that he had carried with him for all these past years was due to the fact that he had been unable to help Anne, unable to stop her in her calculated plan to die.

I had compassion for the gentleman but knew that my immediate situation was peril. My own terror had by now escalated to the point where it had given way to a surprisingly composed sense of purpose, and I tried to think of ways to both resist and escape from the gentleman's grasp.

"Perhaps we should go down, Mr. Price-Jones, and speak more of your love for the Lady Anne," I said calmly, but it was no use, for he had once more passed over to the dark side. He took hold of my arm again and guided me firmly toward the top of the stairs and the bell tower.

"No," I protested strongly, hoping that he would release me, but I knew that he could no longer hear me, and despite all my delaying tactics, we had finally reached the uppermost floor. Mr. Price-Jones seemed familiar with the site and pulled me through a small door that led to the outside of the tower. I could still hear the bells chiming and speculated irrationally that perhaps people on the estate would hear the tollings, wonder at its cause, and investigate.

Mr. Price-Jones took hold of my hand and in the gentlest of manners led me past the bell tower. "Come, Anne," he said quietly. "Come to me forever." He briefly touched my hair. "You have come back to me. You have finally returned," he said lovingly. The now mollified gentleman held on to my hand, guiding me closer and closer to the edge of the snowy, low parapet so that when I looked, I could see over the edge. We were dangerously close to toppling and I tried to shrink back from the brink, but again Mr. Price-Jones forcibly pulled me so that we both were standing there, and I knew that no one could possibly save me—save *us*.

"Come, my beloved. You are mine now, for Mr. Donne is gone forever," he continued, and the tone of his voice led me to believe that he knew of the circumstances of the tutor's disappearance.

It was as if I had to know the answers to all the questions concerning Jeremy Donne. I tried to engage Mr. Price-Jones in calm conversation, hoping that he would reveal the explanation and recover his senses. He paused, and I sensed that he still saw me not as Gwynneth but as Anne, and I lowered my voice so that he could not better distinguish between us.

"What has happened to Mr. Donne?" I asked. Mr. Price-Jones put a finger across his lips and spoke in a whisper.

"Do not worry about him, Anne, for he will never bother us again. I promise you."

"He will come for me," I said, in keeping with what Anne would have said when she lived.

Mr. Price-Jones shook his head. "No, do not worry about him. I tell you he is gone forever."

"What happened to him, sir? Why do you say that?"

Mr. Price-Jones stepped nearer to me and stroked my hand. "Mr. Donne presented himself to me at Cynghanedd a few weeks after your elopement. He asked for my help in contacting you, Anne. But I knew he was not for you. He was not your kind. You need someone strong and with influence, and he was but a poor man—a tutor—who could give you nothing." Mr. Price-Jones continued to caress my bare hand. "You need everything, Anne. Everything. I promise you I will see to it that you lack for nothing in this world." His eyes glazed over and I knew that he was now fully swayed by my impersonation and that he would never again see me other than as Anne Glendower.

"What happened to Mr. Donne?" I asked once more, and this time the gentleman stuck to his recitation.

"He came to me and asked for my help. I told him I would aid him in securing your father's permission to be wed, but I played false with him. I could not let him marry you again." Mr. Price-Jones's face contorted in pain. "You do see that, don't you, Anne? I could not stand to lose you twice in my lifetime." He loosened his grasp on my arm and faced me, seeing Anne Glendower's face and not mine.

"I told him that we would travel to your house together and that I would speak for him to your father, and he believed me." He closed his eyes in doubt and awe. "He believed me and we took our horses and I led him to the moors. He was a trusting person, Anne, too trusting, and he did not suspect anything wrong. I led him to the bogs and told him it was a shortcut to Winter's Light. I pretended that we had to dismount so that we could cross them. I told him that we would be better able to guide our horses if we walked ahead of them in order to move carefully around the sinkholes.

"It was growing dark but still the tutor followed me, and I told him I would go ahead in order to find the safest route. I purposely got far ahead of him, ma'am, and then hid deep within the bog, for I knew that he would lose himself in the mists. I called to him several times to follow me, each time purposely hiding, until finally he was hopelessly lost. I waited for a few more moments to make sure that he would not find his way out, and then I slipped back across the moors, took the horses, and led them back to my stables." Mr. Price-Jones peered into my eyes and I could see that the gentleman had gone quite mad. "I knew they would not find him for a long time, for no one ventures deeply into the bog, not even the local villagers."

I reached out and leaned against the cold, stone frame of the bell tower, hoping that Mr. Price-Jones would think me tired and let up his guard.

"Then the bones and the bits of clothing that were found the next year. . . . ?" I asked.

"They were Mr. Donne's. But by then it did not matter and no one gave it a second thought. By then you—" he said and then seemed confused. "They told me that you were dead, but I knew it was not true. I knew you would return to me once your senses were restored. Once you were no longer blinded by that other person."

I took deep breaths, for at last all was about to fall into place. What had been suspected—that the bones were those of the tutor—was now confirmed indubitably. Nanny had been right, but I did not know if I would ever have the opportunity to tell her so.

Mr. Price-Jones was becoming more agitated, and despite his protestations, I knew it was but a matter of time before he would do something violent. The air had suddenly turned bitter and what light had been in the sky now deepened, so that it almost appeared to be early evening. Several large flakes of snow began to fall upon my cloak and face, yet I was not conscious of their sting. I could only watch as Mr. Price-Jones glanced back and forth as though he was trying to determine what the next course of action should be for the two of us.

I pulled my cape about me, for the wind had become blustery, and I knew that the falling snow would only make for more treacherous footing should Mr. Price-Jones and I have to struggle. I did not know what to do, for the only route of escape—the door to the stairway—lay behind the tormented man. I took another deep breath and suddenly I felt a rush of warm air envelop me and I knew that I was not alone. I remember another time when the force had appeared to rescue me from my tormentors.

"Witch. Witch." The words came back to me and I could only stand and marvel that I was now flooded with a sense of ease. *"Witch. Witch,"* I heard in my mind and suddenly a powerful, womanly laugh seemed to erupt, echoing and mingling with the ringing bells, and I knew that Lucy Glendower was somewhere about me.

Mr. Price-Jones looked at me and for a moment I thought I had glimpsed a light in his eyes which told me that he, too, had heard the laugh and had recovered his senses, but just as quickly the wildness returned to them. There was no stopping him now—his grip tightened even harder on my arm—then, suddenly, it loosened. He looked away from me, toward the balcony's edge, toward the void beyond the brink.

"Anne." Mr. Price-Jones's voice seemed stunned yet almost prayerful. "Anne," he said the name more tenderly this time. My beloved," he murmured softly, and I understood why he spoke the name in gentle tones for, whether

297

it was in my mind or in truth or a trick of the falling snows, even I could see the spectral figure in green standing suspended in the air just beyond the balcony.

"Anne," the tormented man cried out, and I saw the ghostly being raise her slender arms and beckon to us — to him — and I believe the man no longer knew I was there. "Beloved," he said, and I realized that now, besotted with the apparition, he was moving toward it, getting perilously close to the iced edge.

"Mr. Price-Jones," I cried out to him, but he could not hear me — would not hear me — and I watched in horror as he advanced toward the illusion, made a low courtly bow to it, and spoke in a loving and polite voice. "Your servant, ma'am," he said and I could hear the long-awaited happiness in his voice. "Your most adoring servant, ma'am," he said, fashioning his arms as though he were about to sweep a dancing partner into his embrace.

"Mr. Price-Jones," I cried out to no avail, and I knew that what was to happen next was inevitable. He held out his hand to the air — to the supernatural being that I will swear to my dying day we both saw — and it was as if the gentleman willingly and joyfully walked out beyond the barrier and into infinity. "Anne, my beloved," he said peacefully and then he disappeared from my view.

"No! No, Mr. Charles!" I cried out. Carefully I went to the edge of the slippery balcony and looked over and saw his body lying in the snow. I ran down the stairs and to him and he opened his eyes at my approach.

"Anne," he said softly, a wonderful light in his eyes. I moved closer to him. All about us the snow had begun to fall harder and more densely, yet I could not leave him.

"Anne. Anne, my beloved." Mr. Price-Jones raised his arms to me and I could see the brightness in his eyes. "Beloved," he said again, "I have waited for you." Mr. Price-Jones's chest heaved as he spoke the words. "I have waited all these long years for you, my love. I knew you would return to me . . . return to Winter's Light." He slowly extended his hand to me and I crouched down in the soft snow beside him and held fast to his fingers. "I knew you would return," he whispered and I nodded in agreement with his words.

I held his hands in mine. "I have returned, Charles," I said and lowered my head to his lips so that I could hear him better. He looked up at me and smiled and in my mind the sound of a long-forgotten melody began. I saw the young Anne and the dashing Charles dancing in the ballroom where the young girl had just been presented at the cotillion, and I knew that after today I would never wonder at the music's origin.

As I held Mr. Price-Jones's head in my arms I heard the muffled sound of horses coming my way and soon Owen and Nanny Hoskins appeared in my view. I waved them back with a shift of my head and they took my meaning and stayed in the distance.

"No," I mouthed the words, "no," for I knew that this was a time that could neither be invaded upon nor duplicated ever again. The past must be given its due, and I turned my attention once more to Mr. Price-Jones, who was whispering words of his devotion to the long-dead Anne.

"I have always loved you. Always. You were my sun and earth, my summer and winter," he said and I shivered, not from the frigid temperatures, but because, instead, a flow of warm air had washed over the two of us so that even the falling flakes did not drift onto us. I knew that from somewhere deep in my soul something was urging me to repeat the words to reassure Mr. Price-Jones of the love that he thought existed between him and the young Anne.

"You, too, my beloved, are my sun and earth," I said, and as I saw from the corner of my eyes both Owen and Nanny start, I recognized that my voice had changed timbre, and I knew without being told that I had spoken with the voice of Anne. And yet it did not frighten me. "You are my summer and winter forever," I said, holding fast to

299

Mr. Price-Jones's hands as I felt the strength ebb from the gentleman's fingers.

"I love you . . . I have always loved you," he repeated. Then his face relaxed and all the frowns and lines in his features softened, and I knew he was gone from this earth. I bent close to his face and touched his lips with mine, knowing that Anne, my mother, would have done the same thing in an act of forgiveness. I untangled my fingers from his and gently placed his hand over his heart. In his own crazed way, Mr. Price-Jones had been faithful and loving.

Nanny and Owen came forward then and the young man took hold of his uncle's hand in a parting gesture before he turned to me and put his arms about my shaking shoulders.

"I was delayed, *Gwynneth,* and sent my uncle here with a message to you, but Fergus said my uncle was like a madman when told that you had gone to the chapel. *'I must stop her. I must stop her,'* he was heard saying and when I arrived we could find neither you nor my uncle, and Nanny and I . . ." he said and then bowed his head. "Please do not judge him harshly, for he did many wonderful things despite . . . He was a good man."

"Aye, but a man who loved too much," Nanny replied. She turned to me with a questioning look. "Do you want to speak of something more, Gwynneth?" she asked, and I could only shake my head. I could not explain what had happened just now—that I knew both Anne and Lucy Glendower had come to protect me. I could only wonder if Lucy had had to atone for having been unable to help Anne—the young girl's decision and desire to die had been stronger than Lucy's ability to protect, and it had been a battle of wills won sadly, but inevitably, by the gentle Anne. Perhaps because Lucy had failed with Anne she had attached herself to me in order to atone. Whatever the reason, I knew that in the tower I had not been alone. Both of them had joined to protect me.

"No, there is nothing more," I said, brushing at the tears and the snow that mingled on my face. I looked up to the heavens. The dark skies had finally fulfilled the prophecy they had been foretelling all day, and the huge puffs of snow that had begun falling a few moments ago now gave way to millions of tiny, frozen, white flakes that warned of a long and bitter night.

Nanny nodded and turned back toward the house. "It is here," she said with reverence in her voice. She raised her hand and pointed to Winter's Light. "Look to it, Gwynneth, and accept it, for there is no earthly explanation for it." I followed her hand and saw what had been promised me when I first arrived here. The clouded sky had settled into one long streak of darkness so that everything was now seen in silhouette. The blue-grey of the stones of the house appeared shrouded in black and even the glint of the ore embedded in the rocks seemed to be veiled and quiet so that only an occasional twinkling radiated from it. The descending clouds were quickly enveloping everything, and within moments we were into a blinding snowstorm, and yet Nanny continued to point at the house, oblivious to the snow that was settling on her shoulders. The entire landscape seemed hushed; not even the sounds of the animals of the estate penetrated the silence.

"Look to it, Gwynneth," she said, and I finally understood what no one could ever have explained to me. The cold winds swirled about us so that the snow seemed to fall sideways and then cease for just a few seconds, and it was as if the flakes hung suspended high above us. The pale-ringed ball of the luminous early moon appeared briefly from behind the black clouds, sending streams of glittering beams downward to the spot where the house stood. It was as if a mighty heavenly warrior had thrust down spears of flame to earth, for at that moment the whole of Winter's Light sparkled and gleamed and glinted from every speck of mica embedded in its stones and the house seemed to glow in an eerie, frosted brilliance.

"Do ye see it, girl?" Nanny asked and I was too awestruck to reply. I felt a brief bit of warmth encircle me and then desert me to the freezing air. "Do ye see it, Gwynneth Glendower?" she asked, and I shuddered just as the full brunt of the snows descended and the moon slipped once more behind its mantle of clouds so that the outline of the house faded into the frozen night.

I nodded, for now I understood the secret of Winter's Light.

Epilogue

There is something special about a love that endures through time. Philosphers can allude to it only hypothetically. Mere humans can only romanticize it. And the good Reverend Jenkins will not speak of it at all. I once wrote him a letter about all that had occurred at Winter's Light, and I asked him if he believed in its spirits and its wandering souls, in destiny. "Do you, Gwynneth?" he wrote back, and I could make no reply. I could never explain to him what I now know: love is an eternal emotion. It does not die, but continues through the ages, reaching down to the next generation and the next and the next.

Sometimes in the hours suspended between night and dawn when I am awakened by the song of a bird or the sound of thunder in the sky or the flecks of snow that softly strike my window, I believe Anne is watching me. I know she is content in her dimension and waits no longer — for Mr. Donne is finally with her and they are at peace at last.

Of Mr. Charles Price-Jones and his unrequited love, I cannot say. I only know that he truly worshipped Anne with all his heart and his soul. Perhaps he made a bargain with the Devil; perhaps the arrangement was not too dear a price for him to have paid for the opportunity of seeing Anne one last time. I do not know.

I often look at Lucy Glendower's portrait and wonder if

all they said about her was true—if all she had wanted was one more chance at life and if I was that one last adventure. Again, I shall never know.

Sometimes I still hear the echoes of ghostly tunes coming from the music room. I still detect the faint, sweet sounds of the cellos and violas and violins of yesteryear. A fragment of a song . . . a few melodious notes . . . and then I hear laughter, but I do not investigate, for I know it is of no use. I know there is no one there and that it is only the spirits of a love that could not die and could not be forgotten.

I returned once to Daear after the events at Winter's Light. I wanted to go once more to the site where Mathias and Molly lie resting for eternity. I wanted to tell them that all is well now—that I have found my birth mother and father and have a family and friends and people who love me. But I wanted them also to know that I will always remember Daear, my life there with them remaining lovingly in my heart and my memory.

Lady Glendower has completely recovered her health and has returned to her rightful position as the mistress of Winter's Light. She, Nanny, and I have spent many long, happy hours together as I learn of the history of my newfound ancestors and my home.

I do not know if anyone will ever be able to explain the phenomenon that occurs at Winter's Light every year. I believe it is another thing that must be taken on faith, that everything in heaven and earth has its time and place and purpose and season. What is to be will be forever!

And as for me . . . I have not only seen the house that haunted my dreams for all of my life but now I know fully and completely each and every room. I have walked the grounds with Owen . . . and smelled the flowers surrounding it . . . and finally I know where it exists. It is my heritage—my home. It is Winter's Light.